Doorway to Hell

Janet Post

STARGAZER

Printed in the United States of America

Chapter One

Lance shot out of a cold, dark void and into the open, hung suspended for a second, then splash-landed in sewage. He lay on his back trying to understand why he fell asleep in Malibu and woke up shooting through the air.

He struggled into a sitting position and looked around. His nose had informed him correctly. He was in a sewer filled with human effluent. The hunger that had been his ever-present companion for the last ten years gnawed at his gut. His entire being yearned for blood. He needed to feed. The hunger was nothing new, but the reek of raw human waste was.

When he scrubbed the slime-covered bricks next to him with the tail of his Hawaiian shirt, he found an address, 2056 Sacramento Street. That was in San Francisco. What happened to Malibu?

Overcome by weakness, he fell back into the swirling brown water. Close by, he sensed movement. Vermin was all that was left to eat, probably a rat. His race, the Chosen, had fed themselves into extinction.

They hadn't meant to. The first to disappear were humans. When the humans realized extinction hovered over their heads, victims of the overwhelming and growing numbers of Chosen, they went underground.

The vampires fed off the blood of domesticated animals, cattle, horses, pigs, sheep and dogs, a poor substitute. But demons and vampires are not farmers. Soon they finished off the livestock, and all that was left were wild animals and vermin.

The last thing Lance remembered was falling asleep in his crib, a tiny space in the attic of a beach house overlooking Third Point, one of the best spots in the 'Bu to catch a hot, bowly ride. Of course, Lance had to do all his surfing at night, which did not make him happy. He missed the sun sparkling off tubes as he sailed through them, crouched over hugging the rail of his board. He missed the warm, salty air, and getting a tan. Surfers make crappy vampires.

Weak, and too hungry to come out and search for food, Lance slept as his world crumbled, the infrastructure decimated by time and lack of much-needed repairs. Vampires not only don't farm, they do not build or fix things that are broken. At the top of the food chain, their arrogance and their inability to adapt was killing them.

When a rat wandered too close to his hand, he seized it. His fangs zipped out and he buried them in the rat's throat. The rodent's blood was warm and tasted like the sewage around him. Lance gagged but choked down the much-needed nourishment.

The blood invigorated him, and with his curiosity aroused, he pulled himself to his feet, flipped long blond hair out of his eyes and hunched over. Space was limited. The ground suddenly shook beneath his sandals, and he remembered.

When he woke up in his crib, the entire house was shaking. He threw the lid off his coffin and was instantly catapulted out of the attic through a tiny window. Too weak to fly, he'd plummeted into a dark, deep hole. He remembered a loud noise like a high wind howling around his head, a cold, frigid emptiness, and then shooting into the air and landing in this river of shit.

Lance crab walked down a dark tunnel. When he reached an intersection, the tunnel opened, and he stood up. He closed his eyes and listened. Over the slosh of rushing sewage in the culvert, he heard something he hadn't heard in years, the sound of hundreds of beating human hearts.

A sign on the wall said Powell Street. He saw a steel ladder leading to a circular opening above, and a metal door in the brick wall. The door opened to a room crammed with human junk. Old metal beds, trunks, crates and barrels filled the small space. When he opened one of the trunks, choosing it at random, he saw something weird inside, an enormous white and blue glowing egg.

Lance placed his hands on the smooth, white surface. It was warm. Inside, he detected the faint beating of a heart. Animal. He'd

2

sucked the blood of enough animals to last him an eon. Over his head, he smelled humans. He heard their collective hearts beating with a rhythm he couldn't ignore.

As he climbed the ladder, excitement over the intoxicating sound and smell of humans fueled his pace. A manhole cover blocked his path at the top of the ladder. With one powerful thrust, Lance sent the steel cap flying. He shoved himself out of the opening and gaped. Cars raced by filled with people. Lights, almost as bright as day, lit the wet road. Water standing in puddles reflected the brilliant colors of the signs on the storefronts and the lights on the sides of the street.

Where was he? Where he went to sleep, all the humans lived underground or hid in the woods and caves. Something happened during the earthquake. He must have crossed into another world, one populated with millions of people. He was surrounded by food.

Rotating, Lance stood on the top rung of the ladder and stared. His hunger threatened to overcome him. The urge to feed was a primitive call. Killing was not his favorite thing. Lance was a surfer and a philosopher. He loved riding the wild waves, the feel of the wind in his hair and the rich smell of the ocean. Surfing was his religion. But he was also a vampire. And years of fasting and drinking the blood of animals weakened any self-control he might have mustered.

On the sidewalk, he spotted two humans standing in the rain. One looked like a homeless guy. He pushed a cart filled with trash. The other drank from a bottle in a paper bag . . . wino, easy prey and very tasty. His speed slightly impaired by his weakened condition, Lance erupted from the tunnel, sped across the street and snatched the wino. Leaping high, he landed on a balcony with an iron railing, dropped his victim to the concrete floor and fed.

Glorious, hot, sweet blood flowed down his throat and into his shriveled stomach. When he was full, he leaned against the sliding glass door and looked around. The town looked like San Francisco. Well, wherever he was, it wasn't Malibu. The only thing familiar was the humans, the way they smelled and tasted. Maybe he'd been jolted back into a time before his race destroyed their world. Or maybe a doorway to a new world opened when the ground shook.

Whichever, whatever, he didn't care. What mattered was he was here, and here was infinitely better than where he'd come from. All he needed was a nice beach and some primo surf, and he was ready to call this home.

****

Konrad Pengill aimed his Japanese crotch-rocket between two cars, shot into the clear and sped down California Street. The 2018 H2 Ninja was the only thing he owned worth any money. He took pleasure in squeezing the hand throttle and spraying water over the traffic behind him.

It was raining and the fog wrapping around him was thick enough to drink. He was late for his job, a nothing position in the civilian world. He hated every moment of being a civilian. But when you spend three years in the brig and get busted out of the military for beating up your commanding officer, you take what you can get.

Konrad slipped the Ninja between two cars in front of San Francisco Fire Station 10 and dropped the kickstand. The fire station was located on Presidio. The EMTs had a three-car garage and an office next door. After passing the training course, Konrad used his experience in the Army to get himself hired on as an EMT. It was a brutal job working the seven to seven shift in North Beach, China Town and the Marina District. Apparently, they went through a lot of help because they seemed glad to get him.

He swung one tree-trunk-sized leg over the seat of his motorcycle and stepped onto the blacktop. The rain had stopped but fog still covered everything in a wet, gray, cottony blanket. He'd just slung his backpack into his locker when the alarm sounded. He shoved an arm too big for the standard issue sleeve of his uniform jacket and grabbed his medical case out of the locker.

4

Jogging through the building, he ran into Paige Crumbly, his partner for the night. They always partnered him with Paige, a five-foot-nothing femme with dyed maroon hair he could bench press with one hand. She hated all men, including him.

"Hey Paige, sorry I'm late."

"You're always late, Pengill. You just don't give a shit."

Konrad grinned. She did have him pegged. "It was the fog," he said as he opened the door of the Ford E350, climbed in and cranked up the diesel engine.

"It's foggy every day and every night, Sledge. You'll have to think of something better than that."

Paige sometimes called him Sledge because of the size of his fists. She said they looked like sledgehammers. Konrad waved his hand as if shooing her away. "Where we going? I didn't have time to check the radio."

Paige reached over and turned the ambulance radio on. "Powell. Somebody said they saw a man being murdered on a balcony above the Tulip Pistola. According to the witness, the vic is still up there. One of his arms is hanging off the balcony."

Konrad flipped on the lights and the sirens and gunned the van out of the garage and onto Presidio. This was one of the aspects of the job he really enjoyed, running wide open through traffic. Zipping in and out between the cars, mostly tourists and locals heading out to the restaurants in North Beach and China Town for dinner, was easy for him. He liked having permission to go fast, pass people like they were standing still, and force them to give up the right of way.

When they got to the Tulip Pistola, an upscale Italian restaurant, Konrad pulled up on the curb and parked. He grabbed his med kit and ran up the stairs to the first-floor flat. The apartment was empty, like many in town. San Francisco was rapidly becoming a ghost town due to high rent and real estate prices. The landlord was waiting.

5

Konrad, followed by Paige, walked across the parquet floors of the empty two-bedroom flat and stopped in front of the French doors leading to the balcony.

"I could see there was someone out there," the landlord, an elderly, balding white male, said from inside the apartment.

"Did you see more than one person?"

"I might have. You know, I don't see as good as I used to."

Paige glanced at Konrad. "Think we should call for police backup?"

Konrad shook his head. "What could be out there? It's probably just some bum looking for a dry place to crash."

He put his hand on the door handle and squared his shoulders. When the door blasted open in his face, and panes of glass erupted in a thousand sharp pieces of shrapnel, he was stunned and unprepared. He threw up his hands to defend himself from the crazed surfer clawing at his neck.

Konrad felt the familiar rage fill him. He knew what was happening. There was no way to fight it.

He howled like a madman, his strength suddenly tripled, grabbed the blond-haired demon and threw it across the room. Lunging after it, Konrad leaped on top of the creature. From the little he could see it was thin and starved, but strong with fangs and sharp claws. Konrad had no idea what he faced. He just knew the red haze had fallen over his eyes and the lust for blood filled his head.

He wrapped his huge hands around the creature's skinny neck and squeezed. Through the murderous film covering his eyes, Konrad saw the thing turn its head to jam sharp fangs into his hand. Its mouth sprouted needle-like, pointed teeth. Konrad snatched his hand away and the creature slipped out of his grasp like it was greased and ran.

It was fast. So fast Konrad saw only a blur as it shot through the apartment and disappeared out the open door.

"What the fuck was that?" Paige demanded.

Konrad's face felt swollen. He stood bent over with his hands on his knees panting, as the rage inside his chest slowly seeped away. "Don't know. It looked like a surfer. It had a shitload of teeth and it was fast." He wheezed out these few words between gasps for air.

Paige stomped over and grabbed his jacket. "I wasn't talking about that creature. I'm talking about you. What the fuck came over you? Who are you anyway?"

He pulled his jacket out of her grasp, hunched wide shoulders, and turned his back to her. He should have known eventually he'd end up in a situation where his heritage would take over and he would turn into a Berserker. He couldn't stop it. He could trace his lineage all the way back to one of the original Norse Berserkers, Alfer Ulfvarinn.

He'd tried to control the rage. He'd joined the military thinking that would be a good outlet. He'd kill his country's enemies. And for a while, through boot camp and tech school, he'd been physically tired enough to control the urge to kill people who annoyed him like his DI and maintain control while sparring in hand-to-hand combat during training ops. He'd done so well they'd promoted him into Special Forces

While in Spec Ops, he had several episodes that were resolved without incident. Once, when he was parachuting out of an airplane and his parachute failed to open, he'd saved himself by landing in a tree. He was practically Superman when in the Berserker mode.

After basic, there wasn't enough to keep his body tired and his mind engaged. He eventually found his superior officer, Sergeant William St. John, beating a smaller man Konrad befriended. They gave him three years in the brig and a dishonorable discharge for teaching the Sergeant to pick on someone his own size.

"Sledge," Paige walked around him and grabbed his jacket again. The woman had no sense. "What happened to you?"

He looked at her. "I'm sorry if I scared you. When I'm threatened or scared or sometimes just mad, I turn into an ancient Nordic warrior, a Berserker. I can't control it."

7

Paige busted out laughing. She laughed so hard she had to bend over and grab her stomach. "Stop, you're killing me. That's the best story you've told yet, Pengill. Did that thing bite you?"

Konrad looked at his hand. There were two tiny red marks. But his skin in Berserker mode was tough. The creature's fangs had not penetrated. "No. What was it?"

"This is San Francisco, buddy. Could be any number of things. I'm guessing crazy surfer, vampire wannabee. Ever since that show on HBO came out, everybody wants to be a vampire. Let's go do our job and check out the vic."

The victim was extremely dead, drained dry, and he smelled. Paige wrinkled her tiny little nose. "Wino."

Konrad nodded. There was an overtone of wine, but because he was still so close to his Berserker persona, he detected blood, feces, urine and vomit, all the good human odors, and something else. He sniffed the air, bent over and smelled the victim. The haunting scent of patchouli and surf wax still clung to the victim's clothes.

Chapter Two

LeiHua kept her eyes closed as she listened to her captors discuss her fate.

"What's the deal, Lawrence? Why do we have to beat up this pretty little woman? I didn't join the Blue Dragons to beat up girls."

"Red Chua, you would be much better off if you did not question your superiors. We were told to discover the whereabouts of the egg and this woman has it."

Squeezing her eyes tight, LeiHua fought nausea and fear. They knew about the egg and they knew she had it. Her father had entrusted her with the egg and no one else was supposed to know it existed.

"What kind of egg are we looking for?"

"Li Po did not tell me, and we will not ask him."

"Whatever, Lawrence. You're so far up Li Po's ass, you can't think for yourself. Let's get this over with."

The two men jerked LeiHua to her knees and she opened her eyes. Old cinder-brick walls were encrusted with grime, the only light issued from a single bulb dangling from three frayed wires. A thousand spiders had lived and died in the corners of the concrete ceiling. She smelled mold, mildew and dirt. This must be a cellar. Two young Chinese men hovered close to her face.

"We know the drug wore off by now. Tell us where you hid the egg." The oldest one spoke to her in Chinese. A dragon tattoo ran from the top of his head, down one side of his face with the tail disappearing beneath his white T-shirt. Lei recognized the two as Tong.

She pretended to be groggy, closed her eyes and mumbled, "What egg. What're you talking about?"

A stinging slap sent her reeling. Her head swam from the blow as tears leaked down her face.

"We know your father gave you the egg for safe keeping. I can't imagine what he thought you could do to keep it safe. You're just an insignificant girl child."

The older one shook her hard, forcing her teeth to slam together. He punched her in the face again and she dove at him, ramming her thumbs into his eyes. She felt the soft tissue give, one bursting like a grape. At the same time, she kneed him in the groin and then pushed far enough away to jumping, round-house kick him in the side of the head. He screamed as he flew into the stone wall and slid moaning to the floor.

The younger one, Red Chua, grabbed her from behind in an elbow lock, choking off her air. She reached behind her back and groped for his genitals. When she had a grip on them, she squeezed as hard as she could while she stomped on his instep. Red's hold on her neck loosened. She ducked through it, dropped to the floor and drove her fist up and into his groin. He collapsed, whimpering with pain.

With both of her captors on the floor, Lei shot toward the ancient wooden door fortified with large iron straps. It suddenly burst open. Lei stopped short at the point of a gun.

An older Chinese man glared at her. He wore a black patch over his left eye socket. He held the handgun pointed at her chest and surveyed the inside of the cell.

"I see we underestimated you, LeiHua Jiang. You must have spent some of your younger years learning to defend yourself. Get up, you two. You dishonor the Blue Dragons by allowing this tiny woman to defeat you."

Lawrence and Red slowly climbed off the floor. Red couldn't straighten his body. He cradled his privates in both hands.

"I'm hurt, boss," Red said. "I think she broke my nuts."

Lawrence, his entire right eye swollen shut, grabbed Red by the collar. "Stand up in front of your superiors. Take the pain."

10

Lei slowly backed away from all three of them. When her back was against the stone wall, she stopped and waited, her gaze flitting from one to the other.

"Tie her up this time. I want that egg."

"Where's my father?" Lei demanded.

The man with the gun smiled. "I'm so sorry. I forget my manners. My name is Li Po. I am in charge of these pitiful soldiers of the Tong. Your father is beyond help. He is on his way back to China."

Lei's stomach plummeted. They sent her father back to the communists. He would be jailed there for the rest of his life for deserting the army and defecting, if they didn't put him to death.

Shiu Jiang, a colonel in the Chinese Army, was in charge of a small base outside of Keriya on the Tibetan border. On his days off, he liked to snowmobile and hike in the Kunlun Mountains. When he found the egg he defected, hiking miles into Tibet to a monastery where he hid until he could contact her and arrange passage to San Francisco. He must have known they were on to him. That was why he'd entrusted her with the egg.

Lei fought the fear as her mind raced. Her father hadn't told her why it was important or even what kind of egg it was. But she knew he would give his life for it and that was enough.

As she leaned against the wall, her brain scrambling for an escape plan, a tiny tendril of thought entered her mind. She didn't notice it at first. It felt like feathers brushing through her thoughts. Then she heard words, soft as a whisper, inside her head, *Lei, I know you can hear me. Answer.*

Lei spun around. She looked at the three men. They advanced toward her carefully, holding rope. "Don't run away anymore, girl. We won't hurt you, so please don't fight us."

The voice surely did not come from them. "Who are you?" she voiced aloud.

You don't have to talk, just think. I can hear your thoughts and you can hear mine.

Lei was afraid to blink or move. This horrible, weird day had just entered the *Twilight Zone*.

The door to the cell opened again. Lei broke for it, ran past her surprised captors, shoved the newcomer, another Tong member, aside, scrambling as she dove for the stairs right outside the door. Shots were fired. A bullet thudded into the ancient brick wall of the stairwell. She ducked and shrieked as another ricocheted off the metal railing. She saw the newcomer scream, then groan and collapse.

"Don't kill her," Li Po yelled. "I want that egg."

Lei scampered up the stairs. Another shot rang out and burned across the side of her head. She screamed again. Frightened, angry and now hurt, she ran faster, taking the steps two at a time. A hand grabbed the back of her blouse and pulled. The thin fabric of the shirt tore off leaving her running out of the stairwell into the street in her bra and a short skirt.

A flood of rain poured out of the sky, soaking her. Blood dripped down her face from the head wound. Watery red ran across her chest, staining her white bra. A car whizzed by as she raced up Waverly Place, a narrow street running only two blocks. She was grabbed from behind again as she turned onto Sacramento. Putting on a burst of speed, she left the Tong guy with her skirt.

An ambulance with lights and sirens blared down Sacramento toward Waverly Place. Lei, in her underwear, crossed herself, shot a prayer to heaven, and ran out in front of it.

The ambulance driver hit the brakes. Lei covered her eyes. The Tong guy with the red hair yelled, "Oh shit!" and dove for the sidewalk. The ambulance skied across the wet asphalt, spun to the left and shuddered to a stop inches from her. A huge man jumped out of the driver's side and grabbed her arms.

"What the fuck are you doing?" he screamed at her. Then he stopped screaming and looked at her, glanced at the three Tong members hauling ass back down Waverly, wrapped a ham-sized bicep around her and ushered her to the ambulance.

"Paige, put her inside, she's bleeding."

A female EMT with maroon hair opened the back doors and pulled her in. Exhausted, Lei flopped onto the stretcher, dropping her bloody head into her hands.

As soon as she relaxed, the voice was back in her head. *LeiHua, you must help me. I sense something evil close by. It's hungry, terribly hungry and very old.*

Lei lay back on the stretcher and closed her eyes. The female EMT gently wiped the blood off her face with sterile gauze and antiseptic.

"You got a nasty scalp wound, darling," the EMT said. "It gave you a new part in your hair."

Lei nodded. Her mind was busy searching for the voice. *Who are you?*

I am Chomo Lung Ma, the new queen of my people. I am an ice dragon.

Lei rubbed her eyes and the EMT brushed her hands away. "You have a nasty cut here, lady. Let me work on it."

"Sorry," Lei said, folding her hands across her stomach. *Why are you contacting me?*

Your father took me from the hatching sands. You have touched me. He is gone, but you are here. You must save me.

Could you talk to him?

I can only speak to those who are pure in heart and body, virgins. Please save me LeiHua, the evil one grows closer.

The back door of the ambulance suddenly flew open. The giant man stuck his head inside. "Hey, are you LeiHua?"

"Leave us alone in here, Sledge," the female EMT snapped. "The girl is practically naked."

"Oh, and you're not looking," the giant named Sledge responded.

"Yes, I am LeiHua," Lei blushed and covered the small amount of cleavage showing with her hand.

"Something named Chomo Lung Ma is broadcasting into my head, but I think it's talking to you. It says it's in danger and it's a dragon?"

Lei bolted into a sitting position. "But she told me she can only speak to virgins."

Sledge's faced turned a bright crimson. "Aaaah fuck."

Chapter Three

Lance opened the lid of the footlocker. After searching through the small storage room close to where he entered this world, he'd discovered a lovely ersatz coffin. It didn't matter that it was a trunk. All that mattered was it fit and it had a padded lining.

He crawled inside and squirmed around trying to get comfortable. He felt bloated. And he was totally wasted. He hadn't been this tired since his real surfing days. Vamps don't usually get tired.

He dropped the lid and was just about to drift off when he heard the door to the room open.

His hearing was excellent.

"This is the stupidest thing you have ever dragged me into, Sledge."

"I could hear the thing in my head, Paige. Really."

"Please help me look for the egg," Lance heard a third person say. "I left it in here just yesterday. It's in one of these boxes. It's big and white and . . ."

"And egg-shaped?" Lance heard the Paige woman say.

"And you're telling me it's the egg talking?" Lance heard the guy say.

"Yes, it's a queen dragon egg. My father found it in the Himalayas."

"A queen dragon? Not just an ordinary run of the mill, everyday kind of dragon, but a frigging queen dragon. Are we talking drag queen or Queen Elizabeth queen?"

"Come on, Paige. This will only take a minute." Lance opened the lid far enough to see an enormous, square-chinned guy grin and slap a purple-headed woman on the back hard enough to make her take a step forward to avoid falling. He immediately recognized the giant as the EMT he ran into after consuming the wino. It would be hard not to recognize him. He was built like a tank, had a bright, yellow buzz cut and matching goatee, a dominant nose and guileless blue eyes, not to mention the EMT uniform.

"Over here," Lance heard the man say just before the door blasted open. That was the only way to describe it. The force of the blow sent the door crashing into Lance's trunk.

Lance tumbled out just in time to see Vetalas, the oldest vampire from his world, the maker of literally thousands of vampires including him, tear into the throat of a woman with strange reddish-purple hair.

Vetalas ripped the woman's throat out and inhaled the blood like a vacuum cleaner. Blood and gore sprayed the two stunned humans standing against the far wall behind an old metal bedstead. The hot, metallic stench made Lance's nostrils flare. There was nothing as intoxicating to a vampire as the odor of fresh blood.

Vetalas sucked his fill of the woman in seconds, then dropped the husk of her body to the floor. He turned eyes red with blood lust to the remaining items on the menu.

Lance knew what was coming next. He looked at the two humans. They were the ones who had seen him on the balcony. It would be best to allow Vetalas to have his way, drain them, and move on.

"Get out of my way, you puny excuse for a vampire. I have not fed in years."

His motivation still unclear in his mind, Lance moved in front of the humans.

Vetalas waved one clawed finger at Lance. "If the humans are yours, tell me now, or I am going to feed."

Vetalas held the two humans enthralled. They stared at the ancient vampire frozen in place, mouths gaping open.

Lance cleared his throat. Vetalas was huge, almost seven-feet tall. His dark face was hollow and gaunt from years of deprivation, his lips thin and cruel. Long, black hair was drawn sharply back from a pointed widow's peak. He wore a gold neck piece decorated with lapis and turquoise and one matching earring. His face was pitted with the scars of teenage acne. He'd been an Indian who dabbled in dark magic and ended up cursed for eternity. But he'd been blessed with one thing, the ability to spread his curse to others.

"They are mine," Lance whispered, his voice like metal on sandpaper from years of inactivity. "Above ground, there are thousands of humans to feed upon. Leave these two to me."

Vetalas raised his arms over his head. He wore nothing but a golden loin cloth, armlets of gold, and his neck piece. His body shimmered with power. Lance could feel it all the way into his swollen stomach.

"I recognize you. You are of my get. I will honor your request this one time. I do not know where we are, or what world this is, but soon it will be mine."

Lance had no doubt Vetalas was right. He would terrorize this world, populate it with vampires, and drain it of natural resources just as he had done to the one they came from.

Moving too fast for the naked eye to see, Vetalas flew from the small, dingy room into the sewers of San Francisco.

The minute he was gone, the two humans fell to the floor. Released from Vetalas's hold, they crashed back into consciousness.

Lance closed his eyes and sighed. Why did Vetalas have to follow him here and screw up a perfect situation?

*****

"Paige," Konrad cried. He'd failed her. He picked his partner up and cradled her bloody body tenderly. "Paige, I should have saved you."

As the agony of his failure and Paige's death filled him, Konrad's face began to swell. The familiar red curtain fell over his eyes and he growled. He dropped Paige and howled like a wolf. He grabbed the lid of a leather trunk and tore into it with his teeth flinging saliva everywhere. He slammed the trunk lid against the wall and grabbed one of the bedsteads. Konrad bent the footboard into a U-shape with his bare hands and beat on the floor with it, growling and raging.

His heart hammered in his chest. He'd failed Paige. With all his strength and power he should have been able to save her. When he felt a small hand grip his arm, he froze.

"Hey, Mr. Sledge, what's happened to you? There was nothing you could do to save her. You're wasting a lot of energy beating up stuff. That disgusting creature is gone. And the egg is in here somewhere. You need to stop breaking stuff before you accidentally destroy it."

The hate and the anger slowly seeped out of Konrad like air from a balloon. He fell to the floor with his head in his hands and sobbed. "I'm useless. I never get anything right. I have all this strength and it's good for nothing, absolutely nothing."

LeiHua dropped to the floor beside him. She brushed his face with her hand to wipe away a tear. "Someday, you will learn to harness your power. It is a power, Mr. Sledge. You have great strength. I'll teach you if you want. But first, help me find the egg."

Konrad climbed slowly to his feet. For the first time, he remembered the vampire.

Surfer vamp was climbing back into his makeshift coffin. He wore a pair of baggy shorts, a Hawaiian shirt and sandals. Konrad stuck out his hand in an effort to shake the vampire's.

Surfer vamp brushed his offered hand away and flipped a lock of straight, white-blonde hair out of his eyes. "Hey dude, we don't do that, ever."

"I just wanted to thank you for saving us from that, that thing. What was it anyway?"

"Bro, that is your worst nightmare. He destroyed my world and now he's come here to destroy yours." Lance briefly described where he came from, a world decimated by greed and evil.

"Where is your world?" LeiHua asked. "What kind of creature are you?"

"I'm a vampire. My name is Lance. I used to be one of the best surfers in Malibu. That creature's name is Vetalas. He's over 3,000 years old and filled with hate and evil. I'm not exactly sure where my world is, maybe in some other dimension or maybe some other time. I went to sleep in my crib in Malibu, and an earthquake shot me out of bed and into the sewer outside this room."

"Well, Mr. Lance, you can't eat people in San Francisco. It's not right and you could get AIDs." LeiHua returned to lifting lids and looking into boxes. "I know I left it right over here."

Lance climbed back out of his box. "When I moved some stuff around, I saw your egg. I think it's in this corner."

Lance led them to a stack of crates in one corner, pulled several off the pile and opened a large box. Konrad gasped. Inside the box was a glowing, blue-white egg about two feet tall. He could hear the dragon inside breathing.

"She's asleep," LeiHua whispered.

"Well, I wouldn't worry about waking her up. If that devil creature didn't rouse her, nothing will." Konrad laid his palm on the smooth surface. "It's warm." He looked around the room. This was a weird place to hide anything. It was way underground, deep inside the ancient San Francisco sewer system. "Why'd you put it here?"

"My apartment is over us. There's a trap door leading out of the basement into the sewers. In the old days, they ran prostitutes, Chinese female slaves, from one house to another through these tunnels. The Tong is searching for the egg and this was the safest place I could think of to put it."

"Well, little lady, it's been real. Now that you've got your egg, I gotta run. I'm supposed to be working and I have to report Paige's death. I have no idea what I'm gonna write on that report. Someone in authority needs to know about that Vetalas thing. But who's gonna believe me?"

LeiHua grabbed his arm. "Please, Sledge, I need your help."

"Hey, I helped you find the egg. My partner died over it. You're on your own now."

A sudden, biting screech filled Konrad's head. He grabbed both ears and squeezed his eyes closed until the harsh sound in his brain ceased. "What the fuck was that?"

LeiHua stroked the hard, white shell of the egg. "She's awake. She says she's ready to hatch."

Chapter Four

Konrad stopped bending over to pick up what was left of Paige and turned to stare at LeiHua and her precious egg. "The egg just told you she's hatching?"

"No, she says she's ready, but conditions aren't right. I have to take her to a place that's ten degrees above a human's normal temperature. Father took her from the hatching sands, a chamber inside a dormant volcano. The temperature on the sand is perfect for the eggs to hatch. She says dragons have laid their eggs there for thousands of years."

Konrad closed his eyes and sighed. "Lei, I'm having a really hard time believing any of this shit - - the vampire part or the dragon part. And where are you going to find the conditions she needs to hatch? In a microwave? On top of a stove? Come on, Lei, the egg's as big as a collie."

"I'm thinking. What about the beach?"

The water temperature of the Pacific Ocean requires surfers to wear wetsuits even in Southern California. Right Surfer Vamp?"

"My name is Lance, but you got that right, dude. You got to suit up, unless you're a vampire. We like the cold water. At least I do."

"Why don't we just crack the egg and let her out?" This entire conversation bordered on the ridiculous. Konrad was ready to leave. The thought of that horrible Vetalas creature roaming the streets of San Francisco terrified him. Not for himself, but for the people of the city. He could take care of himself.

"No, no," Lei said. "Lung Ma says her body is still attached to the shell. If you crack it she will die. It takes the heat to release her."

Konrad groaned. "Ask her if the temperature has to be exactly 108 degrees, and if it can vary, by how much."

"Ask her yourself, Sledge. You can talk to her. You're a virgin."

"Hey, my man," Lance chimed in. "You really a virgin?"

Konrad growled.

"You might want to think about putting the egg in a hot tub," Lance added. "I always liked a good soak back when I was a human and I came in from a couple of hours of shredding some gnarly curls. Warms you right up and you can set the temperature for whatever you need."

Konrad grinned. "See, good old Surfer Vamp figured it out. Take him with you."

Lance flew across the room and grabbed Konrad by his jacket lapels. The movement was too fast for Konrad to even follow. "I said my name is Lance."

The grip Lance's thin, claw-like hands had on his jacket seemed made of iron. Konrad suddenly felt like an ass. Lance had helped. The least he could do was show some respect. "Sorry, Lance. I guess I'm still a little freaked out about Paige."

The vampire released his jacket. "I could kill you in a second, before you even had a chance to turn into your rad, Viking persona."

"I'm sorry, Lance. Really. But now that you two have your answer, I gotta run."

Lei left the egg and stood next to him. Her eye level was right at his navel. "Please help me, Konrad. I can't do this for Lung Ma by myself. I don't know where to find a hot tub, my car's in the shop, and the Tong is after me."

Konrad picked up Paige's body. She felt like an empty, plastic bag. "I'm really sorry. But you have to see that I need to take care of Paige."

Help Lei, Sledge, Paige would want you to. Konrad heard in his mind. "Like hell she would," Konrad voiced aloud. "You don't know Paige. She didn't even believe in the egg."

"Is she talking to you again?" Lei asked.

"Yes, she is, and she needs to frigging stop. I have to go back to work. I need this job to help pay for my shithole, basement apartment and my bikes. Why did your father bring a dragon egg to San Francisco anyway?"

"He didn't know it was a dragon egg. I didn't know it until she told me. Father thought it was a dinosaur egg. He was going to sell it and make millions. He wanted out of China and the Army. And now he's on his way to military prison." Lei's voice cracked. She bent over and laid her forehead on top of the egg.

"So, how does the Tong know about this egg? Do they know it's a dragon egg or do they think they're stealing a dinosaur egg?"

"You got me. Could you just help me get it to a safe place? After that, I'll leave you alone. I swear."

Konrad was just about to tell her no, when Lance spoke up.

"I hear voices and lots of footsteps. They're headed this way."

Konrad's heart pounded. His face felt full, the skin around his eyes tight. *Not again.*

"Take the egg into that corner," Konrad pointed to a dark spot in the farthest corner of the dingy room. "Hide behind that old sewing machine."

Lei nodded, hoisted the egg and ran to the corner where she squatted down, slanted eyes huge in her white face.

"I guess it's you and me, Lance." Konrad's voice was a growl. He was going Berserker. It seemed like he'd spent the entire evening in this mode. It took a lot of energy.

A dozen black-T-shirt-wearing Chinese men, tattooed and toting automatic weapons, flowed into the room through the door-less entryway. Konrad saw the guns but was already in Berserker mode. He couldn't control himself.

Shrieking, he launched himself at the first Tong member to enter, grabbed the weapon out of his hands before he could fire, and started hosing down the remaining Tong fighters with 7.62 mm rounds. When the magazine emptied, he threw down the gun, took a stance, flexed his biceps and screamed an ancient war cry.

The Tong members turned as one and ran. Konrad and Lance followed them out into the long, brick-lined pathway beside the sluggishly running sewage. Faster than Konrad, Lance caught the last one. The vampire grabbed him by the neck and followed him to the ground. Grossed out, Konrad watched Lance feed for a minute then spun on his heels and stalked back to the storage room.

"Got a cell phone?" he snarled at Lei. "Someone needs to teach Lance a lesson in the dangers of blood pathogens."

Lei handed him a Blackberry. He dialed the City Morgue.

"Baby D," Konrad said into the phone. "This is Paige's partner, Konrad. I have some bad news."

Baby D, real name Deidre Gomez, had always been called Baby by her parents, an African American father and Puerto Rican mother. When she grew up, she became Baby D. She was a forensic pathologist, worked the nightshift at the city morgue and she was Paige's significant other.

Konrad held the phone away from his ear. Baby D was a screamer. "What? What are you talking about, Konrad? Where's Paige?"

"I have her body here with me. We're in China Town. Can you"

Baby D interrupted . . . loudly. "Her body? Oh no, no, no, no." Konrad could hear her wailing, screaming and crying.

"Baby D, I need you to come get me in the meat wagon. Something bad is happening in the city, something real bad. Paige is one of the first victims."

Baby D took a deep breath. Konrad heard it. "Where in China Town are you, Konrad? I can be there in ten minutes. And Konrad, none of this, and I mean NONE, had better be your fault."

Konrad glanced over at Lei. "What's the address on your apartment? I think we better go out that way."

"Thirty-six Pratt Place," Lei said.

Konrad told Baby D and hung up. He handed the phone back to Lei. "Let's go. I'm gonna take you to my place. From there, we'll figure out where to find a hot tub."

"Let's go, Lance," Konrad said.

Lance had dried blood on his aloha shirt. Konrad shuddered.

"Hey, I'm not going anywhere. I entered this world here and this is where I'm staying."

Konrad sighed. "Lance, this crib has no door. Vetalas knows he can find you here, the Tong knows they can find you here, and I live on the beach."

Lance shot Konrad a toothy grin. "The beach? Dude, I'm in."

"Great, you carry Paige and watch the rear. Come on Lei, show me this trap door of yours. We need to get the hell out of here. The Tong will surely be back."

Lei led them out into the main sewer line and down the walkway. Konrad carried the egg and Lance covered the rear carrying Paige's body. High on the walls, sickly yellow lights glowed. The lights illuminated chocolate-colored water running in the sewage canal which reeked and bubbled. Every time a bubble burst, they all groaned and gagged. About fifty feet from the storage room, Lei turned down a dark, narrow tunnel. She stopped. "Anybody got a cigarette lighter?"

"Paige should," Konrad said. "She smoked."

Lance felt through Paige's jacket pockets and pulled out a lighter. Lei clicked it and inched her way down the tunnel where Konrad spotted an ancient metal ladder at the tunnel's end.

Lei scampered up the ladder while Konrad tried not to look at her round little ass in the skimpy panties and failed. At the top of the ladder, Lei threw open a trap door, and light from the room above seeped into the tunnel.

It took only a few minutes for all of them to get out of the sewer and into Lei's basement. From there, they climbed a steep set of wooden stairs, emerging into the main hallway of the apartment building. Lei opened the front door of the first unit and signaled all of them to follow her.

LeiHua's small home was simple and spare, decorated with oak Swedish furniture. They followed her into the bedroom where Lei set the egg down on the bed, which was perfectly made up with a gold and blue coverlet. Lance laid Paige's body next to the egg and

25

looked around like he was lost. There was a computer desk and one chest of drawers in the small room. The curtains on the solitary window were gold, the room painted a light blue.

Lei waved toward the bedroom door. "You guys look out the window in the living room and see if Paige's girlfriend is here yet. I have to get dressed."

Konrad and Lance left Lei alone. Lance wandered lost around her apartment picking up knick-knacks and touching canisters and dishes in the kitchen. "I miss being human."

When Konrad moved the curtain aside on the floor-to-ceiling window, he saw the city meat wagon parked next to the curb. Baby D paced up and down the sidewalk in front of the apartment building like an enraged buffalo.

"She's here."

After Lei donned a pair of jeans, blouse and a jacket, they slipped quietly down the stairwell and out the front door. Baby D saw them, screamed, ran toward them and snatched Paige's body out of Lance's arms.

Baby D was a large woman. She had short, spiked hair, café-au-lait skin and she was wearing a set of blue scrubs. Shrieking and crying, she fell to the sidewalk rocking Paige back and forth.

"What happened, Konrad?" Baby looked up at him, her face drenched with tears. Her huge brown eyes glowered at Konrad.

"She got killed by a vampire."

"What?"

"There's a vampire in the city, Baby D. It's going to be killing a lot of people if we can't stop it."

Baby D stopped crying. "Well, that explains two other bodies that came into the morgue tonight. One's a cop and the other one's a wino. They're both bled dry, big holes in their necks."

Konrad nodded. "It's only the beginning. But Lance here killed the wino. The other vampire must have killed the cop. His name is Vetalas and he's the bad one."

26

Baby D carefully laid Paige on the sidewalk and stood up. Her eyes narrowed. She squared her shoulders and cracked her knuckles. "You said Lance here is a vampire?"

Konrad nodded.

Arms outstretched, hands grasping claws, Baby D launched herself at Lance. "Die you motherfucker!"

Chapter Five

"Whoa, whoa, Baby D." Konrad stepped in front of the woman and held on. She dug in and tried to push him over.

"I'm gonna kill that blood-sucking freak."

"Stop, we have way more problems and we need Lance." Konrad shoved her in the direction of the county coroner's van.

"Who's the girl?"

"Get in the van and I'll tell you everything."

Baby D turned around. "Is that an egg?"

"Get in the van."

"I will. Don't push me."

"Shhhh," Conrad hissed. Every dog in the city had started to bark. Konrad held up his finger to indicate quiet and listened. Then Lei screamed and kept on screaming.

Rats of every size and color streamed in mass out of the storm drains. They scrambled over Lei's boots, Konrad's shoes, Baby D's white clogs and Lance's sandals. Lance was the only one who did not jump up and down to get rid of them.

They dove into the van. The minute Baby had the engine running, the shaking started.

"Earthquake!" Konrad yelled.

A groan issued from deep underground. All around the van, the earth bucked and shook. Buildings swayed and rattled. Glass from hundreds of windows exploded into the street.

"Drive!" Konrad ordered and grabbed the dash as Baby D hit the accelerator. They took off leaving a trail of smoking rubber behind.

"Where we going?" she asked.

"La Playa and Cabrillo," Konrad told her.

"Don't you think we should drop Paige off at my office first?"

A large chunk of railing and concrete-block fascia crashed into the street in front of them. Baby drove around it.

Konrad stuck his head out the window and looked toward the city center where the morgue was located. The buildings still rocked and swayed. As he watched, a forty-story tower tilted and a huge chunk dropped off into the street. "This is a major disaster, Baby. I don't think we can make it."

Baby swerved as a big chunk of asphalt rose in front of them. "Poor Paige. I guess we take her with us. Why we headed to the beach?"

"I live there. We need a place to stop for a minute and think. You have no idea what we've been through in the last few hours."

"It don't look to me like it's getting any better." Baby D piloted the van down Sacramento Street, cut over to Geary and headed toward the beach. The police-ban radio was on and busy as emergency units were dispatched all over the city. When an eruption of chatter, whistles, beeps and alerts lit up the air waves, Baby turned it up.

"That last call wasn't about the quake, Konrad," Baby D said. "They got more DBs in your district and they know you're missing. They're looking for the ambulance. Where'd you leave it?"

"Parked on the side of Powell near a manhole. It's a long story."

"We got time. Why don't you tell me?"

Konrad listened to the craziness on the radio while he told Baby D about the call he and Paige got earlier, finding Lance, then Lei running across the road in her skivvies, and then Vetalas. When he got to the part about Vetalas killing Paige, Baby D began sobbing.

"You okay to drive?"

She nodded. "We got to kill that motherfucker. We got to make him dead."

Konrad brooded over abandoning his job. He needed the money and they would need him right now. The earthquake damage sounded pretty severe. It was a big one, probably a seven or eight on the Richter Scale and it lasted for at least a minute. But he was overwhelmed by the events of the evening, and he found it hard to focus concern for a job he hated. He cared about the people he administered to, but he hated the system.

Baby D drove down 46th, a residential street with old, two-story stucco buildings painted in pastel shades. There was little damage here. The quake seemed to have been centered right where the vamps came through.

Baby turned right on Balboa and headed for the beach. When Konrad looked behind them, he could see a streak of light in the eastern sky. Dawn was coming.

"You sleep during the day, Lance? Or is that a myth?"

Lance lifted his head. "I sleep all day. I have to. I can't be out in the sun. I'll fry."

"I got the perfect spot for you in my basement," Konrad said just as Lei's I-Phone rang. When she answered it, her face lost all its color and she gasped. Konrad heard her say Papa in Chinese and then fire off a tirade of rapid Chinese into the phone he could not follow.

Lance spoke up. "She's talking to her father. He escaped and he's at a monastery in Tibet. They're discussing the egg and some weird prophecy."

Konrad turned around and stared at Lance and Lei. "You speak Chinese?"

Lance shrugged. "I guess us vamps can understand most languages. What, bro? Does that bother you?"

Konrad shook his head. Lei began crying softly as she spoke to her father on the phone. When she finally hung up, she gulped and wiped the tears away with the palm of her hand.

"He escaped and took a train to Tibet. He's hiding with the monks at the Samye Monastery. The monks there are a very isolated and old order of the Padmasambhava and Shantarakshita. Papa said they allowed him to take the egg because the dragon will be needed here. They know of the opening into the vampire world. They said they knew it was coming and felt the tear in the cosmos and the disruption on the spiritual plane when it happened.

"There will be constant earthquakes until the doorway into Lance's world is closed, and the monks say if the vampires are not stopped and the hole sealed, more will come through and they will kill everything in our world, everything."

"So your father knew the egg was a dragon egg all the time?"

"Yes. I can't believe he gave me that story about dinosaur eggs. And the Tong knows. They have contacts in China. They even have contacts inside the monasteries. Not Samye, but in other monasteries close by. The Blue Dragon Tong is very powerful. They have members all over the world."

"So," Baby said as she turned onto La Playa. "Let me enumerate. We have an ancient vampire in the city on a killing spree. We have more earthquakes to watch out for. The Blue Dragon Tong is after us and we got poor Paige in the back. Are you sure there isn't something you missed? I have got to get my head examined. Where you live crazy boy?"

Konrad pointed. "On the corner."

He took his garage-door opener out of a jacket pocket and hit the switch. They drove into the dark interior just as the streetlights flicked out.

Konrad jumped out of the van and opened a green footlocker. It was from his Army days. "Here, Lance, your new home."

Lance looked at it for a minute, shrugged his thin shoulders and climbed in. Konrad dropped the lid.

"I have a spot for Paige, too." He opened a huge chest freezer against the concrete-block wall of the garage and moved some packages around.

Baby D carried Paige, now carefully wrapped in a black, rubber body bag, out of the van and laid her in the freezer.

"That should keep her fresh until we decide what we're doing and get a handle on the situation in the city." Konrad said.

The interior of the garage was home to Konrad's hobby. He rode the Ninja, but he liked to design and modify Harleys. Three big bikes in various stages of reconstruction sat against the outside wall of the garage. A big, blue, Bobcat Welder, a compressor, acetylene tanks and double-decker, red toolboxes were nearby.

Konrad walked by the bikes as he led them into the back of the garage where he had a small apartment. The apartment comprised about a third of the vast two-car garage. Konrad said the people upstairs had been renting out the room since the sixties.

Once inside Konrad's one-bedroom closet, Lei placed the egg on his Lazy Boy and then joined Baby D on the couch to watch the news.

"We need to find us a hot tub to warm up the egg," Lei said.

"Why? Is it cold?" Baby D asked as she accepted a plate of bacon and eggs from Konrad.

"It's ready to hatch, Baby. It has to be 108 degrees. Got any suggestions?"

"The Four Seasons on Market. Me and Paige went there for our anniversary. They have a spa on the fourth floor with saunas, mud baths, hot tubs, aromatherapy and massages. It was heavenly."

"I'm in," Konrad said. "We might be able to use the sauna instead of putting the egg in a hot tub. Where is the hotel?"

"Market Street, the Yerba Buena District."

Lei suddenly gasped and pointed at the screen.

All eyes focused on the TV. Vetalas stood in the middle of the devastation on Mission Street in front of the Museum of Art. The camera paused on him.

"That's him," Lei pointed.

"Who?" Baby D asked.

"The vampire that killed your girlfriend. He's right there."

Baby D stood up and stared at Vetalas. "I'm coming for you motherfucker."

Chapter Six

Li Po sat behind his desk on the fourth floor above his highly successful tourist-trap of a restaurant. The restaurant was called the Golden Mountain. Only Chinese understood the significance. Golden Mountain was what Chinese in China called the U.S., especially if they wanted to immigrate.

The desk was a heavy, old, mud-brown-metal, military-style monstrosity. Papers cluttered the surface along with a green felt blotter, an anachronism if there ever was one, a desk calendar with all the months but December 1981 torn off, and a black rotary phone.

Behind Li Po, gray file cabinets sprouted papers and manila folders shoved full of more paper. On two leather couches arranged against walls covered with peeling, olive-green paint, six Tong warriors waited patiently for Li Po to tell them what to do.

The dingy room was lit by a single, forty-watt, lightbulb on a long cord descending from a hole in the off-white ceiling. The cord had half a roll of electric tape wrapped from top to the bottom where it connected to the naked bulb. Two, filthy, floor-to-ceiling windows allowed weak, gray, early-morning light into the room from the fog-shrouded sky.

Li Po stood up and surveyed his men. His vision was restricted because of the eye he lost, plucked out by a Singhalese pirate when he was thirteen. The six Tong captains in front of him were a motley assortment of street thugs and newly-immigrated men from his hometown of Shanghai on the Wong-Poo River.

Shanghai, a huge seaport, was notorious for crimes of all sorts; piracy, kidnapping, smuggling and murder-for-hire were all everyday occurrences. It was easy to recruit the best of the worst and easier still to get them out of China and into the U.S. with Li Po's many contacts. Blue Dragon Tong was strong in Shanghai.

While loving and revering his homeland, Li Po had a perfect understanding of what it was like to live in China. He'd made a life for himself here in the United States and would never move back there and undergo the restraints and restrictions the communist government placed on Chinese citizens. Poverty in China was not just a word, it was a cruel reality. Getting out of the country was the only solution for most.

"I just spoke to my superior back in our homeland. Huizhong Chang has received a communication from the monk Chimey Dorjee of the Seramey Monastery in Tibet. From this monk, he learned the dragon's egg is still in the hands of the daughter of an Army colonel. Of course, this is something we already know.

"The colonel was on his way to prison in Guangdong, but he escaped. Chang has information that Colonel Jiang is hiding in a monastery in Tibet.

"Chang says we must obtain the egg, or if it hatches the infant dragon, at all cost. This dragon is special. It is a queen and possesses the ability to bring life to the dead. It has many other great magical powers as well. If we control this dragon, we will be wealthy beyond our wildest dreams."

The men all smiled as if on cue.

"The monks have kept the secret of the dragons for centuries. They say there is an evil force entering our city right now that only the queen dragon can stop. This may be true, but it only increases her value to us. If we control her, just think what the authorities will pay for her services. Or better yet, we use her to protect only us. We will own everything."

Li Po stopped talking and took a deep breath. It was this thought, the one of power over the authorities that intrigued him the most. He had long desired to have such power, since his days as a young man in the streets of Shang-hai. He'd seen what power could give a man, not just monetary wealth, but respect. Women would fall all over themselves to kiss his turtle head.

"The earthquake last night has the city under the control of the National Guard, but this will not interfere in our hunt for the egg. We will begin at LeiHua Jiang's apartment, question anyone and everyone, and discover where she has taken the egg. I expect results. If there are none, every one of you will be replaced. There will be no repeat of last night's disasters."

Li Po opened a desk drawer and looked at Red Chua. "I should kill you now, Chua. You failed miserably and are partly responsible for allowing the girl to escape. Li Po pulled a Russian-made Pistol Makarov out of the drawer. Without hesitating, he shot Lawrence Ching in the head with one shot. Ching, a look of terrible surprise on his face, dropped to the musty, brown carpet instantly, a hole the size of an American dime right between his rolled-up eyes.

"I shot Lawrence because he was responsible for Red and he failed to impart the urgency and importance of this mission to Red. He failed to train Red properly. As Red's commander, Ching was at fault."

All five remaining soldiers stared at Ching's quivering body. As one, they looked up at Li Po, mouths agape.

"Please take this as a warning. All of you have ten men under you. You are responsible for their actions as well as your own. Red Chua, you are now the lieutenant of your unit. If it fails, you die. Take your men and find that egg. Please remember, failure is not rewarded."

*****

Across the city, Vetalas lay in the back seat of a black Chrysler 300 parked deep underground on the bottom level of a parking garage. After draining the car's owner, Vetalas had shoved him out of the way under the car.

Unable to stop the action, Vetalas burped. His stomach was full of blood. He felt more alive than he had in five years. His brain seethed with plans to rebuild his empire here in this new world. In the front seat, his first "child," a young man he'd pulled from under the rubble of a big building following the earthquake, slept. The man had been stunned, but unhurt. Vetalas had enjoyed his sweet, fresh blood, draining him until death hovered over the young man's face. Then Vetalas had sliced open his own wrist and fed his newborn child.

The newly-made were easy to control. They were terrified of their new form, queasy about hunting and feeding, and open to all instruction and guidance. It took several years for them to gain independence. Vetalas planned to build a huge army of new vampires and take over this lovely, fog-bound city.

Rebirth for Vetalas from near-death in his old world, had presented him with a new outlook on life. He felt like a newly-made vampire again. This world teemed with humans. It would take centuries to use the natural resources. Centuries he would fill with hunting, killing, and sex.

Even though it was around noon in this world, the sun barely broke through the heavy layer of fog. Vetalas loved the fog. He could stay awake much longer here than in Southern California where the heat and the harsh sun forced all vampires to take shelter as soon as the sun crested the mountains.

Sated with blood, Vetalas contemplated his other need. His newly awakened sex-drive needed feeding just as he fed his lust for blood. There were more women and young men in this city than Vetalas could use up in a hundred years. He stretched and closed his eyes. When he woke, he would find an appropriate home. The back of a car, even though it was a luxury model, was just a temporary solution.

Vetalas wanted something large, like a castle, isolated and quiet, but close to the city. He liked underground spaces, the fog and the ocean. He would begin his hunt for a home tomorrow. After all, he had plenty of time.

Vetalas rarely thought about time. Not since he was a young man in India in 3000 B.C.E., where he'd been worshipped as a god. Later, he'd moved to Egypt, where he'd built a temple to himself. But those were the good old days.

He should never have invoked Shezmu. The Egyptian demon loved slaughter, blood and red wine. He'd put a curse on Vetalas changing him into a blood-sucking vampire. Shezmu laughed while he granted Vetalas the gift he craved most, immortality. He said all things came with a price.

Vetalas closed his eyes. So much for regrets, humanity was highly over-rated.

*****

Red Chua led his men down the steps of LeiHua Jiang's apartment and into the basement. The large room beneath the old building was sectioned off with chain-link fence to form storage space for the tenants. Each little storage room had a padlocked, chain-link door.

He and his men threaded their way down the narrow alley between the storage compartments until they came to the end. The board floor of the basement ended in a bricked-up wall. The trap door was right there next to the wall.

Red lifted it and they all climbed down the rusted, metal ladder. The ladder dropped them in a dark, narrow alley with the board-floor of the apartment building forming the ceiling.

The stench of the sewer was overpowering. Several bricks had fallen off the walls following last night's earthquakes. But these sewers had weathered worst quakes than that one.

The beam of Red's flashlight licked the damp, slime-covered brick walls as Red slowly walked down the narrow alley to its exit in the main tunnel of the sewer. When they came to the junction, Red flicked the beam to his left. The room where LeiHua kept the egg was there. He flicked the beam to the right and stifled a scream with his empty hand.

Red turned and shoved his men back into the alley, bent over and vomited. Terror gripped his guts and squeezed. He was afraid he was going to shit himself. He now knew what the terrible force entering the city was and he knew exactly where it would enter.

He'd seen a swirling black hole in the wall of the sewer only ten feet from the alley leading to LeiHua's building. The hole was disturbing to look at. It swirled and churned in a stomach-turning way. Nausea made saliva flood his mouth. He spit to remove the evil.

While the hole had been terrible to see, what came through while he watched was even worse. Three vampires, each skeletally thin, their parchment-like skin pulled tight across their skulls, hair lank and falling out, shot through the hole landing in the sewage-filled canal.

"What did you see, Red?" Timmy Po, Li Po's nephew asked.

"Remember the vampire that killed Wu last night?"

Timmy nodded.

"I just saw three more fly out of a hole in the wall and land in that river of shit."

"*Goupi!*" Timmy Po hissed.

"It's not bullshit. Go look for yourself."

Timmy edged closer to the junction and peered to the right. His yellow skin paled. He fell backward and hurled up his breakfast of noodles on Red's black athletic shoes as the three shit-covered vampires stumbled into their alley.

Timmy screamed. Two men hoisted him to his feet and they charged back down the alley to the trap door at a dead run. They climbed up the ladder and slammed it shut.

Red sat on top of the trap door and panted. "You men go door to door in this building and find out if anyone saw LeiHua leave with that egg."

Not one of them mentioned what they'd seen in the alley as they left to do as he ordered.

Chapter Seven

"We'll leave at dusk," Konrad said to Baby D and Lei. "We need Lance."

Baby D shook her head and pursed her full lips. "Do you think he has a way to contact the other vampire? I mean, he could be setting us up."

"He helped us when we needed it," Lei said. "When that creature was about to suck us dry, Lance made it stop."

Baby D nodded. "Okay, we wait for Lance. But I ain't trusting him. Don't expect me to cozy up to no vampire."

Konrad was worried about Baby D. The woman was taking Paige's death very hard. She'd sat on the couch all night crying quietly and hadn't eaten the bacon and eggs he cooked for her. She'd even gone into the garage, pulled Paige's poor corpse out of the freezer, and kissed her pale white lips. Konrad knew this because he kept an eye on her. He didn't want Baby D going off half-cocked to find Vetalas on her own. That could only lead to her death.

The loss of his job still had Konrad stressed. His mother lived in a group, nursing home in Albany, right across the bay. The government paid most of the expenses, but Konrad brought her treats. How could he afford to buy her candy and copies of the tabloids if he was broke? His poor mother loved to read those trashy rags. They were her way of escaping the sad reality of being partially paralyzed.

"Help me and Lei and I will heal your mother's affliction."

"Hey, stay the fuck out of my head. I already said I'd help her and I will. I don't need false promises and a bunch of bull crap to motivate me. I know I'm doing what's right."

"You plan to abandon us as soon as I'm hatched. Stay with us. Be my bodyguard."

Having a dragon shoving her thoughts into his head made Konrad very uncomfortable. "I'll think about it," he snarled.

"She can help your mother," Lei said. "Lung Ma possesses many powers."

Konrad stood up. "I don't need anyone's help, ever, and neither does my mom. What I do need is for you two to stay out of my brain. What time is it?"

"It's almost six-thirty," Baby D said. "Sunset is in twenty minutes."

At that exact moment, the door to the garage opened and Lance emerged. "Hey dudes, what's shakin'?"

"I thought you had to sleep until sunset." Konrad snarled, and his already dark mood headed straight into the crapper.

"It's the fog, bro. San Francisco is great. You got to love a city that's dark and gloomy all the time."

"Hey, sometimes it clears up midday. You just never get to see it." Konrad grabbed some supplies he'd put together for their journey and stuffed them in a duffel bag. He picked up his Remington, M1911, and packed the 45.-caliber in the bag along with extra clips and boxes of rounds. He packed his M16 with magazines and rounds. During the night, he'd made some stakes. He shoved them into the bag as well.

"Hey, Lance, will a stake through the heart kill Vetalas?"

Lance looked up. His face was white as milk with thin blue veins visible in his neck and cheeks. "Not Vetalas. It might kill me, but it would probably only paralyze me. When you removed the stake, I'd eat your ass."

"How about holy water, garlic, silver crosses?"

Lance shook his head at each item. "Nope, nope and nope."

"Do vampires have to wait to be invited into your home?"

Lance chuckled. "Hell no."

"Are there any other weird and nasty things gonna come out of that hole, or just you vampires?"

Lance looked thoughtful. "Vetalas could bring over the demons."

Konrad shuddered. Of course, it just kept getting better and better. He asked the obvious. "What's a demon?"

"Offspring of two vampires. It's like a whole new race, dude. We call them the Volthok. They're pretty big, really ugly, and they have wings. Oh yeah, and they're sterile, though they do like sex."

"And they have horns, too, right?"

"How did you know?"

Konrad closed his eyes and sighed. "Okay, staking won't work. So, what will kill Vetalas?"

"You'll have to cut off his head and then burn the body and the head just to make sure." Lance watched Konrad putting energy bars, dried fruit, candy and water bottles into the duffel. "You got any bottles of blood in there? I'm kind of hungry."

"No blood. How are we supposed to feed you?"

Baby D slowly backed toward Konrad's small kitchen. "Hey, I seen this in the movies. Is this where one of us has to offer to open a vein to feed the vamp?"

Lance titled his head to one side and rolled his eyes. "I won't eat you, Baby D. I can go without food for a long time. I'm just hungry. Can't I say so?"

"Can you feed off someone without killing them?" Konrad asked as he hefted the filled duffel and opened the door to the garage.

"Of course. Well, if I'm not starving. When I killed the wino, I was out of control."

"I'd go to the blood bank and swipe some blood for you, but I feel sure the earthquake has the hospitals full and a serious blood shortage in full swing. I do have an idea, though."

Lei carried the egg as they trouped into the garage and loaded their stuff into the morgue's meat wagon. Lance stopped to look at one of the bikes Konrad was restoring. It was a 1936 Harley, Knuckle-Head.

He ran his hand over the airbrushing on the gas tank. It was a painting of a sunset, the white caps rolling in and a porpoise leaping in the waves. "This is awesome, dude. Did you paint it?"

Konrad tossed the bag into the back of the van. "Yeah, I restore old bikes. I got that one at a junk yard for almost nothing."

Lance climbed into the back with Lei and the egg. "Hey, bro, you could, like do this for a living. You're good."

"Thanks, I'll take it under consideration. I am currently unemployed."

When Baby tried to climb into the driver's seat, Konrad stopped her. "I'll drive, Baby. You ride shotgun." To illustrate his words, Konrad handed her a Mossberg 5500 MKII, short barreled shotgun.

Baby turned it over and examined it. "This is righteous, Konrad. Is it legal?"

"Barely." He tossed her a handful of shells. "Load it. Hey Lance, will a round from this shotgun at close range kill Vetalas?"

Lance glanced at the Mossberg. "Make a big hole in him, but no, won't kill him. He'll heal up right before your eyes, take it from you, and shove it up your ass."

Konrad sighed. "Will it slow him down?"

Lance pursed his lips. "For a minute or two."

Konrad backed the van out of the garage and hit the button that closed the door. He drove the van toward town thinking about what he needed and how to get it. His first stop was a supermarket on La Playa. The blood mobile was there. He parked. "I'll be a minute," he told his group and stepped out.

He'd donated a lot of blood. The girl taking information had him in the system. In minutes he was hooked up to a pint bag with a rubber ball in his fist. When the pint was filled, the girl slapped a wad of cotton and a piece of stretchy pressure wrap tape over the wound.

"You sure are a big ole thing," she said in a Southern accent. Her Baptist, bosomy, blonde looks did not appeal to Konrad. His type was more of an edgy Asian chick.

She handed Konrad a carton of orange juice with a straw. Konrad yanked the straw out of the juice, discarded the OJ, grabbed his pint of blood, and headed down the narrow aisle of the bloodmobile, squeezing his bulk between reclining, leather seats.

"Mister, you can't take your blood with you," Blondie called, running after him. "It's ours."

"Sorry," Konrad apologized as he swung down the steps. "I've made a lot of deposits. This time, I need to make a withdrawal."

She stood with her hands on her hips and a confused expression on her round, apple-pie face, while Konrad climbed into the van.

"Lance, dinner is on me." He chucked the plastic bag of blood at the vamp, then handed him the straw. "Enjoy. It's still warm."

Lance stuck the straw into the capped tube and sucked. The thick, red liquid flowed into his mouth, visible through the clear-plastic straw. "This is really good, bro. It smells and tastes rough and rugged, just like you. Now that I've dined on your essence, I'll be able t sense you wherever you are. We'll be like real bros."

Konrad growled. "Just what I needed to complete my family, a vamp brother."

"Do you think I'll turn Berserker now?" Lance sucked down the last of the one pint making a slurping sound when the straw hit an empty spot.

Konrad's next stop was an all-night pawn shop in the Mission District. He parked on South Van Ness and got out. "You guys wait here. If I find what I'm looking for, I'll be right out."

Konrad was back in less than ten minutes with a bundle under his arm.

"What is it?" Baby asked.

Lei sat up close to his seat and laid a tiny hand on Konrad's twenty-inch bicep. "What's in the bag?"

Konrad tossed it in the back. "Something we may be able to use, if we get an opportunity."

Lance opened it and drew an official, Marine Corps, dress sword out of the bag, red and gold tassels dangling from the hilt. "You gonna whack Vetalas's head off with this thing?"

"That's the plan."

"That'll work."

Konrad pulled into the parking garage adjacent to the Four Seasons and stashed the morgue van. Baby D was the only one of them who had stayed at the hotel. She led them into an elevator and up to the fourth floor.

It was midnight.

"The spa should be empty this late," Baby D whispered, as the elevator stopped. When the doors opened, Konrad looked out. The hall was carpeted in royal blue and empty. Etched glass doors in front of the elevator read Four Seasons Spa in flowing calligraphy. Silky, white drapes hung on floor-to-ceiling glass walls stretching the length of the hallway on the spa side.

The doors were locked. Konrad hit the glass with his shoulder once and the lock popped open.

Looking both ways one more time, he entered the dark spa, his group right behind him.

"Are we going with the sauna or the hot tub?" Lei asked.

"Let's use the sauna," Konrad said. "I've always enjoyed sweating. Besides, I'm worried about immersing the egg. Lung Ma might drown when she emerges."

Baby D led them to a cedar-lined room furnished with two rows of cedar benches. The controls were on the wall outside the sauna.

"Put the egg in there and I'll dial up 108 degrees," Konrad said.

Lei put the egg on one of the benches and stepped out. There was a window in the door. Baby D, Konrad and Lei jostled for position to see into the room. Konrad won.

"Do you think I should go in there and sit with her?" Lei asked.

"Whatever floats your boat," Baby D replied.

Lei shucked her jacket and went into the room to sit beside the egg.

Konrad looked around. "Where's Lance?"

"I have no idea where that skinny, little, blood-sucking, motherfucker went," Baby D snapped. "He creeps me out."

Konrad left the sauna door and went hunting for Lance. He found him staring at a tanning bed with a wistful expression on his face.

"It'll fry you," Konrad said.

"I know. I just wish I could get a tan. You think I like pasty white?"

"Come on, the egg is going to hatch any minute. I can feel her waking up."

Konrad felt a rustling inside his head, like a breeze blowing through piles of leaves. Lei screamed, and he heard it with his ears and in his head.

They ran back through the spa, by offices, mud rooms, an enormous hot tub and massage tables. A large veranda opened off the room with the hot tub. Lounge chairs and a table sat out on the veranda under the stars.

The sauna door was open. Lei stood in the open door, her face as white as Lance's.

"It's cracking," she gasped.

Chapter Eight

Lucy Hee towed the big stainless-steel cart out of the service elevator onto the fourth floor. She hated working the nightshift. Her only consolation was Cindy Shepard, the shift supervisor, was screwing her boyfriend on the sixth floor which allowed Lucy to do pretty much whatever she wanted.

Grunting, Lucy shoved the cart down the carpeted hallway. It was filled with clean towels and bathrobes, all embroidered with the hotel's logo. It was her job to stock the spa every night.

When she got to the spa door, she froze. The etched-glass doors hung open. Someone was in there. Lucy abandoned the cart in the reception area and slowly crept into the spa. She heard voices down the hallway near the sauna.

No one was in sight, so Lucy looked into the sauna through the window in the door. She had to cover her mouth with both hands to stifle a gasp. An oriental girl was sitting on one of the benches next to an enormous egg. It looked like she was talking to it.

Lucy turned and ran. She raced by her cart with its load of towels and into the hall. She stopped, pulled her cell phone out of her pocket and hit number-one on speed dial.

"Lucy, baby, how many times do I have to tell you? Don't call me every five minutes. I'm busy."

"Timmy, remember that egg you told me you were looking for?"

"Yeah, of course I remember. I'm at the city morgue right now. One of LeiHua's neighbors saw her and a bunch of people load a large egg into one of the coroner's vans last night."

"Timmy," she breathed. "It's here."

"What are you talking about? What's here?"

"The egg, the egg is on the fourth floor right now."

"Of the Four Seasons?"

Lucy rolled her eyes. Guys were so thickheaded. Any woman would have instantly understood what she was talking about. "Duh!"

Timmy Po inhaled deeply. She heard it. "Don't move. I mean stay out of sight and watch the egg. Keep track of it until I get there. Call me if you see anyone or if whoever's got the egg decides to move it."

"I already saw someone. I think it's that LeiHua girl. She's sitting in one of the saunas talking to it right now."

"Did you see anyone else?"

"Not yet. They broke into the spa." Lucy could hear her boyfriend shouting to his Tong captain Red Chua.

"We'll be there in half an hour. Watch that egg."

"Okay, I will. Love you."

He hung up without telling her he loved her. Men were so self-absorbed. Timmy probably hadn't even heard her. No doubt, he'd already punched the end-call button.

Lucy slipped back into the spa and went behind the desk. From this position, she was out of sight and she could hear voices. When a girl screamed, she peeked around the corner into the hall, just in time to see a huge man, a very pale surfer, and a large black woman open the sauna door and rush inside.

*****

The first thing Konrad saw was a tail. Ice blue scales covered Lung Ma's tail which was as thick as his forearm, tapering to the thickness of a woman's wrist.

Lei spoke to the dragon baby in her head. Konrad could hear them both which he found disturbing. Lei laughed and helped shove the top of the egg off the baby dragon. Her eyes spinning circles of silver, Lung Ma stuck her head up and looked around. When she spotted Lance, she hissed.

"He's here to help," Konrad said aloud. He'd about had enough of this telepathy shit. "His name is Lance."

52

We need to leave immediately, Lung Ma thought as she stared up at Konrad.

Konrad tried to fight the incredible attraction he felt for the dragon. She was beautiful. Her wings were wet and when she stretched them out to dry, they glistened a beautiful silvery blue. The thin membrane of the wing stretched between bony supports was an iridescent blue that glowed with red and green highlights like a gem.

But it wasn't her looks that attracted him. It was the feeling he got in his chest when he looked at her. The feeling was like no other Konrad had ever experienced. It swelled inside his chest and up into his throat. Tears flooded his eyes. He felt incredible love for Lung Ma and a terrible protectiveness. He had to swallow a huge lump in his throat.

The dragon's eyes fascinated him. They spun like a kaleidoscope filled with stars. "There is a woman just outside this door. She is waiting for someone named Timmy Po to come with his men and kill you."

Lei jumped off the bench. "There's a woman out there from the Tong," she said to Lance and Baby as she pointed to the spa's reception area.

"I'll get her," Lance said.

Lance returned in seconds with a terrified Chinese girl.

Her name is Lucy, Konrad heard in his head.

"How many men are coming, Lucy?" Konrad asked.

Lucy's eyes were wide, her face as white as Lance's.

"Make her tell us what she knows, Lance." Konrad snarled and took a deep breath. He could feel himself changing into Berserker mode. Something bad was about to happen.

Lance's fangs snicked out and he bared them at the girl.

"Lance here is really hungry," Baby D said. "If you don't talk, we're going to let him have you for breakfast."

She doesn't know, Lung Ma thought. *She only knows he'll be here in seconds.*

Lance dropped the girl. Konrad picked up Lung Ma and they all ran out of the spa for the elevator. It arrived with a ding to announce it before Baby D could hit the down button.

"They're inside," Lei said. "Run."

"Run where?" Konrad snapped as his eyes began to bulge and his face to swell.

They ran back into the spa and stopped by the chairs in the reception area. Ten men poured out of the elevator, all heavily armed with automatic weapons.

That was enough for Konrad. "Here, Baby D, carry the dragon."

No! Lung Ma shrieked into his brain. *Only you must carry me, Sledge. You are the Hammer.*

Konrad roared. He wanted to attack. He was ready. His body rushed with the overload of adrenaline Berserker mode dumped into his blood.

They turned and ran into the spa, down the hall, past the sauna and mud rooms into the open area with the hot tub.

There! Lung Ma pointed her forepaw, armed with long curved talons, at the balcony.

Without pausing, Konrad opened the balcony doors and then stopped. There was no escape this way, only a two-story drop to the pool located on the second floor.

He turned as heavy fire erupted from the Tong bracketing them in bullets.

The leader stepped onto the balcony. "Give me the dragon and I will let you go."

As one, the ten members of the Tong dropped to the ground, holding their ears and screaming. Konrad could hear an angry buzzing in his head.

"She's hitting them with a mental scream," Lei yelled. "It will only hold them for a second. We must jump. She says we must jump into the pool."

Lei immediately turned and leaped off the balcony. Lance followed her. Baby D's eyes were huge, the whites showing all around the brown pupil. "I ain't going off this balcony. I can't fly and I

The Tong was regrouping, slowly pulling themselves upright.

"You have to Baby, just close your eyes. Lance is down there. He'll catch you."

"Noooo," Baby moaned. "You know I don't like Lance."

Konrad shoved her toward the rail. "Do it now."

Baby closed her eyes, keening a soft wail. "Push me, Konrad."

Konrad gave her a shove.

"Harder," Baby wailed as a barrage of bullets hit the glass windows.

Konrad grabbed Baby around the waist and launched both of them out into space. Lung Ma flapped her wings, giving Konrad a slight lift. They floated rather than plummeted which was exactly what Baby D did.

When Konrad looked down, he saw Lance leap high and catch Baby D, setting her lightly into the shallow end of the pool.

The four of them swarmed out of the pool, Konrad carrying the dragon, and raced into the hotel just as Tong members began dropping into the water. Konrad stopped in the doorway as one of the Chinese fighters missed the pool and landed hard on a lounge chair.

"That is going to leave a bruise," Baby D said and turned to run through the locker-room.

It was three in the morning. No one was around to stop them, not a bellboy, a maid or a desk clerk, as they raced through the lobby for the elevator to the parking garage.

In the elevator, Konrad slowly began to decompress. "I can't believe I left all the weapons in the van."

Chapter Nine

Vetalas sank his fangs into the woman's shoulder. He had no idea what her name was. She was tall, exquisitely beautiful, and lying beneath him. At the moment, that was all he cared about.

With his fangs in her shoulder, she shook and shuddered, too terrified to move. A mental image of a stallion mounting a mare with its teeth in her shoulder filled his head as he drove into her over and over again. When he felt himself reaching climax, he jerked his organ out of her, detached his fangs and shoved his dick in her mouth.

The only fluid in a vampire's body was blood. Vampires cried bloody tears and when a male ejaculated, the fluid was blood, only a little different. The blood was filled with male hormones and the purest essence of a vampire. It was the easiest way to turn a human.

He climbed off the bed and shook his loincloth into place while he stared at the naked woman. "Cover yourself. I have no more need of you and your display is disgusting to me."

The woman scrambled off the bed. A thin trickled of blood ran from the hollow of her shoulder across her breasts. He watched her as she pulled a filmy gold wrap over her white body and left the room.

Sighing with satiation, Vetalas sank into his recliner and turned on the TV. This modern society had two great inventions. One was the recliner. He'd sat in hundreds of hard, upright, uncomfortable chairs in his life. Settling down, Vetalas flipped the lever and the footrest popped up. This was such an improvement.

The other great human invention was the flat-screen TV. His was huge, sixty-inches, and the picture was amazing. Through this TV, he could go outdoors and enjoy a sunset or a sunrise. There was even a station that did nothing but broadcast such wonderful sights.

He was comfortable in this house located high on Nob Hill. He'd taken over the Moody Mansion. The interior had recently been redone and was owned by the beautiful woman he'd just violated. Originally built in the 1870s by J.B. Moody, who made his fortune mining gold and then stealing other claims, the house had survived the 1906 earthquake and the fire three days later.

The interior decorating was opulent and dark. The deep maroons and golds of the wallpaper, carpets and upholstery, blended with dark mahogany and bronze accents, exactly suited him. But even with twelve bedrooms and numerous formal and family living areas, the house was not as big as he felt he needed. He'd continue to search for the perfect site.

The knock on the door felt like an interruption. His right-hand man, Marcelus, entered just as the local news came on.

"Master," Marcelus began.

Vetalas motioned for silence.

He'd seen something that captured his whole attention. Several creditable eyewitnesses, and some not-so-creditable, were telling the reporter they'd seen a baby dragon and four people jump off the fourth floor of the Four Seasons. They even had a furry video taken by a camera phone.

Vetalas leaned forward to get a better look, straining to separate the grainy images on the video. Then he sat back and rubbed his eyes. The image was definitely of a dragon, a sliver and blue, ice dragon infant. Not only was there a recognizable dragon in the video, but he also recognized the man holding it. It was the enormous human his offspring Lance had sheltered in the sewer. When the camera panned to watch them climb out of the pool, he saw the Chinese girl from the sewer as well.

"What is it, master?"

"Bad news. That, my friend, is a vampire killer."

Marcelus lifted one eyebrow. "How is it able to kill us, Master? It is so small."

Vetalas leaned back enjoying the comfort of his plush chair and closed his eyes. "It is only a baby. When I was a boy in India, we heard many stories of ice dragons in the Himalayan Mountains. The monks tended these dragons for centuries."

"I had no idea you originated in India, Master."

"Yes, humbly so as well. My parents were Untouchables. We had no hope of bettering ourselves until we died and were reborn. But I dreamed. When the Brahmins held school, I would slip inside, hide and listen to the stories our kind were not supposed to hear.

"There was a temple in Tiruchirapalli, the town of my birth, called Thiruanaikka, devoted to Shiva the Destroyer. On the walls of this temple were paintings of ice dragons. I saw them with my own eyes. Ice Dragons can kill a vampire with their strength and their venom. One bite from an ice dragon and you're dead. It may take a while, but you die."

"How did this dragon get here?"

"We must find out. It is only an infant, probably just hatched. We must find it and kill it before it grows."

"How big is it going to get?"

"Think tyrannosaurus."

"Fuck me!"

"Exactly."

When Marcelus left, Vetalas turned on the Soap Channel to watch the replay of Days of Our Lives. His mind mulled over the problem at hand. He kept returning to Lance. Lance was his child. There might be some remnants of loyalty and constraints he could capitalize on. Later, close to dawn, he would try calling Lance. You never knew. It might work.

*****

Baby D's apartment was tiny. Konrad paced up and down the small space between the sofa and the coffee table. He felt filled with energy he could find no way to release.

When he looked at his watch, he saw it was three in the morning. Baby D was at work. They'd dropped her and the van at the morgue and taken her car to her apartment. The flat was in a small house on Fulton, close to the park.

Lei was asleep with her arm over Lung Ma. The dragon was a bottomless pit. They'd stopped at a grocery store and loaded up on lamb. She'd told Konrad lamb was all dragons ate. In his mind, he'd received a crystal-clear vision of a blue sheep. Lei told him there was a breed of sheep in the Himalayas that was blue.

She'd had to accept twelve legs of lamb bought with the last of Konrad's cash, scarfing the frozen treats up like they were dog biscuits and she a Pitbull. What in the hell were they going to feed her tomorrow?

The dragon had already grown. It was almost like you could watch her growing while she slept. Konrad kicked her discarded first skin as he paced, finally bending over to pick it up and look at it. It looked exactly like a snakeskin only silvery blue. She'd shed it right after they got here, wiggling and squirming and rubbing herself on the rough carpet.

I'm hungry again.

Konrad sighed. They needed to come up with a solution and quick.

Lance walked in the front door and flopped on the sofa.

"She's hungry again."

"She's going to be hungry until she's grown. There's a small herd of sheep in the park. They might not miss one or two."

"If she would eat winos like you, we wouldn't have this problem. Did you dine while you were out?"

"Oh, yeah."

"What else did you do?"

Lance smiled. "You don't want to know."

The phone rang and Konrad snatched it up. "Hey, the fucking morgue is packed with vampire victims," Baby D shrieked. "We got 'em stacked in the freezer like a pile of dead squirrels been run over by a Mack truck. What's going on?"

"I didn't do it," Lance said.

"Baby, I'm going back into the sewer. Either the doorway to the vampire dimension is still open or Vetalas has been working overtime. I think I better check."

"One of these dead motherfuckers rose up off his gurney and tried to bite me. I stabbed it with a trocar and then hacked off its head with a scalpel. Liked to scare me to death. In all my days working in the morgue, not one dead body ever rose up off the table. Not one."

"Tell her it will happen again."

"Lance says watch out, there will be others."

"Thanks for telling me. Find out where they're coming from, Konrad. This is bad, very bad. Hey, if you come by here, grab the police scanner. It's rockin' and rollin' in China Town."

Konrad hung up. "Let's go Lance. We need to find the dragon something to eat and then check out the sewer."

Chapter Ten

The door blasted open waking Lei up. She screamed.

Lung Ma was beside the sofa on the floor snoring, her dragon mouth open with a thin stream of drool puddling beneath it. Lei fell over the dragon in an effort to protect her.

"Get your hands off me," Lei snarled as a black-masked Tong member lifted her up and off the dragon by her armpits.

Lei recognized Red Chua even though he too was masked. You couldn't miss the dyed, red hair. Chua threw a net over the dragon and two other Tong members quickly rolled her over and over enmeshing her thoroughly in webbing.

"Do we take the girl?"

Red glared at Lei. "No. Kill her."

Red left with the dragon and the two young Chinese men pointed their weapons at Lei. She backed away from them until her legs were against the sofa. Her heart thudded in her chest and bile filled her throat.

Suddenly, the two men dropped their weapons and fell to the floor with their hands gripping their ears. Lei heard a buzzing inside her head and realized Lung Ma was sending mental signals to the men, disrupting their brain patterns. It wouldn't last long.

She snatched an AK-47 off the floor and rushed out the door. She was just in time to see Red shoving Lung Ma into a black panel van. He came around the side of the van and Lei fired off a blast of automatic rounds. The weapon's kick knocked her off the steps and into the shrubbery next to the concrete staircase.

Crawling out of the boxwoods, she was just in time to catch Red's parting one-finger gesture. He pulled earbuds out of his ears and swung them around on their cord to mock her. Somehow he'd figured a way to block Lung Ma's transmission. The two downed men she'd left inside raced out of the apartment, jumped aboard and the van laid rubber.

Lei promptly burst into tears.

Don't worry, child, the dragon whispered into her brain. *I may be young, but I can take care of myself.*

How will we find you?

Do not worry. When it is time, I will call for you and the Hammer. He will save me.

What was it with Lung Ma and Sledge? Lei trudged back up the stairs and called Baby D.

"The Tong stole her," Lei said into the phone. "Lung Ma is gone."

"Does Konrad have a cell phone?"

"I don't think so. He never told me about one or gave me a number."

"We need to integrate that boy into the twenty-first century."

"What should I do?"

"Sit tight. What else can you do?"

*****

Konrad drove Baby's car to the morgue and snagged the bag of weapons and the sword. He wasn't going anywhere anymore unarmed. He tossed the weapons to Lance and went back into the van emerging with the police scanner.

"We need to keep on top of things," he said. "This will help."

The vampire shrugged.

When Konrad flicked the scanner on, an immediate array sounded. Two tones, the first one was for the ambulance, the second for the cops. Each tone was distinct. There were others for Hazmat and the fire department. The operator called for them to go to the corner of Stockton and Washington, right in the middle of China Town.

They parked Baby's car on Wetmore, an alley just off Clay, and started walking toward the manhole that led to Lance's sewer.

Konrad carried the sword, a flashlight, and had his pistol stuffed into the front of his pants.

It was just after three and the streets were deserted. Konrad saw two bums sleeping on the sidewalk with their backs against a Chinese herb store. The streetlights cast a sick, yellow haze through the encroaching fog. The hair on his neck began to rise and he felt his face swelling. Even Lance felt the menace in the air.

"Dude, this place feels like it's ready to explode."

Konrad said nothing, just nodded.

They found the manhole cover laying in the middle of the black street. A skeletal vampire stuck his head out of the hole and without hesitating, Konrad sliced it off. The grotesque head went rolling down the street.

Konrad kicked the body back into the hole and shined his police-issue flashlight into the sewer. "Holy shit!"

Another vampire shot out of the hole, grasping for Konrad's throat. He hacked the vamp in two, right about at midsection. Berserker mode took over and Konrad roared. A steady stream of vampires flew out of the hole, surrounding and circling Konrad. Lance took on several and the fight was on.

Constantly screaming war cries from a thousand years ago, Konrad attacked with his sword. The Marines would have been proud of what that baby accomplished. Turning constantly in an effort to keep the vamps off his back, Konrad hacked with clean swipes, dissecting three more vampires. Thick blood sprayed everywhere. Konrad was coated with it.

A vamp jumped on Konrad's back and dug its fangs into his neck. Lance jerked it off and threw it all the way to the sidewalk where it crashed into a Chinese meat market. The glass in the windows shattered and rotisseried Peking ducks flew into the street.

The flow of vamps subsided, and Konrad was able to catch his breath. Looking around, he saw vampire parts everywhere; legs, arms, heads, torsos and lots and lots of blood. He was covered in it and so was Lance. The two bums were awake staring, eyes wide, mouths hanging open. One picked up a duck and stuffed it into his overcoat. The other one just ran.

"Let's go." Konrad's voice was a low growl as he jumped into the hole ignoring the steel ladder. He landed ten feet below in a crouch, sword in one big fist, flashlight in the other. He played the powerful beam down the tunnel and over the walls. No movement. But his hyper-alert senses told him something was going on further down the passageway, toward Waverly Place.

The two of them loped down the tunnel, sewage churning sluggishly beside the walkway. Konrad didn't even notice the smell. All his senses were tuned in to what was in front of him.

They passed the open doorway leading to the room where Lei stashed the egg.

"Slow down, bro, we got company."

Konrad slowed, hugging the wall. He played the beam ahead and snarled. More male and female vampires jogged toward them. They looked like something straight out of *Night of the Living Dead*, hands dangling at their sides formed into grasping claws, jaws open and salivating, lips drawn back in a hideous parody of a smile, fangs exposed.

Taking up a defensive posture, Konrad dropped the flashlight and held the sword with both hands cocked over his right shoulder samurai style. He and Lance blocked the vamps way out, sewage on one side, brick wall on the other.

The first vampire flew at Konrad. He easily took it out with one swipe. But the second and third were on him in seconds. Lance threw one into the sewage, it bounced back like it was on a trampoline. Konrad hacked a chunk out of one and beheaded another. There were five more. Konrad began screaming his war cries and growling, flinging saliva everywhere as he whirled in circles slicing and dicing vampires.

When all of the vamps lay in pieces or floating down sewage river, Konrad bent over panting. The adrenaline rush always left him exhausted.

"Wow, dude that was incredible. You're like some barbarian warrior. You're Konan man, you're fucking Konan."

"We got to go find that hole," Konrad gasped.

"Sure, man, lead on."

It took him a minute to get his wind back. When he could breathe easier, Konrad led them deeper into the sewer. It didn't take him long to find the hole.

"Whoa," Lance said pointing. "That is far out."

Konrad looked at it and his stomach heaved. The hole was the size of a manhole, the inside a gut-wrenching black, swirling, vacuum. Lance just stared as though mesmerized. Konrad had to look away. It made him horribly sick inside his head and in his stomach.

"We gotta close that thing," Konrad said. He was bent over, his hands on his knees when he heard Lung Ma scream into his head, followed by a buzzing he recognized as the defense mechanism she used at the spa.

"The Tong has the dragon."

Lance didn't answer. When Konrad looked for him, the vampire was gone. "What the fuck?"

Chapter Eleven

Konrad had no idea where Lance booked off to. He spent the next fifteen minutes calling the vampire's name and searching dead end tunnels, walking endless miles through a stinking hell, all without ever seeing or hearing a peep out of Lance.

Maybe the vamp went back through the hole he came out of. Or maybe he smelled some delicious human and went off hunting. Konrad didn't know and he was pretty sick of worrying about it.

He finally gave up. That hole needed closing A.S.A.P. The only thing he could think of was explosives, and he knew just the man for the job. Ricky "Junior" Melman, ex-member of the Army bomb squad in Baghdad, an overworked unit that got little sleep and had a very high fatality rate.

Junior presently lived in the Fillmore on Divisadero. During the day he owned and operated a computer networking business that also provided servers for businesses that couldn't afford their own. Really, his employees ran the business. Junior sat on a huge leather couch in the back room where he played endless games of Call of Duty and dabbled in the online-weapons market. At night, he played jazz saxophone in Tiny's Jazz Café on Fillmore.

It was dawn by the time Konrad climbed into Baby's car and headed downtown to pick her up. He figured he'd take her home and head over to the Fillmore and find Junior.

His head ached and he was exhausted. But that hole needed to be blocked off immediately. Every minute it was open meant more vamps could cross into their world.

"Where's Lance?" Was the first thing out of Baby D's mouth when she climbed into the car.

"I don't know. One minute we were fighting off a hundred starving blood suckers, and the next minute he was gone."

"Well, that's weird, but no weirder than the shit I been through last night. I can't do an autopsy without a bread knife on the table next to the stiff. I had to do head-ectomies three times last night. And after you cut off their heads, they still try to get you."

Baby shuddered.

"Until we close the entrance from Lance's world into ours, it's going to get worse. After I drop you, I'm gonna go find a man I know who deals in explosives."

Baby rifled her purse and pulled something out. "Here. Me and Lei decided you need a cell phone. You know the Tong took the dragon, don't you?"

She handed him an iPhone.

Konrad glanced at it and crammed it into his pocket. Great! Now they could find him whenever they wanted. "I figured as much when I heard Lung Ma scream into my head. How's Lei taking it?"

They pulled up to Baby's apartment, Konrad parked and climbed out.

"Ask her yourself."

Lei exploded through the front door. She must have been waiting, watching the street. Throwing herself on Konrad she bawled and blubbered, finally pulling herself together enough to speak.

"They kidnapped her, Sledge. Those freaking Tong assholes wrapped her up in a net and took her away."

"Has she communicated with you?"

Lei shook her head. "Not since they first snatched her. They must be keeping her in some kind of room that blocks her telepathic waves."

Baby D slowly climbed out of the car and up the stairs. "Why don't you two go visit Konrad's friend. I gotta sleep."

"You have a friend?" Lei said as she jumped into the car.

"He's not really a friend, more like an old acquaintance."

"I knew it," Lei said. "You have no friends. With your personality, you're probably lucky your mother loves you."

70

Konrad rolled his eyes. What had he ever done to make her think these things about him?

"You, on the other hand, are clearly possessed of a wide assortment of friends. How old are you, Miss Virgin?"

"Hey," she snapped. "I wouldn't be throwing that in my face if I were you. Maybe I'm saving myself for the right man. What's your excuse? Because buddy, apparently, your love life is as arid as mine. How old are you?"

"Lei, let's call a truce, please. I'm exhausted, and on my last nerve."

She grinned. "Works for me. What happened to Lance?"

They talked about Lance and his weird disappearance until Konrad hooked a left off Fulton onto Divisadero and parked in front of a squat gray building with a blue front door and no windows. A sign on the front said, Melman Networking.

They walked right into the building. The inside was cold and lit by recessed fluorescent lights. The interior was painted the same gray as the exterior, and everywhere you looked huge computer towers glowed with green lights from steel shelving. Confusing nests of wires were bundled and routed under the shelves and behind everything. The place hummed. The humming was a deep vibration you could feel in your feet and as waves of energy all around your body.

"There are some really big machines in here," Lei said.

"You could probably run the National Missile Defense system with Junior's equipment."

An Asian man and a black woman sat hunched over keyboards. Huge flat-screen monitors showed they were working in computer code. The Asian man looked up, his fingers still touching the keyboard. He lifted one thin eyebrow.

"I'm here to see Junior."

The Asian said nothing just tilted his head toward a door in the back, right corner of the room.

71

Konrad knocked first, and then opened the door. Junior Melman was a huge African American. He'd been kicked out of the Army after ten years of disarming bombs for his country because he was out of shape and overweight. He put together this business with his mustering-out pay and proceeded to get even fatter.

Junior saw who was in the doorway. Konrad could tell because his fat fingers stopped tapping the oversized controller for a nano second.

"What you want, Sledge?" He asked without pausing or looking up again.

"I need to buy some guns and maybe some weapons-grade C-4."

Junior's sausage-shaped fingers kept up the continuous tapping on the controller buttons. It sounded like someone with long fingernails working over typewriter keys at eighty words a minute.

"What you gonna blow up, crazy man?"

"I know you spend a lot of time in seclusion, but maybe you noticed the city is being overrun by vampires."

"I heard a lot of weird shit on the internet, but I ain't seen no undead around here."

"There seems to be a hole in our universe located in China Town. It leads to a world populated by bloodsuckers. They've killed everything on their planet and can't wait to get here and do the same."

"Sledge, you talking some crazy shit. But if there's a dimensional hole somewhere in San Francisco, I want to see it."

Konrad had a brief, but hysterical mental image of Junior trying to fit his bulk down the manhole. "It's in the sewer under China Town. I don't think we can get you down there."

"We can use the trap door under my building."

Both Lei's eyebrows were raised as she clearly tried to communicate something to Konrad. He shrugged his shoulders. He had no idea what she was trying to tell him.

"You sure you want to see this thing? It made my stomach turn."

"That's because of the dimensional shift. You're looking into a doorway between our world and another. The place in the middle where the two worlds meet is always going to be shifting and turning. One second you'll be looking into their world and then the door will close and you'll be seeing our world. It's all happening so fast, shifting and changing, the two universes colliding and they're different, it makes for a scene right out of a nightmare."

"How do you know about all this?" Konrad was getting impatient. He was tired, wanted the stuff to blow up the hole, and to get out of there.

Junior stopped playing the game. Konrad could see the fifty-two-inch, Sony, flat screen. He'd paused it. Heaving himself out of the nest his bulk carved in the leather couch, Junior wobbled for a minute, then righted himself.

"Internet, and I actually read. Take me to this hole, Sledge, and I hope you ain't yanking my chain."

*****

Deep beneath the Bank of the Orient, on Stockton Street in China Town, Red Chua and Timmy Po lugged two sides of lamb into a secret elevator accessed through the main vault that led even deeper beneath the structure. When it opened on the bottom floor, they dropped their burdens into a laundry cart sitting on a brick walkway leading to a huge door.

The door was built of cast iron lined with lead. Behind the door was a vault built by the first Chinese millionaire to enter this city from his homeland, Lee Kwan Tsiang. Lee founded the Bank of the Orient and his descendants still ran it. Li Po's mother was a Lee.

Red unlocked the door with an iron key he took off a hook.

"Be careful, Red. The devil dragon may be loose in there."

"Do not worry so much. She is totally subdued now that we put the collar on her."

73

Red took a pair of specially designed earbuds out of his pocket, stuffed them in his ears and attached the cord to a small device in the same pocket. Timmy did the same. When Red turned the device on, a metallic whine filled his ears and his head.

Timmy slowly swung the heavy door open. The ice dragon rose on her hind legs and roared at them. An iron collar was fastened around her neck with a chain leading to an iron ring in the wall. More iron rings studded the lead walls. This vault had been used for many things over the last hundred and fifty years. Detaining important prisoners was just one of those things.

Red picked up half the carcass and threw it into the chamber. The dragon caught it in her powerful jaws and snapped it in half, swallowing one of the halves bones and all. She'd put on over three hundred pounds in the ten hours she'd been here. Li Po had them hauling food to her every four hours. They tossed the other half into the cell and slammed the door shut.

"Bringing her here was a big mistake, Red. Uncle Li is never going to control her."

"Be quiet. You and I don't make the decisions. We just carry out our orders. You saw what happened to Lawrence. Questioning your uncle's commands will get you the same treatment, and I don't want to end up with a hole in my forehead."

Chapter Twelve

Lance tried to stop. He tried to turn around and go back into the sewer and find Konrad, but his feet kept moving up Sacramento Street to the top of Nob Hill. He wasn't even walking. His feet were barely on the ground. He floated to the front of a huge nineteenth-century mansion surrounded by wrought iron fences with sharp spikes. The gates opened and Lance floated up to the front door.

"Come in, Lance. We're expecting you."

Crap and double crap. It was Vetalas's ass-kissing, second in command Marcelus, a vampire Vetalas made when he was in Rome during Caligula's brief reign.

"What's he want with me?"

"I have no idea what anyone would want with you." Marcelus looked down his classic Roman nose at Lance, sneered and turned his head.

Marcelus led Lance through the enormous mansion, up a grand stairway and into a bedroom. Vetalas reclined in a huge chair with his feet on the footrest. He was watching reruns of Dallas.

"I love this show, Lance. I hated to see it end."

Lance felt the pull of Vetalas over him. His entire body leaned toward the ancient vampire. He couldn't stop it. "Why'd you call me?"

"You have made some very interesting friends."

"And?"

"I need to know where the dragon is. Ice dragons are very dangerous creatures. Did you know they can kill a vampire?"

Lance shook his head. "I had no idea."

Vetalas hit the recliner's handle and snapped out of his chair. He wore a black silk robe and his eyes were deep red. He'd fed recently. He paced a circle around Lance.

"Well, they can. Their bite is poisonous."

"The last time I saw the dragon she was asleep on Baby's floor."

"We want her, Lance. And you will deliver her to us."

"I don't think I can do it alone."

"Just call me and I will come."

"How am I supposed to do that? Can you read my mind?"

Vetalas sat back in his chair and nodded to Marcelus. The big Roman opened a drawer in a chest next to the huge mahogany bed and pulled something out. He flicked it to Lance.

Lance caught the tiny cell phone.

"Use that. I'm number-one on speed dial."

*****

Lei trailed behind Junior who followed Sledge up the steps into her apartment building. She closed the door behind them, sending the hallway into gloomy twilight. Once in the basement, she opened the trap door and Sledge leaped to the bottom of the tunnel without using the ladder.

Junior, grunting like some kind of animal, turned around and squeezed his bulk through the trap. When they were all in the tunnel, Sledge held up his hand.

"It should be clear down here. It's daytime. The blood suckers only come out at night."

Sledge smiled at her and she smiled back. She was beginning to feel like he was hitting on her. He flicked on the big flashlight and shined the beam down the narrow passageway leading to the sewer.

"This is some scary shit, man." Junior kept looking over his shoulder at her as he squeezed down the tunnel. "You sure there ain't no vamps down here, Sledge? I'm about to shit myself."

Lei stifled a laugh. That would be gross.

"I can't guarantee anything. Maybe it's night where they're coming from. I got no way of telling."

When they hit the junction and turned down the walkway next to the sewer, Junior groaned. "What is that smell?"

Sledge pointed to the slowly moving brown river next to the walkway.

"Is that what I think it is?"

"Shut the fuck up, Junior. This is the sewer. You live in San Francisco. That's probably your turd that just floated by."

"Awe, man, that's shit?"

Sledge turned around and grabbed the big man by the collar of his orange, four-X golf shirt. "Do us all a favor, Junior, and be quiet. If there are vampires, we don't want them to hear us."

Junior's eyes were wide. He nodded, zipped his mouth with his fingers, and covered his nose with his hand.

They walked for a mile down the main sewer line, Sledge examining the brick walls edging the walkway. He couldn't find the hole.

"I know it was here because of this pipe and all these valves." He pointed to a pipe easily twenty-inches in diameter that exited the wall and dumped its effluent into the sewer. There were a number of valves at the end of the pipe probably to turn it off or redirect the flow.

"Could it have closed by itself?" Lei asked. Maybe the doorway was gone.

A sudden aftershock shook the tunnel. Lei braced her feet far apart and absorbed the mild tremor. Junior planted himself and mopped his forehead with a huge red handkerchief. Sweat flooded from his hairline, down his cheeks and his neck.

"There!" Sledge pointed.

On the wall right behind Junior, a black, swirling hole opened in the bricks. Lei looked at it once and ran to the sewer to vomit. Something about the hole was unbelievably nauseating.

Junior turned and gasped. His chocolate-brown face turned gray and he projectile-vomited everywhere.

Sledge leaped out of the way just in time to avoid being covered in whatever Junior had eaten that morning for breakfast.

"Don't look at it." Sledge turned his head away. Lei straightened up and peeked at the hole out of the corner of her eye.

"If you glance at it for a second and then turn away, you won't be sick."

"Thanks for the warning." Junior said as he wiped his mouth with his big hankie.

"What do you think, Junior? Can we close it?"

"I can't even look at it."

Lei took another quick peek and saw a foot appear. "I think something is trying to come through."

Sledge drew the sword off his back and waited.

A thin female, pale as snow, shot feet first into the sewer. She immediately launched herself at Junior, still wiping puke off his face.

His scream was high-pitched and filled with terror. Junior spun around trying to drag the vampire off his neck. She clung to his face like one of those creatures in Alien, her body wrapped around his bulk.

Sledge followed, trying to get a strike in. The vamp was tightly plastered to Junior, too tight to slice her off.

Junior teetered, he wobbled, and he shrieked, as the vampire dropped her head and grabbed his thick throat with her fangs.

"Fuck!" Sledge yelled and sliced off the vampire's ass. It was the only protruding part of her body.

She let go of Junior's neck and like a snake dove on Sledge. The force of her kicking off Junior shoved him toward sewage river.

Sledge ducked and sliced the vamp through the middle with a powerful stroke. The top half fell right and the bottom half fell left with the legs still churning. He booted the vampire's upper body into the sewage where it landed right on top of Junior.

The sewage was only two feet deep. Junior rose out of it, grabbed the portion of the vamp on him with both hands, snarled and slammed it into the muck.

Lei and Sledge stared at Junior. She had to cover her mouth and look away.

"You're gonna need to go right to the emergency room and get a shitload of antibiotics."

"Ha, ha, Sledge, great choice of words." Junior pulled himself out of the sewage and sat on the walkway. He was covered from head to toe in stinking crap.

"He can't go back through my building like that." Lei shook her head. "He'll get sewage all over the floors."

Junior stood up and started stripping off his clothes. He took off his shirt and pants, his size sixteen athletic shoes and his socks, and kicked them into the sewer. "How about now?"

With clothes on, Junior seemed like a big guy. Standing in his boxer shorts, there were no words to describe him. He'd easily make three of Lei.

Sledge touched the gaping wound on Junior's neck. "I can sew this up for you. Got any antibiotics? If you don't, I'm serious about getting you some shots. Every germ on the planet is floating around in that stew."

Junior brushed Sledge's hand away. "Leave me alone, man. I got it covered."

They headed back down the walkway, Junior's big bare feet slapping on the concrete.

"Can we blow it up?" Sledge asked.

Junior stopped, turned and stared at Sledge. "There ain't no "can we" about it. We gonna shut that motherfucker down. I don't care if we blow a crater in the middle of China Town two blocks wide."

Chapter Thirteen

Konrad felt really bad about loading Junior, stinking like he was, into the back seat of Baby's tiny Honda hatchback. Lei covered the seats with towels from her apartment out of respect for the upholstery, but the car would never be the same.

"You won't have to worry about vampires biting you now," Lei said. "Shit has got to be a natural vamp repellant."

Junior snorted. "Thanks, like I don't know I stink."

With all four windows down, Konrad drove them back to Junior's business. When they pulled up to the curb, Junior climbed out and stalked through the blue door. He was majestic in his nakedness.

"That is quite a sight," Lei said as she and Konrad climbed out and trailed after him.

"Be quiet, Lei. He's gonna help us close the hole. Personally, I think we should be grateful to the vamp that dumped him in the shitter. It sealed the deal."

Junior disappeared into a bathroom inside his rooms and emerged twenty minutes later decently covered in a voluminous pair of baggy jeans and a gigantic white T-shirt. He unlocked a door and Konrad and Lei followed him through it. When he flipped on the light switch, Konrad gasped.

Gun racks lined all four walls of the twenty-by-twelve space, and each slot in the racks was filled with a weapon. Trunks and ammo cases were stacked everywhere. Konrad picked a handgun off a shelf under the racks and turned it over in his hand.

"Holy shit, Junior, this is a Metal Storm. Where did you get it?"

"Internet, dumb ass. You need to bring your big white-boy, butt into this century. And don't be touchin' my shit."

Junior snatched the gun out of Konrad's hands and placed it reverently in its box.

"I've heard of the gun, but I thought it just came as a machine gun. How many rounds will the handgun fire a minute?"

"Sixteen thousand and without making a sound."

"How many rounds does the mag hold?"

"I had to modify one to fit it." Junior tossed him a clip. "This one holds twenty rounds. I got a bigger one. It holds fifty."

"Wow! We could cut a vamp in half with this thing. Might be better than a sword." Konrad could not believe Junior possessed this kind of technology. The machine gun was new, but he'd never heard about any handgun.

"The grip has a handprint detector. No one but me can fire it unless I change it."

"What else have you got in here?"

Junior held up a Cornershot. "This baby can shoot around corners." He picked up a knife. "This knife holds five .22mm rounds. And this," he held up an ordinary-looking cell phone. "This holds four .22mm rounds and you fire it with the five and the eight key."

Konrad spotted something he'd always wanted, a Wasp. The knife was used mostly by divers. It could inject a freezing ball of gas the size of a basketball at 800psi, dropping any of the world's largest predators. "Hey Junior, this baby might be just what I need if I get cornered by one of those big bastards."

"Take it. I got five more in the locker over in Oakland."

"Thanks, man," Konrad said, and shoved the knife in his pocket.

In addition to the new technological marvels, Junior also had quite a collection of ordinary weapons. "You could arm fifty guys with all this shit."

Junior nodded his head. "This is just my personal collection. I have a storage container in Oakland with the saleable merchandise."

Junior opened a footlocker and lifted out plastic-wrapped lumps of C-4. He handed two to Konrad. "This should be enough to close down that doorway to hell."

Konrad looked at his watch. "We better hurry. It'll be dark in four hours. I know we don't want to be down there after dark and besides, Baby has to be at work at ten."

Junior opened a black, lacquered, wooden box and handed Konrad something inside a black silk bag. Konrad untied the silk strings and slid a samurai sword out of the bag. The katana was encased in a black enameled Saya with a dragon enameled in white along the entire length. When Konrad pulled it out, he whistled. The handle was woven with red silk.

"For you, my man, for saving my life."

"Thanks, Junior, double-edged and sharp as fuck. Just what I need."

Junior chucked the C-4 into a bag along with a handful of detonators and an electronic ignition switch and handed it to Lei. "Be careful with this shit."

She nodded.

"Let's go blow that motherfucker."

They drove back to China Town through lunch traffic. Everyone and their brother seemed to be headed down Sacramento. Konrad parked in front of Lei's apartment and they climbed out.

"Look," Konrad said to Lei.

Down the street, two Chinese men in white T-shirts sat in a black Kia Soul, watching her apartment.

Lei gasped. "That's the Tong. What do they want? They already have Lung Ma."

"Maybe they're tired of feeding her and want to give her back."

The three of them entered Lei's building and went straight to the basement. Once in the sewer, they double-timed it to the wall with the doorway. All business, Junior slapped C-4 around the edges, careful not to look into the doorway, and connected them with wires to his detonator.

"We need to be way down the passageway before we blow this thing. I ain't getting any more shit on me."

"Will it blow the building up overhead?" Lei asked.

Junior raised himself up to his full height. "What do you take me for? An amateur? I got this thing set to blow the doorway shut, and that is it. Theoretically, it won't even disturb shit river over there. But I got no idea what kind of energy is contained in this doorway, so we better find someplace safe to hide."

They decided to use Lei's little storage room. Once inside, they all hit the ground and covered their ears while Junior triggered his bomb.

When it went off, the roar down the tunnel was intense. The ground shook, and dust and dirt collected over the last hundred years rained out of the bricks in the ceiling. A thousand rats ran chattering down the passage past their hiding place.

Junior stood up and dusted off his shirt. "That should have done it."

The three of them walked slowly down the walkway. Konrad expected to see the wall destroyed and the hole blocked off. It hadn't worked that way.

"Fuck me!" Junior's mouth hung open and he ran to vomit into the sewage.

Warned by Junior's reaction, Konrad glanced quickly at the wall, turned and gasped.

"It's bigger!" Lei snapped. "You made the fucking hole bigger."

The blast had opened the hole from two feet in diameter to eight-feet wide, encompassing the entire section of wall.

"We better get out of here," Konrad said. "It'll be dark soon and I have to get the car back to Baby."

"What are we gonna do now?" Lei asked as they climbed through the trapdoor into her basement.

Junior's lips were drawn into a thin line, his eyes narrow. "Get a bigger bomb."

*****

The alarm woke Baby. She slapped it off. It was six o'clock, time to get up and get ready for work. Shoving her feet into fuzzy slippers, she thought about how much she missed Paige. Paige always had coffee ready when she got up. They both worked the nightshift.

When she had a steaming cup in her hand, she sat on the couch to watch the news.

"The town is jumping folks," Jimmy Baynard, the Channel Seven news anchor said. "Last night, SFPD had over twenty-three complaints of vampires. Seven bodies drained of all blood were taken to the city morgue."

Baby nodded, and they weren't all dead.

"Vampires have been sighted all over the city, but the largest concentration seems to be in China Town."

Jimmy began a series of interviews with people on the street.

"It came out of nowhere," a fat Chinese woman said. "It looked like something out of Night of the Living Dead, all skinny with big fangs and hands like claws. It killed Uncle Wang, sucked all the blood out of him and tossed his body aside like it was a banana peel."

Jimmy turned to interview an obvious street person wearing two or three coats, and Baby decided it was time to shower and get dressed. Maybe she should wear a couple of cloves of garlic under her scrubs.

She dropped her robe, slung back the shower curtain and screamed.

Lance screamed, too.

"What the fuck are you doing in my shower?"

"Sorry, Baby." Lance edged out of the bathtub and around her. "I needed a place to crash."

Baby struggled to cover her bulk with a towel. "Get the fuck out of my bathroom. I got to get ready for work."

She whipped off her fuzzy slipper and threw it at him, whacking him in the back as he exited the bathroom. "Fucking pervert vampire. I bet you been waiting in here all this time just to sneak a look at my goodies."

Her heart pounded. She took a couple of deep breaths to slow it and got into the shower. Men were all the same. And the fucking vampires were everywhere.

Chapter Fourteen

After they dropped Junior and took Baby to work, Konrad sat in the car with Lei and stared at his hands on the steering wheel. He knew what he wanted to do but didn't know if he could get up the nerve to do it. It was laughable, a man like him turning into a slobbering idiot in front of women.

"Uh, Lei, Uh."

She looked at him. Her almond eyes glowed in her cute little face. Her hair was long and straight and her skin like silk.

"What, Sledge? What is it?"

He turned his head and looked out the window. As long as he could remember, he'd felt like an oaf, a giant, glumping, clumsy dork, every time he tried to speak to a woman about anything personal.

"Want to go get a bite to eat?" There! He'd said it.

She laughed. "Sure, anything but Chinese."

He smiled and grabbed her hand. "That's really great. How about pizza?"

"Okay," she said quietly, looked down at her lap and allowed him to hold her hand.

Konrad felt a huge bubble of happiness grow inside his chest. He pasted a big, goofy grin on his face and drove toward the Marina District. "There's this great pizza place close to the waterfront where me and Paige eat, I mean ate, once in a while. The pizza is good and I think I can swing it on what I have left after the last Lung Ma grocery run."

"I wonder where she is?"

"I'm sure she's somewhere in China Town. The Tong have her locked up good and tight."

"I miss her."

Konrad had no idea what to say to that. He wasn't good at being supportive and he never knew what to say when people were hurting. "We'll get her back. Or she'll find us. I think she's going to grow.....a lot."

They arrived at Palio's. It was in an old building facing a group of docks. Lights lit up the network of walkways and pilings. Hundreds of sea lions reclined across the old boards. Konrad could hear them barking and talking to each other.

Lei paused for a moment after she climbed out of the car to watch the animals and listen to their constant racket. "Seals. I've never seen so many at one time."

"They're always out there. When the fishing boats come in, the fisherman clean their fish on those tables and toss fish guts in the water."

Konrad took her arm and led her into the restaurant. She was so tiny. He wanted to hold her in his arms and protect her.

They found a table in a corner and sat down. Konrad was starving. They ordered an FTM, fresh tomato, mushroom pizza and two drafts. When the drafts came Lei lifted hers. "Here's to finding Lung Ma.

"And closing up that hole."

They drank deeply, Lei wiping foam off her upper lip with her arm. Konrad watched as she licked the remaining residue off her lip with one flick of her tongue. Oh boy.

"I don't know much about you, Lei. What do you do for a living?"

"I go to school. I'm a grad student at SFSU."

"Wow! How do you manage?"

"My mother's family made a lot of money in Hong Kong off real estate. She was a Tang. The Tangs owned land in Hong Kong back when the British first arrived on the island during the opium wars. They allowed her to marry my father. He was from a good family in Guang Dong.

"Her family saw the Communist takeover coming and put all their money in Swiss Banks. She died six years ago, and her family, my grandparents, my aunts and uncles, all look after me. My dad never got over her death. He got transferred to an outpost close to the Tibetan border and spent a lot of time in the mountains. That's how he found the egg. I think, but I'm not sure, that he was also spending a lot of time at the Samye Monastery studying with the monks."

"How did you get out of China?"

"My mother knew China would resume control of Hong Kong when the British lease expired. She took advantage of her position as a resident, flew here when she was pregnant, and had me. I'm an American."

"Why did she go back?"

"She loved my father very much. She took me and we lived with him until she got sick. He sent her away so she could get care for her disease. She had leukemia. We came here and lived. We have relatives in Oakland. I donated bone marrow, but her body rejected it."

Konrad saw tears in Lei's eyes and changed the subject. "That's some story. What's your field of study?"

She smiled and wiped her eyes with her hand. The glow in her smile sent shafts of energy straight to Konrad's heart . . . and lower. "Anthropology."

The pizza arrived and the mood lightened. Konrad served them both slices. He grinned at her over the top of his slice and signaled the waitress to bring more beer.

"I've been doing all the talking," she said. "Tell me about Sledge."

"Not much to tell," he began. "What you see is what you get. Big man with a control issue."

"What about your parents?"

"I had two."

She laughed. "No, tell me about your parents. I told you about mine."

Konrad shrugged. "My father was like me, big and out of control. He had the same Berserker genes. He was in the military, the Marine Corp. I should have joined. They tolerated his outbursts, and they taught him how to control himself with willpower. The Marines are big on willpower."

"What about your mom?"

Konrad felt his expression soften. It always did when he thought about his mother. "She's great. She loves horses, but one threw her six years ago, and she was partially paralyzed. She lives in Albany in one of those group homes. They take good care of her. I try to get by as often as I can, but I know it's not enough. She likes to read trashy magazines, you know, stuff about the celebrities and who they're screwin.'"

Lei reached out and touched his arm. Her fingers felt like flower petals brushing his skin. "What happened to your dad?"

"He was killed in the Gulf War. The first one. They said he went out like a hero. Rescued nine guys from a firefight and died with sixteen rounds in him. They gave him the Medal of Honor. He deserved it."

Lei took another piece of pizza from the pan and shook her head. "You're just like him."

Konrad stopped chewing and swallowed. "No, I'm not like him. I wish I could be half the man he was."

Lei giggled. "I have a very impertinent question to ask you, just from an anthropological point of view, understand."

"Shoot." Konrad had a feeling he knew what she was going to ask.

"So, crazy man, why is a big handsome guy like you still a virgin?"

He'd known she was going to ask, and the part of him that wanted her to be his first took it as a come on. The part of him that rejected all come-ons out of fear of what might happen cringed. He wished his dad had stayed around so he could get advice about things of this nature. There was no talking to his mom about shit like this.

"It's the Berserker thing," he finally said. "I have no idea what will happen if I get . . . you know, aroused."

He could feel his face flaming and he couldn't believe he just said that to a woman. But Lei made him comfortable. He felt like he could tell her this and she would not judge him. She might even be able to help.

"Wow! I never looked at it that way." She took a sip of her beer and Konrad watched her face and the way her lips fit the edge of the glass. "What happens when you kiss a girl? You must have done that before."

"A couple of times, not a lot. The military kept me tied up for four years and I was in the brig. Every time I tried to kiss a girl, I'd start to feel the Berserker change coming on, so I'd run off."

"I bet those girls thought you didn't like them. One kiss and poof, he runs away." She laughed and Konrad felt encouraged. His revelation hadn't freaked her out.

"Yeah, I bet they did. So, I told you why I'm still a virgin. It's your turn. Spill."

Lei shoved her plate aside, the slice of pizza half eaten. She wrapped both hands around her beer glass and tilted her head. Then she looked him right in the eye.

"I haven't found the right man yet."

Chapter Fifteen

Konrad paid the bill, then threw his arm around Lei's shoulders as they left the restaurant. "Want to take a walk?"

She nodded so he steered her toward the dock. There was a stiff chop on the bay, the water lapping against the pilings. Overhead, stars were visible between banks of clouds, and for once, the ever-present fog was gone, probably due to the breeze. Lei shivered.

"Cold?"

"A little."

He pulled his jacket off and added it to hers. It hung down to her knees.

"Better?"

"Lots. What's going to happen now, Konrad? With the vampires, I mean."

"Junior is going to plug up that doorway or die trying."

"I mean with the ones that are already here, and that bad one, Vetalas."

"First things first, I always say. We'll have to deal with that after we get the doorway closed."

She nodded. "Where do you think Lance went?"

"Tonight, or last night?"

"Both, I guess. What's he up to? Do you think we can trust him?"

"I don't trust anybody, Lance included."

"How about me?" She stopped walking, turned and looked into his face. "Do you trust me?"

He bent down, wrapped his arms around her and picked her up. When her face was on his level, he kissed her. It started as a tentative touching of the lips, then deepened.

When he put her down, they were both breathing hard. He didn't say a word, just took her hand and started walking for the car.

When they got to the car, she stopped. "You didn't run away."

"No, I didn't."

"So, what does that mean?"

Konrad opened the door of the car and she climbed inside. When he was in the driver's seat, he took her hand. "It could mean I found the right girl. How about you?"

She grinned and he saw a delicate rose creep into her cheeks. "Ditto."

*****

"Honorable Li Po, we must move the dragon right now. If she grows any larger we won't be able to get her out of the vault." Red Chua chose a finger at random and gnawed on the nail.

Li Po stood behind his enormous, antiquated desk, black eyes glinting. "Impossible."

Red squirmed in his chair. "Ask Timmy. He's your nephew. Believe me, she's huge."

Li Po lifted one eyebrow and glared at Timmy as though daring the man to contradict him.

Timmy stood up and cleared his throat. "Gracious Uncle, it is as Red says, she has tripled in size. She eats all the time. How big do ice dragons get?"

Li Po picked up a ledger book and slammed it on the desk with both hands. "Then we must move her. I don't know how big dragons get. Moving her will be very risky. I will consult with the seer. She will tell us the opportune moment to move her. and I will try to figure out where to take her."

Red shook his head. "Honorable Boss, you better do it fast. She grows after each feeding and she's roaring for food right now."

Li Po's face contorted and turned red. "Then don't feed her! Why am I surrounded by imbeciles?"

Li Po fumed as he stormed down the steps at the end of the hallway and through the backdoor of his restaurant. That damn dragon had the potential to make him emperor of the world. With her under his control, he would be richer that Bill Gates, Ted Turner or all of Saudi Arabia. But controlling her was beginning to be an issue. There had to be a way.

He stalked between the tables of his restaurant, sparsely populated at this late hour. It was after eleven. Once on the street, he headed down the sidewalk toward an herb shop on the corner.

He was just about to knock on the red door of the shop when something grabbed his shoulder. It spun him around. Li Po found himself staring into the red eyes of a skinny woman. She bared her teeth and fangs popped into view. Li Po's heart pounded. This was one of those vampires people were talking about.

She hissed at him and lunged for his throat. Li Po whipped his butterfly knife out of the sheath on his belt. Snapping it open with the one hand in a practiced gesture, he stabbed her in the side of the head, sinking the knife in all the way to the hilt.

She screamed and pushed him away, taking the knife with her as she fell to the sidewalk. Li Po saw an old broom laying in the gutter, broke the handle in two over his knee, and staked her through the heart.

The female vampire froze. Her eyes were wide open, her limbs splayed. Interesting. He pulled his knife out, wiped the blood off on his black pants and sheathed it. She seemed to be alive, just paralyzed.

When he put his finger close to her eye, she didn't blink. When he moved the finger, her irises followed the movement.

"Can you hear me? Move your eyes to the left if you can."

She obeyed.

He sat back on his haunches to think. This vampire was at his mercy. How could he benefit?

"If I release you and find you food, will you promise not to attack me again? Look to the right if you agree."

95

She looked right.

He pulled the knife back out of the sheath and held it ready.

"If I pull out the stake, will you be able to move again. Look right for yes."

Another quick glance to the right.

He pressed the knife against her throat.

"I can slice your throat very quickly if you make any sudden moves of aggression."

Li Po yanked the stake out. A gout of dark blood flowed briefly, then dried to a trickle and stopped. He allowed her to stand but kept the knife at her throat.

"Come with me." Li Po led her down a dark alley off Washington Street. He knocked twice on a green door set down two steps in a recess. A single light bulb lit the doorway. It dangled three feet from an overhang on a cord wrapped with black electrical tape. The vampire waited in the alley.

A thin woman wearing a high-necked dress under a ragged sweater and slippers answered the door. When she saw it was Li Po, she stepped out of his way.

He led the vampire inside. A cloud of sweet, dusty smoke filled the room. Tiers of bunks, five deep, lined the walls. Skeletal Chinese men filled each bunk. They lay on narrow cotton mattresses in deep opium dreams with a single pillow beneath their heads.

Li Po stepped back so the vampire could see. "Pick one."

She looked at him, her hair, lank and dark, fell over one corner of her face. Her skin was like white porcelain. She lifted a sculpted eyebrow. "Any of them? It doesn't matter?"

In a movement too quick for him to follow, she attacked one of the dreamers. Tearing out his throat, she inhaled the blood.

Li Po briefly wondered if the blood would make her stoned. These old addicts had been smoking opium for years. Their flesh and blood must be permeated with the drug.

When she was through feeding and the man a dried husk, she stood up. Her white skin now held a pink glow and he saw she was beautiful.

"I'm still hungry," she whispered. "Can I have another?"

"Come close." Li Po spoke directly into her shell-like ear. Her lips were covered with blood. She licked it off with her small, pointed tongue.

His own tongue felt thick in his mouth. "What is your name?"

"My name is Shanya."

"Shanya, you may eat the old woman."

The vampire was on her in seconds. The old woman crumpled beneath the attack, falling to the floor beneath Shanya without a sound. It was best to eliminate her. She'd seen him turn the vampire loose in here to kill and feed.

When Shanya was finished, Li Po took her hand. "I was on my way to speak to the seer. I want you to come with me."

She fascinated him. "Where did you come from?"

She explained the hole between the two worlds to Li Po. He listened riveted.

The arrival of the vampires presented endless possibilities. Maybe Madame Xing Would have some ideas about how he could benefit.

Back on Washington, Li Po led Shanya to the red door of the herb shop. It was after one, but the old lady was known to keep late hours. She better answer the door. He paid her well enough.

Madame Zing came to the door after only one quiet knock. Li Po smelled pungent, green tea and smiled. She was brewing Dragonwell. He took this as a good omen.

They bowed to each other when he entered, Li Po bowing lower, even though she was basically his employee. He needed to show her respect because he believed she could control his destiny. When she saw the vampire, she frowned and backed away so Shanya could enter. When they were inside the herb store, she shut the door.

"Honorable Li, why are you here at this late hour?"

"I came for your advice, old mother."

She led him through a beaded curtain separating the shop from her living space. The smell of the shop and her small rooms was a rich blend of incense, cedar, spices and strong roots and leaves.

Li Po and Madame Zing sat at a round table in her tiny kitchen and she poured two cups of tea. "The bloodsucker can wait inside the shop."

They drank the tea. He enjoyed the flavor of the expensive blend of leaves.

"She's not just a vampire," Madame Zing said over her tea. "She's Vjeszczi, a demon that devours the souls of its victims."

Nodding, Li Po swallowed another sip of the tea. Just what he needed to hear. But she could still be useful and she was so beautiful.

When the tea was gone, Madame Zing took out a lacquer-wood tube and removed the lid, shaking out the dragon sticks, each stick eight inches long, tipped in red and inscribed with symbols.

She held them in her hand and made Li Po choose five, one for You, Children, Money, Job and Mother. Returning the rest to the tube, he took the five from Li Po and laid them across the table.

Frowning, she read each stick.

Li Po felt the sweat rolling down his sides from under his arms.

"I see a powerful force in your life, a dragon. She will either kill you or make you rich beyond your wildest dreams. The power of You and the Mother is greater than the power of Job and Money. This is a good omen for you. But beware of those without souls. They can help you. But if the dragon kills them, they will turn on you."

"The dragon can kill vampires?"

She nodded. "Ancient dragons cleansed the world of vampires long ago. I see the bloodsuckers returning now through a rent in the fabric of the universe."

He leaned forward, his heart hammering. "Tell me if I will control the dragon."

Madame Zing removed two more sticks from the tube. She screamed as both sticks burst into flames.

Chapter Sixteen

Lance left Baby's apartment and wandered down Fulton. Across the street, the dark forest of Golden Gate Park beckoned. Deep inside the woods, he saw the faint glow of streetlights. He knew if he flew through the park, he would come out on the sand dunes and the ocean. His soul craved the deep, black waters of the Pacific.

Vetalas had ruined everything. The old demon could control him, call him to do his bidding. He didn't want to find out where the dragon was. He wanted to dine on a wino and then go surfing. He was even willing to polish off a couple of squirrels, maybe a pig or even a stray cat in deference to his human friend's wishes. He'd discovered a weird thing. He liked people. But instead of following his own agenda, he had to scour China Town looking for the little dragon.

Feeling stronger than he had in years, Lance flew toward the Marina District wondering where Konrad was. He felt no loyalty to Vetalas. The Berserker had shown him mercy and friendship. Maybe he should confide in Konrad, tell him where Vetalas was and explain about the dragon. The trouble was he had no idea where to find Konrad.

Without a real plan or idea, Lance flew to China Town. Circling above Lei's apartment, he got lucky. Baby's car was parked on the street out front.

His enhanced hearing allowed him to listen in to what was going on in Lei's place. Konrad was in there with her and they were making out. Lance still liked sex, but what he had to tell Konrad was more important. He knocked on the door.

*****

Konrad had no real idea what would happen when he and Lei got back to her apartment. He knew what he wanted to do, and he thought they should take it slowly. But once he and Lei started kissing on her lumpy, green sofa, things quickly got out of hand. Clothes flew off and in minutes they were in her big bed ready to lose their virginity.

Konrad felt Lei's fear. His face was swelling and his hands were grasping her arms too hard.

"Stop, Konrad, you're hurting me," she whispered.

Her voice cut through the red film covering his eyes and ears and he leaped off the bed.

"I can't do this, Lei. I'm losing control."

A knock at the door was a welcome interruption for Konrad. He feared seriously hurting the tiny woman with his passion.

"Fuck!" She sat up and pulled the sheet under her chin. "You can't do this to me, Konrad." She called after him. "I don't want to be a virgin anymore."

He threw the door open buck naked.

"Dude," Lance put his arm over his eyes as he walked into the apartment. "Cover yourself."

"Where have you been? I spent half an hour in that sewer hunting for you."

"Bad news," Lance said as he flopped onto the green sofa. "I got called."

"Hold that thought. I'll be right back."

Konrad pulled on his jeans in the bedroom and bent to kiss the irate woman sitting on the bed.

"What's he want?" She hissed.

"I don't know, but I think he might have something interesting to say. Just a feeling."

"He effing better."

Konrad returned to the living room chuckling. Lei really wanted to get laid. And so did he. He just didn't want to kill her in the process.

"Hey Lance, you eaten yet?"

"Didn't have time, bro, something I gotta tell you."

Konrad pulled a cold bottle of beer out of the fridge and snapped off the cap. "Shoot. You were telling me you got called. What's that mean?"

"Vetalas made me a vampire. He has the power to compel me to do his bidding. Right now, I'm fighting it so I can be here and talk to you. What I need to find must be close, or I wouldn't be able to be here at all."

"Vetalas, he's the bad-ass vamp that ate Paige, right?"

"Yeah, you could say he's bad ass. He's really old, the oldest demon in our world."

Konrad sucked down half the beer in one chug and wiped his mouth. "What's he want with you?"

"He wants me to find the dragon."

"What?" Konrad glared at Lance. The surfer seemed to be straight-talking. He seemed to be genuine. But there was always the trust issue with Lance. He was a demon.

"Why does he want Lung Ma? I thought the Chinese were the only ones interested in her."

"She kills vampires. He wants her dead."

"How can she kill vampires?"

"She's venomous. Her poison is deadly to demons."

"Okay, I can see why he's afraid of her. But she's only a little thing."

"She's gonna grow, man, and fast. Remember all the lamb? Every time she eats, she grows."

"What's he want you to do? Kill her?"

"No, I'm just supposed to find her for him. He'll take care of her."

"If we kill Vetalas, will all of the demons go away?"

"I don't know what kind of weird movies you been watching, man. If you kill Vetalas, you kill one demon. But he controls many and killing him might change the complexion of your infestation."

"Infestation, nice way to describe it. Where's Vetalas now?"

"He's living in a mansion on top of Nob Hill."

"Likes the high life, huh? Does he have a lot of soldiers?"

Lance nodded. "He's got quite a few old vamps and some new ones living up there with him."

"Best time to get him be during the day?"

"Maybe, but he doesn't always sleep during the day. He doesn't have to. His minions will be asleep."

Konrad went back to the fridge and took out the box with the leftover pizza. He picked up a thick slice, sprinkled cheese and red peppers on it and went back to the couch.

"Ahhh, man, you have to eat pizza in front of me?"

"Sorry. I didn't know you gave a shit."

"Pizza was my favorite food, back in the day."

"Where you think they have the dragon?" Konrad polished off the pizza and wiped his hands on a paper towel.

"She's around here somewhere. I can sense her."

"Can you hear her?"

"Don't know, I haven't tried."

"Well do it."

Lance closed his eyes to concentrate. The bedroom door opened and Lei came out in jeans and a baggy sweater. Konrad held a finger to his lips.

"Shhh, he's trying to hear Lung Ma."

Lance sat frozen in a trance for twenty minutes while Konrad put on a shirt and ate more pizza. Suddenly the demon opened his eyes. They glowed a vivid red in his white face.

"She's roaring for food about three blocks from here."

"Are you going to tell Vetalas?"

"I have to, man. He's laid a compulsion on me. I don't want to go anywhere near him, but I don't have a choice."

Konrad grabbed his jacket. "Let's go see if we can find Lung Ma and then I'll go with you to Nob Hill."

Lance was already at the door. "Really? You'll go with me?"

"I said I would."

Konrad hugged Lei and kissed her cheek.

"When are you coming back? We have some unfinished business, remember?"

"Maybe we should wait until I'm really tired."

"Damn it, Sledge." She dropped her voice to a whisper. "I want you."

His face flamed. He could feel the heat from his groin rising into his stomach.

"I want you, too, babe. I told you, we're gonna have to move slowly on this thing. I almost hurt you bad in there. I could kill you accidentally. It's not a joking matter."

"You can control yourself, Sledge. I know you can."

She ran her hand over his jaw and touched his lips with her fingers. He kissed her fingers. "I'll be back in a little while. We have to pick Baby up at seven."

He walked out the door behind Lance and looked back once to see her standing in the living room, her head tilted to one side, her eyes smiling.

Chapter Seventeen

After stopping by Baby's car to pick up the katana and his pistol, Konrad followed Lance on a zigzagging course through three alleys and out onto Stockton. The two of them stood on the curb and stared at the impressive façade of the Bank of the Orient.

"This bank has been in China Town since the 1800s," Konrad said. "I bet it has a vault somewhere deep underground that's lined with lead. If they have Lung Ma in it, I won't be able to hear her."

Suddenly, as clear as a bell, the dragon's thoughts blasted his brain. *Sledge, I know you are close. The door to my cell is open and I can hear your thoughts.*

"I can hear her," Konrad said to the vampire.

"Where is she?"

Lung Ma, tell me where they're keeping you.

I don't know. It's underground. I'm hungry, Sledge, they won't feed me.

A black Kia Soul pulled up to the front of the bank. Two Tong members climbed out.

"This is our chance," Konrad whispered to Lance.

The demon looked up. "Say what?"

Konrad loped down the street and slipped up behind the two Tong members. His Berserker persona was right there inside him. It was as though he could touch it. He reached inside himself and slipped Berserker mode on.

Roaring like a lion, Konrad grabbed both Chinese men and smashed them into each other. Dazed, they wobbled in two directions. Konrad grabbed one, flipped him upside down and drove him into the concrete sidewalk.

When he looked for Tong member number-two, Lance was quietly feeding on him.

Konrad stripped his Tong guy, then pulled the man's medium T-shirt over his 2-X shoulders. The black fabric split across his back. The guy's black, baseball cap was adjustable.

"Get dressed," he said.

Lance's face reflected shock. His mouth actually fell open.

"Hurry up, man. How else are we gonna get in there?"

"Dude, they're never gonna think you're a Chink."

"All I'm gonna need is a second of hesitation to convince them."

Lance pulled on jeans, black T-shirt and the Tong member's hat. He refused to part with his sandals.

Konrad found a big wad of keys inside the Tong dude's jeans. After several tries, he opened the front door of the bank.

"Lung Ma said she's underground. Hunt for an elevator."

There were two. One needed a key. Konrad chose it, fishing through the bunch to find a key shaped like a Chinese character which opened it.

Standing inside the elevator, he looked at Lance. "You ready?"

"Hey, Dude, I'm immortal, remember?"

"Right."

Konrad hit the switch closing the elevator doors and punched a button labeled with another weird Chinese character at the bottom of the array. The doors clanked shut and the elevator swung back and forth as it began a groaning descent.

"This thing is older than me." Lance grabbed one of the rails lining the sides of the cab and hung on.

"Get ready," Konrad said as he felt for his alter ego. For some reason, he could touch it and feel it ready for him to use. When the doors clanked open, he growled, crouched low and opened his meaty hands.

Two Tong members looked up when the doors opened, faces registering extreme shock when they saw who was inside. Konrad grabbed one by the throat and cracked his neck like a twig, tossing the corpse into the empty elevator.

Lance let him pick up the second one, backing out of the way. Konrad didn't bother breaking the other one's neck. He just tossed him into the elevator after his friend. The two jogged slowly down a long hallway dimly lit by old-fashioned light fixtures placed at twenty-foot intervals.

They passed several closed doorways. Konrad tried them all. They were locked and Lance couldn't hear anyone on the other side. When they got to the end of the hall, it hooked a sharp right. At the end of this new passage, they saw a huge, locked, iron door.

A Tong member leaned back snoozing in a chair with his feet propped on the door's locking mechanism and a rifle resting on his legs. Lung Ma had to be inside.

A loud ding announced the arrival of the elevator. The bell woke up the snoozing guard. He grabbed the automatic weapon laying across his legs and pointed it at Lance and Konrad.

"Hold it or I'll shoot."

Konrad leaped high, pulled the katana free of the scabbard across his back and sliced the guard from shoulder to waist with one swipe. Half his body fell away, the look of surprise still plastered on his face.

"Run," Konrad shouted to Lance.

Racing back down the hallway, they rounded the corner. Coming down the long hall directly at them were ten Tong members with AK-47s in their hands. Frantic, Konrad hammered his shoulder into the first doorway he came to. When it popped open, he pulled Lance inside and slammed the door.

There was a well in the corner of the room. The floor was damp concrete and the well little more than a hole in the floor with a two-inch raised rim. Konrad picked up Lance and threw him into the well.

"You're already dead. See if you can find an outlet."

Lance quickly dove into the dark water and disappeared. The Tong began banging on the door. It wouldn't take them long to open it. He didn't have time to wait for Lance to return.

Konrad dove into the well. Swimming hard, he headed deeper and deeper in the icy water. He discovered in Berserker mode he could see in the dark. At the bottom of the well, there was a tunnel and still no sign of Lance.

Konrad pulled himself into the narrow passage kicking strongly. He barely fit. The rough stone lining the passageway scraped his shoulders. His lungs began to burn. Up ahead, he saw the tunnel end. Lance's face suddenly appeared in the opening. Lance beckoned him on.

Konrad felt when he ran out of oxygen but refused to let go. His chest spasmed and he still held his breathe. He reached the end of the tunnel and shot up. Lance got behind him and pushed. Together they hurtled toward the surface.

He blacked out and woke up minutes later with Lance pushing on his chest.

When he opened his eyes, Lance grabbed his shoulders and slammed him back to the rocks. "You made it!"

The vamp picked him up again and hugged him hard. "I thought you were dead. I can't do mouth to mouth, no air." He pointed to his own skinny chest.

"Stop, you're gonna kill me." Konrad gave Lance a weak shove.

Lance flopped over on his butt and sat next to Konrad. "You gave me such a fright. I really thought you died."

"Didn't know you cared, asshole. Where the hell are we?"

"I checked around. I think this is an old cistern. There's a pumping station over there looks a hundred years old. This has to be the original water system for China Town."

Konrad felt his Berserker persona. It was so weird to be able to touch it mentally and know it was there. He felt his control over it had reached a new level. Maybe it meant he could spend the night with Lei and not worry. With his strength flooding back, Konrad clambered to his feet.

"Did you happen to find a way out?"

Lance hopped up and grabbed Konrad's hand. "This way."

"Hey, just because you saved my life doesn't mean you can hold my hand."

Lance laughed and led him to a shaft leading up. Konrad couldn't see the top. It had to run six stories at least.

"What's up there?"

"A manhole cover."

Konrad groaned. "I'm getting pretty sick of running around under the streets."

When they were back above ground, Konrad scanned for a street sign. They were on Washington. "Let's go find Vetalas. You have news for him."

"You really going with me?"

"I want to case the joint. I might be returning tomorrow, when it's light."

Chapter Eighteen

"We can get to Vetalas by heading up Washington," Lance said. "He lives at the top of the hill."

"Let's take the car." Konrad turned to walk back to Lei's apartment.

Lance grunted. "Can't go back there. Vetalas is calling me again."

Konrad had to run to keep up with the vampire. His feet barely touched the ground as he sailed straight up the steep hills of Washington Street to the top. At the top of the hill he took a left on Hyde and cut over to Sacramento.

Huffing and puffing to keep up, Konrad fell back and watched as Lance floated through a wrought iron gate that opened for him, down a drive bordered by immaculate shrubbery and up to the front of a columned mansion. Konrad was just able to bolt through the gates before they closed. Lance was already moving into the house.

There didn't seem to be a need for him to go inside, especially at night, so Konrad walked the grounds. The interior was lit up like Christmas. Vampires must not like the dark. He could see into the home through tall windows and French doors that opened up on several small balconies.

In his Berserker mode, he saw the demons inside lit from within by an eerie white light. It made their skin ghostly and translucent. He could clearly see the red of their borrowed blood in their veins and their hearts. He shook his head. Looking at them also made his stomach churn.

Among all the vampires, a few humans circulated. They looked to be in a trance. A few people he saw seemed to be halfway between one state and the other. They glowed but were not translucent. These must be some of Vetalas's new conscripts.

Konrad hid in the shrubs and watched Lance speak to a tall demon with short, curly brown hair and a patrician nose. The two were heading up a wide staircase when Konrad felt a hand on his shoulder.

He whirled, sliding easily into Berserker mode, and drew his sword in one slick motion. He faced an enormous demon with glowing red eyes, wings like a bat and horns. The demon towered over Konrad. It opened its mouth to reveal long fangs dripping with some kind of slobber or venom and then it shrieked.

Oh shit!

The noise was loud enough to wake the dead. Konrad didn't have to look into the house to know the demons inside heard. Howling like a wolf, Konrad slashed an arm off the demon. It kept up a continuous shriek like a siren on steroids, the loss of its arm slowing it not one bit.

The demon clawed Konrad, ripping the Tong T-shirt off and tearing five ugly stripes across his shoulder. The wounds burned like they were filled with acid.

It lunged at him, teeth bared, breath smelling like two-day-old roadkill at high noon. Konrad backed into a clump of juniper. The branches clung to his jeans and scratched his skin. He had only inches to go before he was against the mansion's outer wall. One of the windows blew out and the demon had friends.

Red completely covered Konrad's eyes. He'd never been this immersed in his Berserker persona. His body swelled; his pants ripped at the seams. He swung the katana like the blades of a saw, tearing chunks out of the demon as he ripped right through it into the open where he faced ten vampires. They jumped on him all at once, carrying him to the ground under their weight.

He kept hacking at anything close enough to get his sword into. It was snatched out of his hands. A vampire grabbed his throat and ripped out a chunk. Blood from the wound spouted and the vampire sucked it down.

"Get thee off!" a voice called from far away. Konrad's vision blurred and his hearing was fading fast.

Something burned across his neck and the bleeding stopped.

"Take him into the dungeon and chain him. He is something I have not seen in centuries."

Konrad saw Vetalas wipe his finger through the blood on his shoulder and put it into his mouth. "Or tasted. I would examine him."

Another of the big winged demons picked Konrad up and tossed him over his shoulder. He was carried inside, down a flight of steps into a basement, and then through a narrow door, and even further down into a stone chamber. Back under the city.

It was dark and they lit no lights, but Konrad could see. He must still be a Berserker. He couldn't tell. He felt like he was floating. They chained him to a stone wall inside a cell and left him there. He was glad to see the big winged son of a bitch leave. How many of them were in the city?

He'd only been chained for a few minutes, when he sensed something else in there with him. A girl crept down the stairs and into his cell. She looked about fifteen, pale and blonde, her hair like a halo of fine silk floating around her head. There were no bite marks on her neck and she appeared to be scared out of her mind. Her eyes like saucers darted this way and that.

Hugging the stone wall, she made her way slowly into his cell.

"Who are you?" she whispered. "Why didn't they kill you and eat you?"

"I got no idea. Who the hell are you?"

"My name's Kenna. This house belongs to my mom. The vamps don't know I'm here. You got any food on you? I'm starving."

Konrad shrugged his massive shoulders. "Sorry."

She sat down on the stone floor. "Shit, I haven't eaten in two days and I'm dying for a cigarette."

"Could you help me out of these chains?"

She shook her head. "Oh no, no, no, no, then they would know I was here. You sure you don't have anything on you, no cigarettes, no gum, nothing."

She began patting his pockets, pulled his Wasp out of his jeans pocket and the wad of keys he took off the Tong member.

"What's this do?" She held up the knife.

"Be careful, it has a gas cylinder inside it that shoots poison."

"Will it kill a vampire?"

Konrad shrugged. "I never tried it."

The door at the top of the stairs opened and a thin beam of light illuminated the bottom step. Konrad looked up at the door and when he looked down, Kenna was gone and so was the Wasp.

A thin figure in black slunk down the steps. When Konrad recognized the blonde hair, he grinned.

Lance grabbed his chains and broke them off at the wall. "We gotta get out of here, dude. You have royally fucked this up."

Konrad's enhanced vision enabled him to spot Kenna hiding in the shadows. "We have to take her with us."

Lance saw her and hissed. "Where did she come from?"

"Her mom owns the place. I guess Vetalas has her mother under his control."

Kenna came out of hiding. "Who are you? You look like a vamp."

"His name's Lance. He's a friend of mine. We're leaving. You want to go?"

"What about the vamp?"

"I told you, he's my friend."

"You're not going to try to have sex with me or sell me or anything, are you?"

"Let's go, Lance."

"Hey, this is the city, you know. I have to look out for myself."

"You're obviously doing a fine job."

They slipped up the steps and into the main basement. Lance led them to a tiny casement window. "This is the only way out. Every other door and window has a guard."

Konrad shook his head. "I can't fit through that."

"Try, man, it's the only way."

Lance easily slipped through the window, and so did Kenna after a healthy shove. Konrad found his Berserker persona and slid it on. His entire body vibrated with energy as he felt the power fill him. He got his head through the window and one shoulder, flexed his muscles and destroyed the concrete block wall. The window fell aside and he leaped out of the basement.

Konrad knew Lance could fly. "Lance, carry the girl and fly back to the car. I'll go through the grounds. It's almost dawn. You better hurry or you'll get caught by the sun."

"I'm not going anywhere with him." Kenna crossed her arms over her flat chest and glared at both of them.

"I'll meet you at Lei's," he said to Lance. "I'll carry her."

He grabbed the girl and threw her over his shoulder. She squirmed and fought.

"I'm perfectly capable of walking." Her whisper sounded more like one of Lance's hisses.

"I'm going to run."

"I can run."

Konrad took off for the gate at a gallop. "Not as fast as I can."

When they reached the eight-foot-high, black, wrought-iron fence, Konrad put her down.

"How are we getting over that?"

He held up his hand. "Be quiet."

Konrad grabbed a limb off a cedar growing next to the fence and swung up into the boughs. He stuck his hand down. "Come on."

She grabbed his hand and he pulled her up with him. Leaning way out over the fence, he dropped her to the street and followed her down.

The two jogged across Hyde and headed for Washington. Konrad turned the corner to look down the hill into China Town and stopped.

"Would you look at that?" Konrad said. Baby's car was racing full speed up the hill on Washington, zigging and zagging all over the road.

Lance pulled up to the curb and they both jumped in.

"I didn't know you could drive." Konrad said as he ratcheted the seatbelt tightly around his bulk.

"I can't."

Chapter Nineteen

"So, who do we have here?" Baby asked Lei as she climbed into the back seat beside Kenna.

"Her name is Kenna. Her mother owns the house Vetalas is using as vamp central."

"I see," Baby said. "Where's Lance? He ain't sleeping in my bathtub again, is he?"

"I dropped him off at my apartment. He's in the footlocker. How'd your night go?"

"The city is under siege. I had thirty-five DBs last night. The freezer is full. They are stacked two-deep in the hallway. I got the techs checking for signs of exsanguination, if they're bled dry, we cut off their heads. I am not having the village of the damned in my morgue."

"What's the cops' take on all this? You hear anything about their theories of what's going on?"

"Five O is throwing all kinds of shit at the wall to see if anything sticks. The inside scoop from what I hear is there is no inside scoop. For the first time ever, the San Francisco PD has no comment. I mean the entire force is zipped up tighter than a straight man's asshole in a gay bar. They are dumbfounded, completely blown away. I know what they're all thinking. They're thinking vampires and all kinds of supernatural stuff including aliens, the devil and the end of the world."

"Would they believe the truth if they heard it?"

"I can't say, but I've been doing a lot of thinking. Sledge, did your boy Junior get anywhere today on blowing up the doorway?"

"He's got ideas. He ordered some kind of heavy-duty shit that's supposed to work well in tunnels. He said he heard about it in the Army."

Baby leaned forward so her brown face was next to Konrad's shoulder. "Listen, Sledge, we need to tell the authorities about the doorway. Maybe they'll be able to close it. Some of the cops I work with aren't complete assholes. I'll make some calls when I get home and hook you up with one you can take into the sewer. We can't keep this to ourselves any longer. It's too big a responsibility."

"Okay, I'm fine with coming out of the closet. Just make the appointment for later on this afternoon. I need to get some rest."

Baby snorted. "Hey, I do not appreciate the homophobic allusion. I have been out of the closet all my fricking life."

"Speaking about coming out of the closet, you need to pick up Paige and give her a decent burial. I'm sure she's got folks that will want some closure and eventually the company I worked for will want to know what happened to her."

Baby threw herself hard against the back seat and dropped her head into her hands. "No parents," was her muffled reply.

"How about brothers, sisters, aunts or whatever?"

"Just a brother in St. Louis who told her he never wanted to speak o her again after she moved in with me."

"Baby, you can't leave her in my freezer. It just ain't right."

Konrad could hear her muffled sobs. "I'm not ready to say good-bye."

When they arrived at Baby's apartment, Konrad tried to send Kenna with her.

The tired coroner stuck her head in the driver's side window. "I'm going to sleep, Sledge. You got her. You keep her."

"Awe, Baby, can't she stay with you? She needs a woman's care."

"What did you just say?"

"Well you know more about taking care of a girl than I do."

"Lei will know just what to do for her."

Konrad could see what little sex life he had going up in smoke.

"Hey, asshole." Kenna leaned forward and stuck her head between him and Lei. "I'm not deaf and I don't appreciate being

120

treated like a nasty relative who dropped in uninvited. You took me from my home. Remember?"

Baby backed out of the window with a big smile on her face. "Good luck, there, Sledge. See you at seven."

All he needed now was for Lei to get pissed off and his day was made. When he glanced over at her as he was hooking a U-turn on Fulton, he saw that ship had sailed.

"I had to bring her with us, Lei. Her house is overrun with demons, big ugly demons with horns and wings."

Lei snorted, crossed her arms and stared out the window.

"Hey, Kenna, what kind of a creature are they?"

"You talking about the ones with wings?"

"Yeah, I think I killed one in the shrubbery."

"Vetalas's crew uses them to guard the place. They call them the Volthok. I think they brought them along from their world. They eat people, their flesh I mean."

******

Li Po flopped back on the bed gasping for air. He felt as though he had died and gone to heaven. Never had a storming of the jade gate been so pleasurable. Shanya was everything a woman should be, soft, athletic, with skin like silk and very, very tight.

When his breathing slowed, he rolled over and laid his hand on her alabaster abdomen. She reclined against a throw pillow on the top of his silk duvet.

He'd brought her up to his private apartment over the Golden Mountain. His wife lived with their four children in Golden Gate Heights on Kirkham close to Grand View Park.

"That was marvelous, my darling," he whispered.

"I know. Even now, I am becoming a virgin for you all over again."

His eyebrows flew up. "How can that be?"

So quick he never saw it coming, she rolled over on top of him. "It is my nature to heal, so I heal."

Her fangs zipped out. "It is also my nature to feed."

She held him pinned to the bed upon which they so recently made love.

"But you promised you would not kill me if I kept you well fed."

"Well, there you go. Demons are liars."

Her face was so close, he smelled the peculiar odor he now associated with her kind, a musky sweetness, like an overblown rose.

"But you have been good to me, Li Po, in your way. I offer you a chance to live . . . forever."

"Anything, yes, anything, just don't kill me."

"Well, Li Po, first you must die."

In the streets below, he heard a gong. That gong had been rung only once since he'd owned the restaurant, during the earthquake of 1989. His cell phone was laying on the nightstand. It rang and then it buzzed. He was getting a call and a text message at the same time.

"Shanya," he begged. "Please. My phone."

She wagged a finger tipped with a crimson, inch-long nail back and forth and shook her head. "Dying time is here."

She lunged at him and there was nothing he could do to stop her. Naked and helpless as a baby, he lay still beneath her while she drained him. The gong sounded again as he grew weaker and weaker, finally closing his weary eyes. The last thing he saw was Shanya lifting her mouth from his throat, fangs dripping with his blood.

Chapter Twenty

Vetalas took another hit off the bong. He sprinkled more white powder from the tiny glassine envelope onto the burning ember of weed, and felt the harsh smoke circulating deep in his chest. The bong water bubbled as he hit the pipe one more time. The DMT rushed into his brain and he smiled. What a fantastic new drug.

Around him, his minions stoked the bong with more marijuana and DMT and passed it around. Laughing and sighing with pleasure, they fell back on cushions and pillows tossed on the floor, to enjoy the high. It didn't last long, but for him and these other creatures of his making, feeling close to death was very special.

"What is this shit?" Marcelus asked as he shivered with pleasure and laid back to enjoy the euphoria and the visions brought on by the drug.

"It's something new," Vetalas said as he snagged the bong and hit it again. "It simulates a near-death-experience. According to research, DMT is released by the pineal gland right before death. This is as good as it gets, my friend. We can never die, but now we can enjoy the drug produced by the body to make it easier. We can get close to actual death, an experience we will never have."

He'd put a big-screen TV in here for everyone's enjoyment. Oohs and aahs issued from his small circle of associates as they watched the sun rise over the Bosporus in HD. DMT made the vivid colors of the sunrise explode across the flat screen.

"I never thought to see a sunrise again," Marcelus said. "This is fantastic."

Vetalas closed his eyes. He loved this room of the mansion. It was the hunting room. The original owner, J.B. Moody, had been a big hunter. Vetalas snorted at the thought. He'd brought dead animals to San Francisco from all over the planet , had them stuffed and mounted. Over the big stone fireplace, a huge elephant head stared out of glass eyes beneath a set of crossed sabers. The elephant's legs sat beside the door filled with canes and umbrellas.

A rhino head, an elk head, an entire jaguar and a hyena were mounted on the west wall. A huge grizzly bear towered over the room. Its complete body stuffed and mounted, teeth bared, fake red tongue visible inside the preserved mouth.

When the DMT began to wear off, he stood up. "We will now go hunt us a dragon. Marcelus, have you collected the necessary bait?"

"Yes, Master. Three entire human carcasses cut into bite size pieces are bagged and waiting for you in the foyer."

"That is perfect. We need to spoil her purity so she is vulnerable to my weapon of choice. If she eats humans, it will effectively destroy her inner balance and place her in direct opposition to her most sacred directive. Her mission in life, and the mission of all dragons left on this planet, is to protect and serve humanity. She will be weakened and we will kill her"

Vetalas opened a gun cabinet and removed a rifle. He held it to his face and stared into the huge bore of a 450 Nitro Express. He recognized it from his days as a great Indian prince, when he carried weapons like this for tiger hunting. He had to do all his hunting at night, but he had great night vision.

The gun was invented in the late 1800s specifically for shooting elephants. He grabbed a handful of cartridges from a box in the bottom drawer and shoved them into the pockets of his khaki pants.

Vetalas liked the new roomier style of clothing in this world. These pants were not only roomy but contained several large patch pockets with Velcro closures. He wore a black pair of Doc Martin boots, also comfortable and serviceable, and a Guayabera shirt. Suits and ties were a thing of the past. Comfort reigned in this world and Vetalas liked it.

Four of the Chosen climbed into the back of the Cadillac limo parked under the porte-cochere, and two Volthok sat in the front. The biggest Volthok, Lineus, drove, his huge wings folded into the space between his bulk and the seat. Vetalas climbed in and they were ready to go.

"Where to, Master?" Lineus asked.

"Stockton Street, the Bank of the Orient building to be exact."

Lineus drove slowly through the dark streets, heading the big vehicle down the steep hills into China Town. He parked behind a black Kia Soul.

"Lineus, two guards. Kill."

The huge demon rose out of the front seat, expanded its wings and flew across the hundred feet to the two guards smoking in front of the bank. They turned, shock registering on their young faces. One raised his weapon and fired directly into Lineus. The demon fell back for a moment, grinned, showing a mouthful of fangs, and attacked again.

The remaining guard took off running. He ran towards the limo. Vetalas laughed out loud. The four members of the Chosen caught the guard, a thin yellow man with black hair gelled into a shiny spike and long sideburns trimmed to points. His mouth opened and he screamed. No sounds issued from his ruined throat as the four members of the Chosen fed off his fountaining blood.

The Volthok ripped the sturdy bank doors off their hinges and the Chosen carried the bags of human parts into the bank behind them. Vetalas took his time entering the bank with the Nitro Express resting in the crook of his arms. He felt like a big game hunter. He was going after the biggest game of all, a dragon. There was no more terrible beast on this planet, or the one he'd vacated. Left over from the time of dinosaurs, dragons were intelligent and possessed magic and power as well as poison to kill demons.

An elevator to the lower floors didn't carry them all the way to the subterranean tunnels where the dragon was kept. It opened into a vault area with offices and a time-locked, modern vault.

They took several moments and more wasted time searching for another way down. Vetalas felt the impatience and anger firing up inside his head. His fangs popped out as he cursed the Chosen for their stupidity. The vampire Lance had told him there was an elevator to the tunnels.

They went back up and found the correct elevator, but it was locked and Vetalas had no keys. He ordered the Chosen to go back outside and search the two dead guards. They returned quickly carrying a massive wad of keys.

The elevator plunged into the depths beneath the city creaking and groaning. The Volthok remained on the street floor to watch and guard their backs. He had plenty of manpower.

It took only seconds to dispatch the three guards waiting at the doors of the elevator. They flew down the tunnels, passed closed doors, taking a sharp right. At the end of the passage, Vetalas saw the vault. There was one man guarding it. He had red hair covered by sound-reduction head gear and he crouched behind a .50-caliber Browning machinegun.

A hail of large caliber bullets tore into the four vampires ripping them to pieces. The sound was incredible, eating into Vetalas's ears. Vampire parts splattered over the concrete-block wall and the floor. The sacks containing human body parts carved into appealing roasts split open, spreading gore and chunks of flesh everywhere. Bullets ripped pieces of the concrete blocks and masonry off the walls and sprayed shrapnel across the ruptured corpses.

Vetalas dove around the corner in time to avoid being dissected by bullets. He hunkered against the concrete wall panting. The smell of sulfur filled the enclosed space and a layer of smoke rolled out of the tunnel toward the elevators.

Marcelus dragged his destroyed body around the corner and lay whimpering at Vetalas's feet. He would live. His head was still intact. There was nothing left of the other three.

Ratcheting a huge bullet into the single-action Nitro, Vetalas peeked around the corner. He was totally unprepared to see the red-headed Chinese man open the vault door and release the dragon.

She exploded from her confinement, barely fitting through the door. Roaring like a hundred lions, she charged.

Vetalas hoped she was hungry enough to stop and taste one of the pieces of meat he'd brought as he flew down the long tunnel, into the elevator, and back to the ground floor. He never even fired the elephant gun. It wouldn't have done any damage to her. She had to eat the meat first.

Back on the ground floor, he debated taking the Volthok back down and sicking them on her. But it seemed so wasteful. He had so few and he needed them.

Waving the gun, he signaled the Volthok to head back to the car. He was in a black mood. It was time to move into his castle. With the dragon loose in the city, he'd need a fortress to protect himself and his minions. The three of them dove into the limo. Vetalas indicated to the Volthok they should not drive off but wait.

"Maybe the bitch dragon will eat some of the meat and come out the bank doors. You never know. I could get lucky."

****

"She's awake." Lei sat up in bed and shook Konrad's shoulder.

He groaned and rolled over. They'd crashed and slept right through the entire day. Damn! He'd wanted to go back into the sewer. Baby's cop might have called, but he'd slept through that, too.

"I hear her," Konrad said. "She's screaming something about demons."

"The Tong must have set her free or she escaped. We have to go find her."

"She's mumbling about being hungry, too. I can hear it."

The bedroom door flew open and Kenna stuck her head into the room. "There's someone screaming in my head about being hungry. What the fuck?"

Lei scrambled out of bed, pulling on her jeans and a clean sweater. "That's Lung Ma. She's a dragon. We hatched her from an egg."

"Why's she shrieking in my head? I don't know her."

Lei led Kenna out of the bedroom allowing Konrad to get up and dress. When he had his jeans on, he walked out into the kitchen and began making coffee. Lei turned and stared at him. He looked around confused. "What'd I do?"

He saw her swallow hard. "You need to put a shirt on. There's a young girl in here."

A huge grin split his face. He flexed his muscles as he walked back into the bedroom, making his left pectoral dance. Lei looked away, her cheeks red.

When he was decently covered, he returned to the small living room and sat on the couch. Lei poured him a cup of coffee and carried it to him. "She can hear Lung Ma."

"It's probably just residual overflow or something. The dragon was screaming. Half the virgins in San Francisco must have heard her."

"She was being attacked, Sledge. We need to get out of here right now and find her."

"Let me slug down this cup of coffee and we'll go."

The three of them piled into Baby's car. The coroner had the night off. She'd called as soon as they got to Lei's apartment to tell them she was not going in. Lei climbed into the driver's seat and Konrad rode shotgun. He pulled the cell phone Baby had given him out of his pocket and checked it for calls.

There were two. One was from Baby around two that afternoon and the other from a number he didn't recognize. He called it and got a cop, Roger Munoz.

They chatted for a few minutes. Munoz and two of his friends would meet Konrad the next morning in China Town at Lei's apartment for a reconnoitering trip into the sewers.

"She says she's still in the tunnels," Lei said pulling up in front of the Bank of the Orient. The front door hung open and two badly mauled and very dead Tong members sprawled across the sidewalk out front.

128

Konrad still had the keys. They jumped out of Baby's car and ran into the building. In minutes they were descending to the subterranean chambers in the creaky old elevator.

When the doors opened, way down at the end of the tunnel, they saw Lung Ma's tail. Konrad jogged down the passageway. When he turned the corner, he saw Lung Ma feasting on meat spilled out across the floor of the tunnel.

Dragging behind, Kenna turned the corner and spotted Lung Ma and the mess.

"Gross. What is that?"

"She's an ice dragon," Lei said.

"Well she's eating parts of people. I saw the Volthok cutting them up in the basement. They were laughing cause they were trying to carve up chunks of human to look like pieces of beef."

"We've got to get her out of here," Lei said. "Lung Ma, stop eating right now. You're eating human flesh."

The dragon lifted her head, blood and meat chunks hanging off her sharp teeth.

"My God! She's as big as a Chrysler." Konrad couldn't believe how much the dragon had grown in just a few days.

I don't feel well, her voice echoed inside Konrad's head. And with it came a wave of extreme nausea.

Lung Ma turned toward the vault at the end of the tunnel and projectile vomited. Lei knelt against one wall and vomited with her.

Konrad fought the nausea. Beside him Kenna wobbled. "I think I'm gonna be sick."

"Run to the elevator and get the door open. The further away from her you are, the better you'll feel."

The girl turned and took off toward the elevator. A red-headed Tong member sauntered down the hallway, Browning machinegun over his arm. The gun was huge and the Chinese guy wasn't. He looked like he was struggling to carry it.

"Take her," Red said. "She's been nothing but trouble. My boss won't answer his phone and I'm sick of her."

Lung Ma, no longer blue-gray but a hideous shade of green, lunged at him.

Konrad grabbed her tail and pulled on it. "Come on you giant horse. He's telling us we can go."

A wail of agony pierced his brain. "Stop, Lung Ma, you're killing us."

I ate human flesh. I've gone against the first principle of all dragons. My powers are gone. Soon, I too will die.

"Fuck me!" Konrad had just about had enough. "Hey, Red, grab one of her legs and help me get her out of here."

The Chinese man put down the machinegun. "I will help you as long as she doesn't puke on me."

Konrad examined his feet and the concrete floor. A huge puddle of partially digested meat and green bile slowly spread down the hall toward the vault. The stench was indescribable. "Lung Ma, no more hurling. Lei, can you help?"

Lei nodded, slowly pulling herself off the floor, using the wall as a support. Her face was the same color as the dragon's scales.

The three of them dragged, pulled and carried parts of the dragon to the elevator. Lung Ma moaned the entire way. When they had her on the ground floor, she vomited again. They all leaped clear of the ghastly fluid.

I'm so weak. Let me die for my terrible crime.

"No fricking way," Konrad snarled. "You're here to help us kill demons and we need you."

They pulled her out of the bank and down the steps. Then it hit Konrad. He was driving a Honda hatchback. There was no room in it for elephants.

Red seemed to understand his problem. "I'll get the restaurant's delivery truck."

He was gone for a few minutes. Down the street, a black limo crept closer and closer. Konrad saw it too late. A huge blast echoed through the dark street. Lei screamed. Lung Ma's shriek inside his head forced him to grab his temples.

A hole appeared in the center of the dragon's chest. Blue-green blood gushed into the street. The noise in Konrad's head stopped and Lung Ma collapsed.

Chapter Twenty-One

Konrad shot into Berserker mode as the limo slowly accelerated away from the curb. Snatching his sword off his back, he raced for the limo, leaped on the hood and stabbed the katana through the windshield in one swift, brutal move.

He heard a satisfying scream come from the car. The limo swerved hard to the right, Konrad had to stretch out across the hood and hang on as it climbed the curb and crashed through a noodle shop window. Glass rained around him. He shook slivers out of his blonde, buzz cut and jumped off the car.

The backdoor opened and the old demon Vetalas leaped out. Konrad was ready, crouched, sword held in two big fists at his waist. The vampire launched at him so fast Konrad barely saw movement, but his heightened senses picked up the flash of khaki and he slashed with the katana.

Thick, black blood gushed out of the vampire. It screamed a horrible wail. One of those big demon things erupted from the passenger side, grabbed the hacked vampire and started running. Then he heard Lei. Not with his ears but inside his head.

Sledge, please come quickly. Lung Ma is dying.

Well, that was a new development. Sending a comforting thought to her, hoping she would get it, he turned his back on the disappearing demons and ran to help Lei.

He found Kenna and Lei lying across the dragon weeping. Lung Ma rested on her side, blue-green blood, now a trickle, dripped out of the wound.

Konrad picked up the dragon's head and stared into her eyes. They spun like discs. The spinning stopped and he saw her struggle to focus on him. Her eyes were the color of swamp water, murky-brown and green.

"Lung Ma, stay here. Don't leave us. We need you."

Give me your strength.

"How?"

He felt a probing deep in his brain, then his entire body quivered. His Berserker power flowed into Lung Ma.

Now all of you, give me your purity. Mine is poisoned and lost. You must help me replenish it.

Black, evil thoughts filled Konrad's head. He saw killing and death and all kinds of hideous demons fighting and tearing each other to pieces. He saw thousands of dead humans partially eaten, missing limbs and heads, scattered like leaves, dead on a barren plain between two, snow-capped peaks. He saw dragons flying across the sky spraying a liquid from their jaws across the demons. When the liquid hit them, smoke erupted from their scaly skin and they boiled. He smelled the stench of the dying and the reek of burning flesh.

Lei and Kenna must be experiencing the same thing. Lei screamed and Kenna whimpered and cried. Both women passed out. Kenna's eyes rolled back in her head and she began to convulse. Lung Ma thrashed beneath them, rolling and growling.

Konrad fought the black thoughts. He held on to his consciousness and tried to push good thoughts over the evil. He thought of fuzzy puppies, Sunday mornings, holding his mother in his arms, and kissing Lei. He thought of pizza, and beer, and winning battles. He began to feel the slime retreat. He thought of blue water and clean, white snow.

He stood up, grabbed Lung Ma and forced her eyes to open. When they did, he saw they were icy blue.

Red rolled up to the curb in a Golden Mountain truck and jumped out.

"Help me load her into the back," Konrad said to the Chinese man.

Gently, he moved Lei and Kenna off the dragon. They both flopped on the sidewalk breathing heavily. Kenna's eyes returned to normal and all that remained of her convulsions was a slight trembling in her arms and legs.

"Lung Ma, help us get you off the street. We need you to get up."

The dragon heaved herself to her feet. The wound on her chest was a black, shriveled hole. More blood leaked out as she stumbled to the truck. Konrad held her head in his arms and carried it as she climbed slowly into the back of the delivery van. He jumped in ahead of her and pulled her in one foot at a time. When she collapsed onto the floorboards, he collapsed with her, panting.

"You weigh a ton."

The Chinese man sat next to him. "My name's Red Chua. What's yours?"

"Konrad, but my friends call me Sledge."

Red laughed. "Sledgehammer fists, right?"

Konrad laughed with him. "Yeah, right."

"Well, Sledge, what do we do with her?" Red pointed at Lung Ma.

"I guess we'll have to put her in my garage for now. She's too damn big to get into the apartment."

"I'll drive you, but I have to hurry. I can't get a hold of my boss. Something is bad wrong with every fucking thing right now. I'll need to get back here and see if I can find him."

*****

The Volthok galloped through China Town carrying Vetalas.

"Go back to the mansion," he gasped, then gagged as a huge flood of blood erupted from his mouth.

The demon turned up Stockton Street and began the steep climb to Nob Hill.

"You need food, Master. Allow me to procure it."

He set Vetalas down and pushed through the doors of the China Town Interfaith Community Shelter and Meals. He returned in seconds carrying a baby. A woman followed him out screaming.

He handed the child to Vetalas. Vetalas held the infant for a moment, staring into its frightened eyes. He waved a hand over its face and the baby's crying ceased as the Volthok grabbed the woman and threw her through the shelter's window.

Holding the tiny body in his arms, Vetalas guzzled the sweetest blood known to a vampire, infant blood. The blood of a baby, a human at its purist, healed and nourished a Vjeszczi like no other. He didn't drain the baby, just drank enough to restore himself and then laid it on the street. It might live if it received medical attention. He hated to kill his cattle. It was why he created so many vampires. It seemed wasteful. But in the end, his mercy destroyed his world.

"I still am unable to walk," he told the demon. "Carry me."

The Volthok scooped him up and began chugging up the hill. Vetalas was furious. He hurt and his anger was a living thing inside him trying to burst through his chest and his skin. He couldn't remember being this angry . . . ever, not in three thousand years of life.

The Berserker was dead. He just didn't know it yet. Vetalas stewed on his vitriolic thoughts as his body healed itself. Halfway up Nob Hill, he stopped the demon.

"Votor, put me down. I can walk."

The huge demon set him carefully on the sidewalk. "When we get back to the mansion, we will begin the move to our fortress."

"Master, allow me to go back and kill the human who did this to you."

"No Votor, I have need of you and your brothers. Go to the doorway and call them. I need more Volthok. You must bring them through the gate and then to the mansion. We will have an army the likes of which no one has seen in eons. The races of this world will cower before us and you shall have all the human flesh you desire. Promise your brethren this and they will flock through the portal to this land where the human cattle flourish just to feed our kind."

"Yes, Master. I will go and I will call them."

They arrived at the black, wrought-iron gates of the mansion. Vetalas waved his hand, the gates swung open and he walked through. His demon slave turned and headed back to China Town to call his fellows through the doorway into San Francisco.

Once inside the Moody Mansion, Vetalas summoned his minions to the hunting room.

"It's time for us to move to our new home. We will build an impenetrable fortress. The humans will find it impossible to drive us out, and we will flourish and multiply until we rule this world as we did the last."

"Where is Marcelus?" The Roman's woman, a human swiftly turning into a member of the Chosen, asked.

"Marcelus is where he fell, woman, fighting humans and the dragon. If he lives, he will find us. The Chosen tend to themselves. Worry and concern are human emotions."

Vetalas examined her. Her name was Paige. She was pretty, and small with sharply defined muscles, and an acid tongue. Marcelus found her wandering the streets by the beach, half dead. He'd fed her some of his blood and she'd strengthened. In several years' time, she would grow into a full Vjeszczi, but not if she didn't learn to mind her mouth.

"Tomorrow night," Vetalas began as he turned in a circle to examine them all, to make eye contact with each of his minions. "Tomorrow night we will begin the move to our new home on Alcatraz Island."

Chapter Twenty-Two

Konrad climbed out of his own bed and stared at the alarm clock. It was eight. He was supposed to meet Roger Munoz at Lei's apartment around nine. He'd decided to sleep in his own digs. Constant contact with Lei was making him unbelievably horny. And there she was with the girl six inches up her ass, so no action until that loose end got tied up.

Rubbing his hand across his rough, spiky hair, he tried to tally up the hours of sleep he'd managed in the last week and was unable to come up with any kind of number healthy to human survival. He stared into the bathroom mirror and pulled at one of the bags under his eyes. They were as big as suitcases.

He pulled on a pair of semi-clean jeans pulled from the semi-clean pile and found a fresh shirt hanging in the closet, the last one. Running around after demons and dragons put a hurting on your regular life. He'd just found the time last night, late, to fetch his bike from the fire-station parking lot.

When he went hunting in his fridge for nourishment, all he found was six-day old pizza crust and leftover Chinese take-out from over a week ago. He'd shared some with Paige before the shift ended and brought home the leftovers. Thinking about Paige made him want to see if she was okay inside her icy coffin.

With his jacket on and wearing his favorite pair of boots Konrad chugged out the door into the garage. He looked around at his project bikes and felt bad. He hadn't worked on them in over a week. The Knucklehead was coming along well. It ran great. He just needed to finish the sanding and varnishing of his artwork.

He opened one of the saddle pockets on the Ninja and pulled out an energy bar. Munching on his breakfast, he flipped open the lid of the freezer. He stopped chewing. *Fuck me running!*

How in the hell was he supposed to tell Baby that Paige was missing? Where could she be? Did someone steal her body or, and this was a really terrible thought, had she opened the lid and climbed out under her own power?

Konrad kicked the footlocker Lance liked to sleep in. It sounded hollow, so he opened it. No Lance. There was something that didn't jive about surfer vamp. Whose side was he really on?

He reached Lei's apartment right around nine and parked the Ninja out front behind a black Monte Carlo. The morning sun was doing its best to burn through the fog and give San Franciscan's their hearts' desire, a sunny day. He clomped up the steps to the apartment, running several scenarios through his head where he told Baby Paige was not in the freezer. None of them came out well. Most had Baby trying to choke him to death.

Roger Munoz waited for him with some guy in a suit, a black dude Konrad figured was another cop.

"Good morning, I'm Konrad Pengill." He shook hands with both men.

"Nice to meet you, Konrad," Munoz said. "This is Special Agent Dexter Wright. He's the FBI agent assigned to look into our little problem."

"You guys armed?"

Konrad found his katana in a corner of Lei's bedroom and strapped it to his back.

"Yeah," Munoz said.

"With what?" Konrad stared Munoz in his shiny, black eyes.

Wright looked confused. He glanced at Munoz. "I'm wearing my service revolver."

"Well, Special Agent Wright, service revolvers don't do shit to any of the perps you're looking for."

"What are we supposed to carry?"

Konrad tossed Munoz the Marine Corps dress sword. "One of you can carry that. I guess the other will have to be able to run very fast. Which one of you two can run the fastest?"

Munoz pointed at Wright. "Him."

Konrad surveyed the pair. Munoz was thirty-something, five-ten and at least two hundred pounds. Wright was over six-feet and couldn't weigh one-ninety, but he was well over forty. "I believe you are correct. Keep the sword."

Konrad kissed Lei good-bye as they headed for the basement and the trapdoor into the sewer. He had a bad feeling about this. Something was down there. His Berserker persona kept pushing him aside, trying to assert itself.

At the bottom of the ladder, he gathered his troops. Munoz was ready to listen to anything he had to say. It was obvious Officer Munoz had recently seen some bad shit. Wright, on the other hand, was skeptical.

"What are you two so afraid of?' Wright asked as they trotted down the walkway beside sewage central.

Munoz shook his head but said nothing. Konrad grinned. The policeman was worried about keeping his job. If nothing appeared down here, he didn't want to look stupid.

"We're looking for vampires, demons and anything else weird and ugly you can think of. They're strong and hungry when they come out of that hole. Be ready."

Konrad approached the doorway slowly. When they were fifty feet away, he stopped his group to pass out instructions. "Don't look into the doorway. It'll make you sick, very sick. If anything comes out, Munoz, you hack it into with your sword. I'll be right there with you. Agent Wright, you better be ready to haul ass."

Wright shook his head and pulled his pistol. FBI issue .45-caliber Glock 23.

"If you see something coming through the hole, unload the whole clip. Aim for the head and neck. Ignore the tempting torso shot, it won't do a thing. If you can strafe the neck and dislodge the head, you'll disable the monster for a few minutes." Konrad saw movement up ahead and held his hand out for the other two to stop.

"Something's going on."

"It's daytime." Munoz hissed.

Konrad held two fingers up in front of his eyes, and then turned them toward the doorway. Munoz nodded. The FBI guy was fiddling with the safety on his weapon.

Berserker mode crept over Konrad. He could see more clearly, hear better and even feel the air flowing around his body. Hugging the wall, he moved slowly. Then he saw something so weird, he almost turned and ran. The ugliest demon he'd ever seen, apparently kin to the one he'd killed outside the Moody mansion, with wings, horns and red eyes, was singing. It hovered just off the ground right outside the doorway, wings outstretched. The song was something Konrad heard inside his head like Lung Ma.

Suddenly, a big, green foot popped through the doorway. It had claws and looked like a Predator foot. The scaly leg followed and then the thigh. Konrad looked away as an enormous set of genitals swung through and then the torso and head. A loin cloth emerged and flopped into place to cover the huge balls and big green dick.

Screaming his Berserker war cry, Konrad drew his sword in one slick motion, lunged forward, and hacked into the singer. The song in his head stopped, but the sword, even as sharp as it was, stuck in the demon's torso and he couldn't pull it out.

Two more creatures fell through the hole and before Konrad knew it, he was surrounded. An insane red light burned in front of Konrad's eyes as he braced one big foot on the demon's belly and yanked out his sword. A flood of black blood flowed onto the concrete pathway.

Munoz approached hesitantly. Konrad saw him through the thick red haze out of the corner of his eye. Leaping high, Konrad swung his sword twenty times rapidly, cutting and hacking. The demons' had unbelievably tough hide.

One grabbed him by the neck, huge claws digging into his skin, and threw him down. Flecks of black blood and slobber splattered him, getting into his eyes as he fought for his life. The katana was snatched away and all he had left was his fists.

One of the demons grabbed him by the throat, choking him. He pummeled its body, big sledgehammer hands punching and kicking anything he could reach. He found a set of elephant balls with his grasping hand and squeezed. Some of the pressure relaxed. He squeezed harder and felt a grinding crunch in his hands like gravel inside a leather sack. The demon on top of him screamed a high-pitched screech that ate into Konrad's eardrums.

But even though the demon was in pain, he kept his hands around Konrad's throat. To his left, Konrad saw Munoz take out one, slicing its head cleanly off its body. With his hearing fading and his vision blurred, Konrad barely heard Wright firing his pistol over and over again. Another demon joined the first. Two of the monsters had him down and were finishing him off. It suddenly seemed as though there was a thousand of them. More must have poured through the doorway.

A hand grabbed his foot and pulled. He managed a hard right to a demon's face, found the handle of his katana with his left hand, slashed, and hit something. He rolled to the left and landed in sewage river.

Munoz jumped in after him. The flow, higher than usual due to the recent rain, carried them away on a rushing tide of shit.

Konrad looked back and saw Agent Wright pounding back down the walkway beside the concrete culvert toward Lei's apartment. *Fuck*, was all he could think as he and Munoz sped along in the reeking torrent. What if the demons followed him into her apartment?

Chapter Twenty-Three

Red Chua pulled into the parking lot behind the Golden Mountain. Getting rid of the giant lizard was a huge weight off his shoulders. He'd finally dropped her at an apartment off Fulton, stuffing her giant ass through a set of French doors on a balcony. The apartment was owned by a very angry black woman, who cursed like a construction worker when the dragon fell across her coffee table and squashed it flat.

That accomplished, Red had to find Li Po. Something very bad was happening here in China Town. The place was overrun with bloodsuckers and demons and Li Po seemed oblivious.

Red tried Li Po's cell phone one more time as he ran up the stairs to his three-room flat. He kept an apartment close to the restaurant in a building sandwiched between a dry cleaner and a small Chinese market.

He opened the door slowly almost afraid he'd find horrible demons on the other side. But his rooms were quiet. In his bedroom, he opened a red, lacquer-wood trunk and yanked out an Uzi and an ancient sword.

Red's family was Mongolian. His flat face spoke to that ancestry. It was rumored his line could trace its roots all the way back to Ogedei Kaan, son of Chinngis Kaan. Red was born in a small village in Khentii Province, the birthplace of the great Kaan.

Brandishing the sword with its curved, scimitar blade, Red took a couple of swipes into the air. The crazy white man, Konrad, carried a sword and it seemed like the logical weapon. He'd seen with his own eyes what it did to that demon vampire with the long black hair. But the machinegun worked too. Red decided to cover both bases, stuck the sword in his belt and carried the Uzi.

He ran down the steps and through a dark alley next to the restaurant. There was a set of backstairs leading to Li Po's little love nest. On the eastern horizon, dawn announced its arrival by sending streaks of light across the deep blue sky. Red stopped at the door to Li Po's apartment and took a deep breath. He tried his boss's cell phone one more time. He could hear it ringing inside.

Red scratched politely on the door. He heard movement inside and knocked softly.

The door was abruptly snatched open and Red stifled a gasp. Li Po grabbed Red by the collar of his leather jacket and jerked him inside. Behind Li Po, Red saw a woman with long black hair. She was naked; her body an alabaster vision that almost blinded him with its beauty.

Li Po shoved him to the floor. "Why are you bothering me?"

Red looked up and saw tiny fangs protruding from Li Po's lips, but what freaked him out the most, Li Po had two eyes. Somehow, his boss had re-grown the eye plucked out so many years ago by the pirates. He wanted to vomit. His world was spinning out of control. He needed to stop the spinning and regain his equilibrium.

"I'm sorry, honorable sir, but I have grave news to deliver."

"What?" Li Po's voice was an angry shout.

"The dragon escaped."

Li Po grabbed Red by the neck and attacked him. Red felt the sting of Li Po's tiny fangs bite into his throat. He slid the curved-bladed sword out of his belt and slashed at Li Po's back. His boss screamed and dropped him. Red spun on his heels and dove through the window. Thousands of glass shards followed him to the awning below. He plunged through the awning and into the restaurant's dumpster.

Scrambling out of the garbage, Red threw one leg over the edge of the dumpster and fell to the blacktop. A rare ray of sunshine stabbed the fence behind the Golden Mountain. The sun was up. Red hung over the edge of the garbage bin and retrieved his sword and Uzi. He picked himself up and looked back up the stairs at the apartment. The door slammed shut.

Red wandered back down the alley, his mind swimming in turmoil. Should he gather the Tong members and tell them about Li Po? What would they do? He made his way out to the street and headed toward Waverly Place and Tong headquarters. He felt like it was time to call Shanghai and get in touch with Li Po's boss, Huizhong Chang. Things in China Town were out of control. They needed to know.

*****

Under the city, Konrad and Officer Munoz drifted down shit river. Konrad was freaking out. What if that stupid FEEB led the demons back to Lei's apartment? He pressed his hands over his temples and did the only thing he could think of. He threw his thoughts into the ether, searching for a thread or any sign of Lei or Lung Ma. He got the dragon.

Worried about Lance and his unreliability, Konrad decided not to put the dragon by herself in his garage. Not with Lance its only other occupant. So he dumped her on Baby. At the last minute, he remembered the French doors leading into Baby's living room. It seemed like his only option.

What is it, Sledge? I am still so weak.

Can you get Lei? Tell her to run. More demons are pouring into the city through the doorway. I'm afraid they will find her.

You should be able to speak to Lei yourself. It is only your preconceived limitations that prevent you from making contact. But I will tell her.

Konrad squeezed his eyes shut and tried to visualize Lei. He felt a comforting and familiar thought pattern and sent his thoughts in that direction. A tendril of sweetness flitted across his mind and he knew it was her. But he couldn't pick up any words, just the feeling that she was there.

"We need to get out of this shit soon," Munoz said, interrupting his concentration. "There's a pumping station on Jerrald Street, we musta come all the way across town. That last sign I saw said Third Avenue."

Konrad could hear a roaring noise up ahead. The flow of the sewage had tripled in volume. They were in a flood. He saw a pipe crossing the ditch ahead. "I'm gonna grab that pipe. Hold onto my legs."

Konrad growled and flexed his chest and arms. This was it, now or never. He roared and leaped, snagging one big arm around the massive pipe. Munoz hung on for dear life to his left leg.

"Don't let go, man."

Hand over hand, Konrad made his way across the sewage river to the edge of the culvert. To get out, he had to throw his legs over the pipe. He'd lose Munoz.

"Climb up and hang onto my belt," he gasped.

Munoz grunted and hauled himself higher, grabbing Konrad's belt. Konrad could feel his pants sliding. Before they came completely off, he threw both legs over the pipe and shinnied down the length and onto the concrete walkway. Munoz dropped off and hung on to the lip of the culvert.

"Help," he gasped.

Konrad reached out a paw and snagged Munoz by the shirt, dragging him out of the sewage.

They lay there gasping and blowing.

"You reek, amigo," Munoz wheezed.

"Oh, and you smell like roses, man, a fucking bed of them."

"What we gonna do?"

"Call somebody. You're the frigging cop."

*****

Across town, Lei and Kenna were racing for their lives. The alarm from Lung Ma sent them both running from the apartment.

148

She heard the clang of the basement door slamming and the pounding of heavy feet. When she stopped to look back, she saw the FBI agent erupt from the basement, his face a ghastly white.

"Run," he gasped and waved them on.

The agent raced down the steps behind them, pulled the keys out of his pocket and unlocked the door while he was running.

"Get in!"

Lei shoved Kenna across the rear seat and looked back at her building. Three of the biggest, ugliest demons she'd never imagined, not in her worst nightmares, pushed and shoved at each other to get out of the front door. For a moment, they stuck there, then exploded down the steps toward them at a galloping run.

Agent Wright started the car, jammed it into reverse and raced backwards down the street. He hit the brakes, spun the car in a half circle and shot down Grant Avenue towards the center of town.

"Where's Konrad?" Lei hung over the front seat and pounded on Agent Wright's shoulder. "What happened to Sledge?"

"He fell into the sewage. Him and Officer Munoz. Did you see those monsters? What the fuck is going on?"

"Is he all right? Did he escape the demons?"

"Konrad Pengill is some kind of monster himself. He swelled up twice his size, took on all of them, hacking and slashing with that Jappo sword of his. Black and green blood was flying everywhere. Officer Munoz grabbed Konrad and they both fell into the shit. I have never seen anything like this in my life." Wright crossed himself, pulled a big silver crucifix out of his shirt and kissed it. "Never."

Chapter Twenty-Four

Konrad and Munoz popped out of a manhole in the middle of Third Avenue, a very large street. People stared and backed away rapidly. When Konrad got a good look at Munoz, he understood why. They were covered in brownish-green slime, along with the occasional chunk.

Konrad reached over and flicked a piece of toilet paper off Munoz's left arm.

"What time is it?" He asked.

Konrad rubbed green film off his divers' watch. "One-thirty. That entire fiasco took over three hours."

"You think Wright got away?"

"Hope so. I'm worried about Lei. I'm praying the dumb ass didn't lead the demons right to her door." Konrad fished through his inside pocket and pulled out the cell phone Baby gave him. It was encased in an Otterbox and still worked. He cleaned the screen off with one finger and dialed Lei's number.

She picked up after the first ring. "Sledge, I'm so glad to hear your voice. You all right?"

Konrad looked down at his filthy jeans. "I guess so. I got to get to Baby. I need antibiotics. So does Munoz."

"Agent Wright said you fell into the sewage. I saw those demons, Sledge. They're enormous. What're we gonna do?"

"I can't think right now, doll. I'm standing in the middle of Third Avenue covered in crap. Where are you?"

"Agent Wright is taking us to Baby's. We're turning down Fulton right now."

"I'll meet you there."

A police cruiser came to get them. They piled into the back, sitting on the hard plastic seat.

"Damn!" The driver, Munoz's partner Xavier Perry said, as he rolled down all the windows.

Munoz and Perry were part of the canine forces. Perry's big German Shepard rode beside him on the front seat. The dog turned around, tongue hanging down to his chest, reached out his big black snout and sniffed. Then he growled, his lips pulling back to reveal long, sharp canine teeth.

"Hey, Cujo, it's me, Roger." Munoz stuck out his hand for the dog to smell, and it immediately began barking.

"You stink, Munoz. Stay away from him. You'll permanently fuck up his nose with that stench."

"Just drop us off at my friend's house on Fulton," Konrad said, sitting back in the seat.

"I'm gonna have to get this thing fumigated." Perry said with his fingers pinching his nose closed. He stuck half his head out of the window as he hung a left on Fulton and stayed that way.

When they got out of the cruiser at Baby's, Perry took a can of air-freshener out of a compartment under the seat and sprayed everything, including them. "You're gonna have to throw those clothes away," Perry said.

"I know. Can you go by my apartment and bring me a change?"

Perry nodded. "Only because you're my partner. And then I want to hear all about your trip through the sewer."

Konrad looked up at Baby's apartment. He saw Lung Ma's tail sticking out of the French doors. They knocked and Lei answered. She took a step toward Konrad to hug him, stopped and backpedaled.

"You can't come in here smelling like that. Baby will freak."

"Come on, Lei. We been beat up by demons and half-drowned in shit. We need a shower and clean clothes."

Lei backed up another three steps. "It's your funeral. She's already pretty pissed about the dragon."

Konrad swallowed hard. He still had to tell Baby about Paige.

The two of them stepped into a tiled entryway and stood there. Baby appeared from the bedroom and stared. "Oh my motherfucking god! What is that smell?"

"Sorry, Baby, we fell into the sewer." Konrad shifted his weight from one foot to the other. "Can we shower here, please?"

"Lei, grab those two Chronicles over there. Put some damn paper down. Ain't I got enough grief? I got a dragon in my living room, a vampire sleeping in my bathtub and now you two shitbirds want to use my shower." She grabbed a can of Lysol out of a cabinet and sprayed the floor and gave some generous shots to the air.

"Lance is here?" Konrad was surprised.

Lei began spreading open sheets of the morning newspaper across the carpet heading toward the bedroom and the bathroom.

"He's asleep in the tub. I don't know how you're gonna shower with him in there."

"I'll take care of Lance."

"Do not touch anything. Take those filthy clothes off your ass and hand them out to me." Baby snapped orders like a drill sergeant. "Lei, take the Honda and go get Sledge some clean clothes, and something for his cop buddy."

Munoz shook his head as Lei opened the front door. "I got some coming. Don't worry about me."

They cake-walked through the door into the living room and Munoz froze. "Holy, Mother of God. What is that?"

Lung Ma lifted her huge head, ice-blue eyes spinning like discs. *You smell like demon, Sledge. Did one cut you with its claws or bite you?*

"She's an ice dragon," Konrad explained to Munoz. "She was sent here because she kills demons. We hatched her from an egg."

"How big does she get?"

"Don't know, I never asked her."

"I got clawed up pretty bad," Konrad said to Lung Ma. "This guy here is a cop. He wants to know how big you get."

I can't grow unless I eat and I'm starving. You need to get treatment for those scratches. Demons have poison in their claws and their saliva. You don't get sick at first, but the wound rots and you die of blood poisoning.

"If we don't get some antibiotics, we're gonna die from the crap we just swam through. The demon poison won't get a chance."

I need food, Sledge. I'm starving.

"Is she bitching about food?" Baby stood in the doorway of the kitchen with her hands on her hips, wearing sweats and pink, fuzzy slippers.

"Yes," Konrad said slowly. "She says she's hungry."

"Well, she done cleaned out my fridge, ate all the ribs I was saving for my supper, ate all the Kung Pau chicken from last night and she emptied the freezer. You need to deal with this."

"If she's big enough to fly, I'll let her out tonight, and she can catch her own food. Lung Ma, can you fly yet?"

Lung Ma closed her huge eyes and batted lengthy eyelashes. She tilted her head. To Konrad it looked like she was flirting with him.

Of course, I can fly. Want to go for a ride?

"Not tonight, maybe later. If you can fly, you can hunt. We'll let you out tonight. The zoo's pretty close. They have buffalo, antelope, stuff like that. You can catch your own food for a change."

Lung Ma's eyes spun with pleasure. *Oh, I'll like that. Are there any blue sheep?*

"I have no idea. I never paid much attention to the livestock in the zoo."

"I hear you talking to her," Munoz said. "Is she answering you?"

Konrad tapped his head. "She's a telepath."

"This shit gets fucking weirder by the second."

"You two get your stinking asses out of my living room." Baby pointed. "And when you get in the bathroom, put some paper down."

"Can you get me some antibiotics?" Konrad asked Baby as he shoved Munoz into Baby's tiny bathroom.

"I'll call right now. Put some paper on the floor outside the bathroom and throw those filthy, disgusting rags on it. Don't let anything touch my floor." She grabbed the can of Lysol and sprayed more down the hallway toward the bathroom. "Ain't never gonna get rid of that smell, never."

Konrad opened the shower curtain. Lance slept curled on his side.

"Fuck me, I forgot about him."

Konrad opened the bathroom door. "Baby, got a trunk or a big suitcase?"

"How about this?" She backed down the hall dragging a huge wicker laundry basket.

"Open it."

Baby obliged and Konrad dumped zonked Lance inside. He never woke up. Baby giggled. "Payback is a bitch."

Konrad lifted his eyebrows under the thick layer of muck.

Baby shook her head. "No, no, this is something personal. I owe him."

The big woman shoved the filled basket down the hall, opened a closet and crammed it inside giggling all the way.

When both men had showered, showered again, used up all Baby's soap, shampoo and all the hot water, they wrapped towels around their waists and headed for the living room. Lei was back with Konrad's clothes, so he dressed quickly.

When Perry returned, Munoz dressed and all of them, Perry included, sat around Lung Ma in the living room.

Baby was cooking something. She stood in the kitchen doorway with a wooden spoon in her hand.

"What did you see down there?" Perry asked.

Munoz explained as best he could while Lei spread some kind of salve over Konrad's scratches. Every minute or so, Munoz turned and looked at Konrad for help. It took about an hour, but by that time. Baby, Lei and Perry knew something bad was happening in the city.

"What we supposed to do about this, Sledge? I got to get ready for work. Is it gonna be another night from hell?"

"I imagine so, Baby. It's not getting any better. Tomorrow I'll bug Junior and see how he's doing with his project. He's supposed to get us something called a thermo baric bomb. Hard to get, but deadly in confined spaces. He's the expert. I'm trusting him to close that doorway."

"Great, what do we do with the ones we already have?"

Konrad looked at Perry and Munoz. It seemed weird to him that he was the one answering the questions. He was the one in charge of making all the decisions. Cops were even listening to him.

"I was thinking of hitting the mansion on Nob Hill tomorrow, first thing in the morning. Anyone want to come?"

Chapter Twenty-Five

Konrad and Munoz sat in the front seat of a police cruiser, one of many police cars and SWAT vans lined up outside the house on Nob Hill. Konrad shifted one big ham, twisted his back, and rubbed his forehead with his forefinger and his thumb. They'd been waiting three hours for authorization to raid the Moody mansion. Lei along with Munoz's dog sat in the back with the dog hanging over the middle of the seat, slobbering and panting.

The two of them and Wright spent the morning and some of the afternoon coordinating the raid with SFPD and the FBI. It was a tough sell, and neither Konrad nor Munoz could understand why. Wright had actually busted into blubbering sobs in front of San Francisco Police Commissioner Ralph Campos and still the SFPD hierarchy refused to believe.

"Fuck! Can't these assholes see it's getting late?"

"Calm down, Sledge. Captain Plank is just following procedure."

"Screw procedure, it's about to get dark."

"Well the Captain doesn't really buy that all of these guys're vampires. He thinks they're probably just a bunch of Goth weirdoes."

"About a hundred really ugly demons and vampires are about to sell it to him."

"It's a hard concept to grasp, Sledge," Lei said. "Our city is being overrun by demons. I mean, would you buy into this if you hadn't seen it with your own eyes?"

Konrad turned around and looked into her lustrous, dark eyes. "No. and if you told me about it, I'd think you'd lost your mind."

She smiled, reached forward and grabbed his hand. Hers was so tiny it disappeared into his huge paw.

Streaks of orange light across the western sky were all that remained of the day. Konrad sipped coffee out of Munoz's ancient thermos. It tasted like dirt, but it was hot, and it helped him deal with the waiting. He shouldn't have brought Lei, but he'd thought she'd be safe. He thought they would attack the vampires during the day when they slept. That ship had sailed. It wouldn't be long before dark. Soon all his worst fears were going to materialize. The possibility of a blood bath on Nob Hill grew as night closed in.

Voices erupted from the radio connected to the dashboard.

"Position one, you ready?"

"Ten-four, position two what's your twenty?"

"We're situated at the rear of the house waiting for the green light to go."

"Roger that. Position three, what's your twenty?"

"Left side of the house, just under the veranda."

"Ten-four. Command's sending in a robot to look around."

"Jesus," said Konrad. "What the fuck are they thinking?"

"I don't know, maybe they want to videotape the vampires for a new horror film? They could call it Nob Hell." Munoz slapped the dash. His coffee-colored face was white around the mouth and his eyes were glassy and hard.

Slowly, a small gray robot rolled up to the front door. It was a Mark V, the kind always seen on TV disarming bombs. A member of the San Francisco SWAT brigade crab-walked to the wall, pressed himself against the red bricks, reached over and opened the door with one hand. The robot disappeared inside.

*****

Vetalas woke next to Paige, hungry. "Get up, slut, and go grab me something to eat. Something between ten and sixteen-years-old would be nice. I'm craving a little youth after feeding from your old, ugly ass all night."

"As you wish, master."

It was about time the young vampire learned to hold her tongue. It had taken long enough, but he'd finally broken her.

158

Vetalas stalked out of the room naked, drinking in the fresh smell of the night. Boxes and suitcases sat piled on the Italian tile of the entryway. The nest was packed and ready for the move. After they were situated in Alcatraz, it would be time to find and kill that dragon and the Berserker.

Vetalas opened up a kitchen window to look at the night sky. He loved the stars. In the city, the lights made them vague and faded, but he could still see the North Star and Venus close to the sickle moon.

He looked over the grounds and what he saw made him grin. His fangs snicked into view. Food littered his front lawn. The cops were here. Looked like the SWAT team. Black-uniformed officers, Kevlar vests in place, held M-16s aimed at the mansion. They knelt behind every manicured shrub and bush in the yard.

He walked across the tile in the grand entryway just as one of the front doors opened. A small robot with a camera mounted on the top rolled into the mansion. The camera swiveled back and forth. Vetalas bent over and looked into the lens. He saw it auto-focus, waved and smiled showing his well-developed canines.

Paige appeared from the kitchen with a pretty boy. Not sixteen, but still young.

"Forget the food. SFPD has thoughtfully provided all of us with a meal. Wake everyone and get them ready. I'm going hunting."

Vetalas dressed swiftly in his favorite khakis and a golf shirt and stuffed his feet into a pair of loafers. He sped to the gunroom and pulled his elephant gun off the rack over the fireplace. With a handful of shells in his pocket, he grabbed several more rifles out of the gun safe and went back to the hall.

Fifty of the Chosen gathered and ten Volthok. He handed the rifles out and told his armed brethren to find a window and get ready.

"Votor, take the Volthok and go out the upper story balconies. Choose your dinner from the men in the shrubbery. Imitate the Golden Eagle. Drop them and feed from their splattered remains."

When the Volthok raced up the stairs to do his bidding, Vetalas turned to the vampires. "Time to put these insignificant creatures in their place."

Vetalas knocked a hole in one front window with the barrel of the 450 Nitro Express, slammed a huge cartridge in the chamber, locked the bolt and stuck the barrel through the window.

*****

Konrad and Munoz climbed out of the car. "Something's going down," Munoz said.

"Lei, stay in this car and lock all the doors. Don't come out no matter what. You understand?"

Lei rolled her eyes and looked away.

Konrad sighed, but what could he do? He'd thought this would all be over by now.

"Keep Sam in there with you," Munoz shot over his shoulder as they headed for the temporary command post behind the SWAT van.

Captain Plank hung over the shoulder of the tech running the robot controller. A laptop sat open on a small folding table. The view from the robot's camera was on the screen.

Konrad took one look and gasped. Vetalas stared into the lens, his fangs showing.

"Look, one of them Goth idiots has on a set of fake fangs," Plank said.

Konrad felt his Berserker persona filling him. His heart rate doubled, adrenaline flowed through his body like fire. "That's not some Goth idiot," he growled. "That's Vetalas."

The captain laughed. "What's a Vetalas?"

Munoz looked at Konrad. "This is it amigo. We're well and truly fucked, aren't we?"

Konrad nodded, stepped away from the command post and pulled his katana. Munoz whipped the Marine Corps sword free of its scabbard and the two of them slowly advanced through the gates onto the grounds. That was when the screaming started.

The last rays of daylight cut steaming streaks through the fog. A SWAT team member shrieked as he was plucked from his hiding place in the shrubbery by a flying demon. The demon flew a hundred feet into the air and dropped the cop. He fell screaming to the ground where he landed on a fountain and exploded.

All around the grounds, SWAT team members were being yanked out of hiding, carried aloft, dropped, and killed. The demons swooped out of the sky, tore hunks off the cops, some still clinging to life, and shoveled the bloody gobs into their fanged maws.

The officers of SFPD rushed into the grounds firing their weapons at the demons. Suddenly, a huge gun exploded from inside the mansion. Konrad recognized the sound. It was Vetalas and his elephant gun. One of the cops' chest blew out. The bullet penetrated the Kevlar like it wasn't there.

"They're using armor-piercing bullets," Plank shouted as more weapons fire erupted from inside the mansion.

Then the other front door flew open and a hoard of bloodsuckers rushed out. Konrad fought like never before. He slashed the katana, whirled in a circle and cut down demons and vamps like a sickle through wheat.

Out of the corner of his eye, he saw one of the hideous flying monsters grab Munoz. The Marine Corps blade fell to the ground as Munoz tried to free himself from the demon's claws.

Racing at an amazing speed, Konrad headed for Munoz and the demon. The demon rose to thirty feet with Munoz kicking and screaming. Konrad leaped into the air. His legs pushed him to an unbelievable height. He landed on the back of the demon holding Munoz. Gripping it around the waist with his legs, he held the katana in two hands, reached over the horned monster's head and sliced through its neck.

Reeking, black and green blood sprayed Munoz, and the demon dropped. Konrad leaped off its back landing in a treetop. The demon landed hard on the ground with Munoz on top. They bounced once and Munoz flew off.

From his perch in the tree, Konrad saw Lei race into the fray. She picked up Munoz's sword and fought like an ancient Chinese warrior.

*****

Lei saw Munoz get scooped up by the demon. She saw him drop his sword. Her heart pounding like a drum in her chest, she opened the door and jumped out of the car. The dog followed her.

Grabbing Munoz's sword, she used it as she'd been taught in Baguazhang training, the ancient Chinese art of Pa Qua. Whirling and leaping, she slashed at the vamps keeping them as far away from her as she could. She knew if they got close enough to grab her, she was finished before she got started.

She killed two women, cutting off their heads in one stroke. The Marine Corps blade was different from the weapons she'd practiced with, the balance awkward. But it was sharp.

She saw Sledge jump into the air farther than a human man should be able to leap, at least thirty or forty feet, and moved in that direction. When the demon fell and Munoz fell with it, she and Sam raced for the fallen police officer.

Lei stood beside Munoz who was unconscious, feet braced. She held the sword ready in two hands. A demon swooped toward her and Munoz out of the fog. Sam barked hysterically, standing over Munoz. Then Sledge leaped onto the demon out of a tree.

Everywhere she looked vamps and demons fed on the cops and SWAT team. Lei had never seen or imagined anything like this blood bath.

Sledge rode the demon's back, hanging onto its thick, green neck. He grabbed one of the demon's wings and bent it, breaking the bones in the wing structure. The handicapped demon spiraled to the ground where Sledge jumped off and turned to fight. But it appeared as though these demons had learned to respect Sledge and his whirling katana. Fangs dripping with thick white saliva, three-inch long claws extended, the demon circled warily dragging its destroyed wing.

Munoz woke, moaning and grabbing his head. Lei backed toward him and held out one hand, watching the fighting and Sledge. Munoz grabbed her hand and the fur on the dog and pulled himself to his knees.

Sledge and the demon circled each other. Then Sledge leaped up, so high it astounded Lei. He came down slashing with the sword and neatly sliced off the monster's head. The horned monstrosity's severed head rolled ten feet and stopped next to Vetalas's loafers.

Sledge, Lei and Munoz stared into the red eyes of the vampire king. His lips were dripping with the blood of the San Francisco Police Commissioner, Ralph Campos. Campos lay on the ground his throat torn out.

Vetalas stared at them. He pointed a finger at Sledge and Lei, threw back his head and laughed. "You think to fight me and my minions?" He waved his hand to encompass the hoards feeding behind him. "You will lose. I remember you Berserker. Your time has come."

Vetalas shot into the air straight at Sledge. Lei screamed as Sledge whirled with the katana and landed a glancing slice. But Vetalas easily slapped the sword away and grabbed Sledge by his thick neck. Then Sam attacked. The dog grabbed Vetalas by the foot and savaged the vampire's leg.

Vetalas shrieked, dropped Sledge and grabbed for the dog. But Lei was there. She hacked at the vamp with her sword, cutting into its calf. Ruby-red blood gushed out of the cut. Vetalas screamed, flew high and dove for them.

Sledge scooped up an M-16 laying on the ground next to a partially eaten SWAT team member. He dropped to one knee and fired ten three-round bursts at Vetalas. The vamp screamed as the bullets chewed a line across his torso.

"Get out of here," Sledge yelled.

Lei helped Munoz to his feet, and they ran for the gate with Sam at their heels.

Sledge fired off another three-round burst, and Vetalas pointed his clawed finger at him.

"You're dead, Berserker. I'm in no hurry. Look around you. This is your fate." He laughed then, a hysterical giggle that sent chills up Lei's spine and flew into the mansion.

The vampires left their kills or carried them inside to enjoy later. Sledge helped Munoz to his feet, and they walked over to the command center. Campos was gone, but Captain Plank was there along with the computer tech. The tech, Lei read his name badge, Officer Rick Antonelli, shook the captain trying to get him to talk.

Sledge grabbed Plank's shoulder. "Plank, it's over."

Plank's eyes were blank, his mouth wide open. A long strand of drool dripped onto his crisp, white shirt. When Sledge let go, the captain keeled over and curled into the fetal position.

"He's saying something," Munoz said.

"He's been making that noise for the last five minutes." Antonelli looked up at Sledge. "Sounds sorta like ba, ba, ba, ba. That's all I can hear."

"He's catatonic," Lei said. "I've seen it before. He couldn't take the shock."

Munoz snorted with disgust. "More like he couldn't take the blame. This entire fiasco is all his fault."

Chapter Twenty-Six

Konrad, Lei, Munoz and the dog sped toward Fulton Street and Baby's apartment in the SFPD cruiser. Munoz was badly clawed, bleeding and in need of another shot of Cipro. Konrad hooked a left onto Fulton and the small cell phone Baby gave him chirped from his jeans' pocket.

Holding the wheel with one hand, he fished it out and flipped it open.

"Sledge, is that you?"

Konrad recognized the lightly accented voice of Red Chua. "Yeah, go ahead."

"Things are falling apart around here, Sledge. We need to meet. I got some ideas I want to run by you."

The Blue Dragon Tong member wanted to talk to him? Things in China Town really must be in the shitter. Konrad looked at his watch. It was almost eight. Baby would be leaving for work soon. "I got a couple of things to do first. Where were you thinking we could get together?"

"There's a small textile factory on the corner of Washington and Wentworth Place. Meet me there around midnight."

"Midnight? I guess so. The bloodsuckers will be on the prowl."

"Tell me about it."

Red hung up as Konrad parked in front of Baby's apartment. Her car was still there, but Lung Ma's tail was not sticking out the balcony doors. She must be hunting.

They went up and Konrad flopped onto Baby's couch, exhausted. The fight with the demons had worn him out. He could still feel the Berserker inside of him ready to take over at any moment, but the exertions of the battle had drained Konrad.

Baby was already in scrubs, ready for her shift. She brought a platter of sliders out of the kitchen and set them on the table. "You guys look like ten miles of bad road. How'd the fight go?"

"Just like it looks," Munoz said. "Got another shot of Cipro for me?"

Baby examined his scratches while Konrad, Munoz and Lei dug into the tiny hamburgers. Munoz slipped one to Sam as Baby returned from the kitchen carrying a large hypodermic needle and a glass bottle of the most powerful antibiotic around, Cipro.

"Looks like you got nailed by another one of those demons."

Munoz nodded.

Lance wandered out of the kitchen sucking on a plastic bag of blood. He sat across from Konrad on the love seat.

"I hate being a vampire, Sledge. I know you don't trust me, dude, but if I could change back into a human, I'd do it in a heartbeat, if I had one."

I could change him back, if I wanted to.

"Lung Ma just said she could change you back if she wanted to," Lei said to Lance.

"You're kidding. What would make her want to?"

Konrad closed his eyes. The dragon was soaring over the city. He could see the Transamerica Pyramid, the Golden Gate Bridge and Ghirardelli Square through her eyes. Even though it was night, everything glowed, illuminated in blue-white light.

Been hunting? Konrad sent his thoughts to her.

Yes, did you know there is a herd of buffalo in the park?

What does Lance have to do to be worthy of this rebirth deal?

I'll know when it happens. I can't do it until I'm sexually mature, anyway.

What'd she say, dude?

"She says she has to fuck you first." Konrad chuckled over that one. But he was thinking about Paige.

Lance gasped. "Fuck me?"

"I was just yanking your chain. She says she has to be sexually mature to transform you and she'll know if you do something worthy of this great deed."

That set Lance back in his seat. Konrad glanced around. Baby had disappeared into her bedroom.

"Lance, what the fuck happened to Paige?"

Lance's thin, blonde eyebrows shot into his hairline. "Bro, you mean, in-the-freezer-Paige?"

Konrad nodded.

"Nothing. Are you saying she's gone?"

Konrad nodded again. Baby appeared and Konrad casually placed a finger across his lips. Lance ducked his head for a quick look in Baby's direction.

"What you two dumbasses whispering about?"

We were just wondering what business is like at the morgue. Been busy?"

Baby tilted her head and tapped the toe of one gigantic, blue nurse's clog. "We had to borrow three extra coroners from out of county. The assistant we got from Oakland says they're getting a lot of drained DBs over there, too."

That piece of news hit Konrad right in the solar plexus. It was all he could do to keep himself from jumping in the car and running to save his mother. But it was already after nine. No way she was awake. The home she was in locked down tight as an oyster every night at eight.

After Baby left for work, Konrad took a shower and changed into some fresh clothes Baby laundered. He slipped on his denim shirt and bit back a curse. The shirt was stiffer than a piece of cardboard. She'd starched it.

"Lung Ma just told me she's roosting on the roof," Lei said when he came back out into the living room. "She's got a comfy spot overlooking a balcony with a huge pigeon coop."

"Tell her not to eat them. Baby's gotta live here."

Lei laughed and he pulled her off the sofa. "It's time for me to head over to meet Red Chua."

"You're not going anywhere without me."

Konrad sighed. "Where's Munoz?"

Lei winked. "He's asleep in Baby's bed. The Cipro knocked him out."

"She let him sleep in there?"

Lei narrowed her eyes and curled her lips right at the left corner. "I think she likes him."

"But she's gay," Konrad whispered.

Lei rolled her eyes and shrugged her shoulders.

They drove across town in Munoz's cruiser. When they got to the address Red gave him, Konrad parked.

"This is gonna turn out to be a sweat shop, isn't it?" Lei said as they knocked on a side door.

"Probably."

Red let them into a narrow hallway. Lights glowed from a room down the hall and the noise of sewing machines and hushed voices could be heard from inside the building. Red led them up a narrow flight of stairs. At the top, Red opened a door. On the other side a huge room was filled with men and women dressed in loose white pants practicing forms.

The room had mirrors down one side, a polished oak floor and recessed lighting. Each of the martial artists' movements was synchronized as they went through the ritualized motions of the forms, shouting each time they changed position.

Lei and Konrad followed Red into an office, and Red moved behind them to shut the door. A middle-aged Chinese man sat behind the desk. He wore a golden uniform over bright-blue, loose-fitting pants. The yellow-gold jacket was tied with a black belt that wrapped several times around his body. His head was shaven, his ears slightly pointed and his eyes beady and bright. Three jagged scars tore across his face, cleaving his chin into three sections. A broad, curved Chinese sword lay across the desk.

Red bowed. "Honorable Master, this is the man I was telling you about, the Berserker Konrad Pengill. We call him Sledge. And this is Colonel Jiang's daughter."

The man put both of his hands together as if in prayer and briefly bowed his head. "I am Tianyuan Yu Tang, master of this Zen temple. We are Shaolin warrior monks. We believe in the teachings of Zen, but we practice the arts of war as our brethren have done for centuries. Red says you are a warrior of astonishing abilities, Mr. Pengill. He says he believes we need you to defeat the demons that infest this city. He says I can help you become greater than you are."

The door opened and an elderly Chinese woman entered. Both Chinese men turned to greet her, bowing low.

Red waved his hand indicating Konrad and Lei. "Madam Zing, this is the warrior I told you about. Sledge, this is Madam Zing Luong. She's a seer of great power. She asked to meet you."

Chapter Twenty-Seven

Konrad examined the office. Three sticks of incense burned in front of a jade Buddha. The smell permeated the room. The statue sat on a cabinet, the two front doors inlaid and painted with fighting dragons. What Konrad recognized as a prayer wheel sat on the corner of this table.

Every wall in the office was covered with intricate, brightly-colored paintings and wall-hangings. As a smoky haze drifted around his head, Lei took his hand and smiled.

Madame Zing was neatly-dressed and looked about a hundred, with long, gray hair pulled tightly into a bun at her neck. She wore a pale-blue cardigan over a wool skirt that ended below her knees, a white blouse with a round collar and black-canvas shoes. What caught and held his attention was the huge dragon pendant hanging from a thick gold chain around her neck.

The old woman stared at Konrad out of snapping, black eyes. "You're quite a specimen," she said, slapping his biceps with one little hand. She walked around him pinching the flesh of his waist and shoulders. Konrad sucked in his gut. The old lady dropped her right foot back, braced herself and punched Konrad in the stomach with her fist. He gasped and grabbed his belly. The old bat packed quite a wallop. It hurt.

Madame Zing cackled. "Caught you off guard, young man. Never trust anyone. Never let down your guard. I could just have easily stabbed you with a knife dipped in poison. You'd be laying there puking green right now and no one could save you."

"Madame Zing wanted to meet you, Sledge," Red told him. "She's got something she needs to tell you, something she's seen."

"Sit there," she said and pointed to a pair of chairs with a table between them.

A lacquer-wood table sat between the two chairs. As Konrad sat down, he saw the four legs were carved into dragons, their claws holding the top and their wings joining. Madame Zing saw him looking at the carved dragons.

"A long time ago, there were four kinds of dragons on earth. Fire dragons were the most powerful. They breathed fire and lived in Europe. The water dragons lived in the ocean, as you might imagine, and the earth dragons lived underground. They were shorter, stouter creatures that inhabited many parts of the planet where there were mountains and hills. The ice dragons are the dragons of the air. They fly. All of the dragons of earth spewed poison and all possessed magical powers."

Madame Zing sat in the other chair and took Konrad's hand in both of hers. She smiled at him and he saw she had no teeth. Yu Tang placed a steaming cup of tea in front of the ancient woman, bowed and returned to his desk. She dropped Konrad's hand and took a small sip.

"Sledge, you are the last of an ancient breed, just like the dragons. You have inside yourself, all the power needed by the human race to defeat these demons. But it's lying dormant and unused because you don't have the skills necessary to tap it. Yu Tang will teach you what you need to know . . . because if you do not learn, the entire human race will die."

The old lady must be doing the good drugs, because this was certainly a drug-induced fantasy. "What are you talking about? I can't save the human race. I'm just one guy with a bad temper, and an ancestor with an even badder one."

The old woman sipped more tea. "This is very good, Yu Tang. Thank you."

Konrad started to get out of his chair. The woman slapped the tiny porcelain cup down with some force and held out her hand. "Stop! You will listen to what I have to say."

Konrad discovered he couldn't stand, so he sat down.

She leaned forward. "I have seen our deaths. And as you die, Sledge, a cloud of black, angry insects swarm across the planet devouring everything in sight. The sun explodes in the sky and then all I see is black. Day becomes night and night lasts forever."

She leaned back and opened her hands in front of her face, her fingers spread. She held them that way and her eyes rolled back in their sockets. Chills rolled up and down Konrad's spine. Gooseflesh rushed across his shoulders and down his arms. The hag was a real creep show.

"I don't get it. Why am I so important?"

"If you die, Sledge, the human race dies with you. You will fight the demons inside their castle, and if you are not prepared, they will win. And if they win, humans will be just so much fodder for their consumption. You are the only person on this planet with the strength to go into the lion's den and emerge victorious."

Konrad looked at Lei. "She's got me mixed up with somebody else."

Lei stood behind him and put her hands on his broad shoulders. "She's got the right guy. I can feel it. Listen to her, Sledge. Do what she says."

The old woman grabbed his hands again. Her fingers were like bird claws, they dug into his flesh. "The dragon will help you. You command an ice dragon, Sledge. She is the most powerful creature on this planet. Her strength and her magic are at your disposal."

"She's just a baby."

The old woman's voice rose until she was screeching. "Learn how to use your own powers, Sledge. Join with the dragon and defeat the demons. Send them back to hell and slam the door shut behind them."

Madame Zing slumped in the chair. It was as though she delivered her message and died. Konrad leaned over her. "You okay, Madame Zing?"

173

The hag opened one eye. "Do as Tianyuan Yu Tang says. He is a great teacher. You have much power, Sledge. Your rage gives you strength, enough to slow the passage of time or even to stop it."

*****

Konrad closed his eyes, listened to his breathing and the slow, steady beat of his heart. Zen Master Yu Tang sat next to him. They were in the private meditation chamber of the Shaolin Master. The walls were covered with beige silk, the floors with mats. Incense burned on a lacquer-wood tray. A spray of autumn leaves lay across a plain table.

This was Konrad's second day learning to meditate with the master. The first day, he'd gone deep inside himself and discovered he could touch his Berserker persona with his thoughts. He could feel it waiting for him to call upon its strength.

Today, the master told him, he was to practice moving in and out of that persona without needing the rage to trigger it. Konrad chanted the words the master had given him, the chant of the three refuges. "*Buddham saranam gacchāmi*, I go for refuge in the Buddha. *Dhammam saranam gacchāmi*, I go for refuge in the dharma. *Sangham saranam gacchāmi,* I go for refuge in the sangha."

Sweat bloomed across his forehead as he concentrated and chanted, slipping into Berserker mode for the fifth time, no rage needed.

Still listening to his breathing, still measuring each breath, Konrad felt the strength of the Berserker. He felt his muscles grow and his spine tingle with immeasurable power. He allowed himself to become fully immersed in the ancient personality.

His chest swelled, and he opened his eyes. Snow swirled around him and he could see his breathe. He sat on a rock in the center of mountains. The sky was gray and filled with falling snow. He stood up and followed a well-worn path across the top of the hill. Huge

174

gray rocks half-covered with snow sprouted from the earth beside the trail.

It felt like he walked forever. His bare feet were freezing, and snow covered his thin, orange robe. Flakes hung from his eyelashes as he stared into the iron-gray sky. Why was he here? Where the fuck was he? It was like a dream, but he was so cold and the snow and the rocks under his feet seemed so real.

He heard the rider approaching before he saw it. A huge, blue-gray horse crested a hill in front of him and stopped at the top.

The rider was a Norseman. He wore wolf hides and a wolf's head adorned his helm. Long blonde hair cascaded down the rider's shoulders and back. He wore a full blonde beard and stared at Konrad out of glacier-blue eyes.

The Viking held the horse's reins in one big fist, easily keeping the plunging, stamping animal under control. He carried a massive sword which he raised over his head, then he pointed it at Konrad.

Snow swirled around the Norseman and Konrad. "You have the power, Konrad Pengill. You are one of us, descended from heroes, born to fight. I, Alfer Ulfvarinn, tell you, ride against the demons invading your world and defeat them. Bring honor to our name. The key to victory is the beating of your heart."

Konrad had no idea what he was supposed to do. This felt like a dream, but it seemed so real.

"This sword holds great power and the strength to kill demons."

The horse reared, and Konrad's ancestor whirled the huge beast on its hind legs and galloped back over the hill.

Konrad felt the world spinning out of control. The gray sky overhead twisted and turned, then faded to white. When he opened his eyes, he was standing in the middle of the meditation chamber with Ulfvarinn's enormous sword clutched in his hand.

The master was gone and he was alone.

Chapter Twenty-Eight

Paige clutched Vetalas's arm as they flew over San Francisco Bay toward Alcatraz. She hated flying, hated it before she became Vetalas's thing and hated it now. The sun was gone. All that remained of the day was a steak of yellow and pink edging the Pacific on the other side of the Golden Gate Bridge.

A squad of ten demons surrounded them, their huge wings flapping slowly like great vultures. Vetalas didn't have any wings. Apparently, he didn't need them.

Vetalas landed on the roof of the main cell block and thrust her off his arm. She cowered, averted her eyes and studied the asphalt beneath her feet. It was ancient, cracked and covered with bird shit.

"Look, they deliver our meal."

He dragged her to the edge of the roof, and they gazed down at several buildings, the bay and a big white boat filled with tourists drifting slowly toward a concrete slip. To the right, the lighthouse glowed with a high-powered beam aimed toward the Golden Gate Bridge.

The tour boat slowly pulled into the dock in front of what looked like a four-story apartment building. The concrete blocks of the building were yellowed with age, many windows broken. Waves and a gusty wind rocked the sturdy boat as it disgorged its human cargo.

"It doesn't matter how many we killed over the last week. There are no guards on that boat and they still venture out at night. Dine, my friends. Show the cattle who owns them."

The chieftain of the Volthok, Lineus, spotted a tall woman running up the ramp from the dock toward the main cellblock. She towed a small child with her. The big demon took off, his huge wings sliced through the air as he dove toward his prey. The woman stopped in the middle of the hill, turned and saw Lineus. She picked up the child and ran faster. Paige held her breathe. When the woman reached the top, she kept running toward the building found an open door and catapulted inside.

Deprived of his first choice, Lineus circled slowly and made another selection. This time a fat man who stood frozen with fear in the middle of the road. Paige sighed with relief. Lineus could eat all the fat men he liked.

The rest of the demons swooped off the roof. They plucked humans off the dock and the boat, and then dropped them onto the harsh rocks of the island. Screams split the night air along with whoops and grunts from the feasting demons. It seemed as though they could never get enough to eat. And after each meal, they grew larger. Paige wanted to look away, but couldn't. She was so hungry. Her tongue traced her infant fangs and she licked her lips.

"No, my lovely halfling. You may not suck the blood of humans yet. There are centuries enough for that. First you must learn obedience to your master."

The lights came on in the towers. Floodlights lit the dock and the buildings. Paige saw a flock of Vetalas's demon vampires flying across the bay now that it was fully dark. He and the Volthok could tolerate the sun.

A bloody tear coursed down her cheek. She missed Baby and her life. She missed Sledge, the asshole. He was one of the few men she tolerated. Vetalas preened and postured as he watched the demons feed. It was a disgusting sight. Paige was sure he loved it. She snuck a look at him from under her arm and her fangs bit into her lips. One day he would pay. He thought she was tamed. He thought she was his personal pin cushion. He'd learn differently.

The demon vampire grabbed her arm. "Let's explore."

He dragged her through an open door on the roof and into the cellblock. The puke-yellow paint on the long row of cells was chipped and faded. Rust flaked off the walls and bars like metal psoriasis. Scraps of paint and rusty chunks crunched under her boots. The place reeked. Her heightened senses detected mold, mildew, rat shit and ancient sweat. It was the sweat of suffering men, a different odor entirely.

They went down a narrow stairwell to the basement. Thin light illuminated dark cell doors and an aged concrete floor stained with god-knew-what. The smell down here was different. It smelled like terror.

"This was solitary confinement," Vetalas told her as he grabbed her and shoved her into a dark cell with a low ceiling. He slammed the door, locking her inside. "How do you like your new home?"

Paige screamed and Vetalas laughed and laughed.

****

"Hut!" the master of the temple called. All of the students took a step, hit their fists together, side-kicked and resumed the original stance.

"Hut!" Master Tang called again, and this time the students stepped forward picked up their Wu-shu, Darn Dao broadswords and slashed the air several times, wheeled, slashed again and yelled.

Sweat rolled down Konrad's forehead as he fought to control his weapon and alter-ego. Holding the weapon in his hand caused the Berserker to surface. Konrad fought to be the one in command.

Lei slashed her sword beside him as the students all moved together to perform the intricate steps of the forms.

Master Tang clapped his hands and the students raced to place their weapons on a rack and form a circle. It was time to spar.

"You and you," Tang sent Lei and a young male student onto the mat inside the ring. Lei circled her opponent, a taller, slender Chinese boy about sixteen. Once again, Konrad had to control himself. The desire to protect Lei was strong.

Lei leaped high and hit her opponent under the chin with a jumping front kick, whirled and kicked him in the side of his head with a strong sidekick.

The students cheered as the boy attacked her with a series of rapid-fire punches. Lei blocked the punches with her forearms and went low, grabbing the kid's foot when he tried to front kick and flipping him over on his back. She was on him in a second, the outside of her foot against his throat.

The master called them away. Lei bowed to her opponent, who returned the bow with a red face. The master called Konrad into the improvised ring and squared off against him.

Konrad was still learning this Chinese horseshit style of fighting. But Shaolin Kung Fu included grappling and Konrad knew how to wrestle. He'd been state champ in high school. He also had some basic martial arts skills from the Marines.

Master Tang came at him with a flurry of punches, several rapid sidekicks to his thigh followed by a roundhouse kick to the side of his head.

It was as though his attacker fought in slow motion. Konrad reduced the number of his heartbeats through breath control, blocked each of Tang's fast jabs and the kicks. The roundhouse caught him a glancing blow, but Konrad was able to grab the master's foot. Tang leaped high, twisted in the air, yanked his foot free, and landed a hard kick to Konrad's jaw.

Konrad growled, dropped lower in his stance, and raised his hands to block blows to his face. He knew his kicking ability was sub-par. He couldn't hope to compete with Tang in a kicking match. As they circled again, Konrad waited.

Tang moved in with the speed of a striking cobra, two fists to Konrad's head were easily blocked. But when Tang lifted his foot for a kick to his chin, Konrad was ready. He grabbed the master and jerked him off his feet, followed him down, picked him up and threw him out of the ring.

"Congratulations," Tang said later. "You are a fast learner." Tang bowed to Lei. "And you Miss LeiHua are already a master. I believe I detect the subtle training of Master Yang Luchen. If you are indeed his student, you are a lucky young woman. I have never known him to accept a female."

Lei returned the bow. "Yes, honorable Master Tang. Master Luchen trained me as a favor to my father. They were childhood friends in Guang Dong."

Konrad followed the two out of the training area and into Tang's office. While they talked, he stripped off his leg-wraps and draped them over his arm.

"I'm gonna shower," he said to Lei. "We have to get out of here soon. I gotta be in Albany to see my mom before seven or they'll lock me out."

She nodded, and he took off for the men's locker room.

Ten minutes later they were on their way to pick up Baby and take her to work. They dropped her at the coroner's office and headed for the Bay Bridge and Oakland. Konrad worried about his mother. Ever since Baby told them the Oakland Coroner's Office was inundated with sucked-dry DBs, he'd been freaked out. Oakland was adjacent to Albany where his mother lived.

They arrived at the group home on Adam's Street around six-forty-five. Konrad held Lei's hand. She looked up at him and shook her head.

"Are you sure you want me to meet your mother? I'm Chinese. She's gonna hate me."

"Come on, Lei. She's an older woman sentenced to life in a wheelchair. She'll like anyone I like. You got the bag?"

She held it up. They'd stopped at the Lucky Seven Quik-Mart on the way to pick up a pile of Examiners, Enquirers, Globes and a Reader's Digest. Konrad tossed four candy bars into the bag as well. She liked Milky Ways.

"She'll be set for days."

The home was just that, a real house. It was a roomy, two-story, block structure with a garage. The garage had been turned into bedrooms. Inside the front door was a partition. The place smelled like mothballs, pine cleaner and fish. It always smelled like that no matter what was cooking. Lei wrinkled her nose and smiled at him as he rang the bell sitting on a table by the door. A round-faced, woman wiping her hands on a dish towel walked out from behind the screen to greet them.

"Hi, Mrs. Willows. How's Mom?"

"Hello Konrad, your mother's doing great. She'll be so happy to see you."

He bent and pecked the woman's cheek. She had an apple-round face, several chins, wore a tent-like dress and slippers.

"Did you bring her the papers?"

Konrad held up the bag.

"I see you brought a friend. I think this is the first time I've ever seen you with a girl."

Mrs. Willows kept up a string of small talk as she led them to the garage area. His mother had a room on the ground floor for easier accessibility.

Konrad knocked and opened the door. His mom was watching the evening news. When she saw him, she beamed. He bent over and hugged her, trying his best to send her some of his strength and energy. She'd grown fragile in the chair. It made him sad to see it.

She held out her hand. "Where are they?"

Lei stepped forward and placed the bag on her lap.

"Mom, this is my friend LeiHua Jiang. Lei, this is my mother, Francis Pengill."

Konrad cringed, waiting for fireworks. His mother examined Lei for a few moments while no one spoke, and Konrad didn't breathe. Then she smiled.

"I'm so pleased to see Konrad is making friends."

Chapter Twenty-Nine

Konrad and Lei sat with his mother for an hour watching the evening news and talking. His mother was addicted to news. She watched it all day long, switching back and forth between anything she could find on UFOs and celebrities.

"Have they figured out why all these people are dying, Konrad? It seems so strange and horrible, all these people getting their blood drained."

He leaned forward and took his mother's hand. "That's one of the reasons I drove over. Lei and I ran into some of the killers. It's really weird, Mom, they're demons and vampires. They're coming into our city through a hole in the sewer."

"I knew it. I knew there were vampires in the sewers. We been breeding up all kinds of mutant crap down there for years. You should see the stuff Mrs. Willows flushes down the drain. I read in the Enquirer the other day that a thirty-foot long anaconda was found in the sewers of New York. We probably got aliens living down there, too. Why, in the Globe I saw an article about . . ."

Konrad put his hand on her arm. "All that stuff in those rags you read is bullshit, Mom. This is the real deal. I brought you something to protect yourself with."

He handed her the Wasp. "When you stab someone or something with this knife, it freezes their insides. It only takes a small stick and whoever is after you, is dead. So be careful with it but keep it beside you all the time. It freaks me out that you're over here. I heard the vamps spread out and are in Oakland now."

Konrad's cell phone rang. He checked the screen. "Yeah, go ahead Munoz."

He stood up and stepped away from his mother to talk privately. "What's going on?"

"Tomorrow morning the department is going in."

"I thought Captain Plank was sidelined."

"They're bringing in a replacement from Daly City. We're meeting at the Powell Street manhole at eight. These guys got no idea what they're facing. I need you to show up, man. I don't want to go back down there alone."

"Don't worry. I'll be there."

******

Konrad checked his watch. It was already nine in the morning. They'd been standing in the pouring rain for an hour.

"When we going down?" he asked Munoz.

"Don't know, man. I guess as soon as Scary Larry decides to lead us into battle."

A huge gust of wind drove the rain into Konrad's face. He pulled the collar of his leather jacket up to cover his ears and his police helmet lower. They all wore the helmets for safety and because they were equipped with radios. All of the attack force led by Captain Plank's replacement from Daly City, Lieutenant Larry Groves, or as the men liked to call him, Scary Larry, were connected by these radios.

Groves stalked back and forth next to the Powell Street manhole, his hands crossed behind his back, his long black mustache blowing in the stiff wind. Yellow crime-scene tape flapped and blew from poles set up around the hole. Groves ignored the rain as he examined his troops, twenty hand-picked members of SFPD.

He stopped in front of Konrad. "Who the fuck are you?" He turned to his men. "What's the Jolly Green Giant doing in the middle of my crime scene?"

Munoz stepped up. "This is Konrad Pengill, sir. He's the one who discovered the hole."

"What's this, Officer Munoz?" Groves yelled, yanking Munoz's enormous silver cross out from under his uniform jacket. "This isn't police issue."

"No sir," Munoz yelled back. Groves was ex-Marine and even though he'd left the Corps, it had never left him.

Groves moved down the line pulling garlic necklaces out from under jackets and more crosses. "What in the hell is going on here? Dubowsky, is that a stake I see tied to your belt. Finch, what's in the silver flask?"

The officer under the gun flushed. "Holy water, sir."

Groves fingered a dog collar studded with spikes one officer wore around his neck and yanked a red and yellow plastic gun off another man's back. "What's this, Richards?"

"Super-Soaker, sir. I drained the font at St. Anne's."

Scary Larry's face was the color of a ripe pomegranate. "There is no such thing as a vampire!" he screamed. "I repeat, there are no vampires. Demons do not exist!"

Groves pulled a wet cigar out of his pocket and jammed it in the corner of his mouth. "No wonder Plank is in the nut house."

"You gotta hope if the vamps get anyone today, it's him," Konrad said to Munoz.

Munoz grinned. "You got that right."

"You," Groves pointed at Konrad. "Since you discovered this alleged doorway to hell, you go in first."

Konrad climbed down the narrow ladder with a flood of water rushing over and around him from the street. Groves was right above him. When they hit the concrete path beside the culvert, Konrad stopped.

"Sir, the sewer is flooded." Munoz said.

"I don't care if we have to swim. You," he pointed at Konrad again. "Take me to this hole."

Konrad stepped close to Scary Larry. They were about the same height. "My name is Pengill. I'm a volunteer and I'd appreciate a little respect."

Groves chewed away at the unlit cigar and grinned. He grabbed Konrad's shoulder. "I like a man that stands up for himself. Lead on ….Pen-ghoul."

"When we get to the hole," Konrad said into his radio. "Make sure none of you look directly into it. The fucking thing is weird. It'll make you too sick to stand up. You'll be blowing your breakfast into the sewer while some big ugly demon tears you to pieces."

"Ignore that last bit of information," Groves snapped into the radio. "There are no demons down here. Probably just bums and drug addicts."

"Suit yourself. It's your funeral," Konrad mumbled.

Water rushed underground through every storm-drain and manhole. The sewer was overflowing. Waste washed knee deep around their legs as they plowed down the flooded walkway toward the doorway. Every man had a police-issue flashlight blazing away and two men carried huge spotlights. Konrad could see things he'd never seen down here before and really wished he couldn't see now.

Rats, flushed out of their holes, sat on every ledge, cleaned water off their fur or scampered from point A to point B. There had to be hundreds of them. Thousands of cockroaches, driven out of their homes as well, swarmed the walls. Two dead bodies floated by and Groves made them stop so they could catch the DBs and secure them.

Konrad watched with his Berserker senses heightened. They weren't alone in the sewer.

He grabbed Munoz, tipped his head and discretely touched his eyes with two fingers, then pointed the fingers down the pathway. Munoz nodded and they both slipped closer to the wall. Konrad drew his sword, the sword of his ancestor, Alfer Ulfvarinn, and held it in one hand.

The huge sword weighed about thirty pounds. It glowed silvery blue in the glare of the flashlights. Konrad could see a pure white aura surrounding the blade. The hilt was exactly the right width for one of his big hands, with an arced piece of metal at the top and a wide pommel at the bottom of the grip. Runes and strange writing ran down the length of the sword, carved into the metal and then painted deep blue. It was light enough and so well balanced, Konrad could swing it with one arm.

Munoz switched the safety off his M-4 and the two of them eased along the path leaving Groves and his men to deal with the floaters. When they reached the corner before the doorway, Konrad held up his hand. He could hear talking in a strange language, lots of grunting, and that weird singing he'd heard before in his head. One of the demons was drawing more of its kind through the doorway.

The white glow around his sword began to grow. Konrad felt himself swelling with the Berserker rage. He controlled his breathing, slowed his heart rate and chanted his mantra under his breath. The Berserker strength flowed through his veins like never before. He looked at Munoz. The cop nodded and hefted the M-4.

They leaped around the corner simultaneously. Konrad yelled a challenge to the huge demon standing in front of the doorway. The ugly son of a bitch was not alone. Five more backed up and stared at him through red eyes. Screaming a war cry, Konrad waded in with his sword, slashing at arms, torsos and heads while Munoz raked the ones coming through the hole with three-round bursts. Parts of demons and black blood flew across the dark, fetid area in front of the doorway, splashing into the rising flood.

In the enclosed area around the doorway, the large demons had trouble maneuvering due to their huge wings. They carried enormous clubs studded with spikes, but they were so tall, swinging them was difficult in the enclosed space.

The bullets from the M-4 did little damage, but Konrad's sword cut through their thick, scaled skin like slicing through cake.

Munoz tossed his useless gun aside, drew the Marine Corps sword strapped to his back, and stepped forward to help Konrad. But Munoz was no match for the huge demons. A big purple one, grabbed the blade and broke it over his knee, then snatched Munoz and tossed him into the rush of sewage headed for the bay.

Konrad caught all this out of the corner of his eye as he took on a big green monster with horns and a wicked scar running down the right side of his face.

Groves rushed forward and emptied the magazine of his weapon at a vampire coming through the doorway. The three-round bursts cut into the vamp but didn't kill it. The skeletal, bloodsucking demon kept coming.

Scary Larry drew his sidearm, an enormous Colt .45 with a pearl handle, and fired five quick rounds directly into the vamp. The huge bullets slowed the vamp for a second, but it healed right before Groves' eyes.

"Fall back!" Groves yelled. "Fall back!"

Konrad could hear him screaming inside his helmet through the radio.

"Charlie's got us, fall back." Groves slowed down to shove more bullets into the empty cylinder of his pistol and fired all six rounds right into the vampire's face. Its head exploded and it fell at Groves' feet.

Six other men rounded the corner and opened up with their M-4's. A huge demon slapped Richards' weapon aside. The cop pulled the Super Soaker and sprayed it with holy water. Smiling widely, the demon revealed rows of long fangs, the demon wiped the liquid out of its red eyes, picked Richards up and threw him through the doorway.

Finch leaped forward, snagged Richards's boot and held on. The poor cop's entire body, except for his left foot was on the other side. Finch screamed for help as the foot slowly moved into the hole.

Two more officers raked the demons with bullets, but the sight of the hole was too much for Finch, he had to let go of Richards to vomit copiously into the racing water. A demon grabbed Finch by the neck, twisted, and tore off his head just as three more vampires exploded from the hole. One carried Richards's head, holding it by his brown hair.

Konrad heard all this and saw some of it with his peripheral vision, but he couldn't help. Three demons had him pinned and he needed his concentration. He lifted the sword high and sliced the arm off one of the ugly monsters. It fell at his feet, while its arm disappeared into the disgusting shit river.

The water rose swiftly. It was almost to Konrad's knees. He sliced into another, cutting its torso in two. The top half fell into the water and the bottom remained planted with black blood gushing into the swirling sewage.

"Fall back!" Groves shouted over and over again into the headset until his voice was a tiny squeak. "Fall back. Charlie's got us. Retreat!"

The police officers broke away, turned and ran back down the walkway, slogging through the hip-high flood. Konrad backed away, protecting himself with the sword. He glanced down the sewage flood, hoping to spot Munoz, and saw his friend clinging to a wall support, sitting on a six-inch ledge.

One of the demons saw him, too, leaped into the sewage, swimming like a killer whale toward Munoz. Konrad screamed his battle cry and went after him.

Munoz's helmet was gone. Konrad could see the raw fear in his eyes as the demon closed in. Konrad reached for more Berserker power and felt everything around him slow, the flood of sewage slowed, the demon slowed, Munoz was screaming in slow motion.

But Konrad was still moving fast. He reached the demon, grabbed its foot and hacked it off, grabbed the other foot, swung his sword again and removed the entire tree-trunk leg at the hip. He let the monster go and caught a pipe next to Munoz. The level of sewage in this part of the tunnel was so high, the ceiling along with its network of pipes, was easily within reach.

"Come on, Roger, grab onto me. It looks like we gotta go on another ride through the sewers."

"No, leave me here. I'd rather die."

"Don't be such a wuss."

Munoz let Konrad pull him into the flow. He was shaking like a leaf, his lips blue and his teeth chattering.

"I'm gonna need another shot of Cipro," he managed to squeak as they shot through the tunnels on the raging torrent.

The rainwater flooding into the sewer raised the level of shit river so quickly it lapped the top of the pipe. With only inches between their faces and the filth-encrusted pipe, Munoz and Konrad had to hold their heads back to get any air.

Even in full Berserker mode, Konrad could do nothing to save them. The rushing tide of crap was going to drown them both in seconds.

As the water covered his head, Konrad felt no fear. Fear was not an emotion he ever experienced in his Berserker persona. He was only filled with rage. He reached behind and grabbed Munoz's arm. He'd reached the end of his air, his lungs bursting with the need to breathe, when he was suddenly sucked up and into a pipe. He felt Munoz pushing against his feet. Together, they shot through the duct leading to the surface. Konrad felt like he was going a hundred miles an hour when he erupted from the pipe at the head of a huge geyser of sewage and flew fifty feet into the air.

He and Munoz fell to earth in the middle of a grassy field and lay on their backs gasping for air. Munoz lifted himself up on one elbow. "Holy shit, Sledge, we're in the city spray field."

"What's that?"

Sprinklers suddenly came on, shooting brown water in arcing circles. Konrad

sniffed. "Oh man, more shit."

"You got that right." Munoz crawled a few feet and clambered to his feet. "We

better run. They put the buffalo in here."

"We're in the park," Konrad said. "Let's find the fountain, wash off and head for

Baby's. It can't be that far from here."

190

Chapter Thirty

Konrad slipped up behind Lei and wrapped his arms around her. "When can we go to bed?"

She turned in his embrace and pushed him away. "Not now, not tonight," she said and pointed at Kenna watching TV on Lei's tiny flat screen.

Konrad lifted her chin with one finger and stared into her lustrous eyes. Her long hair fell over her shoulder in one thick braid all the way to her waist. He wanted to kiss her so badly. He could feel her lips on his, even though right at this moment, they were pursed into a frown of disapproval.

"Lei, being close to you like this every day is torturing me. I'm starting to turn purple. I want you. I mean, I really want you."

She smiled and looked down; her cheeks flushed a rosy red. "I want you, too, but I can't, not with her here."

She allowed him one short kiss, absolutely no tongue.

"When?"

She pushed him away and turned around to finish loading the dishwasher. "Baby, you know if we . . . uh, if we do it, we won't be able to hear Lung Ma ever again. She says something terrible is happening in the city. Many people are going to die if she doesn't grow big enough to use her powers soon. We need to be able to speak to her."

"We could write her notes."

Lei laughed. "We could, but she can't write us back." She wiggled her thumb. "Dragons can't hold pens. No thumbs."

Konrad stalked into the living room, grabbed the remote from Kenna and changed the channel to extreme sports on ESPN. He loved to watch snowboarding. He spent time in Canada at Whistler every year where he hit the half pipe.

"Lei, Konrad stole the remote," she yelled. "He changed the channel on me. I was watching Twilight."

"Change it back, Konrad. She loves that movie."

"You'd think she woulda had enough of that weird shit after living in vamp central for a week."

"These are nice vampires, not mean ones. Besides, Edward is so hot."

Konrad handed her the remote and began pacing. He couldn't stop thinking about the demons roaming the city, the doorway to hell under China Town, Lance, Baby, and Junior slaving away over the thermobaric bomb. So many things were going on. He hadn't seen Lung Ma in two days.

"How big is the dragon?"

Lei put the dish towel down, turned around and leaned against the counter. "She's big, really big."

"Compare her to something for me. I need a picture. Is she as big as an elephant or a stegosaurus?"

"Think Mack Truck. Think garbage truck. Think tyrannosaurus rex with wings."

"Wow! What's she been eating?"

"She ate too many of the park's buffalo. They started shooting at her. The rangers were waiting up for her night raids, so she started hunting out to sea. I guess she found a pod of killer whales and ate a few, then found a humpback whale and ate that. Well, she said it was too much and very fatty, so she just ate half."

"She ate an entire whale?"

"Konrad, you don't listen. I said she couldn't finish it. It contained too much fat and it was too big. That was yesterday's meal. Today, or tonight I should say, is another day."

"Do you have any idea how big she's going to get?"

"She says she's about full-grown. Her poison glands have begun to develop. She should be able to spit poison next week. And she's been able to perform some small feats of magic, like teleporting herself around the city."

Konrad grabbed her and kissed her thoroughly, even though she fought at first. When she finally melted into his embrace, his head spun with desire. He set her aside, turned and smirked at Kenna.

"I've gotta get out of here. I think I'll go for a ride on my bike."

Outside in the brisk air of a San Francisco fall evening, Konrad pulled his leather jacket out of the center compartment, shrugged it on over his massive shoulders, threw his leg over the saddle and cranked up the Ninja.

Konrad shot down Geary, the cool, damp air caressing his face. He ramped up the rpms and felt the bike respond with speed. Zipping in and out of traffic, he headed toward his apartment and the beach, crossed La Playa, hit the sand and stopped.

The Pacific Ocean boiled onto shore in mid-size swells. Under the night sky and the half moon, foam glistened and sparkled at the top of each wave. The rich smell of saltwater and marine life floated on a stiff breeze hitting him in the back as he climbed off the bike and started walking down the beach. It was deserted except for a small pod of seals sleeping close to the water.

His black, motorcycle boots sank into the wet sand. He walked and he thought, pondering all the problems surrounding him. He worried about his mother across the bay alone, and about Baby, and Lei. He thought about Paige. Where was she? Should he tell Baby she was missing? Should he tell her where he thought she might be and what he thought she might be?

He found a large driftwood log and sat down close to the water's edge. The waves rolled onto shore in sets of eight, each consecutive wave bigger. The moon came out from behind a cloud and Konrad saw something skimming across a wave in the moonlight. At first he thought it might be a seal, then he saw it was a surfer. The eerie half-light glinted off white hair. He stood up to get a better look and started laughing. It was Lance.

"Lance," he yelled running toward the water. "Lance."

The surfer looked up. He was crouched low on his board. Lance quickly executed two sharp turns, zipping back and forth, and stayed on the wave until it was almost on the beach, where he stepped off into the knee-deep surf.

"Yo! Konrad, dude, did you see that last ride? All the way to the beach, man. I'm like, stoked. Great offshore breeze tonight. Waves are holding up. Nice, clean curls. This place has been closed out for the past three days."

"Closed out, is that surfer talk for something?"

"Blown out, closed out, it means the waves were so big and the onshore wind so strong, the surf didn't curl. Just lots and lots of foam, man. Can't surf it. What're you doing here?"

"I was out walking and riding my bike. Trying to get some shit straight in my head."

"Know what you mean, man." Lance carried the board up the beach and tossed it on the sand. The two of them sat down, Konrad on his driftwood, Lance on his board.

"Lance, tell me about the demons and the vampires. I need details. I don't know the rules, and ignorance could get me killed."

Lance dried off on a towel, gouging it into each ear. "What do you want to know?"

"I already get holy water, garlic, stakes, none of that shit works, right?"

"I told you, a stake through the heart paralyzes a vampire. Miss the heart and he'll get you. But, yeah, all the rest of that stuff is bullshit."

"Okay, how about the myth that says if you kill the maker, the vampires he made all die too."

"I wish. No, man, none of them die, but if the maker dies, the ones that haven't fed from a human or killed and fed from a human, turn back into their normal selves."

"So, there's no hope for you? I mean, even if we kill Vetalas."

Lance shook his wet hair. "My only hope is Lung Ma. And she won't help me unless I do something extraordinary."

"Like what?"

"She didn't say."

Konrad stood up. "Thanks for the info. Guess I'll head over to my apartment and catch some zees."

A sudden wind gust blew sand and dirt into a swirling cloud. *"Sledge!"*

The booming voice inside his head was so loud Konrad grabbed his forehead. A roar resounded over the noise of the wind and waves. Konrad looked into the sky as an enormous shape blocked the light of the moon. Holy crap! It was Lung Ma and she was huge.

The beat of her glistening, blue-white wings stirred up tornadoes of sand as she slowly settled. Konrad found himself facing the dragon's head. It was as large as a pickup. Her massive nostrils opened and closed as she sniffed him.

You smell like Lei.

"I just left her. She misses you, but she said you were eating well."

Lung Ma licked her lips and ran a big, blue tongue across her long front fangs. *Shark tonight. A great white was feeding on the seals. I ate it.* She smiled revealing more rows of teeth. *I love those fat little things. They're so cute.*

"What, the seals or the sharks?"

Seals, Sledge. They're the cutest things. I love to watch them play. I went swimming with them earlier, diving and rolling around in the waves. That's when I saw the shark. She licked her lips again and picked something from between her teeth with the tip of one claw. *It won't be bothering them anymore. Hey Sledge, wanna go for a ride?*

Konrad looked at Lance who shrugged his shoulders. "I gotta skip man or I'll miss my dinner. It's wino time again."

Konrad climbed on Lung Ma's front leg. From there, he slipped in front of her wings, and sat at the junction of her front legs and her neck. She had a rough line of spiky, stiff hair like a mane running down the crest of her neck. It was dark blue in the moonlight. He crammed his feet in her armpits and hung onto the mane as she leaped high.

With two long strokes of her wings, she gained enough altitude to really scare Konrad. The open ocean was a long way down, the water glistening shades of deep blue and silvery gray in the moonlight.

Let's go explore the city.

"Sure," Konrad managed to squeeze out between shaking lips.

The dragon banked hard to the right. Konrad held on, laying his head on her scaly neck. His face was so close he could make out individual scales the size of quarters covering her back. When she picked up speed, his stomach knotted and rolled. He thought he was gonna hurl. When she folded her wings and dived, he screamed like a girl. He couldn't help it. It was either scream or pee his pants.

They soared over the city, the lights of the Transamerica Pyramid and the city center glowing below. As he grew more accustomed to his seat and the movement of her wings, he was able to sit back some and enjoy the view. It was a good thing he wore his jeans. Lung Ma's scales were rough, and it was cold.

After ten minutes, he was hanging over her leg, checking out the sights. "Hey, Lung Ma, fly over Alcatraz."

With two huge flaps of her great wings, the dragon shot over the marina area and out across San Francisco Bay. The beam from the lighthouse on Alcatraz drew them like a beacon. In the distance, the Golden Gate Bridge looked like a golden bracelet on a bed of black velvet.

Lung Ma circled Alcatraz, soaring lower. Konrad could see demons moving around the rock, up the road, and across the open compound. There were people everywhere, humans, not vampires. He could tell the difference. Vampires and demons carried a sickly yellow aura around them. One big demon glowed with an inner green fire. As they swooped closer, it looked up, and saw them.

The demon ran ten yards then took off, its huge green wings lifting it toward them.

Should I kill it? I think my poison is strong enough now.

Konrad grabbed mane. "No, just dust his ass. It's better they don't know what you can do yet. You'll be our secret weapon."

Chapter Thirty-One

"Where have you been, Marcelus?"

Vetalas sat in his favorite Lazy Boy with his feet in Paige's lap. His minions discovered a series of caves under the prison and moved his favorite things into them. The new quarters beneath Alcatraz were dark all the time so he was able to be up and about whenever he pleased. They even brought the stuffed and mounted collection of trophies from the Moody Mansion, along with the huge flat-screen TV, Moody's collections of guns and of course, the pair of sabers. He felt quite at home.

"I was seriously hurt in the corridor beneath the bank, Master. I had to crawl into a dark hole and recuperate. It took a while."

"I'm hungry, Paige, and so I imagine is Marcelus. Bring us something young and tender."

Paige rose from her cushion on the floor, cast one frightened look at Marcelus and ran from the room.

"Paige is mine," Marcelus growled.

"Yes, she was, but you left her with me and now she's my property."

Paige returned with two young women, both in such deep trances they walked like zombies. When she turned to leave, Marcelus lifted a finger. "Stay here. I have something to say to you."

Her eyes flicked from Marcelus to Vetalas.

"I'm not going to hurt you. I just want you to tell Vetalas all about the Berserker."

Vetalas sat up, snapping the handle on the side of the lounge chair. "What could this woman know about such a man?"

"She was his partner. Or didn't she tell you?"

"Partners in what?"

Marcelus pulled one of the women close and pushed her blonde hair off her neck. His fangs slid out and he was ready to dine. "They worked together for the city as emergency medical technicians. Didn't you, Paige?"

Vetalas was on Paige in a second. He wrapped his hands around her neck. "How could you keep this from me? You know how much I loathe him. I could snuff out your miserable life in a second."

Slurping noises grabbed Vetalas's attention. "Marcelus, enjoy your meal elsewhere. And take this other wench with you. I've quite lost my appetite."

When Marcelus and the two women were gone, Vetalas pulled Paige into his bedroom. He tore off her clothes and pushed her to her knees. "Now, unless you wish to be violated, humiliated and then killed, you will tell me all you can think of about Konrad Pengill, the Berserker."

*****

It took Paige twenty minutes to tell Vetalas everything she knew. Crying silently, tears flooding her cheeks and running across her breasts, she told him about Konrad's apartment, his passion for motorcycles, his years in the service, and she told Vetalas about Konrad's mother and where she lived.

Then he forced her to have sex with him while he fed off her. She'd never hated men as much as she hated Vetalas. In her mind, he was the epitome of all that was bad about human males. She wanted to kill him, but knew it was impossible. Impotent rage filled every fiber of her body. Her hands clenched at her sides and tears of frustration flowed down her face.

Weak and drained of blood, she lay on the big bed and wished she would die. But that was the wimp's way out and Paige could never be a wimp. Closing her eyes, she tried to think of a weakness in Vetalas or in his current defenses. Nothing popped into her mind, but as she lay there in pain, she vowed to discover either a way to escape or a way to kill the evil vampire king.

*****

When Vetalas was finished with Paige, he pulled on a comfortable pair of khakis and his black, fluffy slippers.

The information he'd gleaned from Paige had given him an idea. She'd revealed a weakness in the Berserker . . . his mother.

He called Lineus. The huge demon squeezed his wings into one of the Lazy Boys and Vetalas turned on Wipeout. It was Vetalas's new favorite show. It was amazing what humans would do for money. It was hard for him to imagine he'd been one.

He retained memories of the poverty in his small village. But he remembered also, karma and the caste system. He was born into the lowest caste. His family had meekly accepted their fate was to live as untouchables until rebirth when they would climb up the caste ladder. That was their karma.

"Lineus, I have a job for you. Across the bay in a town called Albany, there is a house on Adams Street." Vetalas gave Lineus the numbers on the house. "Go there, find Francis Pengill and bring her to me."

Lineus laughed out loud as one of the contestants on the show fell off the bouncing, red balls for the second time and belly-flopped into muddy water in glorious HD. "Yes, Master."

"Oh, make sure, she's unharmed. She's the Berserker's mother."

*****

"Show me again how it works," Konrad said to Junior.

"The first thermobaric explosion probably took place in a flour mill." Junior sat in the deepest pit of his leather couch with a box at his feet. "The explosion was caused by the rapid burning of the flour in a confined space. They also call this a vacuum weapon.

201

Flamethrowers were the most primitive vacuum weapons. This bomb," he held up a simple black box the size of a milk carton, is going to shut the black hole."

Konrad took the box from him and carefully examined it. "But it's so small."

"A primary explosion releases a cloud of explosive material. The secondary explosion ignites the cloud, and boom, you get a massive blast and a pressure wave. Think of it like this. You open a box of hand grenades in a small room, toss the grenades into the air while you're pulling the pin on another grenade. They all explode at one time. Get it?"

"No shit?"

"Inside that tunnel, the blast will be magnified, and the combination of the explosion and the pressure wave should go through the doorway and into the other world effectively closing the doorway from the other side."

"I get it," Konrad said. "I still think this is a small box."

"It doesn't have to be big. It just has to work. Sometimes these thermobaric bombs are unpredictable. You're counting on a cloud of explosive material igniting and doing what you want. It could destroy a city block or even the entire sewer system."

"I'm gonna have to call Munoz. I can just imagine what Scary Larry is gonna say. But the cops have to know what we're doing."

"When do you want to deploy this thing?"

"I'll have to get back to you after I talk to Munoz."

"We need to close that doorway, Sledge."

"I know. If SFPD nixes the idea, we'll blow it ourselves. We may have to move to Vermont, but we're closing that doorway."

"You might want to consider Mexico. Vermont has long winter nights. There's no way all these demons and vampires are gonna just disappear. I think they'll be around for a long, long time."

Chapter Thirty-Two

Francis Pengill finished her bagel while she watched the morning news. One of the papers Konrad brought her lay open on the table beside her wheelchair.

"I really miss Diane Sawyer, don't you? I can't believe they sent her to do the nightly news. She's such a pretty thing." Mrs. Willows picked up the empty tray and leaned on the back of Francis's chair to watch.

Francis pointed to the open newspaper. "There've been more alien abductions in the city. You better make sure the house is locked."

"Poo on that, Francis. You need to stop reading those rags. There's no such thing as aliens."

A crash from the front of the house startled Mrs. Willows. "That damn foreign maid I hired musta knocked something over again. Foreigners, I swear the country is crawling with them. Pretty soon there won't be no room for the folks that were born here."

She stomped out of the room. Francis could hear her heavy footsteps as she walked down the hall screaming for Pepita.

Another crash and a scream froze Francis. Her heart beat so fast she was afraid it would explode. She touched the knife Konrad gave her and prayed it was just the clumsy maid.

When the doors on the other bedrooms in this section of the house were hammered open one at a time, she knew it was her worst fear....aliens. Black dread filled Francis as she listened to someone heavier than Mrs. Willows stomping down the hall toward her room. The aliens were looking for her. They'd finally come. Unable to get up because of her paralyzed legs, she was a sitting duck.

She gripped the left wheel of her chair with one hand and clutched the knife with the other as her mind scrambled to remember what Konrad told her about it. He said it injected a ball of gas the size of a basketball. Maybe it would work on people from outer space.

Her door flew open and Francis screamed. It was an alien. A huge monster ducked its horned head to enter her room. It folded enormous wings behind its green scaly body and touched the nametag on her door with one long claw.

"Francis Pengill?" The monster rasped in a low guttural growl.

Francis's whole body shook, the fear like a wild animal trapped inside her breast. Bile rose into her throat, but she held onto the knife. Her entire life had been devoted to working with horses before her injury. Large animals are dangerous, and you have to be brave to face them every day, go into their stalls, train them and ride them. Francis was no sissy.

When the hideous creature leaned over to pick her up, she grabbed its big right ear with her left hand as though he was a recalcitrant mule and twisted. The monster howled with pain as she stabbed it in the genitals with the knife.

Immediately a frozen ball of gas shot into the creature at 850 psi. At least that's what Konrad had told her.

What she saw was the ugly green alien howl and pull up its loin cloth. Francis gasped. She'd seen a lot of stud horses, but this nasty character was hung like a mule. Its enormous Johnson was an icy blue, contrasting wildly with its green body. When it touched its equipment, the grotesque penis broke off in its hand and fell to the floor in three pieces.

Horrified, she tried to wheel away and get out the door. But it reached out one enormous clawed hand and grabbed the back of her chair. She tried to push the wheels, but the monster's grip was too strong.

When she looked over her shoulder, she saw it gently gather up the pieces of its frozen appendage and place them in a leather pouch hanging from a brass-studded belt. Then it roared at her, its red eyes shooting hate, and scooped her out of the chair.

Francis screamed and screamed as the alien carried her through the house. Everywhere she looked, the residents lay butchered. She didn't see Mrs. Willows, but Pepita's disemboweled body was spread across the living room.

The creature carried her out the door, opened its huge wings, and vaulted into the air. The slate roof of the house and the tops of Mrs. Willows' evergreen trees grew smaller and smaller as they flew over the house and hill behind it. When they cleared Albany Hill with its huge cross, the demon headed for the bay.

Francis forced herself to retain consciousness as cold, wet air rushed through her nightgown chilling her to the bone. Even though she was freezing and scared out of her wits, she wanted to be awake when the creature took her up to its spaceship. She'd always known she'd be abducted by aliens.

*****

Konrad opened the car door and Lei stepped into the damp evening. He couldn't take his eyes off her. From thigh-high boots, to a short, leather skirt, lacy white top and leather jacket she was the hottest thing he'd ever seen. She even carried the katana on her back in a nifty leather scabbard designed especially for her by Master Tang. It was all Konrad could do to control himself.

Their forced abstinence was taking its toll. But tonight, Kenna was staying at Baby's and they had the apartment to themselves. Lung Ma told them to go ahead. She'd find some way to communicate with them.

"Dinner was lovely," Lei said as he took her arm and helped her up the stairs to her apartment.

"Yeah, I always wanted to eat at the Waterfront."

"It cost a fortune, Konrad."

"I know. Had to break into the savings account." He put his arm around her in front of the door to her apartment and drew her close. "But I wanted this night to be perfect."

She lifted her face and they kissed. Konrad groaned. *Finally.*

He kicked the door closed, scooped her into his arms and carried her to the bedroom. She giggled like a schoolgirl as he dropped her on the bed and grabbed the heel of one boot.

"How do you get these damn things off?"

Lei pushed him away, stood up and headed for the bathroom. "Give me a minute and I'll change into something more comfortable."

Konrad stripped off his silver tie and shrugged his big shoulders out of the gray, raw silk jacket, tailored to fit by Red Chua's company. He tore off his black shirt and flexed his muscles.

Lei tripped out of the bathroom in a filmy white thing and Konrad dropped his trousers. Just as his pants hit the floor, the cell phone rang.

"No fucking way!" Konrad growled. His Berserker persona was always lurking just under the surface of his consciousness. He felt the anger and blew it away in a cleansing breathe.

"Don't answer it," Lei said.

He closed his eyes as the insistent chirp kept on and on. "I have to. It could be important."

When he pulled the phone out of his pocket, he saw it was Munoz. "Hey, I'm kinda busy. Is this important?"

"Could be. Didn't you say your mom lived in Albany?"

Konrad felt the rich food he'd eaten for dinner rise in his stomach. He burped. "Yeah, she lives on Adams Street."

"Eight-twelve by some chance?"

Konrad closed his eyes. Not Mom, he prayed. Don't let it be Mom. "What happened, Munoz? Tell me before I destroy this fucking phone."

"I can't say right now if your mother was hurt, but one of those big demons tore through there, trashed the place and killed a bunch of old people. The report says the caretaker of the place, a Mrs.

Katherine Willows, was incoherent, babbling on and on about aliens and big green monsters."

Chapter Thirty-Three

"I have to go," Konrad snapped. "It's my mother. Demons tore up the group home."

"I'm going with you." Lei ran back to the bathroom to change.

Konrad followed her. "No, babe, if something happened to Mom, I'm going after them. I don't want you involved. It's gonna get ugly. This is personal."

She grabbed his shoulders. "I want to be involved. I love you."

He pulled her close and rested his head on her hair. "I love you, too, and you're not going."

He stomped out of the bathroom, cursing as he searched Lei's bedroom for clothes. All he had to wear was the fancy get-up. Shrugging the shirt and pants back on, he stuffed his size sixteens into his good shoes and headed for the front door. Lei followed.

"Are you sure you don't need me? I have skills."

He stopped at the door and pulled her into his arms for one last kiss. "If I need your help, I'll come get you. But I'd rather you went to Baby's and stayed out of the way."

She nodded, her eyes huge with fear. They touched palms, then he kissed her fingers and ran down the steps and out of the building.

Konrad pushed the Ninja, flying through rain-dark streets and across the Bay Bridge, weaving in and out of traffic, his heart pounding with fear. When he pulled up in front of his mother's group home, the whole place was cordoned off with crime-scene tape. Ambulances, cop cars and meat wagons, yellow lights on, filled the narrow street and all the close-by parking lots. Flickering emergency lights gave the entire scene a disturbing, surreal quality.

This was his worst nightmare. Somehow, he knew it was his fault. Vetalas found out about his mother and came after her because of him.

He parked the bike between a cop car and a coroner's van with the back door open. He peered in as he walked by, but it was empty. When he got to the front door, he was stopped by a uniformed member of the Oakland Police. "This is a crime scene, sir. I have to ask you to leave."

"My mother lives here." Konrad's voice was a low snarl.

"Sorry, sir, you'll have to wait on the lawn while I get the Sergeant. I can't allow you to contaminate the scene."

"When did all this happen?"

"We got the call around three. The mailman came by. He had a package and when no one answered, he opened the door and I guess that's when he called 911. They said most of the blood was either dry or drying, so I'm guessing this all went down in the morning."

Konrad easily elbowed him aside. The cop grabbed his shoulder. "Please . . . you don't want to go inside. It's, it's awful."

"I have to know."

Konrad shoved his way past a gurney carrying a black, bagged body pushed by a white-faced EMT. "I need to check," he said unzipping the bag. "My mother lives here."

"There's no head on this one," the female EMT said. Her voice cracked. "I couldn't find it."

When he unzipped the bag, he recognized the Velcro-sneakered-feet of one of his mother's fellow inmates. That's what she called the other residents, inmates. He zipped it back up and stared with a dead heart and blank eyes at the chaos in the living room.

A coroner knelt on the carpet taking scrapings. Parts of the home's new maid were scattered across the tan rug.

Terrified of what he might find, Konrad slid by more crime-scene specialists and down the hall to his mother's room. The door hung open, her empty wheelchair half in the hall. He paused for a minute. All he could think about was the maid's guts spread everywhere. *Not Mom, please.*

He pushed the chair aside, entered the room, and breathed a huge sigh of relief when he saw no blood, no body parts. Fingering the open Enquiring Mind on Mom's table, he walked through the small space. Mom's bed was made, so it happened sometime after nine. He grabbed the remote and turned on the TV. When it came on, he saw it was set on her favorite morning news channel.

Her breakfast plates were gone, so she'd already eaten. That moved the time of the attack up to ten. He looked at the floor and froze. The Wasp lay under the table. He picked it up and saw a black stain on the tip and sniffed. Demon blood. When he looked up, he gasped. *Vetalas!*

Carved into the inside of his mother's door was a huge V. Konrad touched it. The V wasn't carved as much as it was gouged. It looked like the letter was raked out of the wood with a claw.

Konrad tore back through the group home, knocking cops and crime-scene personnel aside as he went. His Berserker persona lurked just under the surface of his consciousness, trying to take over.

Jumping on the bike, he gunned it down Adams Street heading back to the city. He knew from Munoz that Vetalas had cleared out of the Moody Mansion. No one knew where he'd gone but there were suspicious reports of tourists being savaged at Alcatraz and he remembered the ride on Lung Ma, and the demon he'd seen. It looked like the big, ugly green customer that hung with the head vampire, the one with the scar.

There was only one way to be sure. He had to find Lance.

It was after eleven when he hit the beach, sliding to a stop, spraying up gouts of wet sand. If he was early enough, Lance should still be surfing.

Konrad stalked down to the water line and scanned the waves. They were pretty small with a heavy chop, not at all ideal for surfing. The moon, rising over the city, cast yellow light off the glistening waves. Seals played in the water, slicing through the surf as they searched for fish.

Farther down the beach toward the point, he saw the surf improved, the chop lessened, and the breeze blew more off shore. He headed that way, hoping the surfing vamp was there.

He was almost to the point when he saw Lance coming toward him on the point break, the vampire's white-blonde hair a beacon in the moonlight.

Konrad took off running and waving his arms. Lance kicked off the wave and paddled out to catch another. The sets rolled in, each one bigger. By the time Konrad reached the point, Lance was zipping along on another wave.

"Lance!" Konrad called knowing the vampire had super-hearing.

Sure enough, the surfer looked up, hooked a sharp right and then another turn to the left and dropped off the wave. He paddled in, fell into the beach break, whipped his long, wet hair out of his eyes with a flick of his head, and ran onto shore with the board under one arm.

"Did you see that last wave? It was awesome."

Konrad grabbed Lance's arm. "Man, I need you to help me. Vetalas has my mother."

Lance shook him off and grabbed a towel from a chunk of driftwood. "I can't help you, dude. Vetalas will kill me."

"This is important. He'll kill my mother if I don't find him and get her back. Is he on Alcatraz? I heard one of the boats never came back. They've canceled tours."

Lance's head jerked.

"He is, isn't he?"

"I can't have nothing to do with this, dude. I'm telling you he'll send me to demon hell and that's no joke."

Konrad leaned into him and hissed in his ear. "Remember Lung Ma. You need to do something extraordinary to get her to turn you. Helping me could be it. Don't you want to surf in the bright sunlight again? See the sun shining through a tube as you zing along at forty miles an hour?"

Lance sat on his board, skinny knees hanging out of baggy board shorts. "Don't make fun of surfing. You have no idea what it's like."

"I know it means a lot to you. I see you out here every night on your board. But no, I don't get what you see in it."

Lance spread his arms wide. "It's like communicating straight with Mother Nature. She breathes in and the waves flow out. When she exhales, the waves rush onto the shore. It's elemental, man. You're like out there with the sun, the waves, the dolphins and the fish, even the sharks. And then you feel the power of the ocean under your board. It's a fucking spiritual experience."

Konrad moved closer. "Then help me, Lance, and I'll put in a good word with Lung Ma."

"What would I have to do?"

"Take me out there. Show me where he's living."

"He fixed up a place underground, beneath the prison. I can't take you down there. He's got hundreds of vampires and demons guarding the island. He'd catch us in seconds and then that'd be all she wrote for good old surfer Lance."

"I flew over the Rock on the dragon the other night. There's also a lot of humans walking around. You could pretend to be taking me in as a prize for Vetalas. He might as well of left me a note saying he has her. He wants me to come for her, Lance. He had his demon carve a V in my mother's door."

Lance gulped and his white Adam's apple bobbed in his stick of a neck. "I could pretend to turn you over to him, but when he found out the truth," Lance drew a finger across his throat. "It'd be straight to demon hell for Lance. No more surfing, no more nothing."

"It's not going to be pretend. We'll find him and swap me for my mom, even. Come on, Lance, take a chance. Help me out. I'm going out there with or without you."

The surfer closed his eyes and shook his head. "You'll tell the dragon I helped you?"

"I'll call her right now. She can fly me over."

Lance jumped up. "No, Sledge, don't make me do it. I heard there's a special hell just for vampires, straight from Dante."

"You're a good soul, Lance. God will forgive you."

Lance shivered. "God doesn't like vampires, dude. He ain't gonna forgive shit."

Konrad kicked the sand off his good shoes. He needed to go home, put on some jeans and grab his leather jacket before he did this. "Make up your mind. I'm gonna head over to my apartment and change. I need to load up on weapons before Lung Ma gets here."

"No, you ain't because you can't take any with you. What are you nuts? They see one sword or pistol and we're both dead."

"Maybe I have something he can't see, something small and deadly."

"Like what?"

"I don't know. I haven't figured that out yet."

Lance picked up his board. The resin in the fiberglass sparkled shiny green with pink and white flecks in the moonlight. "You promise to put in a good word with the dragon?"

"You know I will. I'll make out like you're the biggest hero ever walked the planet."

Lance punched him in the arm. "Hey, don't lay it on too thick."

"You going with me?"

Lance sighed, turned around and stared for a moment at the ocean. "I guess so.

Chapter Thirty-four

After Sledge left, Lei changed into jeans and wandered the apartment. She felt like she'd been abandoned. She felt useless and her stomach would not stay out of her throat. Terror for Sledge and what she feared he planned would not leave her alone. It gnawed at her insides and forced tears down her face.

Brushing her cheeks dry for the tenth time, she paced like a caged tigress back and forth across the room. When her cell phone rang, she dove on it.

"Lei, this is Red Chua. I have some important news for you."

Annoyed at Red for not being Sledge she snapped. "Fine, tell me."

"No, no, can't tell you anything over the phone. The Tong is in chaos. Li Po has turned into some kind of monster. He's running everything with a hideous ghoul named Shanya. The guys are all quitting and looking to me for leadership. Even the Blue Dragon leader, Huizhong Chang, is calling on me to take control. I need to talk to you in person."

"Sounds like Li Po is a vampire. You got blg problems."

"No shit. Can you come down to North Beach and meet me at the Starbucks on Kearny Street?"

Lei glanced around the apartment. If she stayed here, she'd probably go crazy. She could go to Baby's and hang out with her and Kenna, but she doubted if that would be a calming influence. Red had news for her, so she better find out what it was. It might be something that could help Sledge.

"What time?"

"I'll give you an hour to get there. How about 10:30?"

Lei agreed and hung up. She'd go hang out with Baby later.

She was so happy to finally be in her own car again. With the transmission fixed, her little Toyota ran like new. The ride to the North Beach went fast with light traffic at this hour. When the rain finally stopped, the ever-present fog descended like a brick to cover the entire town in an eerie blanket.

Before demons invaded the town, she'd liked the fog. It gave the city atmosphere. Now she felt like something horrible was going to jump out and attack her every time she turned a corner.

Kearny Street was close to the water. The fog closed in around her like a soggy blanket when she climbed out of the car.

Red waited at a small table in the corner drinking something steaming and tall. She ordered chai and went to sit across from him. Her heart banged in her chest. She was worried about Sledge and now Red wanted to tell her something she had to hear face-to-face.

He stood up when he saw her, and she plopped into the empty chair. "Tell me, Red. What's going on?"

He sat back down and took her hand. She noticed he wasn't bad looking. It was just his dyed hair. He had large almond-shaped eyes without much of an epicanthic fold, a strong, square chin and a heavily-muscled neck. A tattoo of a dragon ran up his thick forearm all the way to his shoulder. The tail came out of his shirt and wrapped around his neck.

"It's your father."

Lei gasped. "Is he dead?"

"No, no, he's on his way here. I got a message from Honorable Chang and he told me Colonel Jiang is on his way to the U.S. He's in London right now and should be in San Francisco in two days. He said he's bringing a monk from the monastery to take Lung Ma home."

Lei leaped to her feet. "He can't. I mean the monk, he can't take the dragon. We need her here."

"That's not the worst of it. Honorable Chang is coming here as well. He doesn't believe anything I've been telling him about Li Po. He wants to see for himself."

Lei couldn't believe her father was on his way. She hadn't seen him in over five years. "Where does my father plan to stay?"

"No one told me. I guess with you."

*****

Konrad called Lung Ma. He sat on the lid of the toilet in his apartment with the door closed and his head in his hands. In his postage-stamp living room, Lance surfed the channels on the TV. Concentrating, he sent out messages for her with his brain. He'd never felt so stupid in his life. He used all the powers he'd been taught by the Zen master. He controlled his breathing and focused on a picture of the dragon he held in his mind.

It finally worked. The return message from Lung Ma sounded like her mouth was full. *I'm eating Sledge. Call back later.*

Don't have time. Vetalas kidnapped my mother. I need a ride out to Alcatraz Island. That's where he's holding her.

Sledge, I just snagged a thirty-foot shark. It's delicious.

Please, Lung Ma. Come quickly. I'll meet you on the beach.

Her grouchy answer made him smile. He left the bathroom. "Lance, she's coming after she finishes off her snack."

"What's she eating, an elephant?"

"No, she's taken a liking to seafood, a shark."

They met the dragon on the beach. Thick fog covered everything. Moisture-laden cotton was the only way to describe it. The sodium-vapor lights on the street made the cloaking cotton a sickly yellow.

Lung Ma arrived out of nowhere, dropping in front of them like a silent Huey. She sniffed Konrad. *You smell like anger and sweat. I will attack this island and kill all the vampires.*

You can't. There are too many and they have demons to protect them, big ugly horned ones. And they will surely kill my mother if you do.

217

It's your party. I guess we'll follow your rules. What would you have me do?

Konrad told her while Lance pulled his hands behind his back and secured them with a thick chain and a padlock. Then he wrapped some really thick chain around Konrad's neck. It was two-inches in diameter. After padlocking it under his throat, Lance had a nice leash about three-feet long.

They climbed aboard Lung Ma and Konrad closed his eyes for the take off. Lance screamed with delight as they flew above the fog, crossed the Golden Gate Bridge, only the top visible, and headed for the Rock.

Drop us on the side facing the bridge. Konrad told her.

Alcatraz was wrapped in foggy invisibility like everything else. Konrad hoped it would be an advantage. He had Lung Ma drop them on Baker Beach. Waves lapped the rocks as they climbed off the dragon and scrambled up a steep hill to the roadway. The dragon sent him a final message.

I will listen for you, Sledge. Call me if you need me.

Lance picked up his end of the chain. "This is the dumbest thing I have ever done in a long, long life of doing dumb things."

"Stop mumbling. Demons have super hearing, remember?"

Lance dragged Konrad down the road to a cutoff that led to the lighthouse and the main prison. He took the left fork in the road and immediately smacked into a huge green and purple demon Konrad did not recognize.

Konrad fought his Berserker persona. It longed to burst the chains and kill. But he had to find Mom. She was on this rock somewhere. He could feel it.

The demon's voice was so low and so crude, Konrad could barely understand it. "What you doing, bloodsucker?"

"I have a prisoner for Vetalas. This is the Berserker he wants."

Big, green, and ugly held out a clawed hand. "Take him, I will."

Lance snatched the end of the chain behind his back. "Oh no, I want the credit. You'll keep it all for yourself."

Growling, the demon turned and marched away. He lifted one sharp talon and beckoned them to follow. From then on, the pathway grew more and more congested with demons and vampires. They all stopped and stared but big ugly seemed enough to keep them at a distance. Dead bodies lay everywhere. Konrad had to look up to avoid seeing their contorted faces and twisted limbs.

They entered a doorway on the front of the main prison and immediately headed down a steep, dark set of stairs. The place reeked of mildew and rusting metal, with heavy overtones of sweet, coppery blood. It was so strong Konrad glanced at his feet to see if the floors were painted with it.

There were no lights. Apparently, demons didn't need them. Konrad slid into his Berserker persona. Everything became lit by a green glow just like night-vision goggles. The demon leading the way pulsed with a yellow-green aura. Lance radiated a nice sea green, grossly clashing with the bile-yellow walls surrounding them.

The stairwell ended at a huge door with a grilled window. The demon shoved the heavy door open with his shoulder. Screams echoed off the metal walls. Konrad tried not to think of who or what made them.

They followed the demon through a long tunnel. Pipes crisscrossing the ceiling dripped orange-tinted water. Some were wrapped in what Konrad felt sure was asbestos. When the walls of the prison ended, the tunnel continued. Carved out of bedrock, it sloped down. The ceiling dropped in places forcing the demon and Konrad to stoop. Lance got tangled in the demon's wings and had to stop, swiping at the segmented span with his free hand, each boney support topped with a claw.

When a light shone up ahead, Konrad growled. His strength built. Snapping the chains would be a cinch, but all he could think about was Mom. She was down here somewhere in this hole, helpless and scared. Thinking about it for even a minute, made him even madder.

The demon stopped in front of a carved, wooden door painted red and fitted right into a wall of rock. The pattern cut into the wood swirled with an unsettling design. It made his stomach churn just like the doorway to the other dimension in the sewer. Their big ugly leader scratched at the door with his claws.

It swung open, and Konrad leaned forward to see thick, blood-red carpet and rock walls covered with silk hangings and trophies. The heads of an elephant with its trunk raised, a huge boar, a cape buffalo and a rhinoceros hung haphazardly between scarlet silk tapestries of unbelievable scenes.

"Come in, come in. Lance, you have brought me the Berserker. I will reward you well."

Surfer vamp looked at the demon and smirked. It growled a reply Konrad couldn't understand.

Lance yanked on Konrad's chain and he followed the vampire into the room. His head pulsed with anger and Berserker strength. He had to fight to control it.

Vetalas reclined in a vast green-velvet lounge chair. His mother sat in a small chair; her wasted legs were crossed at the knee. Konrad stared. She was kicking her left foot. Her eyes were scared and when she saw Konrad, she smothered a scream with the back of her hand.

Konrad scanned the room. He spotted the big green demon with the scarred face. His skin loin cloth was gone. In its place, he sported a huge bandage covering his privates. He lifted his chin in the green demon's direction. "I see your sex change finally came through. You and Vetalas plan to get married?"

The demon roared and charged. Konrad crouched, hands clenched, as he waited for the hit.

"Lineus, stop! You may not kill the Berserker. He is my toy."

Konrad smiled, enjoying the demon's discomfort and impotent rage.

"I fed your mother a little of my blood," Vetalas said. "As you can see, her legs now work. Our blood has tremendous curative powers.

But I did not dine on her. She is still very much a human. Your mother is not my chosen victim, as I'm sure you've figured out. I want you Berserker."

His mother leaped to her feet. "No, Konrad don't do it."

Vetalas backhanded her. She fell into her chair whimpering, a huge bruise forming on her cheekbone. Konrad lunged forward, hit the end of the chain and stopping.

"Chain, good thinking Lance. Have I already told you I will reward you?"

Lance nodded.

"Berserker, if I let your mother go, will you stay here, and of your own free will become my vassal?"

Konrad roared and strained in the chains. He felt how easily they would burst under his power. But what good would such a show do him? His mother would be murdered and eventually so would he. He couldn't kill all of the demons on this island, though he'd love to try.

Konrad dropped his gaze, shielding his hate by looking away. "Let my mother go."

"Not until you give me your word, Berserker. You for your mother. Even trade."

Konrad glanced around the room one more time. More and more vampires and demons dribbled in through the open doors. Many of the undead carried automatic weapons or holstered pistols. Looked like they planned to fight a war. There was no way for him to get out safely with his mother. He had to submit to Vetalas's ultimatum.

Taking a deep breath, Konrad let it out slowly and nodded. "Okay. I'll do it."

Vetalas laughed. "Lance, take Mrs. Berserker away. You are free to use her as you will. She is your reward."

"No! You fiend!" Konrad strained against the chains. He felt them giving and backed off. He had to trust the surfer. Breaking loose and killing a demon or two before they swamped him and killed him anyway wouldn't save his mother.

Konrad watched Lance lead his mother out of the chamber on her own power, her legs strong as when she was young. Then he turned to Vetalas and his eyes narrowed into slits. The demon king's time would come. He planned to make sure of it.

When the door closed behind his mother and Lance, ten other blood suckers emerged from behind one of the hangings. Vetalas stood up, lifted his chin, closed his eyes and inhaled deeply. "I smell your blood, Berserker. It has a scent all its own. Soon, your power will also be mine."

Konrad's heart raced. Vetalas and the ten vampires formed a circle around him and closed in. He spun around trying to keep all of them in his view. Then they attacked, fangs bared, as one. He bellowed as he went down under their weight and felt the sting of their fangs driving into his flesh.

He fought, throwing off two, then throwing off another, but they kept coming back. He grabbed an older vampire with long curly hair and tore off its head. But the rest kept coming. His strength waned and he gave up the struggle. The last thing he thought of was the dragon. *Lung Ma, save my mother.*

Then everything went dark.

Chapter Thirty-Five

Lung Ma sat quietly on the rocky shore while Sledge's mother climbed onto her back. Lance was beside himself. He wanted to tell the dragon where to take her, but he couldn't communicate with the dumb beast.

He pointed toward the glowing yellow, fuzzy city across the bay. "Take her to Baby's," he yelled at the top of his voice

Lung Ma's silver-blue eyes spun.

"You are the stupidest animal I have ever encountered. Take Sledge's mom to Baby's."

Francis Pengill seated herself firmly in front of the dragon's wings and smiled. "Don't worry Lance. I'm sure she knows right where to take me. Such a lovely big creature she is."

Francis rubbed Lung Ma's scales and the stiff mane of bristles on the ridge of her neck with one hand. The dragon lifted a foreclaw and tapped Lance on the top of his head.

Backing off, he watched the dragon launch herself into the sky, stretch her huge wings and gain altitude. He'd done the best he could. Maybe she understood him. With one glance back at the prison, he grimaced and took off, flying for the beach. He wasn't hungry, so maybe he could get in another hour or two of surfing before sunrise.

*****

Francis felt right at home riding the dragon. It wasn't a horse, but riding is riding. She pushed her heels down, balanced her seat and grabbed a handful of stiff mane. Even though they were flying, it felt a lot like riding a horse bareback. The scales under her behind were rough, but the discomfort was small when compared to the joy of being freed from the prison.

The air brushed by her face and she lifted her chin to enjoy the cold breeze. She rubbed the dragon's neck ridge just like she'd rub a cranky horse. A mother horse does the same thing with its teeth.

The surge of Lung Ma's powerful muscles beneath her felt wonderful after years of sitting in a wheelchair. She hated that Konrad was forced to sacrifice himself for her but had faith in his abilities to handle any situation, even one as dire as being held captive by Vetalas. And look what her trip to the vampire's lair gave her. She could walk again.

Somehow, she knew Konrad would survive and defeat the demons. His Berserker blood was very strong. Only she knew how strong. Her great-grandfather was also a Berserker. She'd never told anyone but her husband, Harald, about her ancestor. Harald knew what they bred. He recognized Konrad's strength even when their child was only a baby.

The dragon flew low over the foggy city. Francis held tight to the deep blue bristles as Lung Ma dropped to a rooftop. Apparently, this was her stop. She reluctantly left the dragon's back. The kind creature made her feel safe, sheltered from all evil, and filled with optimism. With her feet on the roof, the horror of her recent experiences cascaded through her and tears filled her eyes.

Konrad's little Asian girl ran out from the open stairwell doorway. She grabbed Francis and hugged her.

"Lung Ma told me she was bringing you here. What happened to Sledge?"

*****

When Lung Ma contacted her and told her she was bringing Konrad's mother to Baby's house, Lei was overjoyed. The dragon didn't tell her Konrad wasn't with her.

"Konrad had to give himself to that horrible vampire king to free me. I couldn't stop him."

"No!" Lei screamed. "They have Sledge?"

Agony shot through her. Her heart felt ready to explode with anger, terror and fear. What should she do?

A soothing voice flowed across her mind. *There is nothing you can do. Don't worry. The Hammer can handle himself. It was his choice to make. He gave up his life for his mother's.*

"What are you talking about?" Lei shrieked. "Is he dead?"

Sledge is now with the undead. Vetalas wishes to control his strength and to absorb some of it for himself.

Lei fell to her knees and pounded on the gritty asphalt roof. "I'll save him. Take me to the island, Lung Ma. Take me now."

The dragon's eyes spun as she stared down at Lei. *Yours is the first voice I ever heard, little one. I will not take you to your death. Listen for Sledge. He will call you. Hear his inner voice. You can if you try.*

Francis bent over and put her arm around Lei. "Come on, darling. Konrad will be fine. He's stronger than you know."

"How could you just leave him there? He's your son?"

"I didn't have a choice," Francis said. "Do you think I wanted to leave my only son in that hell hole? Konrad chose to give himself up to free me. I couldn't throw his sacrifice away by getting us both killed. And here, with you and the dragon, maybe we can plan something that will help him."

"What?" Lei cried. "How can we help him when even Lung Ma says it's hopeless?"

I didn't say it was hopeless. I said Sledge can handle himself. He's a halfling vampire, now. His future is in his own hands.

Lei allowed Francis to comfort her, but inside the ache of Konrad's absence and potential loss hurt unbearably. She let the pain fill her and harden her resolve to somehow save him. Tears rushed down her face. "How can you be so sure he'll make it out of there alive?"

Francis hugged her. "I know my son."

They walked into the stairwell arm in arm. Lei led Francis down the steps to Baby's apartment. Kenna was there waiting with Baby. When they walked through the door, Baby shot out of her seat on the couch.

"Mrs. Pengill, where's Sledge?"

Baby and Lei helped Francis to the couch. She sat down and smiled at Kenna. "Hi, who are you?"

"My mom's a vamp. Vetalas took over my house, filled it with flipping demons and turned my mom into one of them. Konrad saved me."

"Yes, he is a good boy."

Lei grabbed Francis's hand. "Tell us what happened."

"When they first snatched me, I thought they were aliens. One of them big green demons carried me to Alcatraz. I've never been there before. Lived in the Bay Area all my life and wouldn't you know, the first time I go to the Rock it's under the arm of some green monster. But they wasn't aliens. They're demons and vampires and they think they're going to take over this city."

Baby perched on the arm of the love seat. "Well, Mrs. Pengill, I hate to tell you, but if something doesn't happen quick, they're gonna do it."

"Konrad will think of something."

"What else happened out there?"

"They took me under the big prison. Stinks like death down there. All the vamps are starting to wear guns and act like they're bad. They took me to a big, fancy room way underground and stuck me in a tiny little closet with some other half-way to vampire girl. Her name was Paige and she treated me real nice. I think she wanted to have me for supper, but she told me Vetalas hasn't been allowing her to kill or feed off human blood. The first time she feeds off a human she's killed, she can never go back to her former self."

Baby leaped off the arm of the chair. She ran stiff fingers through her short spiked hair and closed her eyes. She looked like she was praying.

"What's wrong Baby?" Lei asked.

"What did the vampire named Paige look like?" Baby's voice quavered as she asked the question. Lei understood immediately. Baby was hoping the Paige vamp was her lover.

Francis looked thoughtful. "She was very thin and tiny, about five-feet tall, pretty with fine, mahogany-red hair."

"It can't be." Baby paced back and forth from the bedroom to the living room of the tiny apartment. Her eyes were wide, the whites showing all the way around like a crazy person's. She grabbed Lei by the shoulders, her brown eyes full of tears. "Do you think it could be my Paige?"

"I thought she was in the freezer in Sledge's garage."

"We have to go there right now and check."

"But what about Sledge? Shouldn't we try to save him?"

Baby had her clogs and her coat on. "Listen to his mother. If she thinks he'll be okay, then he will. I've got to find out if Paige is in that freezer. She could still be alive, Lei. I have to know."

"I'll go with you. Mrs. Pengill and Kenna can stay here."

Kenna grabbed Lei's arm. "Why you always dumping mc? I wanna go."

Lei glanced at Baby. "Can she come?"

Baby shrugged. "Get your shoes on. I'm outta here right now."

Francis waved them on with one hand. "Go ahead. I'll be fine here. I'm so tired, I think I'll just nap on the couch. I haven't slept a wink since that ugly green son of a gun snatched me out of my room."

Baby squeezed herself into the front seat of her purple, Honda hatchback. Kenna dove into the rear seat behind Lei as Baby peeled out of the driveway and tore through the quiet streets toward the beach as fast as the little car would go. She hit La Playa, slid the car into the driveway, and shot over to Konrad's apartment. Lei had the garage-door opener in her purse. She grabbed it and hit the button as soon as Baby pulled in.

The three of them leaped from the car and raced into the garage. When they got to the freezer, Baby held out her hand. "Wait."

She rubbed her face and took a deep breath. Lei put a hand on her arm. "Want me to open it?"

"No, I'll do it." Baby took another deep breath, and slowly lifted the lid. The only thing inside the freezer was meat, frozen white packages of meat. No Paige. No body bag.

Baby let the lid fall. "What could have happened to her? How did she get out of here and then to Alcatraz?"

"I think I can answer that."

They spun around in unison. Lance stood in the garage dripping water, his surfboard under one arm.

Baby leaned forward, her face contorted with anger. She lifted her forefinger and waved it at Lance. "You knew? And you didn't tell me?"

Lance examined his bare feet. Outside, the shrubbery and the open lot across the street were enshrouded in shadowy gray. The sun was rising. "Konrad and I decided you'd be better off thinking Paige was dead, safe in the freezer. He didn't want to upset you."

"Upset me?" Baby shrieked. "Upset me? I'll show you what upset is?"

She launched herself at Lance, who as quickly as only the undead can, shot head first into his footlocker and slammed the lid. Baby hammered on the top of the trunk. "I'll get you for this Lance."

"It wasn't me," issued faintly from inside the trunk. "It was a vamp named Marcelus. He found her. She got out of the freezer on her own. Vetalas gave her the gift of life. Marcelus took her to the mansion on the top of the hill and now Vetalas has her. Will you let me go to sleep, please?"

Lei grabbed her arm. "Come on, Baby. There's nothing you can do to Lance, and you know it. He was just trying to be kind. Paige is out there with Konrad on that island. What we need to do is collect an army and go out there and save them."

Baby allowed Kenna and Lei to tow her back to the car. "Where you gonna find you an army? Last time I checked they didn't carry armies at the A&P."

Lei shook her head and hit the button closing the garage door. "I have friends."

Chapter Thirty-Six

Konrad opened his eyes and blinked. Everything looked different, clearer, brighter, the colors more intense. He was in a huge shower room. Thirty feet above him, sky lights let in sunshine. The light cascaded through the glass in a rainbow of electric color. The tiles, green in places with algae and mold, glistened in the sparkling rays, his vision was so acute he could see individual algae plants and the pores in the off-white tile. When he tried to move an arm, he discovered he was weak. He could barely move his feet or legs.

The glare hurt his eyes. He closed them and returned to the comfort of oblivion. When he woke up again, he was kicked into consciousness by a big, green, calloused toe with a long, hooked nail.

"Quit, I'm awake." Konrad tried to grab the foot, but he was still too weak to move his arms. He remembered waking up to painfully bright sunlight. It was now dark, and the shower room lit by mercury-vapor lights encased in wire cages. The yellow of the lights was so vivid and so concentrated, he closed his eyes against the glare.

He sniffed, smelling mold, mildew, rusted metal, blood, and filthy demon, a disgusting blend of bizarre musk, body odor and garbage. When he scented the blood, his incisors ached. He ran his tongue over them and felt sharp little points.

"Vetalas wants you."

Konrad couldn't believe it. He understood the growling, guttural snarls of the demon. The words were as plain as English.

The demon picked him up, tossed him over his shoulder and carried him out of the shower room. They went down a long white hallway, the paint peeling and ancient. The windows were barred, the old iron worn thin and broken in many places.

The hall ended and the demon took the steps of the wrought-iron, circular stairway two at a time. It kept going down. The further underground they went, the more comfortable Konrad felt. It grew darker and darker, but he could still see as clearly as in the lighted areas.

He struggled in the demon's arms, searched inside himself for his Berserker strength and couldn't find it. It was as though that part of him was gone, dead. He felt for anger to fuel his strength and found nothing. What was going on?

He remembered the vampires attacking. Vetalas shooed them away, lifted his head and tore into his throat. He recalled being thirsty, his throat dry as dust and he remembered drinking something warm and sweet. And that was his last memory until he woke up in the old shower room.

The demon kicked open a door, walked through a crowded room and opened another door. It dropped him on crimson pillows piled high on blood-red carpet. He was able to lift his head. Vetalas sat in a green lounge chair. His feet encased in fuzzy slippers rested on the foot.

"Konrad, or should I call you Sledge?"

Vetalas lifted a wine glass filled with red liquid. "To your health."

The demon king finished off the liquid and smiled at Konrad. His teeth were coated with a red film. "That was the last of your blood, Berserker. I now possess all your strength, while you can't even lift a finger. Well maybe a finger, but surely not your hand."

Konrad growled and struggled to pull himself into a sitting position. But it was useless. Vetalas was right. He was too weak.

The vampire used the wooden handle on the side of the chair to set the footrest down and leaped to his feet. "I feel like a million dollars."

He grabbed the big green demon, easily hefted him over his head, then threw him ten feet. "I'm stronger than a vampire. I'm stronger than the demons. I'm stronger than you. I am a god."

Konrad closed his eyes. What had he done?

Vetalas knelt beside him, bared his canines and punched a hole in his own wrist. He held it out to Konrad. "Drink and be stronger."

Konrad shook his head as he stared into Vetalas's red eyes. This couldn't be happening. He'd never thought Vetalas would turn him. Kill him, yes, but turn him into a demon, never.

"Drink, Sledge, or you will die. I already possess your power. Eat so you can live forever and fight by my side."

Konrad could smell the blood. His body screamed for him to take what was offered. He felt the points of his canines and knew the truth. He was dead. Vetalas had taken his life and turned him into a monster.

Then he remembered what Lance told him. If he didn't kill and feed off humans, and then he killed Vetalas, he could have his life back. He bent his head toward the offered wrist and sucked greedily, slurping loudly as he swilled down Vetalas's blood.

There was an almost instantaneous result. He felt stronger as the blood flowed into his body. His hands tingled; his legs twitched. Vetalas snatched his wrist away.

"Not so fast, Berserker, you get only what I am willing to share. Paige, feed our guest."

Konrad couldn't believe his eyes. Paige Crumbly knelt beside him and offered her throat. She turned her head away from Vetalas and lifted a finger to her lips. Her eyes begged him for silence. He put his mouth close to her neck and whispered. "How long have you been here?"

She put her finger to her lips again and he stabbed his fangs into her jugular vein. Her blood tasted like warm honey. With every sip, his strength increased.

"That's enough." Vetalas placed one fuzzy foot on his forehead and pushed him back into the pillows.

Konrad wanted to resist. He had some strength, but knew it wasn't enough. He lay back as Paige, head bowed, slid from the room. It looked like she was Vetalas's personal slave. He needed to talk to her, to find out what she knew and to ask her how to get out of here.

Resting his head on the pillows, Konrad closed his eyes and searched his body for his Berserker persona. When he felt it deep inside his chest, he rejoiced. Vetalas seemed to think he'd stolen it. But he'd only borrowed some blood. By making Konrad a vampire, Vetalas had given Konrad as much power as he had, maybe more because Vetalas would surely lose the gift of the Berserkers eventually, while it was Konrad's gift for life.

He laid there and flexed his hands, making fists. He moved his feet, curling his bare toes under and stretching them. The door to the opulent room opened and two naked women crept in, their eyes watching Vetalas as they approached his chair.

The dark-haired woman was Asian, she looked a little like Lei. Vetalas grabbed her by the neck and threw her toward Konrad. "Take her, she's yours to enjoy."

The woman stumbled in his direction and dropped to her knees. Her breasts were small, and she was so thin her ribs showed. Konrad sat up and pulled her toward him. He could feel the need for sex like a hungry animal in his crotch. He looked over at Vetalas. The demon king pushed the red head down on the big bed in the corner and mounted her. The sight of a naked Vetalas was all Konrad needed to destroy any sexual appetite.

The door was only a few feet away. He leaped to his feet and headed for it pulling the girl along with him. The red head screamed from the bed, a horrible high-pitched wail that chewed a hole in Konrad's enhanced hearing. He figured the Asian girl would be glad to leave with him, but she hung back, digging in her feet. "No, no, I must stay here."

Konrad dropped her hand. He hated to leave her, but this looked like an opportune moment for him to get the hell out of Dodge.

When he opened the door, he discovered the room on the other side was filled with gun-toting vampires, including one he recognized, Li Po. The leader of the Blue Dragon Tong leered at Konrad.

"Look, the Berserker is just like us."

A demon moved from the corner of the room and stood in front of Konrad with its scaly green hands on massive hips. Its message was loud and clear.

"I was just looking for the girl who left a minute ago. Her name is Paige."

"Vetalas wants you watched."

Konrad grinned and felt for the Berserker. He was able to slide into it like a familiar jacket. "I imagine he does. Are you supposed to be my watchdog?"

The demon growled, and Konrad noticed its scar. This was the demon he'd run into so many times before. He wore a loin cloth, not a bandage, but it was the same one. Whatever injury he'd sustained must have healed.

Konrad pointed to the demon's crotch. "Got it all back in working order? The demon maidens must be celebrating."

"My name is Lineus and as soon as Vetalas gives the order, you're a dead man."

Konrad turned his back to Lineus and moved through the room. Li Po stepped in front of him. "Sooner or later he will bring all of San Francisco into the nest."

"Might get a little crowded, and who would feed all of you then? Got to save some of the cattle or you'll starve. From what I understand, that was the problem where you fucks came from. Conservation is the key."

Li Po hissed and lunged for Konrad. Stopping him was easy. He grabbed the Asian vamp by the throat and held him while Li Po struggled. Lineus strode over, grabbed Li Po's arm and ripped it off. Konrad dropped him.

The Asian bled profusely for a second, the flow dried up and right in front of Konrad's amazed gaze, a new arm began to grow out of the stump. Konrad backed up. His head swam and he felt nauseous. This place reeked and was packed with one weird, ugly creature after another. He wanted to run but knew there was nowhere clean and pure on this island.

He found a corner in the room and sat down on a bench. He centered himself and began to count his breaths, matching them to the beat of his heart. He pushed energy up and down his chakras, folded his fingers, ring fingers pointed up and touching and opened the crown chakra. He was immediately surrounded by a field of violet. Power rushed into his mind and he reached out with his thoughts for Lung Ma. He was shocked when he heard Lei.

Konrad! I can feel you in my head just like the dragon. Where are you?

Don't talk to me. You'll be polluted. Vetalas has taken my humanity. He's made me a vampire.

Let me help. Tell me where you are, and I will come to you.

The feel of Lei with him here in this nest of evil was wonderful and horrible at the same time. He wanted her safe, far from Alcatraz and far from him.

Just tell Lung Ma I want to escape. Tell her to listen for me tomorrow night. I'll get out of here somehow.

I love you, Sledge.

He groaned. He'd become a monster. When she saw him, her love would die, and he wouldn't blame her.

Vetalas has changed me into a vampire. There can be no more love between us. When he changed me, he took away my humanity. I can't love, but I can hate. I'm filled with hate. I'm going to destroy Vetalas and send him back to the hell that spawned him.

He cut the mental connection, rose from the bench and stretched. Strength flowed through him. His enhanced vision caught Paige sneaking from Vetalas's room leading the red head.

He looked for Lineus. The demon was gone. When he followed Paige, he moved faster than he'd ever been able to before. He literally flew. The other vamps didn't even see him as he followed Paige through the exit and out into a hall. The underground tunnel was built of brick. It must be some of the original work done during the Civil War. Chains hung from rails overhead. Pipes crisscrossed the ceiling leaking rust-colored water which pooled in hollow spots on the floor.

Paige scampered deeper underground towing the faltering red head. Konrad caught up with her in a split second, grabbed Paige, tucked her under his arm and turned to head for the surface. The redhead fell into one of the puddles on the stained concrete floor.

Paige slugged him. "If you're trying to escape, you can't. There's no way off this island. Put me the fuck down!"

He stopped. "Oh, and you've personally checked the entire rock, the prison and the subterranean chambers."

"No, she said, smoothing her hair out of her eyes. "I haven't. But I've been here for weeks and no one gets out alive. There's over a hundred demons stationed in the lighthouse and in every possible corner."

"You might not be able to get out, but I can."

She rolled her eyes. "Still the same old Sledge, I see. Arrogant and full of yourself. You're not Superman, you know."

Konrad flexed his muscles and growled. "No, Paige, I'm stronger than Superman."

Chapter Thirty-Seven

Konrad put Paige down and headed up the tunnel toward the stairs. She grabbed his hand. "You can't get out, Konrad. You have to stay here and do as Vetalas says." She glanced rapidly left and right. "If you don't, he punishes you." Her voice was just whisper.

"I ain't worried about him. As soon as I get my strength back, I'm gonna be stronger than he is. He thinks he's taken my Berserker power, but he hasn't. I'm still Sledge, the Berserker, and now I'm a vampire as well. He created a monster when he made me, a monster that's going to come back on him with a vengeance. I'm gonna kill the bastard and he won't be able to stop me."

Paige shook her head. "No, Sledge, you can't kill Vetalas. He's older than you can imagine. Every minute he lives, he gains strength. If you go up against him, he'll kill you."

"I'm not listening, Paige. I'm going topside now, and I'm leaving Alcatraz. Are you with me, or not?"

She took his hand still shaking her head. "I'll come with you, but it's a fool's journey."

They ran down the dripping wet tunnel. Konrad hit the ancient circular staircase running. He got halfway to ground level when two demons on the way down blocked the steps.

Konrad pushed Paige behind his body and growled. He allowed his Berserker power to fill him, feeling his strength triple. Screaming a Norseman war-cry, he launched himself at the first demon, a stocky, bright blue sucker that smelled like roadkill.

He hit the demon in his big gut, hoisted him over his head and slammed him down on top of the other one.

"Konrad, they're coming up from below!" Paige screamed as she was grabbed and carried back down the steps into the tunnel.

The demons ganged up on Konrad. His strength was great, but he was still weak from being turned. His vampire power was not as strong as it would be.

"Konrad, it's Lineus!"

Lineus shouldered his way from the ground level past his brother demons and grabbed Konrad in a bear hug and squeezed. Ribs cracked, his body crushed in Lineus's embrace and he passed out.

When he woke up, his crushed ribs were miraculously healed. He was back in the shower room and sun streamed in through the skylight.

Konrad rubbed his burning eyes. He lay in a beam of sunlight, his skin smoking. After he moved into the shadows, he looked around. Paige lay in a crumpled heap next to one of the monstrous columns running down the center of the room. Each tiled column held four shower heads.

Shading his eyes, he tried to gage the time by pinpointing the location of the sun. It looked late in the day, maybe around three. He needed to make his escape while the vamp element on the island was asleep. He knew the demons were awake, and Vetalas could maneuver in sunlight, but most slept during daylight hours.

"Paige, wake up. We got to make a run for it now."

She moaned and opened her eyes. "I can't go out in the sunlight. I've been turned too long."

Konrad spotted one of the many drains running down the center of the room. Each drain was a round, perforated metal seal about two feet in diameter. He shoved his fingers through the holes and pulled. Grunting with the effort, he twisted the drain cover and finally, with one mighty yank, pulled it off. He flew backwards, tossing the cover six feet.

"Do you have any idea where this goes?" He looked into the hole. His enhanced vision enabled him to see the drainpipe led to a larger pipe below, much like the sewers under San Francisco.

Paige shook her head. "Vetalas kept me close. I haven't had a chance to do any exploring."

Konrad sat back and rubbed his chin. "I wonder why he put you in here with me. He knows I'm going to try to get away."

"Maybe he thinks he can control me and keep an eye on you. Maybe he wants you to be free, so he can manipulate you through me. I don't know what's on his mind, Konrad. I do know whatever he's thinking is evil. He's the devil sent to punish all of us for our sins."

"Well, girl, I don't really care what he's thinkin'. I'm outta here."

He dropped into the hole and looked around. The drainpipe was four feet in diameter, plenty of room to maneuver. It stank of mold, rat piss and ancient, wet insulation. A thin trickle of water ran through the pipe. Holding up his arms, he called to Paige. "Come on down. I'll catch you."

She dropped into his arms. The pipe angled slightly. Konrad chose to go with the flow and headed downhill.

They duck-walked, hunched over for a hundred feet. The pipe ended abruptly, opening to a larger pipe dropping into darkness. When the stream flowed over the edge, it separated into shining droplets. There was no ladder. Konrad stared intently into the depths. He could make out the glistening movement of water far below.

"We've got no rope and it's a long way down. I'm going to try to walk my way down, but if I fall, don't worry. I'll be fine."

Paige nodded as Konrad dropped into the pipe, forced his back against one wall and rammed his feet against the other in the classic technique of chimney climbing. The sides of the pipe were covered with slime. He inched his way down fighting to keep from losing his grip. Halfway down, he slipped, dropped a few feet, caught himself for a second and then fell. He landed feet first in deep water. Surfacing, he blew like a whale and waved to Paige.

"Drop, I'll catch you."

"No, Sledge. I can't, it's too far."

"I never thought of you as a candy-ass, Paige. Baby will be so disappointed when I show up at her apartment without you."

"Fuck you, Sledge." She yelled, held her nose and dropped. Konrad, treading water, caught her in his arms. They both plunged under the water with the force of her weight. When they surfaced, she slugged him.

"Ow! What was that for?"

"Just GP," she snapped.

"You hit me for general purposes? What'd I do?"

"I was scared, you dumb ass." She shoved her wet hair out of her face and looked around. "So, bright boy, where do we go now?"

It did look hopeless. There was no way to go back up, no doors, it was dark, and the water was deep.

"Stay here while I go exploring."

"No problem. Where would I go? I can't fly, yet."

Konrad dived deep and swam hard. His enhanced vision and his super speed and strength helped him reach the bottom of the pipe, about twenty feet down, find a connecting tunnel and follow it. He even had air left when he popped out in a room filled with enormous metal pipes, big open tanks of water, and the mother of all water heaters.

He returned for Paige and dragged her behind him to the exit. They climbed out of the pool and sat on the metal edge to dry off and plan their next move.

"Where the hell are we?"

"I think this is the cistern room. The Rock has no springs or water sources. They had a catchment system. All the water from rain on roofs and concrete was funneled into these big tanks." Konrad pointed. "I think that's the biggest water heater I have ever seen."

Paige walked over to it and touched it. A huge whoomph, blew the smell of gas into the room and a jet of flame followed. She screamed and leaped into one of the tanks. Konrad followed her.

The gas fire under the water tank pulsed. It was enormous. Konrad rubbed his face. His eyebrows were singed, but even as he felt the crispy edges, they grew back.

"Okay, Superman, how do we get out of here?"

There were no doors in this room. The water tanks were connected to each other by a mass of pipes overhead. Konrad bent over and looked under the heater. He could see an open room on the other side. The pipes running back and forth across the ceiling passed over the water heater with inches to spare. No way they could squeeze through.

"I guess we wait for the water heater to go off and go under it."

"Through the fire?"

"If it's like any other water heater, when the water's hot enough, it'll cut off."

"Can't we turn off the gas?"

"I'll check." He found a valve that could be attached to the gas supply and started turning it. Flakes of rust crumbled off the valve into his hands. It screeched and complained as he forced it to the right. The height of the flames died but didn't go out. When it was as tight as his great strength could make it, he stopped.

The room was getting very hot. "I think I made it worse. Now the water will take forever to heat, and the flame will never shut off."

"Great, genius, what do we do now?"

******

The members of Blue Dragon Tong waited patiently for Red Chua to speak. Red stared out at them from behind Li Po's ancient desk. It was early in the morning, many balanced paper cups of tea or coffee from Starbucks on their laps. The sun sent weak, late-autumn light streaming in through the filthy windows. Below them, the clash of pots and pans announced the arrival of the prep staff in the Golden Mountain.

Chua tried to gather his chaotic thoughts. He needed to tell them something to the point. But what was the point?

"You men must be aware that our honored leader, Li Po, has been taken over by a demon. As second-in-command, it is I who must now make the decisions and lead our Tong."

Timmy Po stood up. "Honorable Red, where is my uncle?"

"He was last seen cavorting with a white woman in the opium den near Washington Street. I believe he left China Town and now lives with the round eye demons, maybe out at Alcatraz. I heard the demon king has a nest on the Rock and is building his forces to take out San Francisco."

"Shouldn't we try to save him? He is our leader." Po sat down next to Chen Wa, a fierce fighter in both hand-to-hand combat and in the use of swords.

"You are right, Timmy, and Honorable Huizhong Chang has ordered me to do this. Which of you will volunteer to go to Alcatraz Island and find him?"

None of the ten men arrayed on leather couches and in folding chairs raised their hands or their voices.

"Not even you, Timmy?"

Timmy stood up again. "Red, hey man, there's vampires out there. My uncle is a vampire. They ate all the customers in the opium den, all of them. I saw with my own eyes what vampires and the demons can do in the bank vault. We need help if we're going out there to take them on their own turf. Why don't you approach Fong Jing and ask him to bring in the Chee Kung Tong."

Red thought for a moment. "I will ask Little Pete is he's interested, but to be honest, I believe we will have to enlist the aid of the round eyes. I'm gonna go talk to Lei Jiang. Her father is due to arrive any day. She and the Berserker and the dragon are who we should be talking to. We need their help."

When the meeting was over Timmy stayed behind as the other men left to take care of business. He wandered up to Red, his hands in the pockets of his baggy black jeans. "If you don't mind, I'll go with you."

Chapter Thirty-Eight

"I'll think of something," Konrad told Paige as he stared around the huge chamber. All the walls were brick. The water heater took up a huge amount of space and he counted four brass tanks leading to the underground water supply. Old brass pipe came out of the concrete floor, ran to the ceiling and branched off into many smaller pipes running in all directions.

The walls were stained black and green from years of gas fumes, mildew and mold. The place had to be toxic. The smell of gas and mold was overpowering.

He got up and examined the walls, tapping on them to see if there was open space behind them, or to see if they were thin or thick. He tapped on all three available walls and couldn't tell the difference between any of them. It was like trying to find a ripe watermelon. Who the hell knew what the right noise was?

He sat on the floor in front of one and crossed his legs. He rested his hands on his knees, palms open, thumb and forefinger touching, and chanted, concentrating his breathing to match his heart-rate. When he felt his vampire self-merge with his Berserker persona, he leaped to his feet and hunched his shoulders. Power raced up and down his spine, he funneled it all to his head and rammed his skull into the bricks.

Paige screamed. "Are you nuts?"

Konrad's head blew a hole in the wall and he followed it with his body. He dug in on the other side as he teetered at the edge of a huge chasm.

Mortar and brick dust covered Konrad's T-shirt. He brushed it out of his hair and looked back at Paige. "Are you coming?"

She stepped through the hole and stared into the rocky gorge. "That was insane, by the way, and what the fuck is this?"

"I got no idea. I can hear waves crashing on rocks. Can you see the bottom?"

She bent over. "All I can see is rocks, lots and lots of rocks."

"I think this might have been the original quarry where they got the material to build the first prison back in the 1800s."

"If it was a mine, there has to be a way down."

He looked up. The ceiling was solid rock with charcoal smudges from ancient fires. He could still see individual pick marks where the builders or maybe the prisoners hacked this mine out of bedrock.

A narrow ledge ran along the wall behind them. It ended in one of those brick-lined tunnels. They inched along the ledge and popped out on the ancient concrete floor of a low passageway. The tunnel was less than six feet high. A thick layer of dust covered the concrete, which swelled and cracked in many places. A rat came out of a fissure in the rock wall. Konrad picked up on the movement and its red eyes.

"Hungry?"

Paige scowled. "Always, but not for rat."

Konrad flew toward the rat and had it in his grasp before the rat could twitch its whiskers. He bit a hole in its neck, slurped some of the blood and handed it to Paige. "Eat some anyway. You know you can't kill and feed off humans. If you do you'll be stuck a vampire forever."

Her fangs popped into view when she smelled the blood. She lapped up a little and threw the corpse into the pit. "I didn't know that. How do I get changed back?"

"We have to kill Vetalas."

"Oh, is that all?"

They walked into the low, dark tunnel which ended at an iron-barred door. The bars were rusted and gone in places. They pushed through the door and the tunnel opened up. A row of rusted, metal doors with tiny barred windows lined each side of the hallway.

"This is probably the original cellblock."

Konrad pushed open one of the doors. Inside was a skeleton with manacles on each wrist. They opened all the doors. Nothing remained in any of them but the dead inmate and his chains.

"I can't believe they left these guys here to die. The Civil War must have ended, and they just walked away."

The hall dead-ended in another brick wall.

"Going through this one?" Paige lifted one eyebrow in her pale face.

"Konrad rubbed his head. No, think we'll try the mine. Maybe there's a way out in that pit."

They raced back down the hall, stopping at the edge. When Konrad looked into it from this angle, he thought he saw water at the bottom and two drainpipes.

"Over here," Paige called.

She'd found a narrow trail into the pit. Faint wheel tracks were worn in the rock. "They must have brought up the stone in carts."

Halfway into the hole, a rock fall covered the trail. It took them ten minutes to climb over it.

"It's got to be dark out by now," Paige said. "The vamps will be waking up and they'll find us."

"No shit, Paige. Got anything else positive you want to add?"

They scrambled down the rest of the trail. At the bottom, Konrad looked up. He didn't see anything, but his Berserker senses combined with the enhanced vampire abilities were screaming at him to run.

The water in the bottom of the pit was shallow. It covered sharp rocks with ankle-breaking holes, and it smelled of the ocean. "Wait," he told Paige.

"They're here," Paige whispered.

Konrad looked up. Fifteen vampires led by Li Po stood on the rim of the chasm. Shots pinged off the rocks and Paige screamed.

Two ancient drainpipes covered with dripping, slimy green moss loomed in front of Konrad. He saw blood oozing from Paige's torso, right below her breasts. The bullet slowly popped out of the wound which closed behind it. Weird shit seemed to be an everyday occurrence.

"Come on," he yelled.

She flew to him and together they dove into the pipe on the right. It was a tight fit for Konrad. His shoulders were mashed against ancient concrete made with rough, rocky aggregate. Thank god for the slime. It lubricated his journey. Sliding and shoving, he made his way into the dark. The smell of the ocean kept getting stronger. They hit salty water and the level rose as they moved further into the pipe.

When the water was up to his nose, he stopped. "Wait here, I'll see if this is going to take us out of here or get us killed."

"Sure, you go on ahead. I don't mind waiting. The demons can't fit in here and I can fight off any vamps."

Konrad had to look over his shoulder to check her expression. Sometimes he just couldn't tell if she was ragging him with sarcasm or being straight. She lifted an eyebrow.

"Okay then, I'll be right back."

He shot into the tunnel. When the water closed over his head, he pushed harder and faster. The tunnel finally ended in a barred grate. Desperate for air, he slammed into it with all his strength, blew it into the water and swam for the surface.

The pipe exit was about ten yards offshore. He could see the lights of the cell block and the guard towers. The lighthouse was on the other side of the island, so this must be the south shore. Treading water, he looked toward the city. It was a rare starlit night and the city shone brightly on the horizon.

He took several huge breaths and dove back into the dark water. He never would have found the pipe opening without his vampire-enhanced vision. It was overgrown with barnacles, algae and covered by rocks. He shoved his way in and popped out in front of Paige gasping for air.

"They're coming," she cried, eyes round with fear. "I can hear them splashing through the water."

Konrad nodded, and backed out of the tunnel with her following, their faces close. He burst into the windy, cold, night air with relief, Paige beside him. The swells lifted him and dropped him. The tops of each swell slapped water in his face.

"What do we do now?" Paige screamed over the wind. "I can't fly out of this."

Konrad held his finger over his lips. "Be quiet. They might follow us out here. Hold tight to my back and don't let go or you'll be swept away on the current."

He knew about the current in the bay. It headed straight to the North Pacific Ocean at about three miles an hour. They'd already moved past the island. He watched the shifting surface of the water for a few minutes, but no heads appeared.

"I guess vamps don't swim. I'm gonna call the dragon."

He sent out a mental scream for Lung Ma. It took several attempts, but he finally located her. She was far out to sea hunting for killer whales.

I need you dragon, he called. *I'm floating around in the bay with Paige. Can you come get us?*

He heard her mental complaint. *I'm hungry.*

Dammit, Lung Ma, we're drowning.

All right, I'm coming. Lei will be so glad to see you.

It only took Lung Ma ten minutes to find them by homing in on Konrad's mental signal. All he could think was if he and Lei had consummated their relationship, how would he have been able to contact Lung Ma? He and Paige would have been forced to swim to San Francisco. They might make it, but who wanted to try?

When Paige saw the dragon, she screamed and dug her fingernails into his back.

"Be quiet, she's the dragon we hatched out of the egg. Remember?"

"That thing came out of that little egg?"

"She grew."

"No shit."

The dragon's huge wings stirred the water as she settled. Konrad swam over to her and climbed up on a wing. "You're bigger," he said. "A lot bigger."

She turned her head and batted her eyelashes at him. *And you've turned into the undead. How could you let them do that to you?*

He settled in front of her wings and grabbed hold of her bristly mane. "I had to save my mother. Where is she?"

She's with Baby and Lei at Baby's apartment.

Paige hauled herself up behind Konrad. Lung Ma hissed. *You've brought another blood sucker with you? I don't want her on my back, Sledge.*

"Come on, Lung Ma, please don't give me any shit. I've about had it up to here." He held his hand up to his forehead. "This is Baby's girlfriend, Paige. She's still a halfling like me. As long as we don't kill and feed, we can change back into humans. All we have to do is kill Vetalas. And that's currently number one on my to-do list."

The dragon snorted and lifted her wings, slowly rising out of the water and into the cold air. Paige shivered and clung to Konrad's back as Lung Ma swept across the water toward the city.

Where do you want to go?

Konrad leaned forward so he could scream into the dragon's ear. "Take us to Baby."

Chapter Thirty-Nine

Konrad and Paige rode Lung Ma high over Baby's apartment. Two Kia Souls, Lei's beat up Toyota, and a cop car were parked on the street next to Baby's purple Honda. It looked like she was having a party.

The dragon dropped them on the roof and flew off. *I need to finish my dinner,* she explained as the updraft from her wings pelted them with gravel and pigeon droppings. They shielded their eyes as they watched her fly toward the ocean.

"She's beautiful, isn't she?"

The silver blue of Lung Ma's scales sparkled in the city lights. "I never thought of her that way," Konrad said. "I guess she is kind of graceful when she's in the air. On land, she's an elephant. So . . . are you ready for this?"

"As I'll ever be. Oh, Konrad, Baby's gonna be so pissed. I'm a vampire."

They knocked on the apartment door before entering. The smell of barbecue filled the small hallway.

"She's cooking," Paige whispered.

He shrugged. "What's that mean? She's always cooking."

"She only cooks when there's a bunch of people over or she's really upset."

Konrad smothered a laugh with his hand. "Then she's always upset."

Paige nodded her head. "I know."

Lei answered the door and shrieked when she saw them.

"What?" Konrad asked.

Lei covered her mouth with her hand, her eyes wide with horror. "You look terrible."

"Well, I've been through a lot in the last two days. You gonna move over and let us in?"

She tried to hug him, and he gently pushed her away. "No, Lei, I'm not Konrad or Sledge anymore. Vetalas changed everything."

He took Paige's hand and pulled her into the apartment. Bloody tears ran down her face. Her mahogany hair was glued to her head and stiff with salt. She wore the skimpiest of skirts, a see-through blouse, and was bare-footed. It hadn't mattered to either of them until now.

They stopped in the living room. Konrad's heightened senses picked up voices in the bedroom. Munoz was in there with Baby talking about work and the CDC. Lance had one corner of the couch; his mother sat in the other corner. The place was packed. Red Chua and Timmy Po sat on the floor talking to Kenna.

"What's going on here? Looks like you're planning something or having a party."

Baby stuck her head out of the bedroom. "Who came in, Lei? We ain't got much more room."

When she saw Paige, she screamed, covered her mouth, her eyes rolled back in her head, and she dropped like a stone to the hall floor. Paige ran to her.

Lei tried to follow, but Konrad grabbed her hand. As soon as his flesh touched hers, he snatched his hand away. She felt so warm and alive and he knew what his skin felt like. He'd bumped into Lance ften enough.

"Leave her alone. She's changed and she's been through hell. Let 'em work it out by themselves."

"Talk to me, Sledge. Tell me what happened to you."

She tried to take his hand again and he shook her off. "Vetalas turned me into a monster. That's what happened. I gotta go talk to Junior, have him put the bomb in the sewer and get him to set me up with some weapons and plenty of ammo. I'm gonna get the sword of my ancestors and sharpen it until I can shave with it. Then I'm going back, and I'm gonna kill that bastard if it's the last thing I do."

Munoz came out of the bedroom. "I heard what you said, and you ain't going alone, amigo. I'm going with you."

Red spoke up from the floor. "That's why we're here man, we want in."

Baby pushed Munoz aside, planted her feet and glared at Konrad. "I'm pissed at you, Sledge. Why didn't you tell me Paige wasn't in the freezer?"

She put her arm around Paige's shoulders and squeezed. When she looked at Paige, her eyes softened, and tears rolled down her round cheeks. "Thanks for bringing her back to me, Sledge. Thanks."

Paige pushed Baby's arm away. "I'm not the same girl, Baby. I still love you, but Vetalas changed me. I'm going with Konrad to Alcatraz. We're gonna kill that fucker or die trying."

Konrad's mother, Francis, moved through the crowded room to stand in front of Konrad. "I knew you'd make it out. What'd that ugly son of a gun do to you?"

Konrad kissed her cheek. She put one hand on his face. "You're ice cold. He turned you into one of them vamps, didn't he?"

He nodded. "Don't worry, Ma, I'll fix it."

She nodded. "You're just like your father, you know. He would have said the same thing."

Baby stepped into the middle of the living room and lifted her hands. "Okay, folks, listen up. Before we eat, I have to bring everyone here up to speed. There have been some new developments in the city. Last night, the CDC quarantined the entire Bay area. They think the demons are a disease."

Konrad shook his head. "You're kidding?"

"No, and they've taken over my morgue. Last night alone, fifty of the newly undead walked out because I wasn't there to stop it and they wouldn't listen to me about using the trocar and the butcher knife. On their way out, the vamps ate most of the CDC pathologists, the orderlies and the clerks. Munoz says they're calling in the National Guard."

"What are they supposed to do?"

"You got me."

A loud knock at the door stopped Baby's rant. Lei answered it. Lt. Larry Groves stood in the open doorway with an Australian, leather cowboy hat in his hand and a .44 strapped to his hip. He wasn't wearing his uniform.

Lei stepped aside and Scary Larry shoved his way into the crowded living room. "I was right. This is where the action is." He stuck out his hand. "Munoz, your partner told me I could find you here. He's outside parking the squad car. We brought both the dogs."

Munoz shook Groves' hand with a stunned look on his face. "Hi, Lieutenant, what did you want me for?"

"I want to be part of the action. I want in on the kill. Those paper-pushing, sons-a-bitching, desk jockeys in charge of this city couldn't plan an attack on a nursery school. Perry told me you were friends with the Green Giant, and he has all the intel on where to find the hive, or the nest or whatever you call the place where those commie, motherfuckers are hiding."

Groves pulled a cigar out of his pocket and stuffed it in the corner of his mouth. "So, when we hitting them?"

Konrad glared at Roger Munoz.

"Hey, it's not my fault, man. I didn't invite him."

"Groves, I can't allow you to get involved in this. It's way too dangerous."

"I know what you're thinkin'," Groves said. "You're thinkin' I cut and ran down there in the sewers. And you're right. But I wasn't prepared. I never seen anything like those big, ugly, green bastards. Give me another chance." Groves pulled his enormous .44 out of the holster on his belt and stroked the barrel. "I won't retreat on you this time."

Lance grabbed Konrad's arm. "I'm in, too, bro. When you planning to go for it?"

"Probably tomorrow afternoon. We need to hit them while it's still light to be the most effective. You'll have to wait until dusk. I can still go out in the daylight. I just can't stay out in it for long."

"Ah, man, you're leaving me out."

"I'm not, Lance. As soon as you can get there, you're welcome to throw yourself into it on our side. We'll probably need you."

Konrad shook his head. What a group. "Munoz, ride with me to Junior's. We'll load his van with weapons and make us a plan."

"You ain't going nowhere without me," Groves said.

Red and Timmy got off the floor. "Can we go? We got weapons but nothing like what we're gonna need to fight the demons. I talked Little Pete into joining us, which means we'll have the Chee Kung Tong on our side, too. China Town is overrun. If you got a weapons guy that has what we need, we got money." Red pulled a huge wad of cash out of his pocket and waved it around. "We got some AKs and a few shotguns, but we need something bigger and better if we're gonna attack the Rock."

"I guess you can come. Munoz, you drive."

Lei grabbed Konrad's arm as he tried to walk out. "Sledge, please don't shut me out."

Konrad had to look away. The pain in her eyes gouged a hole in his soul. "We'll talk when I get back."

She held on to both his shoulders and made him look at her. "Promise?"

"Promise."

They met Munoz's partner, Xavier Perry, coming up the steps. "Where you guys going?"

"Guns," Munoz said. "Konrad's taking us to his dealer."

Perry punched Munoz's in the shoulder. "Well, that's a switch, us having to go to an illegal arms dealer to get weapons."

"Tell me about it."

"Hell, the government is all wrapped up in thinking we got a disease in the community," Perry said. "They're worried about fucking looting, mass hysteria and what they're calling the 'infection.'

They got SFPD patrolling the streets with rubber bullets and riot gear."

"Most of the guys are carrying big knives and swords," Munoz said. "I tried to tell them. Groves tried to tell them. Until you've been in the sewers and seen the problem up close and personal, it's hard to comprehend. You coming with us?"

"Sure, Why the fuck not?"

They took two cars. The Tong guys drove theirs and Munoz drove his squad car. They left the drooling hounds in the extra police vehicle, windows down.

They pulled in front of Junior's business around ten. "I bet he's playing sax at the club," Konrad said, but rapped on the door anyway.

When no one answered, they loaded back into the two vehicles and drove to Tiny's Jazz Café further into the district on Filmore. The door to the café was locked and the neon sign over it out. Konrad knocked and someone opened the peep hole and looked through.

"Who is it?"

"I need to talk to Junior. Is he playing tonight?"

"You got any walkers out there?"

"What's a walker?" Konrad asked.

"The walking dead, one of them vampire things. The city's full of them. You know what I mean."

"Just get Junior."

"He's playing a set right now. Come on in." the door was thrown open by a huge black man, bigger than Junior, bigger than even Konrad. When he saw Konrad, he stepped back and eyed him up and down.

"I know you. I seen you before. But you don't look so hot."

"I got into some trouble with your 'walkers,' but I'm here to talk to Junior about dealing with them."

The big man backed away. "Stand your asses over by the wall and don't talk to nobody."

The club was jumping, packed with people drinking and listening to the loud music. A choking cloud of cigarette and marijuana smoke hung in the air. The lights were low and the alcohol flowing. Junior's big ass swallowed the stool he sat on as he played his saxophone.

Konrad's group backed up against the walls as instructed and waited for Junior. When the set was over, he put his sax in the case and snapped it shut. Konrad elbowed his way through the crowd. "We need to talk."

"What you bring that herd of fucking weirdos into my place fo?" Junior squinted at the men lined against the walls, arms crossed, waiting. "Is that Scary Larry? You crazy bastard."

"You still sore over getting busted for stealing that dead guy's identity?"

"Never proven. I got off without even a slap on the hand."

"Junior, you two finished yakking about old times, 'cause we came here because we want to fight the demons. And at this point, I'm taking all the help I can get. We need weapons, Junior. Lots of them."

"Whoa, You think we should be talkin' 'bout this kind of shit in front of Five-O?"

"Don't worry about it. They're with me and we're all in this together."

"You got cash? Cause I ain't no charity organization."

Konrad nodded. "We have plenty of money."

"You ready for me to plant the bomb?"

"Tomorrow."

"Bout fuckin' time. Let's go get my van."

Chapter Forty

Junior took them across the Bay Bridge into Oakland. They had to wait in a long line of traffic to go through two security checkpoints and get over the bridge, and each time, Konrad hid in the back of the van. The National Guard manned the posts, searching each vehicle for 'infected citizens.' The idea being to keep as many of them as possible bottled up inside the city.

"Don't they know vamps and demons fly?" Junior asked as he turned into a U-Store-It facility. Junior keyed in his pass-code and the gates opened. After driving to the back of the fenced-in block of storage units, he parked.

"They think it's an infection," Scary Larry said from the back of the van. "They still aren't buying into the fact we're infested with blood suckers. And that was after friggin' Plank stormed the Moody Mansion and half the force was jumped by demons and Plank ended up in the loony bin. Fucking, dumb-ass, bastards wouldn't even believe we had a disease in the city if we hadn't gone down in the sewers."

"You were no different, you didn't believe it either. But these guys, they wouldn't believe it even if we took pictures," Munoz said. "The bureaucrats and the assholes running this city never leave their offices. Most of them would have a heart attack and die on the spot if they ran into a demon."

"You got that right," Perry added.

They slid open the van door and climbed out. Junior slowly hauled his large rear end out of the driver's seat and picked through a huge wad of keys.

"I keep most of my saleable merchandise here," he said. "It has twenty-four-seven access and no cameras."

He unlocked the garage-type door and rolled it up. Red and Timmy walked in like zombies, eyes wide as they stared at the rows and rows of weapons.

Munoz and Groves looked into the storage unit and then stared at each other. Groves shook his head. "I can't believe it's come to this."

They followed Junior into the storeroom. "Now, I ain't gonna be with you guys, but I pretty well know what you need."

He headed into the back with the two Tong guys following him, their heads swiveling left and right as they tried to absorb the quantity and quality of the merchandise.

Konrad sniffed and smelled the overpowering aroma of coffee. "You ship this shit with coffee?"

Junior nodded. "Yeah, the weapons come in with the beans. The smell confuses the dogs." He pulled two big boxes out of a back corner and threw them open. "Here," he said to Konrad. "I'm giving you these two Browning QCBs. I didn't pay for them and you're gonna need 'em. You know, you can shoot the head clean off a vampire in twenty seconds with one of these things. I got about ten cases of cartridge belts. You'll have to pay for those."

"No problem, Red said. "We'll pay."

Konrad walked over to a rack and pulled down a strange-looking gun, square-shaped, with a bent barrel and a pop-out LCD screen. "Corner gun. I want this, Junior. I'm going down into the tunnels after Vetalas. I need it."

"Man," Junior whined. "That thing cost me a fortune. I had to bribe like three supply officers to get it. It's state-of-the-art, you know. That screen is really a video camera."

"It's not state-of-anything," Konrad snapped. "Anyone can make one of these things in his backyard workshop. And I need it. You don't happen to have a corner-shot grenade launcher do you?"

Junior's eyes popped open. "Uh, no."

Konrad grabbed the large man by the collar of his voluminous Hawaiian shirt and growled. "I don't have a lot of control."

Junior backed away, arms raised, hands flat. "I can see that. The grenade launcher is over there."

Groves stepped forward. "I'll take that."

Junior handed the grenade launcher to Scary Larry.

"Now this is a fine piece of equipment. Could have used this back in Bagdad."

When the deal was sealed and all the weapons and ammo packed in the van, they headed back across the bridge. "This could be tricky," Junior said as they neared the first checkpoint."

Groves pushed his way to the front of the van. "Pull over. I'll get us through."

With Groves driving the van, they flew through both roadblocks and cruised back to Junior's shop. The dark streets were empty of traffic. Occasionally, Konrad picked up movement, a vamp running across the road or flying overhead. He knew none of the other passengers saw anything.

They distributed the weapons at Junior's.

"We're outa here," Red Chua said after loading the back of the Kia. "What time do we meet up?"

"Three tomorrow afternoon at Golden Gate Tours' dock. Stay in your vehicles until we're all there. We gotta commandeer a boat and I'm not sure what kind of resistance we'll face."

Red nodded. "We're bringing over a hundred men. Better make that two or even three boats."

"I know there's at least ten working out of that dock. We'll see what's available."

When the Tong element departed, Konrad turned to Junior. "You set that bomb to go off at eight tomorrow night."

"At night? What? You crazy? I ain't going down there in the dark."

"I don't care when you plant the damn thing. Just set it to blow at eight. The streets will be empty because of the curfew, and you might snag some vamps and demons going in and out. Night is the best time."

261

"We had another earthquake yesterday. Aftershocks been shaking the city ever since. Is it safe to go down there?"

"You're just gonna have to bite the bullet, Junior, and take the risk. You've been in worse situations in the Army."

"I know, but I had backup."

"You want me to send someone with you?"

Junior thought for a minute. "No, I be all right. I'll take my own man; I'll take Tyrese with me."

"Is he the bouncer?"

Junior nodded. Konrad stuck out his fist. Junior bumped it with his. "Good luck. Call me if you don't get it set in time or if anything goes wrong."

With Junior ready to do his part, and the Tong armed to the teeth, Konrad climbed into Perry's squad car and they drove back to Baby's. Baby's purple Honda still sat in front of the apartment. She and Lei must be waiting for them to get back.

Groves and Munoz stashed the weapons in the trunks and back seats of their cars and put a dog in each one to guard the munitions. Then they all trouped up the steps.

Lei opened the door before they even knocked. Her eyes were red from crying. Konrad felt like his heart was going to explode.

The place reeked of barbecue. Groves was the first one to notice. He grinned at Baby. "You got food?"

She slapped her hands on her hips and tapped her foot. "I made pulled-pork sandwiches and French fries." She eyed them up and down. "There might be enough. We already ate."

Konrad was starving but couldn't eat. His body could no longer digest food. He was technically dead. He'd been fighting the craving every minute he'd been in and around his friends. He knew he had to eat soon, or he would be too weak to carry off a fight with a blood-fat Vetalas. But what? What could he consume and what did he have to avoid? He wasn't sure. He needed to talk to the expert on being a vampire, Lance.

"Where's Lance?" he asked Baby.

"He's in my shower. He likes it in there. Don't ask me why."

Konrad pulled the shower curtain aside and found Lance watching porn on a tablet.

"What the fuck are you doing?"

"I'm trying to be good. Lung Ma told me if I was good and did good deeds, she'd change me back to human. That means no raping women, no mesmerizing them or glamouring them into having sex with me. It's what we do. How else do I get a woman? I'm horny. Where am I supposed to find a woman that will voluntarily have sex with me? I'm a skinny little vampire wearing board shorts."

Konrad shook his head. This was way too weird to even begin to comprehend, not that he wanted to. "Fine, close the screen for a minute and talk to me."

Lance swiped the screen shut.

"What can I eat if I want to stay clean and become human again when I kill Vetalas?"

"Animal blood is okay, no human blood, unless they're halflings like you. And definitely don't kill humans and feed off them. What you can really eat the most of is vamps, man. Drink all the vampire blood you want. It won't destroy your humanity and it'll make you, like, stronger."

"Vampires? I can kill all I want?" Konrad was freaking out inside. He could definitely handle that.

"You got it, bro. Now, can I have some privacy?" Lance yanked the curtain closed.

Konrad left the bathroom, slamming the door shut behind him.

"Baby," he said, when he found her in the kitchen filling hamburger buns with pork and sauce. "Do not go into the bathroom."

"What you talking about?"

"Don't ask."

Chapter Forty-One

While Scary Larry, Munoz and Perry scarfed up barbecue, Konrad pulled Lei into a corner. "We need to talk."

"Fine, just don't push me away." When she took his hand, he let her hang onto it. "I don't care what Vetalas did to you. You're my man. Let's go back to my apartment and I'll prove it to you."

Konrad felt her urgency in a new and more exciting way. He could actually feel her need for him. His heightened senses gave him the power to be aware of all her emotions. It affected him so strongly, he was afraid he'd lose control and take her right there.

His desire was ten times what it had been before he was changed. Vampires must really like sex.

"You're sure?"

She nodded, half-closed her eyes, and licked her lips. Konrad couldn't take his eyes off her tongue.

"Baby," Konrad called. "Paige, we gotta go."

He dragged Lei with him to the kitchen where they found Baby washing and Paige drying the dishes.

"We're gonna head out to Lei's apartment. You okay for the night?"

She wrapped an arm around Paige's shoulders. "Sledge, my man, thanks to you, I'm the best I been in a while."

They stopped in the living room. "Ma, want me to take you to my apartment?"

His mother took one look at him and Lei and smiled. "No, son, I'll stay here with Kenna. You go on and go to bed. You look like you could use a good night's sleep."

He felt his face flush. His mother knew. "Uh, thanks, I'll be back by in the morning."

Konrad broke all the speed limits driving to Lei's place in China Town. She sat on the console between the seats, kissed his cheek, his lips and his neck, stroked his chest, and drove him crazy.

He parked out front, ran around to the passenger's side and opened the door. Before she could set foot on the sidewalk, he had her in his arms. He carried her up the steps, holding her close while she unlocked the door. His desire was like fire burning in his gut and up into his throat.

He kicked the door open and she slammed it shut. They were naked on the bed in seconds with him fighting for control over raging passion fueled by the Berserker blood and now his vampire nature.

He lay on his back and counted breathes while Lei kissed him and touched him.

When Lei straddled him, rubbing her body along the length of his, squirming and wiggling, he growled. "Are you ready?"

She pressed her hands on each side of his face and guided his mouth to her breasts.

"I'm taking that as a yes," he whispered. "Tell me if I do something you don't like, or if you want me to stop."

When it was over, and he could breathe again, they lay entwined on the bed. He held Lei's small body as close to his as he could. If he could have absorbed her into himself, he would have. "I love you," he whispered into her ear.

Her hair was spread around her like a cloud. How had it come undone? He couldn't remember a lot about their lovemaking, only that it was the most wonderful experience of his entire life.

"I love you, too," she breathed into his ear.

A loud knock at the door crashed into their mood and shook Konrad out of his post-coital lethargy. He was almost asleep.

"Who the fuck is that?"

Lei jumped up and shrugged on a silk kimono. "Just stay there. I'll see who it is, get rid of them, and be right back."

Konrad smiled and fluffed his pillow. His smile faded when he heard who was at the door.

Papa," Lei shrieked in Cantonese, a language Konrad now clearly understood. *Holy shit, her father is here.*

He leaped to his feet, pulled his jeans and T-shirt back on and disappeared into the bathroom where he splashed water on his face and ran stiff fingers through his buzzed hair. He noticed dark circles around his eyes, and the pallor of his skin. He needed to feed.

Boots and jacket back on, he went out into the living area.

A Chinese man of medium height dressed in a saffron-colored monk's robe stood in the living room. His air of disapproval radiated from him like a gas cloud. His head was shaven, he wore a set of sandalwood beads wrapped around his wrist and another around his neck. Lei's dad was apparently traveling as a Buddhist monk.

Lei grabbed his hand and pulled him toward her father. "Papa, this is my boyfriend, Konrad Pengill. Konrad this is Shiu Jiang, my father."

Jiang didn't bow or say anything to Konrad. He turned to Lei and began to rant in rapid-fire Cantonese. "How could you dishonor our name and yourself by bringing a guai-lo into your home and sleeping with him? How could you dishonor me in this way?"

Konrad felt his face flame and his blood boil. *No, Konrad, you can't eat your girlfriend's father.* "Excuse me, Shiu Jiang, but I understood every word you said. Lei and I love each other."

Jiang backed away from Konrad, his eyes wide. "There is something wrong with you, your skin color, your eyes...what are you?"

"Dammit, Lei, why didn't you tell me I look strange?"

"It doesn't matter to me, that's why." She turned on her father. "Why have you come here? What do you want with me? We're in the middle of a war with demons and vampires. I don't have the time or the energy to answer to a Chinese colonel with nineteenth century ideas about morality. This is my home and you will not come in here and push me around."

Colonel Jiang bowed to Lei. "I am sorry, you are right. This is your home. But he," Jiang pointed at Konrad, "Is not human."

267

Konrad turned away, his mind churning with anger and embarrassment. Jiang was right, he wasn't human. He'd never been human. His Berserker blood made him different enough, now he was a monster, just like Vetalas.

"I'll leave," he said.

Lei grabbed his hand. "No, you can't leave, I won't let you. Father, why did you come to America? Why are you here? I thought you were staying with Monks in Tibet."

"They sent me to fetch the dragon. The old queen is dying. The dragons must have a queen and each queen only lays one queen egg. Lung Ma must return to Tibet and take her place as the leader of the Ice Dragons."

Lei's eyes flew open. "Oh, my god, Lung Ma, Konrad, we can't talk to her anymore. What're we gonna do? Papa, you can't take the dragon. This town is infested with demons and vampires. She's our greatest weapon. We plan to attack their nest tomorrow. Oh, Konrad, how could we have been so selfish? Who's gonna talk to her now?"

Jiang pushed Konrad aside and faced his daughter. "What are you talking about? Demons and vampires here in this city?"

"Yes, Papa, I just told you so. They've built a huge nest on Alcatraz. Konrad is heading a raid on it tomorrow. The Tongs are even behind it. Blue Dragon Tong and Fong Jing and the Chee Kung Tong are supposed to meet us at the docks tomorrow afternoon."

Jiang rubbed his bald head as though he weren't used to it being that way and paced around Lei's small living room. "The monks told me the history of the Ice Dragons and their capabilities. But how could I believe it to be true in this time, right now? Where did these monsters come from? The monks possess ancient records that say all vampires and demons in our world were exterminated in the nineteenth century. Why are they here now?"

Lei started to explain. "There's a hole between..."

Jiang interrupted. "You!" He turned on Konrad, arm extended, finger pointing, his face a mask of anger, eyes narrowed, jaw thrust forward, mouth a thin line. "You brought her into this." Jiang grabbed Konrad's arm and stared into his eyes. "You're one of them."

Jiang reached into the folds of his robe and yanked out a short stabbing sword. "Die, demon!"

Konrad flew backwards to avoid being beheaded by Jiang's first swipe. Fighting to restrain his Berserker persona and the vampire inside him, Konrad counted breaths and kept backing out of beheading distance while he held out his hands. "Stop, Colonel Jiang. I know what I am. But I've been told I can regain my humanity as long as I don't feed off humans. I would never hurt Lei. I love her."

Jiang stood with his feet wide switching the sword quickly from one hand to the other. "You've already put her in grave danger. Even a lummox such as you should be able to perceive this."

Konrad hung his head. "I know she's in danger because she's with me, but I also protect her. Who are you to come in here and accuse me of putting her in danger after you left her on her own for years?"

Lei held out her hands and stepped between them. "Stop this right now. I love Konrad, Papa. He did not put me in danger. When you sent me that egg, you inadvertently involved me in this war with the demons. And now, I am going to finish it. He needs me."

Lei ran to Konrad and buried her face in his chest. "And I need him. Together we will fight the vampires that have taken over our city and we will win."

Konrad disentangled her arms and kissed the top of her head. "If I'm gonna be worth a shit tomorrow, I have to feed. Lance told me what to do. You stay here, work things out with your dad and get some rest."

"You'll take me with you tomorrow?"

Konrad sighed. "I wish you'd stay here where it's safe."

"I can fight."

"Yes, you can."

"What are we gonna do about contacting Lung Ma?"

"I think I'll ask Lance. Surfer vamp knows a lot of things. Maybe he can talk to her. He's been a vampire since the sixties. But don't worry about it, baby. I'll think of something."

They kissed, a light lip-brushing, both of them horribly aware of Colonel Jiang glaring at them.

"Will you be back soon?"

"As soon as I can."

Chapter Forty-Two

The hunger inside Konrad churned and clawed at his gut. He felt it in his head. His whole body ached with need. No wonder vampires killed when they suffered the thirst. It was unbearable. The only thing keeping him from snagging the first person he saw and draining them was his Berserker persona. The strength of his ancestors was going to give him back his humanity.

It was weird the one thing that made him a monster all his life would bring him back where he never felt he belonged. The horrible cravings explained so much. Now he understood why so few prevailed and destroyed their makers before they made a human kill. The blood thirst drove them to it. It destroyed their humanity and turned them into killers.

Paige told him the only reason she still hadn't killed was Vetalas. He'd denied her human blood to torture her, and maybe his evil nature would be the one thing that saved Paige.

Konrad shot down Geary headed for the beach. He had to find Lance. He hoped the surfer finished his business in Baby's tub and went to enjoy outdoor sports as opposed to indoor sports.

With his heightened senses, more acute eyesight and hearing, he was able to push the Ninja to even greater speeds as he hurtled through the empty streets. Even with the fog at ground level, he kept the bike above ninety, sometimes hitting one-thirty in the straight-aways. He knew what was ahead. His hearing told him the way was clear and his sight pierced the thick fog like never before.

When he arrived at the beach, he parked and walked out on the wet sand. The ocean sparkled like a million tiny light bulbs. The stars overhead were so clear and beautiful, he stopped and stared. He could see them right through the fog.

It was easy to find Lance. Surfer Vamp floated on the swells, one leg on each side of his board. He waved and screamed the vampire's name. The off-shore wind grabbed his words and carried them out to Lance, who waved back at him.

Konrad admired Lance's style as he caught a small curl and headed for the beach. His pale skin glistened as he ran toward Konrad carrying his board.

"What's up, dude?"

"How do you keep sane after all the years of blood sucking and killing?"

"It's the waves, man. It's where you lose yourself and then you find yourself. It's my religion. Back when surfing first got going in the early sixties, I was just a kid. I learned on a ten-foot board in crappy surf. Now I got this primo little six-footer. I can cut up a wave. Mother Nature teaches me new stuff every day about being human, even though I'm not. If you don't love or respect anything else, bro, you got to respect her."

"You're really something," Konrad said, and he felt it. Lance was special. He hoped Lung Ma would recognize his great qualities and give him back his life.

"You out here to admire my skill on the waves, or you need something?"

Konrad didn't want to tell anyone his new secret. If he'd been able to, he would have blushed. He ducked his head and dug the toe of his boot in the sand. "I can't talk to the dragon anymore and neither can Lei."

Lance burst out laughing. His chuckles and giggles rose high and were snatched by the wind as he slapped his knees and guffawed. "You did her, didn't you?"

Konrad glared at Lance. "Hey, that's none of your fucking business, but, yes, we did it, and now we can't talk to Lung Ma. I came here to find out if you can."

Lance shook his head. "Hell no. I tried and tried to hear her out there on Alcatraz when I was putting your mother on her back. I couldn't hear a peep."

Konrad's heart sank. "Damn! What are we supposed to do now? We need her tomorrow and I don't even know where she is."

He stuffed his hands in his pocket and stared at the black Pacific and the sparkling foam-topped waves. Lance moved close to stand beside him. Together they watched seals playing in the surf.

Suddenly, Lance turned and smacked Konrad's shoulder. "Dude, the little chick can talk to her."

"Who?"

"Kenna, the girl we rescued from the Moody Mansion. I know she can hear the dragon."

"Now why didn't I think of that? You're right, she can. You figured it out, man. Thanks, Lance."

*****

Li Po skimmed through the dark tunnels and passageways beneath Alcatraz with a grim smile on his face. One of his Tong members, Corey Sing, newly turned, showed up on the island only hours ago. Po just received the message minutes before and was following his informant, a skinny Tong-wannabe named Kenny.

He found Sing laying on a metal cot in one of the cells on the first floor of the main cell block.

"You look like shit, Sing."

The Tong member lifted his head. "That you boss? Where's your eye-patch?"

"My eye grew back when I was turned."

Sing smiled. "I need to feed, Honorable Li. Do you have any human women around here?"

"Everything you need is on this island, but first you will tell me all you know about the Tong and what's going on in China Town."

Sing propped himself up on one elbow. Li Po grabbed him and tossed him against the cell wall.

"Stand up and show some respect. You disgust me, laying there in the presence of your Tong captain as though he were any other man. I am Li Po. And now I am strong enough to kill you with one finger."

Sing slowly climbed to his feet. His head hung and one of his arms was crooked, probably broken when he hit the wall. "Please forgive me Honorable Li. I forgot my place."

Li Po smiled. "Yes, you did. Sit and tell me about the Tong."

Sitting together on the cot, Sing quickly filled Li Po in, telling him about Red Chua joining with the Berserker, Little Pete and the Chee Kung Tong. He told Li Po all about how the Berserker planned to raid Alcatraz the following afternoon.

Li Po stood up and rested a hand on Sing's shoulder. "You have done well." He waved a hand toward Kenny. "He will find you a place to rest and a woman."

Filled with this important news, Li Po raced through the tunnels toward Vetalas's chambers. He had never been allowed close to the head vampire. His head swam with possibilities. Vetalas might reward him for his information with more power. It was possible he might be able to get closer to Vetalas himself.

When he got to the red door with the crazy design, he scratched politely. A huge green demon opened it and Li Po, bowed his head. "Honorable sir, I have important news for the master."

The demon growled and spoke in his rough voice. "What could you know that would interest the master?"

Li Po felt real fear facing the giant monster, but he'd heard the Berserker tore off its genitals. "I was told the Berserker is going to attack the nest."

The demon grabbed Li Po by his throat and held him at eye level. Li Po whimpered, so scared, he would have shit himself, but he didn't do that anymore.

"You better not be lying blood sucker."

Carrying Li Po by the neck, the monster stalked through the opulent apartment and knocked on another door. Marcelus, Vetalas's right-hand man answered.

"Need to speak to Master Vetalas. This putrid piece of filth says he has news of the Berserker."

Vetalas instantly appeared at the door. "Bring him in."

Once inside, the demon dropped Li Po. He stood in front of the greatest creature on the planet and stared. He'd never been allowed this close. Vetalas sat in a green lounge chair, hit the handle and reclined. He wore furry, black slippers. Two naked women groveled on the bed, both more beautiful than any woman Li Po had seen. He gawked.

Vetalas leaned forward. "You're not here to stare at my women, China man. Tell me what you know."

It only took a few minutes for Li Po to fill Vetalas in.

Vetalas snapped the handle on his recliner and whipped upright. "What time are they going to attack?"

Li Po bowed his head. "I am so sorry, Master, my pawn did not tell me the time. He only said in the afternoon."

"His name is Corey Sing?"

Li Po nodded.

"Lineus, bring him to me immediately. Whatever he knows about the Tong and the Berserker we will know. If they plan to attack tomorrow, we must prepare. Li Po, I'm putting you in charge of gathering our warriors and arming them. Let the Berserker come, we'll be ready."

Chapter Forty-Three

Junior Melman pounded on the door of Lei Jiang's apartment. It was ten in the morning. Behind him, Tyrese Johnson blocked the weak light of the sun breaking through the fog.

The door was finally opened by a Chinese guy dressed in a robe the same bright orange as Junior's golf shirt. Junior slapped on his dealing-with-white-folks smile. Even though the man was Chinese, he had an air of authority about him clearly visible in his posture and his sharp-eyed stare.

"May I help you?"

Junior grinned wider and ducked his shoulders twice. "Hey, I'm just looking for Konrad or Lei. Either one of them around?"

The man turned and yelled into the apartment. "Lei, you have visitors."

"Just a moment, please. I'll go get her."

The Chinese guy actually shut the door in Junior's face and left them standing in the hall.

Tyrese pursed his lips and waved his index finger back and forth. "Why are we here anyway? It was my understanding that we have to take the bomb into the sewers."

Junior turned and looked Tyrese up and down. "Oh, and you think you can squeeze your big, queer ass through a manhole? There's another way down and this lady has the key."

The door opened and Lei stuck her head out. When she saw Junior, she smiled. "Oh, it's you. My father said there were two large black men at the door, and I couldn't imagine who he was talking about."

"Uh, Lei, we need to get into the sewers through your cellar. Ain't no way we can fit through no manhole."

"Sure, let me get the key to the basement. You guys want me to come along?"

Junior swung his big head back and forth. "Fuck no. Konrad would remove my, uh, my package and feed it to me."

The tiny Asian woman led them to the trap door and opened it. "When you're done, stop by and tell me how it went."

Junior nodded, pulled his backpack off and found a high-powered flashlight. "I'll sure do that."

When Lei was gone, Junior shined the light down the ladder. It seemed darker than the last time. "You got both swords?"

Tyrese dropped his big pack with the thermo-baric device, dug around in it and pulled out two Samurai swords. The katanas were wrapped in silk. When Junior bent over to pick them up, he noticed Tyrese's shoes.

"You wore white, Steven Madden's to go into the sewers? What were you thinking, Tyrese?"

"I was thinkin' I got to look good. I always look good."

Junior shook his head. Tyrese was about to get the surprise of his life.

They quickly descended into the tunnels. Junior fell down the last three feet of the ladder, while Tyrese, more nimble in spite of his great size, scampered down the ladder with ease.

The beam from the light licked the slime-covered walls as they lumbered down the narrow corridor and took the right turn toward the hole. A huge rat leaped off one of the pipes overhead, landed on Tyrese's shoulder and dove into a hole.

Tyrese's scream echoed throughout the tunnel system. Junior dropped the flashlight and covered the bouncer's mouth with his hand. "Shhhhhh. Shut your fucking mouth. You gonna be quiet?"

Tyrese's eyes were wide, showing white all the way around the iris. He nodded. When Junior removed his hand, Tyrese shuddered. "That was a rat, man, a big, fucking, ugly, slimy, hairy, rat."

Junior played the beam from the light over the walls. "Look, Tyrese, we got hordes of roaches, we got rats, and see that brown stuff floating in the ditch, it's shit."

Tyrese's eyes got bigger and bigger. "You never told me about all this when you asked me to come down here."

"I figured you knew. It's the mother-fucking sewer. And when we get there, don't look directly into the hole."

"I know, Junior, you already told me five times. Looking into the hole makes you sick. I can't imagine why you seem to think I can't remember the simplest thing. You're always nagging me, Junior, nag, nag...."

Tyrese's words died away. Ahead stood the biggest purple and black demon Junior had yet seen. This one was even bigger than the green one he and Konrad fought here before.

"Stop," Junior whispered. "Get me the BFG."

"What the hell is that?"

"Big Fucking Gun. Hand me the AR-15."

Tyrese dropped the pack quietly as they hugged the sewer wall. He pulled out the rifle fitted with the Elcan scope and handed it to Junior.

"Is that what I think it is?" he whispered.

"I don't know what you're thinking, Tyrese. That is a big motherfucking demon."

"Oh, my fucking god. Don't let it get me, Junior, please don't let it get me."

"I don't plan to let it get either of us."

Junior handed Tyrese the pack and sited down the barrel. The demon was about a hundred yards away, standing with its feet spread and its huge hands on its hips. He appeared to be watching something. Junior prayed it wasn't an entire family of weird ugly creatures coming through the doorway.

He fired two three-round bursts, placing the rounds in the demon's neck. Its big head blew off, completely severed by Junior's accurate shots, the surprised look still on its face. A fine mist of black blood sprayed the bricks and the concrete floor.

"Good shooting, Junior. Remind me to take you next time I go clubbing."

"Tyrese, if you talk about clubbing down here, you know I can't be responsible. Carry both them packs. I got to be ready. And hand me my sword."

Junior led the way toward the doorway. He carried the AR-15 in one meaty hand and the Samurai blade in the other. Rifle for demons, sword for vamps, you have to be prepared with the right weapon for the job.

When they got to the doorway, Junior shot a quick glance in the direction of the doorway. He didn't see anything coming out. The demon guard was dead, so he laid his rifle and sword down.

"Now hand me that bomb."

Tyrese stood two feet from the demon's headless corpse staring. "That's one ugly sum-bitch."

"Move away from the body. You're getting black blood on them white shoes."

Tyrese jumped out of the way and began pawing through the pack. He pulled the box with the bomb out mumbling a string of curses. Still talking to himself, he handed it to Junior.

"I don't know why I let you talk me into coming down here. It's filthy, crawling with bugs and it smells. In fact, I ain't never smelled anything this bad in my whole fucking life. I shoulda known better when you said you'd pay double. You don't pay double for nothing. I shoulda listened to my momma and never started hanging out with your sorry black ass in the first place. You ain't nothing but trouble. Now I'm standing next to a river of doodoo holding a bomb and trying not to look at the dead body of some night-walking . . ."

"Shhhhh, you know, there might be more of them."

"WHAT?" Tyrese handed Junior the bomb. "Then hurry, the fuck up."

Junior secured the bomb to the top of a huge pipe right over the doorway. He connected the detonator, set the timer for eight and backed slowly away. He was careful not to look directly into the opening, just a quick glance to reassure himself nothing was coming through.

"Let's go." He picked up the rifle and his sword and backed down the walkway.

Tyrese carried the packs as they slogged their way toward the ladder. When they were through the trap door, Junior took out his cell phone and sent Konrad a text. "The package has been delivered and set to blow at eight."

Tyrese bent down, wiped his shoes clean with a white handkerchief, lifted the trap and dropped the stained hanky into the darkness. "Praise Jesus, we got out of there alive."

Chapter Forty-Four

Konrad stared across the bay at Alcatraz Island. He could just make out the lighthouse poking through the thick bank of fog hanging over leaden water. This was the thickest fog he'd ever seen in the Bay area.

Thirteen tour boats bobbed on the rough water tied to slips inside a network of docks. Bumpers made of old tires protected them from smashing into the wooden walkways in the choppy seas. There was one big, fifty-foot craft. It looked like it would hold a hundred men. The rest of the boats were twenty-feet long or so and could maybe hold fifteen men and their gear in the rows of seats behind the captain's console and the wheel.

A chain-link fence and a gate ran across the dock to protect the boats. The gate was closed and padlocked. Golden Gate Tours must have shut down.

A square woman in a security-guard uniform rolled out of a small white building next to the dock. There was a big sign on the front of the building advertising tickets for tours to Alcatraz. The guard had stuffed herself into green pants two sizes too small. The loaded, black, Sam Browne belt cut her in two bulging halves then crossed her chest where it cut into her shoulder. She carried a telescoping baton and spoke into a radio as she swaggered toward Konrad.

Konrad walked to meet her as the ghostly shapes of white panel vans began pulling into the parking area.

"Why you hanging around the boats?" The security guard asked, as she repeatedly smacked the baton into her left hand. "These boats belong to Golden Gate Tours. If you're looking for a tour out to the Rock, service has temporarily been suspended due to some illegal activity out there on the island."

Konrad figured something like this would happen. He smiled and forced his vampire-enhanced mind into the woman's. Immediately, his own mind was filled with all kinds of crazy thoughts. She was thinking about whacking him with the baton, and seemed to believe she could subdue him because she'd taken some self-defense courses at the local Y. Her thoughts circled around her dinner, which was growing colder by the second in the white building and hitting him in the nuts with the baton.

"Where are the keys to the boats?"

Her eyes rolled back in her head and Konrad gave her a shake. Her thoughts focused on protecting a safe inside the building. The keys must be there.

As soon as she dropped her arms to her sides and her eyes glazed, he pushed her, and she fell over backwards. He grabbed her under her arms and dragged her into the building. Sure enough, a small key safe hung on the back wall.

Konrad smashed it with his fist, crumpling the door. He pushed the gray metal door aside, grabbed a handful of keys off the little hooks, and stashed the guard. As he ran back to the docks, he scanned the sky for Lung Ma. Kenna stood close to the locked gate concentrating.

"I don't know what you expect me to do," the teen complained. "I've been thinking the dragon's name, and I've been burning up my brain cells trying to contact her. This is just plain stupid. You're nuts if you think I can throw my thoughts in the air like tiny carrier pigeons. I can't do this."

"Stop bitching, Kenna, and keep trying. You heard her inside your head before. You can talk to her. Without the dragon, we got no hope of defeating Vetalas and the demons. You know this."

She un-squinted her eyes and glared at him. "I know we can't beat that killer with or without the dragon. You don't understand his power. I lived it. I saw with my own eyes what he can do."

Even with her pessimistic attitude, Kenna went back to squinting and digging her fingers into her temples. Konrad prayed the dragon would hear her.

Lei emerged from the fog and walked down the dock. She wore her kick-ass boots, a short, black leather skirt and a thick ribbed sweater. Her footsteps echoed off the boards.

When she reached him, she held her face up for him to kiss. "You look terrific," she said. "Your color is coming back."

Konrad looked away. His color was back because he'd trolled the Marina District late last night catching vampires. The vamps were preying on the prostitutes hanging out on the streets and draining them. Not only was his color heightened, but he was even stronger.

"Has she spoken to Lung Ma yet?" Lei asked as she moved closer to him and leaned against his side.

"She says she hasn't heard anything, and she doesn't believe she's gonna. I told her to broadcast a message telling the dragon we're headed for Alcatraz and to join us in the fight."

As Lei scanned the sky, wrinkles of worry creased her smooth forehead.

"We shouldn't have done it, Konrad. Our selfish act could have doomed the entire world."

"There's no point in crying over spilt milk. What's done is done. Is your father coming?"

She flicked her head." He's in one of those vans talking to Little Pete. They're the same age and seem to know a lot of the same people. I never knew China was so small."

"Little Pete?"

"Fong Jing, leader of the Chee Kung Tong. Everyone calls him Little Pete."

"How many men did they bring?"

"About two hundred."

Konrad slid the huge sword of his ancestors out of the scabbard on his back and swung it a few times. "Tell them to load into the boats. We're going with or without the dragon. We can't wait any longer."

Scary Larry, Munoz and Xavier Perry pulled up in a police car, climbed out and headed to the dock. Everyone was here but Lung Ma.

Larry parked himself next to Konrad, opened a package of Red Man chewing tobacco and pulled out a big wad. "Want some?" he mumbled as he worked an enormous brown wad into one corner of his jaw.

"No thanks."

"How about you guys?" Larry offered the package to Munoz and Perry. "I always go into battle with some chew. Helps get rid of the butterflies and keeps you alert. I remember back in Nam, I think it was in 71, I was just a kid. We were on this patrol and we got jumped by Charles. I swallowed half a bag of this shit. We were getting the holy crap shot out of us and I was shagging my dehydrated eggs into the bushes. But I still managed to take out five of the enemy."

Munoz actually accepted Larry's offer, taking a small clump and cramming it into a corner of his mouth. Konrad stared.

"What?" Munoz grinned. "I dip now and then, too. Takes the edge off just like Larry said. And it gives you one hell of a rush"

Konrad used his sword to cleave the chain locking the gate in two and push it aside. He and Larry jumped into the bigger boat. Munoz and Perry headed to others, keys in hand. The Tong swarmed the dock and quickly filled the boats.

When the boats were all started and idling, Konrad gave the signal to cast off. He backed the big boat out of the slip, turned it slowly and headed for the island followed by twelve smaller boats bursting at the seams with the Tong.

Lei, Kenna, Larry and Colonel Jiang crowded into the pilot house beside Konrad. They scanned the horizon as Konrad guided the boat across the choppy, gray water. A stiff westerly breeze kept pushing the boat toward the Golden Gate Bridge and the Pacific

Ocean. The current wanted to drag the craft that way as well. Konrad fought the driving forces of nature and kept the boat on a steady course toward Alcatraz.

Halfway across, Konrad spotted large shapes leaving the island flying in their direction. His stomach sank. He knew what he was seeing...demons.

With his enhanced vision, he made out the large green demon his mother had emasculated. The frightening creatures flew toward his armada on huge wings, legs dangling, arms outstretched.

"Tell the Tong we got company," Konrad said to Larry.

"Roger that," Larry said as he backed out of the small cabin.

"What are they?" Colonel Jiang demanded.

"Demons, Papa, big, ugly, green, and purple creatures that can fly."

"They eat people," Kenna added.

"I see they can fly. Where did they come from?"

"Through the doorway in the sewers. I explained all this to you."

Jiang shook his head. "I never imagined anything this terrible. They are so big."

The Tong readied their weapons in the open boats as the demons grew closer.

"Where's the dragon?" Konrad mumbled to himself. "Lung Ma we need you."

When the demons were close enough, the Tong opened fire. Konrad tried counting the nasty creatures and stopped at fifty. He saw one demon drop into the Bay. Then the screaming started as the ugly creatures snatched Tong fighters out of the open boats. Konrad increased his craft's speed, sending up a huge wake.

Larry stuck his head into the cabin. "They're dropping them into the water," he screamed.

Konrad looked behind just in time to see a Tong member plummet from the sky and crash into one of the boats with enough force to go right through it. Water rushed into the damaged craft and the Tong members inside leaped into the sea.

"They knew we were coming," Konrad screamed over the wind and the sound of gun fire.

"You got that right," Larry said. "They were tipped off."

Munoz circled the swimmers, plucking them out of the water into his already crowded boat. Perry must have figured out what Munoz was doing because he turned his boat and raced back to help.

More demons swooped down on the open boats. Scary Larry and three other men went to the stern and sprayed the demons with large-caliber bullets. Two more demons dropped into the water, guts hanging out, heads exploded, spraying black blood and gore across the seething Bay.

The heavy fire finally drove the demons back to Alcatraz as Konrad turned the boat to skirt the island and head for the docks.

"Look," he said to Lei, pointing at the water tower, the guard towers and the lighthouse looming out of the fog.

Hundreds of vampires hung out the windows. Each was armed with a rifle. When they turned the corner of the island and could see the dock, Konrad gasped. Demons and halflings like himself, crowded the dock and the road leading to it down the steep hill.

"Where is Lung Ma?" Lei cried.

Scary Larry stuck his head in the cabin. "You see that shit?"

Konrad shook his head. "If the dragon doesn't show, we're screwed."

Chapter Forty-Five

Konrad spun the wheel, turning the boat away from the dock toward the south. "Fuck the docks. We'll land the boats at Baker's Beach."

"That ain't a beach. It's just a small opening in the rocks," Larry held his hands flat like a ref saying no score. "We can't land these boats there. The rocks'll tear the bottom out of the bitches."

Konrad snarled. His Berserker persona was so tightly woven into his psyche, he felt like he was always in it now and could turn it on and off like a light switch. "I don't give a fuck. That's where we're going in. It's right behind the main cellblock and those assholes," he pointed at the army of half-vamps and demons waiting for them at the dock. "We'll have to trot across the island. We should have at least a few minutes to land without being massacred."

The boat shot forward as Konrad mashed the throttle lever. Behind their big boat, the rest of the armada turned and followed. When they got to the point where Konrad and Paige had emerged from the underwater pipe, Konrad pushed Larry toward the wheel.

"Take 'em in, Larry. I gotta go after Vetalas."

"You're gonna let us go in without you?"

"I'm still counting on the dragon showing up. This is the only way I'm gonna catch Vetalas with his pants down. I have to go in the back door."

Konrad made sure his sword was secure in the scabbard on his back and headed for the stern. Lei grabbed his arm. "Where are you going?"

"You know what I have to do. I'm going in through the drainpipes."

Her face crumpled. "No, Konrad, please don't do it. Stay with us. We'll make it into the prison. We'll get into the tunnel system."

He held her arms. "I'll be fine. I know the way in, and all their attention will be on you guys. I have to kill Vetalas or I'll never regain my humanity. Please understand."

Tears streamed down Lei's face. "I love you."

She held her palm out to him and he pressed his much-larger hand against it. "I love you. Stay close to your father and don't do anything stupid."

He turned, pushed his way through the crowd of Tong members, and dove over the stern.

*****

Lei watch as Konrad sliced through the choppy water. He turned once, waved and then disappeared beneath the turbulent gray sea. Feeling like her heart was a bleeding sore, she trudged back to the pilot house. Larry and her father stood close to the wheel arguing about the best spot to unload the men. Overhead, more demons dropped out of the fog and attacked the boats. This time they had guns.

Gun fire chopped into the men on the top deck. Screams erupted and the Tong returned fire. Lei hunkered down on a small bench in the back of the pilot house beside Kenna and covered her ears.

The girl's face was streaked with tears and her eyes huge. Lei wrapped an arm around the girl's shoulders. "You hear from the dragon?"

Kenna shook her head and sobbed.

Suddenly the roof exploded and the body of one of the green demons dropped into the wheelhouse. It was still alive. Colonel Jiang ripped his curved sword out of the scabbard at his waist and neatly sliced off its big repulsive head. Stinking, black blood flooded the floor.

Below, the bottom of the boat scraped a rock. Lei heard an ugly, rasping, grinding sound and the men on the bottom deck started screaming. When she looked out the window, she saw they were still twenty feet away from the island.

"Abandon ship," Larry yelled as he gunned the engine driving the boat forward onto more rocks.

Lei's father grabbed her elbow. "Get off the boat, girl. Now!"

Lei held Kenna's hand and they stumbled out of the wheelhouse.

The other boats had shallower drafts and were able to move closer to the beach. Anchors were tossed overboard, and men swarmed into the shallow water and up on the rocky shore. The big tour boat sank swiftly into four feet of churning bay. When Lei jumped in, the cold water was a shock.

She held her sword in one hand and tried to find her feet on the slippery, algae-covered rocks. Kenna clutched her arm, dragging her into the water. They both found some stable footing as Larry grabbed one of her arms and her father grabbed Kenna, towing them onto the rock-strewn beach.

The ten-foot strip of beach was edged by a wall of jumbled rocks. The army of Tong scampered out of the water and up the tumbled mass. Lei followed her father, still wearing his saffron-colored robes, now wet and dripping sea water, up the hill.

It was a difficult climb. Some of the rocks were so large they had to maneuver around them. At times they were able to move rapidly. When Lei looked up, she saw the first halfling vampire waiting at the top.

Larry pulled his .44 and fired five rounds from the big gun, all into the vamp's head. It exploded, and Larry grunted. "One down, five hundred more to go."

More vamps followed, and a dark shadow passed above Lei. She glanced behind and screamed. A huge demon reached for Kenna, claws extended. Without thinking, she drew the Samurai blade and sliced its claws off. Black blood sprayed her face and her lips. It tasted like putrid flesh. Gagging, she wiped her mouth.

More and more vamps and demons arrived. The Tong was pinned on the side of the rock face taking on heavy fire while the demons picked off one man after another, hauled them out to sea, and dumped them.

Larry and Colonel Jiang forced her and Kenna to hide beneath them in the shadow of a huge boulder. Larry used his rifle to destroy one demon but more kept coming.

It looked like they would have to retreat to the boats as casualties mounted and the fog-shrouded sun sank toward the horizon. When it was dark, the true vampires would come after them and they would be overrun.

*****

Konrad hated to leave Lei and Kenna. He felt like he could do so much more if he entered the nest from below. Maybe he would surprise Vetalas, catch him napping and kill him quickly. And this move might be their only hope of winning the war. If Lung Ma didn't show up, his being on the inside was their last secret weapon.

He shot one final look at Lei's sad face and dove beneath the choppy sea. It took him several attempts, but he finally found the algae-covered pipes. The green, waving, hair-like tendrils of algae completely covered the opening. He shot to the surface, took several deeps breaths and saw the big tour boat round the point and head for the miniscule stretch of beach. Then he dove deep and shot into the pipe.

It was easier this time. He made it out of the pipe and into the tide pool at the bottom of the mine without running out of air. He was stronger, much stronger. With sword in hand, he clambered over the scattered rocks, found the cart path and climbed.

At the top, he stopped to listen. He was in the deepest part of the island's underground system, but he could still hear activity above. He decided to try the wall at the end of the ancient cellblock he and Paige explored in their trip through these tunnels.

He could see without the aid of a flashlight, picking up his and Paige's footprints clearly in the dust as he strode toward the bricked-up wall at the end of the row of cells.

It looked formidable, the bricks faded, chipped in places, and worn. Old graffiti from the 1800's stood out in black charcoaled swipes. Sergeant Bradshaw had carved his name in a corner and there were a lot of black hash-marks. Endless days chalked off one by one.

He placed a hand on the wall, feeling for vibrations, then he tapped. It sounded thick. Oh well, this was no time to lose confidence or worry about headaches.

He got a running start and charged the wall. Using his broad shoulder instead of his head, Konrad rammed the bricks. The wall exploded from the strength of his impact. He went right through, hit a woven, wall-hanging, smashed into a huge slab of wood, went through that and fell into a king-sized bed with a black, velvet coverlet, wall-hanging wrapped around his head.

Tearing the tapestry off his face, he scrambled out of the bed and crouched low with his sword ready. But there weren't any vamps in the room which he quickly recognized as belonging to Vetalas. He'd rammed through the wall behind the king vamp's bed and taken out one of the weird pieces of fabric art.

He recognized the opulent décor, the crazy wall hangings, and the thick carpet. A pair of black, fuzzy slippers sat neatly lined up at the foot of the huge bed. He'd seen them before on Vetalas's big, vampire feet.

When he glanced behind, he saw bricks scattered across the black velvet cover. The door to the room was closed and luckily there were no women sleeping in the bed. The big green recliner was empty and the flat screen TV off.

Konrad placed his ear against the closed door. The room on the other side had teemed with vampires and their slaves the last time he was here. He didn't hear a thing. All of the vamps must be either sleeping or massing for an attack on Larry and the forces.

He checked his watch. Shit! It was already five-thirty. Only ten more minutes of daylight remained.

Sucking in a big lungful of air, he opened the door a crack. It immediately smashed into him with so much force he flew backwards.

"I see you have returned, Berserker."

It was Marcelus, Vetalas's second in command, the one who turned Paige. Konrad growled. He had a score to settle with this asshole. Crouching, he held the huge blue-silver sword of his ancestors in his right hand. The runes along the blade glowed with white fire.

"You'll be the first vamp I take out with this little sword of mine. I can't wait to slice off your ugly head."

Marcelus laughed and swooped across the room like a streak of lightening. It was an obvious attempt to flank him. Konrad turned just as fast as Marcelus and faced the vamp.

Not laughing any more, Marcelus hissed and dove for Konrad. The vamp's teeth were out, and his face drawn into a mask of hate, eyes slits, nostrils flared. Konrad stood ready, his sword in both hands. When Marcelus closed on him, Konrad switched the sword to his right hand and sliced deep into Marcelus's left arm. The sword hung for a second in the vamp's shoulder blade, then sliced off Marcelus's arm and half his shoulder.

The vampire screamed as red blood sprayed across Konrad, but he didn't stop. He flew at Konrad snagging a choking hold on his throat with the one hand he had left. Inch-long claws dug into the flesh of Konrad's neck. The pain and the strength in the creature's hand were incredible. Konrad ignored it, moved his grip higher on the sword and stabbed the vamp in the stomach, driving the blade deep and upward.

Marcelus's scream of agony was cut short as the sword of Konrad's ancestors emerged from the vampire's mouth. The hand around his throat relaxed as Konrad grasped the hilt of the sword with two hands and sliced upward again, this time cleaving the vampire's stomach and chest in two. Flames erupted from Marcelus's open mouth. Konrad leaped out of the way taking his sword with him as the vampire exploded sending globs of melted gore everywhere.

Backing up, Konrad stared at the sword. "Now that's what I call a weapon."

He stood staring at the dead vamp for a minute thinking. Marcelus was Paige's maker. Maybe his death freed her. And then maybe Vetalas had to die to free all of them. He didn't have time to ponder the philosophy or vampire mechanics.

A sound from the other room grabbed Konrad's attention. He turned his head just in time to see Vetalas shove through the door dressed in a black, gilded-leather breastplate strapped on over a black and gold silk tunic. Dressed for war, Vetalas stood in the doorway.

The king vamp carried a huge sword in one hand and a smaller Roman gladius in the other. "Well, Berserker, I see you have come to try to best me." His smile showed long incisors and a mouthful of other sharp teeth. "Many have tried, and all have failed."

Chapter Forty-Six

As the sun slid beneath the ocean, Lei's hopes for a swift victory died and her heart sank. Far out to sea, roiling black clouds sent jagged shafts of lightning toward the water. The clouds looked to be headed this way.

Half of the two hundred Tong members were close to cresting the hill when hundreds of vampires attacked. The vampires smothered the Tong in a wave of fangs and claws. Tong fighters plummeted down the hill, sucked dry, their throats torn to shreds.

"We have to retreat," Munoz yelled to Larry.

"In what?" Larry screamed and pointed to the big tour boat, half underwater, sloshing back and forth in the waves.

"The other boats won't hold all of us." Scary Larry grabbed two grenades off his equipment belt, pulled the pin on one and lobbed it as hard as he could up the hill. The explosion sent parts of demons and vampires spinning down the hill.

He tossed the other one farther. It flew over the top rocks and exploded. A wave of vamps flew into the air. But the Tong was still being overwhelmed. Fighters turned, scrambled and fell down the rocky cliff.

Red Chua had an RPG. Larry saw Red load a round in it and jumped three rocks to grab his arm. Lei heard him scream at Red over the sound of shouted orders, dying Tong members and shrieking vampires.

"Fire high or you'll kill your own men."

Red nodded, his eyes huge. Larry laughed, then shot a wad of brown juice out of his mouth. "Fire away, pal."

The Tong leader dropped to one knee and pulled the trigger. The missile shot up the hill, over the top, and seconds later the earth shook as it detonated.

Red fired his two remaining rounds, tossed the useless weapon aside, and shouldered his way toward Larry and Munoz. "My guys are getting destroyed. There's too many of the bastards. We need to fall back."

Lei poked her finger in Red's chest. "We have to fight. Konrad is down there somewhere looking for Vetalas. We have to hold on until he succeeds in killing their maker."

She might be a woman, but Lei was a fighter. Hiding under a man didn't suit her style at all. Pulling the samurai sword, she turned to Kenna to tell her to stay on the hillside with Colonel Jiang.

When she saw Kenna, she froze. The girl stared off into the distance, her eyes wide and her mouth hanging open. Kenna blinked and looked up at Lei, blue eyes misted with tears. "I hear her. She's coming."

Lei grabbed Kenna's black T-shirt. "Who's coming?"

Kenna pointed toward the Golden Gate Bridge and the ocean. Lei squinted. Against the backdrop of angry dark clouds one black spot moved swiftly toward them. In seconds, Lei saw huge wings and the icy-blue body of Lung Ma.

Lei punched Larry. "She's coming!"

"Who?" Larry yelled.

Lei pointed and her father, Larry, Munoz and Red all stared.

"The ice dragon has heard our call," Colonel Jiang said.

As Lung Ma swooped closer, Lei saw the dragon carried a rider. Pale, blonde hair gleamed in the failing daylight. The sight of the dragon winging its way toward the island sent goosebumps shivering up and down her arms. Her heart lifted, and she screamed with joy. "We're saved."

Lance left Lung Ma's back and flew toward them while the dragon swooped low over the island spraying something out of her mouth. Vampires that were hit by the liquid smoked and screamed at the same time.

"You brought her, Lance," Lei yelled over the noise of battle.

"Yeah, she was out there playing in the surf with the seals. I saw her first thing when I woke up and I thought, dude, isn't Konrad attacking Alcatraz tonight? So, I got my board and paddled out. Turns out she can hear me fine, she just don't like the way a vampire's mind feels in her head. So, she was ignoring me that day I was trying to tell her about Konrad's mom."

Lei hugged the surfer. "You did a wonderful thing bringing her here, Lance. I guess she couldn't hear Kenna."

"Oh, she said she could hear her, she just thought it was some kid messing with her mind. She says she has a lot of voices in her head all the time, mostly children. She was, uh, she was wondering why she couldn't hear you and Konrad anymore."

Lei felt her cheeks heat. "I know, Lance, we shouldn't have done it. Many men suffered and some probably died because we were selfish. I'll have to live with that for the rest of my life."

"I wouldn't let it bother you, Lei. You had to become a woman some time. And, uh, you know, like, Konrad loves you."

Lung Ma's arrival turned the tide of the battle. As Lei watched, a bloodsucker coming over the top of the hill got sprayed. It immediately spun in a circle, face twisted in agony, then burst into flames. When the spray hit humans, nothing happened.

"What's in the venom?" Lei asked her father.

"The monks told me the dragons were bred to kill demons. Over the centuries, their venom has become so deadly the tiniest drop kills a vampire but is harmless to humans. I have no idea what the chemical components are. I imagine there is more than a little magic involved because as you must know, the dragons are very magical creatures. They are among the few left on this planet."

With the dragon spraying venom over the vampires, Red led his fighters over the top of the hill. Lei, Kenna, Lance and her father followed. Scary Larry and Munoz were in the front of the soldiers swarming onto the road leading around the island.

"Be careful, Lance," Lei said as they climbed the hill. "Lung Ma can kill you, too. And I'd hate to see anything happen to you."

When they reached the top, Lei saw Lung Ma dive low across the open parade grounds filled with demons and vampires. She sprayed venom over them, and the ones hit burst into flaming ruin. It looked as though the Tong fighters would win. The forces of light would conquer the forces of evil.

The first rumbles of thunder shook the island and Lei felt a few splatters of rain. *Great, just what they needed, a storm.*

Lei saw Red fighting with a demon and ran forward to help him with her samurai sword in hand. He fired several bursts into the creature from his rifle, but it kept coming for him. When she scanned the skies for the dragon, Lei saw there was no hope she would arrive in time to save Red from the huge demon. Lei raced to his aide as another rumble of thunder shook the heavens and a jagged bolt of lightning illuminated the sky.

It took only two swipes from the razor-sharp sword to sever the ugly creature's head. Red grinned at her. "Thanks. I lost my sword back there on the hill. I thought I was a goner."

They stood side by side catching their breath and watching Lung Ma clear the island of demons. Suddenly, the dragon seemed to stutter in mid-air. Her wings looked as though they were unable to work together. Lung Ma began to fall and spin in a death spiral toward the rocks near the lighthouse.

Lei gasped. "What's wrong with her?"

Red scanned the horizon. "There," he pointed. "It's Li Po. He's got some kind of machine in his hands."

A vampire Lei recognized as the ex-leader of the Tong stood on the roof of the main cellblock holding a black box.

Lung Ma lay on the ground squirming and clawing at her head. A whining noise built inside Lei's mind. It sounded like a thousand bees and it hurt. She grabbed her skull. "Li Po is killing Lung Ma with whatever's in that box. We have to stop him."

Red shoved a fresh clip into his rifle. "I'll go."

The pain in her head slowly lessened, and the sound faded. She looked for the dragon. Lung Ma stood on the road next to the main cellblock weaving back and forth. But she'd stopped trying to claw her head off.

"I'll go with you."

They jogged up the road leading to the big two-story, concrete-block building. The old blocks were yellow with age, the windows broken. Lights illuminated the roof, and floodlights set all across the island cast an eerie yellow glow. With the dragon down, the fight escalated. Lei could hear the screams of the wounded, the shrieks of the demons, and Scary Larry roaring his battle cry.

"Hurry, Red. We have to get to Li Po."

When they got to the door of the main cellblock, their way was blocked by three female vampires. Red opened up on them with his rifle and Lei swung her sword. The two of them blew through the group at the door and raced up the stairs. When they reached the small doorway leading to the roof, Red stopped.

"This is my fight. Li Po was my leader. I must be the one to kill him."

"Take the sword," Lei said.

Red grabbed the sword from her, and they pushed through the door. Black tar and gravel covered the flat roof. Sheets of rain poured out of the sky creating puddles on the asphalt. Li Po stood alone at the edge of the roof fiddling with the controls of a black box.

"Hand me the box, Li Po," Red yelled.

Li Po looked up and grinned, showing long fangs. "It is you, Red Chua, my trusted lieutenant." Li Po glanced down and turned a small knob on the side of the box. "We have defeated your secret weapon, Red. The dragon is down. Soon she will die and Vetalas will lead us to world domination."

"I can't let that happen." Red circled to the left of Li Po trying to get behind him.

Lei inched toward the low concrete-block ledge around the roof. When she was close enough, she saw Lung Ma struggling to rise. An enormous green demon strode toward her carrying a gun. Lei recognized it as the gun that almost killed the dragon back in China Town.

"Red, they're going to shoot Lung Ma!" Lei screamed and turned to run back through the door and down the steps. But more vampires had emerged from the cellblock. They closed in on Red and Lei.

"You'll never get off this roof in time to save her," Li Po said. He set the black box down on the ledge and turned to Red. "It no longer matters whether the thought disrupter works or not. Lineus will finish her off and then all of you will die."

Red lunged at Li Po with the sword, but the vampire was quick. He circled behind Red and grabbed him by the throat, clawing at his face and neck. Red slashed Li Po with the sword, hacking a chunk out of his head. The vampire didn't stop or slow down even when his brains spilled onto his white, button-down shirt.

Red hacked again and again as Li Po buried his fangs in Red's throat. Li Po's left arm flew off, and blood sprayed everywhere. Lei screamed and bashed the vampire's open skull with the butt of Red's rifle, then turned to destroy the horrible box.

Li Po fell to the roof and Red followed him with the sword, hacking and chopping until the vampire shriveled up and turned black.

Lei helped Red to his feet, then grabbed his hand and dragged him to the roof edge. They stared helplessly as Lineus took aim and fired at Lung Ma from ten feet away.

Chapter Forty-Seven

Vetalas seemed so confident, dressed in his opulent Roman armor, carrying two swords like he was some kind of ancient hero. Konrad raised the sword of his ancestors. The runes on the side sparkled like diamonds. They circled, weapons held ready.

Konrad struck first. He swung with lightening swiftness at Vetalas's head. But the vampire was gone.

When he whirled around looking for his target, Vetalas struck him in the shoulder with his short sword. Blood leaked out of the open wound and down Konrad's shirt for a second then dried and the wound closed. Konrad backed against the wall as Vetalas advanced on him.

"You're no match for me Berserker. I possess your power and the strength of my three thousand years. You're an insignificant speed bump in my plans to take over this world. Pray now to whatever gods you believe in because you'll be joining them soon."

Konrad refused to be drawn into Vetalas's glamour spell. He knew the vampire was trying to use the sound of his voice and the magic of his mind to hypnotize him.

"Shut the fuck up, Vetalas. That shit doesn't work on me." Konrad lunged at the vampire with his long sword, caught him by surprise and nicked his fancy armor. When the tip of the sword touched Vetalas on the neck, he screamed and fell back. Konrad saw an angry red burn where the sword just brushed the vampire's flesh.

Feeling he had a temporary advantage, Konrad pushed forward swinging and slashing with the big sword. He felt for his Berserker strength, slid into the familiar rage, growled and flew across the space between them, sword ready.

Vetalas was shocked when Konrad took off, flying towards him. Konrad saw the surprise in Vetalas's wide opened eyes and mouth.

"I can fly, too, you son of a bitch." Konrad slashed his big sword and felt it glance off the vampire's leather breastplate.

Turning at the wall, he stopped. Vetalas was on the other side of the chamber, swords ready. He took off shooting straight at Konrad. Konrad took off at the same time. They clashed in the middle of the room with a huge clang of metal on metal. Konrad's Berserker strength filled him, and his big sword broke the vampire's long sword.

Vetalas turned and darted out the open door. Konrad flew after him. In the antechamber, Vetalas turned and flew at Konrad again. Konrad was in full Berserker mode. He screamed and shook his head sending saliva everywhere. Then he began counting his breathes, matching them to his heartbeat. When Konrad slowed his heartbeat, time slowed.

Even at top speed, Vetalas could not move fast enough to avoid Konrad's sword. Konrad had changed the speed of passing time. When he swung, he hacked part of Vetalas's left arm off below the elbow. The vampire's shriek was earsplitting. The flesh of Vetalas's forearm sizzled and smoked. The vampire whirled and flew out of the antechamber and into the dark tunnels beneath Alcatraz.

Konrad followed the vampire using his enhanced vision and senses. He smelled the coppery odor of Vetalas's blood and burnt flesh trailing like an intoxicating aroma through the damp underground passages. The vampire shot through tunnel after tunnel, gradually heading toward the surface. Vetalas flew up a steep stairwell and emerged into the night in what had to be the building housing the prison generators, huge squat monster machines from the forties. A smokestack sat next to the building.

Across the Bay, Konrad saw the lights of the city shimmering through sheets of heavy rain. A clap of thunder startled him, and he looked up in time to see lightning flicker and arc across the sky.

Vetalas was running from him. The knowledge made Konrad's head spin. The oldest most powerful demon on the planet was afraid of him. When Vetalas took to the sky, Konrad lost him in the rain and clouds. Freaking out, filled with the fear that all his hopes for redemption would vanish with the vampire, Konrad put on a burst of speed. He finally spotted the evil creature heading toward the city so fast he was only a streak of gold and black.

Konrad closed the gap between them an inch at a time. Air rushed by his head at high speed. His eyes ran with tears and he squinted to keep from losing his quarry. He held his sword ready as he streaked toward the escaping vampire.

When he pulled next to Vetalas, they both hurtled through the air at high speed. Konrad slashed at Vetalas, and landed a hard blow across the vampire's leather covered back. Vetalas screeched, held his short sword with both hands and lunged at Konrad who had his silver sword raised over his head. Lightning struck the two blades sending sparks flying and a jolt of electricity through Konrad. Blinded by driving rain, he spun out of control and plummeted toward the black water.

Once again, fear of losing Vetalas, forced him to find more power. He reached deep, chanted his mantra, and touched his Berserker self. The lightning strike seemed to be adding to his store of energy. Using every bit of all his strengths, Konrad hit the water dove deep, and turned toward the surface. He shot back into the sky chasing Vetalas.

Far ahead, he saw the vampire shoot into the city, move closer to the ground, rush through the streets and slow. He even saw Vetalas look over his shoulder. Vetalas must think he'd lost Konrad in the dark and the driving rain. But that was good, because Konrad was able to catch up and keep track of him. At Embarcadero, Vetalas shot underground into the Bay Area Rapid Transit (BART) system.

It was getting late. Konrad saw the big clock on the wall in the BART station. Five minutes until eight. Junior was supposed to blow the doorway at eight.

Vetalas hesitated at the entrance to the subway tunnel and Konrad closed in. He grabbed Vetalas by the ankle and pulled. They tumbled and rolled with Konrad coming out on top. He swung his sword, but Vetalas was able to catch the bigger blade on his short sword and shove it aside.

The vampire shrieked and attacked, grabbing and pushing Konrad under him with a huge burst of strength. Konrad fell back onto the rails of the subway, his sword beneath his body. Vetalas sank his teeth into Konrad's shoulder. Konrad roared with fury and threw the creature off. As more power flowed into him, Konrad leaped on top of Vetalas, grabbed his throat and started to tear off the vampire's head.

With a mighty heave, Vetalas rolled away and escaped Konrad's grip. The vampire ripped a metal door off its hinges, tossed it aside, and dove into the dark opening. Konrad was right behind him.

They jetted through the tiny passages with Konrad tight on Vetalas's heels. When the tunnels opened into the sewer, Konrad saw a sign on the wall, Powell Street. The doorway must be close by. If Junior detonated the bomb now, they could be caught in the explosion.

Vetalas pressed his arms to his side and increased his speed, flying along next to shit river. Konrad followed. He saw the room where Lei had hidden the egg. They flew by the corridor leading to her basement. When the passage opened up and the doorway into Vetalas's world appeared, the vampire didn't hesitate. This must have been his plan all along. Hide in his own world, then come back and continue to feed off Konrad's people.

Vetalas looked over his shoulder once, laughed showing long fangs, and then dived through the doorway. Konrad didn't even have to think. He shot through it after him. If Vetalas didn't die, Konrad would never be human again.

*****

Lei covered her eyes and screamed. The sound of the huge gun going off echoed across the island.

Red grabbed her arm. "Lei, look, one of the vampires took the bullet for the dragon."

"What?" Lei opened her eyes. "Oh god, please don't let it be Lance." When she looked, she saw the surfer vamp lying in a crumpled heap on the ground. "No, no, no, not Lance."

Lance must have stepped in front of the gun. He lay shattered in front of Lung Ma.

"I have to go to him." Lei picked up the samurai sword and raced for the doorway. In no mood to be stopped, she attacked the four vamps and a demon guarding the exit. Lei tore into them whirling, slashing, kicking and hacking. The first one went down sliced in two with one wicked stroke. The second one attacked her with its fangs bared. Lei roundhouse kicked it in the head as she struck the demon in the shoulder with her sword.

Red came to help, wasting the last two vamps with a barrage of large caliber bullets. The two ran down the steps and out into the open. Red protected her as she ran to Lance. Lung Ma cradled the destroyed vampire in her claws.

The dragon's beautiful eyes spun as she gazed at Lei. Kenna ran up with Colonel Jiang. "She says Lance gave his life for her."

The demon was a smoking ruin behind Lei. She looked once and saw the elephant gun laying in a puddle of black goo.

"She says she killed Lineus for Lance and she says she's going to give Lance his dearest wish because he made the ultimate sacrifice."

Lei looked around. "She better hurry. We're surrounded."

Vampires and demons circled them, slowly closing in. Scary Larry and the Tong were still fighting further down the road. Lei heard the screams and gunshots.

The dragon covered Lance's face with one huge claw and closed her eyes. Lance immediately stirred and groaned. Lung Ma gently laid Lance on the ground and launched her big body into the air. She swooped down on the surrounding vamps and began hosing them.

Lei sat beside Lance's head and lifted him into her lap. Lance groaned and rubbed his forehead. "What happened?

"You saved the dragon's life. You jumped between her and Lineus."

"I did? What was I thinking?"

"Lance, you saved her. She said she gave you your dearest wish."

Lance lifted one hand and looked at it. He pinched himself. "Ow! That's really intense. It hurts. Put your hand on my heart, Lei. Can you feel it beating?"

Lei laid one hand on Lance's chest. "I sure do."

"How 'bout my eyes? Are they red?"

Lei looked closely into Lance's eyes. They shone bright blue with clear whites. "Nope, they're blue."

"She made me human." Tears, clear tears, ran down Lance's cheeks. "I can surf in the sun again. I can eat cheeseburgers. I can get a tan." Lance's eyes opened wide. "Bummer man, now I can die."

Chapter Forty-Eight

Konrad rolled across hot asphalt into Vetalas's world, and leaped to his feet, braced for the worse. He had no idea what was on this side of the doorway. When he looked up, he saw Vetalas standing in front of him with his hands on his hips and a big grin plastered across his gaunt features.

Vetalas held both fists in the air and yelled. It was a scream of victory. Apparently, his forearm and hand had grown back the minute he entered this plane.

Konrad stared at the world around him. Rusted cars and trucks were piled on top of each other against the curb in an effort to clear some kind of trail. It looked like he was on a major road. Smoke billowed from homes and apartments to the west. Skeletons and skulls were scattered everywhere. A huge full moon flooded the road with eerie blue light out of a sky filled with puffy cumulus clouds. Drifting smoke billowed and then cleared away on the sea breeze. He could definitely smell the ocean through the stench of death and smoke. The Pacific had to be close by.

"You're in my world now, Berserker. Here, I have unlimited power. You will not best me in my house. Your only choice is to join me."

Vetalas closed the distance between them in a single move. Vampires and demons appeared from behind the cars and open doorways. They circled Konrad and Vetalas. Their starved faces and hungry eyes followed his every move.

Inside his head, Konrad felt Vetalas push, worming his way into inner thoughts as though searching for secrets. His eyes grew unbearably heavy. Vetalas was telling the truth. He must have twice the power here as he had in Konrad's world. Konrad tried to shove Vetalas out of his mind and failed.

When Vetalas saw he'd successfully glamoured Konrad, he strolled over, his footsteps quiet in the Roman sandals, and threw an arm around him. "When we go back to your world, we'll work together. If I could, I'd force you to kill and feed here, but there's a sorry lack of humans in this world and feeding on a rat just won't do the trick. When we go back through the doorway, you'll still be under this spell and you'll help me defeat the dragon and populate your planet with more of the Chosen."

Konrad searched inside his soul for the power to expel Vetalas from his mind. It was as though here, Vetalas gained strength, while Konrad's slipped away. He couldn't find enough power to throw off Vetalas's hold, so he fed his Berserker persona rage.

"I will never work with you," Konrad ground out between his teeth one word at a time. He fed more anger into his soul, thinking of all the things in his life that had pissed him off, starting with his father's death, his mother's accident, and ending with Vetalas feeding on Paige. As his fury grew, so did his strength. He balled it all up in a corner of his mind until he had a seething mass of hot, ferocious rage boiling just out of Vetalas's control. He blocked out Vetalas's words, forced himself not to listen, and when his anger was strong enough, he released it.

Roaring like a wild animal, Konrad exploded out of Vetalas's grip, turned his sword toward the vampire and hacked, aiming for his head. Vetalas parried swiftly, his blade up and ready for the huge blow. The clang of the two swords meeting was deafening. Konrad attacked again and again each blow harder. Vetalas parried every one, just managing to keep Konrad from cleaving his head in two.

On the last stroke, Konrad saw the dial of his watch. It read eight o'clock. Shit, shit, Junior was going to blow the doorway any second and he'd be stuck here with this crowd for all eternity.

His momentary distraction allowed Vetalas to enter his mind again. This time the ancient vampire's push cleared all of Konrad's thoughts away. All he could hear was Vetalas's voice echoing inside his head.

"Come with me, Berserker. Together we will rule your earth for all eternity. Just you and I will possess all the power in the world. Every woman will be ours. Every man will fall at our feet as either food or new conscripts to our army of demons and vampires."

The hypnotic tone and the overpowering presence of Vetalas in his mind smothered Konrad's ability to think. He felt warm all over and the nagging thoughts of destruction and love floated just out of reach. He couldn't grab them and hold onto them.

The moon burst from behind a cloud and a sudden shaft of moonlight struck the blade of his sword. The bright light hit him in the eye and broke Vetalas's glamour spell.

In a blinding instant, he was fully aware of his situation, the ticking clock and the crowd of hungry bloodsuckers closing in. Leaping into action, he swung hard and smashed the unsuspecting vampire's gladius with so much power and strength, the thinner blade of his ancestor's sword shattered, breaking into two pieces. He was left with a short blade about a foot long, with a jagged point.

Vetalas's evil laugh rang out when the sword broke. "I see that fabulous sword is really nothing but a piece of shit. You're mine now Berserker."

And the vampire was on him, moving in for the kill.

"If you won't work with me, my child, then you will die."

*****

"Where's Konrad?" Lance asked, weaving to his feet. He leaned on Lei. "Where's big old Sledge?"

Tears sprang into Lei's eyes. "I don't know. He dove off the boat. He said he was going to find Vetalas."

Rain poured out of the sky. Wet, scared, and worried, Lei took Lance's arm. "Come on, let's get out of the rain."

Lei led her little group to the nearby shelter of the abandoned residential apartments. Her father, Lance, Kenna and Red stood shivering under an overhang protecting the front door while Lung Ma

311

swooped back and forth across the island with single-minded determination, hunting vampires and demons, and spraying them with venom.

"I think I need to find Sledge," Lei said. "I can't stand not knowing what's happening."

A bright flash of lightning briefly illuminated the island. In the brief moment of illumination, Lei saw two figures shoot out of the generator building at the island's other end and head for the city. One of the figures was huge and unmistakable.

"Look, Sledge can fly." Lance said, grinning.

Lei's father growled and shook his head. "I told you he was a demon. He's probably joined up with that other bloodsucker."

"Don't ever talk about him like that." Lei snarled, stormed out from under their sheltering nook and headed across the island. "Come on, Kenna. Let's go find Scary Larry and get off this rock."

It didn't take long to find Larry, Munoz, and Perry. They were high-fiving each other, celebrating their victory. Larry pulled cigars out of his inner vest pocket and handed them out. "To victory."

He lit his cigar and passed around the lighter so all his friends could fire up their stogies.

Lei grabbed Larry's elbow. "Lieutenant, Konrad flew off the island after Vetalas. We need to find them." She looked at her watch. It was five minutes to eight. A shiver rippled up her backbone. Junior said he set the bomb to blow at eight.

"If the Jolly Green giant can fly, how the fucking hell do you expect me to find him?"

Tears sprang into Lei's eyes. "I don't know, but I have a really bad feeling. That bomb is set to go off in five minutes."

Larry wrapped an arm around Lei's shoulders. "Darlin', we can't stop it and why would we want to? Do you think Konrad went into the sewers?"

She sniffed and wiped her nose on the back of her sleeve. "I don't know. I just have a really bad feeling. I think something awful is about to happen."

"I'm gonna round up my men and get off this rock," Red said. "You guys coming?"

Larry nodded. "Damn right. I've had enough of these bloodsucking, sons of bitches for one day.

Lei allowed herself to be led toward Baker Beach and the boats. "Paige and Baby will want to know what happened."

Kenna walked along beside her as they headed toward the rocky hill leading to the beach. "I can't believe Paige didn't come. She said she wanted to be in on the kill."

"Baby refused to part with her darling."

Lung Ma swooped to the crest of the hill and parked, tail swishing, eyes spinning.

Kenna froze, her head tilted to one side. She grabbed Lei, her eyes wide with horror. "She says Sledge has gone through the doorway."

*****

Konrad stared at the broken sword for only an instant. If he didn't get his ass out of this world right now, he was going to find himself a permanent resident. His only hope was to slow time again. Measuring his breathes, he felt time slow to a crawl. He could see individual droplets of sweat flying in slow motion off his arm as he lunged for Vetalas with his broken sword.

Vetalas screamed and swung his short sword at Konrad's head. With time slowed, the sound was deep, and the scream lasted forever, while Vetalas's right arm slowed to a crawl. Konrad saw the blow coming, easily dodged it, and hacked off the hand holding it. He chose his target carefully and drove the jagged point of his blade deep into Vetalas's heart. When he snatched the broken blade out of the vampire's chest, a thick, gout of black blood erupted from the hole. The black blood looked exactly like demon blood and smelled just as terrible.

313

When Vetalas dropped to the asphalt, Konrad turned, hunting frantically for the doorway. He saw a disturbed spot in the air above the road, a rippling motion kind of like heat off a desert highway. Desperate to get back to his own world before Junior's bomb permanently closed the door, Konrad dove for the spot.

His big feet tripped over a skull and he fell forward. He stopped himself from taking a nasty header with his hands, one still holding the broken blade. Konrad saw movement behind him reflected in a puddle of water. He flipped over and flung the broken sword as hard as he could. It flew straight as an arrow shot from a cross bow into Vetalas's right eye. The vampire erupted in flames and a jet of fire blew out of his screaming, open mouth.

Konrad felt weird. Maybe he was changing back into a human. Terrified he would not make it through the doorway before Junior's bomb blew it shut, he slowed his breathing and his heart rate, and stopped time yet again. He gathered his strong legs under him and propelled his body through the doorway.

Just as his head passed into the gate between worlds, a huge explosion ripped the very fabric of the universe. Konrad was shot into nothingness. His ears roared with noise and pain as he was consumed by an intense black void.

Chapter Forty-Nine

Lei leaped off the boat at the dock, checking her watch again. It was almost ten o'clock. It had taken them forever to load all the injured men on the boats and then travel the rough bay to the tour company's dock.

Red ordered his men to meet them. Timmy Po ran down the dock when he saw the first boat tie off in a slip. He was out of breath when he got to Red and Lei.

"Honorable Red," Timmy gasped. "A huge explosion rocked China Town at exactly eight. Powell Street collapsed at the Clay Street intersection."

Lei grabbed Timmy's leather jacket. "Did you see Sledge?"

Timmy carefully disengaged Lei's grasping fingers. "Uh, no. Were we supposed to be looking for him?"

The floating boards of the dock began rocking. Lei felt Scary Larry come up behind her.

"Don't worry, Lei. We'll go look for him right now," he said. "Just give me a minute to evac the wounded.

Lei turned and buried her face in Larry's big chest. "I'm so worried. I don't want to live if Konrad is dead."

He patted her awkwardly on the back. Her father came up and took her in his arms. "Everything will turn out exactly the way it's supposed to, my daughter. There is little you can do to change the course of fate."

Lei pushed away from him and brushed the tears off her face. "So that's your philosophy. I guess that's how you explain leaving me and Mother alone all the time while you did your duty to your country. A country that tried to have you arrested and tried for desertion after all your years of loyal service. You were helpless to buck the tide of fate. Well, I happen to believe you can change fate. I believe we hold our destinies in our hands, and we can alter them at any time by right actions and by caring. I love Konrad and I won't leave him to his fate."

She stormed down the dock, grabbed Larry's hand and dragged him off the dock.

"Take me to China Town, Larry. I have to look for Sledge."

"Don't forget me," Kenna called, running down the dock.

When the wounded Tong members were loaded into the white vans, Lei and Kenna walked over to the police cars. They climbed into the car with Larry and Munoz. Perry drove the other car and they all headed to China Town. Kenna sat in back with Munoz's big Alsatian while Lei sat between Larry and Munoz. The dog slobbered all over Lei's neck from the back seat as Munoz navigated the dark, empty streets.

They drove into China Town on Washington. When they reached Stockton, they were stopped by police barriers. Munoz got out of his car and pushed the barriers aside so they could drive into the cordoned-off zone. Lei rolled down her window and stared at the destruction as Munoz drove slowly down Washington toward Powell. Bricks, glass, signs and concrete littered the road. They were forced to drive over some of the debris.

The Powell Street intersection was as far as they could go. A collection of police cars and three fire trucks clogged the street, preventing them from going any further.

Lei climbed out of the car while Munoz got the leash. He and his dog headed toward the center of the destruction.

"He's not a cadaver dog, but maybe he can help," Munoz said.

"Wait here, Kenna. I don't want you out in these streets. You could get hurt," Lei told the girl.

"I'm so tired, I don't think I could go anywhere anyway." Kenna laid down in the empty car with her jacket under her head. "I think I'll take a nap."

With Kenna safe, Lei followed Larry and Munoz in a daze. Perry ran past her with his dog. Larry, chewing on a cigar end, put his arm around her. "Don't worry, Lei. If anyone can make it out of this mess alive, your boy Sledge can."

*****

Konrad woke to the sound of shrill screams. His head hurt like hell. When he opened his eyes, he shut them immediately. Apparently, he'd been propelled by the force of Junior's bomb straight out of the sewers into someone's bathroom.

Broken, white, three-inch square tiles lay scattered all around his shoulders which were firmly wedged in the bathroom floor two inches from the toilet. A Chinese woman of about eighty stood in the middle of a claw-footed tub clutching a tiny towel over her ample body. Her screams ate into Konrad's ears.

Summoning his Berserker power, Konrad erupted from the floor, shattering more tiles and knocking the toilet over. When water began fountaining from the severed line, the Chinese woman's eyes rolled into her head and she collapsed into the tub. Konrad turned off the water going into the toilet, grabbed the housecoat laying on the broken throne and tossed it over her.

He slapped his black jeans to remove the tile dust and opened the bathroom door. Apparently, he was back in China Town in his own world. When he looked out the window of the small apartment, he saw Powell Street and the flashing lights of a herd of cop cars, fire trucks, and ambulances.

Grinning from ear to ear, Konrad went back into the bathroom to check on the elderly lady. He averted his eyes as he helped her to her feet. She continuously exhorted him in rapid-fire Chinese, of which he understood not a word. His grin grew even bigger. If he couldn't understand her, he was no longer a vampire.

When the lady was wrapped up and sitting on her bed, Konrad ran out of the apartment and into the street. He was still looking around for someone he recognized, when a huge dog leaped on his chest and almost knocked him over.

Munoz jumped on him after the dog. "You're alive! Damn it if I ain't glad to see you."

Konrad slapped Munoz on the back. "Not half as glad as I am to see you. Where's Lei?"

"Back there somewhere with Larry. How'd you get here, man? Last time I saw you, you were jumping overboard out there at the Rock."

"Long story, Roger. I'll be glad to tell you after I find Lei. I know she's worried."

"Go on, then. She's way past worried. She hit full-on hysterical about fifteen minutes ago."

Konrad pushed his way through a throng of residents, all out of their houses fearful this was a massive earthquake and an aftershock could hit any minute. He heard them talking and understood their fear. But he knew it wasn't a quake and there wouldn't be another one. Junior's bomb was a once-only deal. With all this destruction, the doorway had to be closed.

He spotted Larry first. His arm was around Lei. Konrad stopped when he saw her. His heart filled with love and tears rolled down his face. He knew the minute she spotted him because she screamed his name.

"Sledge!"

He ran toward her with his arms outstretched. She leaped into them and he swung her around. "Lei, I'm so glad to see you're safe."

"Did you kill Vetalas?"

He buried his face in the fragrant hollow of her neck. "Yeah," he whispered.

"I knew you would. Could you lighten up a little? You'll break my ribs."

*****

Konrad borrowed one of the police cruisers to drive to Baby's house. He and Lei left their police buddies at the scene in China

318

Town taking Kenna with them. Larry, Munoz, and Perry decided they needed to stay and help.

"Do you think Paige changed like you did?" Lei asked as Konrad parked in front of the apartment. Baby's purple Honda sat out front, so they knew, even though it was after eleven, she hadn't gone to work.

"I'm praying she did. Baby will be pissed if she didn't."

"Baby's always pissed." When Lei said this, they looked at each other and laughed. Nothing seemed able to burst the bubble of happiness lodged in Konrad's throat. He'd accomplished what he set out to, releasing himself from Vetalas's curse, and he hoped they'd driven the vampires off Alcatraz.

They knocked and stood outside the door with their arms around each other. Kenna was so weary she leaned against Lei. When Baby answered, Konrad knew Paige had changed.

Baby grabbed Lei and smothered her in a huge embrace. When she finished crying on Lei, she grabbed Konrad and hugged him. "She's back. Paige is her same old full-of-piss-and-vinegar self. You did it, Sledge. You gave her back to me. I thought she was gone forever. I can never thank you enough."

Baby drew them into the living room. Paige stood up, cocked an eyebrow and slapped her hands on her hips. "Took you long enough. What the hell happened out there?"

Konrad burst out laughing. "Vetalas was a little tougher than I thought. I had to chase him straight back to hell through that doorway."

"Hell is where that nasty, mother fucker belongs."

"Paige, don't be cussing in front of the girl." Baby wagged an admonishing finger. Paige grabbed it and they hugged.

Francis Pengill rose off the couch. "You're safe," she said as she walked across the living room to grab Konrad in a huge embrace. They hugged for several minutes.

"I'm fine, Mom," he said, pulling away.

"Me too. I can walk again."

"At least something good came out of all this."

His mother held his arms and backed away, searching his face. "I think you'll discover a lot of good came out of all this."

Baby led Paige toward the kitchen where she grabbed the smaller woman and squeezed her tight. Paige pushed her away. "Don't be huggin' on me in front of people, especially the girl. What have I told you about that?"

Konrad watched them playing with each other, Paige her old insulting, irreverent self. His mother well and looking happier than he'd seen her in years. His eyes burned as he looked at Lei. He brushed away the sudden moisture. He was not going to cry again. Not in front of all these people, anyway. "Let's go home," he whispered to Lei.

She looked into his eyes, hers slightly slanted, soft and warm. "Your place or mine."

"We're out of here," Konrad called to Paige and Baby as they walked out the door. "You coming Kenna, or you staying here."

"Can I stay?" she asked.

Baby wrapped a meaty arm around Kenna's drooping shoulders. "You look wasted. Of course, you can stay here. From now on, your home is with us. And you can tell that nasty vampire Lance, he can come around whenever he wants."

"Lance is a human."

"Shut the fuck up," Paige said.

Konrad turned and grinned. "He saved the dragon's life, so she gave him his humanity in return."

"Lung Ma says goodnight everyone," Kenna said. "She's taking a nap on the roof. She said she cleaned all the vampires off the island she could find. She even went underground. I don't think she liked that."

Lance suddenly appeared on the stairway. "That fricking dragon is gonna be the death of me."

"Lance!" Baby grabbed the surfer and dragged him into the apartment. "You're human!"

"Yea, and I can tell you, it's gonna take some getting used to. Do you realize I can't fly? I'm gonna have to find a car. I had to catch a ride with Lung Ma to get my skinny ass off the Rock. And she's a maniac in the air. I'm lucky I survived."

"Hey, we're heading out to my place on the beach," Konrad said to Lance. "Come with us. I'll give you the Knucklehead."

"No kidding. Is that the bike with the cool airbrushed painting?"

"That's the one."

"I'm going with them," Lance said to Baby and her roommates.

"Go on, Lance," Baby said, pushing him toward Konrad. "But don't be a stranger."

*****

The hot sun beat down on Konrad's back as he stroked out into the surf on his brand-new, custom-made, Tim Bessell surfboard. Lance bobbed in the three-foot waves waiting for him.

When Konrad reached Lance, he sat on his board, legs dangling and smiled. The fog had lifted and the sun glared down on the shining Pacific out of a crystalline, blue sky. But the water was still cold. They both wore wet suits.

"You know, I miss never being cold," Lance said.

"Come on, Lance, is that all you miss?"

Lance turned his face to the sun and grinned. "Yep, that's all. I'm moving back to the 'Bu at the end of the week. Gonna go back to ridin' the waves for big money."

"Honestly, are you that good?"

"One of the best, bro. I been shredding waves since I was fifteen and that was a really long time ago."

Konrad couldn't believe the difference humanity made in Lance. Surfer vamp was a really handsome human. He'd pulled his white-blonde hair back from his face which sported a chiseled jaw, dimpled chin and a five o'clock shadow. His blue eyes were several shades darker than when he was a vampire and sparkled with life and vitality. He'd put on pounds and muscle.

"You look great, Lance. What's your last name anyway?"

"Van Artsdalen."

"You related to Butch?"

Lance lifted one eyebrow.

"Wow! You were in *Endless Summer.* You really can surf."

Lance paddled hard and took off on a wave. Konrad heard, "It's my life." And then the strains of a subtly changed popular song floated back to him on an ocean-scented breeze. "Are we humans or are we surfers?"

About the Author

 A self-declared military brat from Hawaii, Janet worked as a reporter for years before retiring to write books. Horses and dogs are her passion along with writing adventure for youth and adults.

Tell-Tale would like to thank you for your purchase. If you would like to read more by this or other fine TT authors, please visit our website:

www.tell-talepublishing.com

CPSIA information can be obtained
at www.ICGtesting.com
Printed in the USA
BVHW031753060220
571663BV00001B/42